I0527030

A GATHERING OF GIANTS

JACK KINCADE

For our kids, and the great dogs that love and protect them.

Curious Fact:

Over 600,000 people vanish across America every year.

Where on earth, do they all go?

PROLOGUE

Local Newspaper Article:

STRANGE LIGHTS OVERHEAD!

KANSAS CITY SUN- October 31, 2018 (AP)

Local dairyman Ellsworth Scruggs and his wife Milly David Scruggs were formally listed as missing today by the Cleavesport Sheriff's department.

The spokesperson said that State Troopers discovered the missing farmer's milk cows wandering along Highway 49 unattended. A small child of undetermined age was found traveling amongst the herd. According to rescuers on the scene, the rowdy heifers seemed to actively protect the solitary child as if he were kin. These odd circumstances have left the abandoned little boy in shock and unable to speak and provide deputies with any coherent information to go on.

No sign of the boy's foster-parents has been found after an exhaustive search.

There have been widespread reports that a localized freak weather storm may have played a significant part in the Scruggs family's disappearance. Several witnesses had reported bright lights and funnel clouds hovering directly above their hayfields just before two small tornadoes touched down and then quickly retreated.

No other signs of foul weather or foul play have been reported in the area.

The desperate family members would appreciate any

information regarding the whereabouts of the missing couple.

In another bit of strange Halloween news, The U.S. Government has finally revealed today that UFOs genuinely exist.

That's right, folks; it's official. But who and what they represent, nobody seems to know?

Or at least nobody's talking yet.

-CHAPTER 1-

The One Who Walks Between

"Fire! On fire!"

The creature's mind raged back into consciousness, howling in pain.

Disoriented and confused, the monster sprang up to discover itself trapped in the center of a blazing impact crater. Flames ravaged what remained of its clothes.

These strange, smoldering rags formed a crude straitjacket with thick leather straps and hand-forged buckles running up and down the back. Someone had smeared the entire garment with pine tar and set it ablaze. Now the fuel-fed flames only snuffed out when rammed up against the damp ferns.

"War? Again?"

The seething brute rolled to extinguish the agony.

"Do they surround us still?"

Temporarily blinded, it struggled to right itself.

"Where are they now?"

It had to rise.

"I will slay them all!"

The creature roared onto two legs.

It wasn't until this great, ruined beast stood upright that it resembled anything approaching a human being.

In fact, there was a dark-skinned, ancient man lurking just beneath the disfigured flesh of this monster. By searching the undamaged parts—one could see that he was a striking giant of a fellow, over twelve feet tall.

Here stood an indigenous First Nations warrior from another time and place long ago. A titanic, pre-Columbian giant who once hunted sloths taller than elephants back in the megafauna of the American Southwest. The same legendary colossus who helped the Incas build their stone strongholds above the clouds at Machu Picchu, one staggering boulder at a time.

This titan of a man appeared that singular—that immutable—that timeless.

He was an ancient Time Warrior, lost somehow in this future place, yet still spirited enough to have come smoldering, straight from the heat of his latest battle, less than five minutes before.

Throughout the centuries, anyone who crossed paths with this deadly pre-Columbian marvel only whispered of him in the most reverent tones.

But the ancient tribes who raised him from childhood, as he soared taller every day, knew him simply as Yuma—the Tree.

"What happened? Where am I?"

Yuma forced open his swollen eyes.

"Where are they?"

As the giant struggled to focus, he realized that night was upon him, and he was lost inside a dense forest on the edge of a lake somewhere hauntingly familiar. Above him, the sky buzzed with a puzzling circular glow, giving the entire starlit atmosphere a distorted fishbowl appearance.

The lively little town hugging the bay on the far shores seemed happy enough, in stark contrast to Yuma's solitary agony. The cheerful township celebrated the Fourth of July as homemade fireworks popped and whistled into the sky. The patriotic colors seemed distant, yet close enough to sting the nose.

Yuma recognized the lyrics as the Yankee Doodle melodies echoed across to him.

Why am I so confused? Did I fall into my campfire? Am I dead?

Nothing made sense to the dazed giant, but inside that moment, his pain convinced him he was alive—and still on fire.

The giant thrashed against the suffocating bindings, shedding a trail of sparks. The buckles glowed amber as he ripped and shredded his way free.

Yuma spun around to orient himself, gasping for air.

That festive hamlet lay south, and a commanding range of mountains soared high behind him to the north. The daunting ridgebacks blotted out the stars for miles like an unscalable fortress wall.

Yuma surveyed the peaks. A single waterfall cleaved the nearest mountaintop in two, creating twin veils of whitewater to plunge untouched into the lush forest below.

"Am I home? Was I across the lake tonight? But how? I do not remember how I arrived here. I... I...?"

The battle-scarred giant staggered a few yards before collapsing onto a carpet of ferns. The leafy plants closed around him on contact, soothing his blistered body in their healing embrace.

Yuma lay unconscious beneath the green void for a few moments, dreaming sweet dreams of his wife, Blue Feather, before coming around. Finally, he rolled onto his back, and the ancient stars winked down at him.

"You are right," he replied. "You are always wise. She will be angry. I must wait before Blue Feather sees me tonight. I must heal. I do not want my love to see me this way again. She never likes the bloody parts."

He heard the happy chirps of birdsong collecting high above as the creatures on this side of the lake celebrated his dramatic return.

A trio of fast-moving hummingbirds dove down from the treetops. They hovered over the giant's head, cooling his burns with their invisible wings.

"Zip! Zash! Zee!" Yuma cracked a broken smile as the tiny birds buzzed protectively over him.

He remembered his miniature friends on sight. Their brilliant luminescent appearance reignited more memories of this revered place. Yuma's smile turned into a grin when he noticed a familiar Sequoia towering above all else.

"There is my Little Sister!"

The majestic redwood displayed a distinctive lightning bolt charred deep into her impervious flesh—stretching from earth to sky.

"I have watched you grow tall–no matter the odds."

Yuma shook his head, trying to clear it—muddled about what had happened in his enchanted life only minutes before.

"Wait? The Mission?"

But he startled out of his memories as an ear-piercing scream split open the night from across the lake. Yuma staggered down to the shoreline to pinpoint it.

"That is the sound of terror."

The shriek was unnerving enough, but when accompanied by the crowd's overenthusiastic cheers as another barrage of fireworks thundered the hollows, it was almost too much for the soul to bear.

"What new banshee is this?"

Yuma spotted an oversized fireball screeching high above the other explosions. The calm surface of the lake mirrored its trajectory brilliantly as it blazed skyward.

The sheer size of this shooting star made zero ballistic sense unless it was an incoming missile or a troublemaker's practical joke. But, a split second later, Yuma made the sickening connection.

This blazing comet wasn't some futuristic super weapon or noisy errant firework. It was a burning human being streaking across the sky—screaming for his life.

The partying town across the bay had intentionally catapulted another giant out over the water, just as they had done to Yuma only moments before. Unfortunately, the second victim crashed two hundred yards offshore, this time with an enormous splash and sizzle.

The tar flames drowned on contact as the blistered warrior bobbed back to the surface—lucky to be alive but still trapped inside his waterlogged straitjacket. Unable to use his arms, the sinking giant kicked for his life.

"Yuma! Help! (gulp) Help!" he screamed. "Are you alive? Yuma! Save me! Save us! Use your powers! You swore an oath!"

Badly confused, Yuma waded in to rescue the drowning man.

"No. No. Who is that? What is he talking about?"

The ancient Time Warriors' mind stretched back for answers it couldn't find.

"Wait. I recognize that voice!"

A sudden eruption of bubbles drew his gaze to the center of the lake. The once tranquil waters now shimmered with dazzling bolts of neon green madness rising up from the depths.

Yuma jolted at the erratic light show.

These are the long eels!

"Flee, man! Swim for your life!" Yuma yelled.

Hundreds of electric eels raced up from the blackness, competing for their next meal. These twenty-foot maneaters blazed vivid green in the plankton-rich-waters with every discharge of their lethal powers.

Yuma froze as the swarm hit the man like a nightmare with a thousand snapping jaws. The brutal head-on collision between man and beast sent the giant airborne before splashing down, covered in squirming lake monsters.

"Yuma! Help! Please! I'm eaten alive!"

One last bright thrash and panicked gulp, and he disappeared beneath the shimmering waters forever.

Across the lake, the crowds howled in delight. The brighter the chaotic green bubbles, the louder the cheers rose as their celebrations roared into high gear. This organized display of simple madness and murder only intensified—

feeding off the bloodthirsty frenzy of the little town.

The lake continued to glitter as the fastest eels snapped up the last morsels of immortal flesh. In the end, only the bones and buckles remained to sink to the bottom of the unknown.

"Someone has discovered our fatal weakness," Yuma whispered to himself as he abandoned any rescue attempt. And he was startled when the energized eels turned and jetted for him.

The giant stumbled onto the beach just as the massive swarm launched together.

Snap! Snap! Snap!

The tangled mass landed only inches from enjoying another giant meal. The hungry eels eventually slithered back into the waves, angry and unsatisfied.

Another round of cheers rose across the cruel lake as Yuma heard the next scream gut open the sky.

"No! Stop it! Why are you doing this?"

The distant splash rang like a dinner bell for the eels as they torpedoed for their next snack.

"Yuma!" The newest drowning man shrieked between mouthfuls of water—"Toth? Toth! Yuma! Help!" (gulp). "Help! You know I hate water! I hate it! Hate it!"

Yuma's mind raced now, trying to catch up with itself.

"I recognize that voice! That is Cheenoo! Cheenoo, my best friend! And the other? Toth! That was Toth! From my mother's tribe!"

Yuma remembered everything as his memories reignited—releasing centuries of pain and loss in bright flashes of insight.

The endless wars. The secret meetings. The false armistice. The betrayal. The trap. The poison. The trials. The prison. The torture. The launch. Hurtling through the sky.

"That was tonight! Who did this? Who did this to us?"

Intuition hissed the name into his ear.

"Wixx. Wixx! It was you! Nobody else would!"

He slammed his fists into the sand.

"Nobody else could."

Yuma's head remained bowed when he heard the next terrified screams arcing out over the lake.

At first, he didn't recognize the most familiar voice in the world to him. But then he could hear nothing else.

"No! Nooooo! Not Blue Feather!"

Yuma dove into the water and swam to save her, but it was far too late as her burning body slipped beneath the water, half a lake away.

The Amazonian warrior, Blue Feather, had snapped her neck on impact and never felt the sting of the first teeth as her electrocutioners bit into her.

Yuma struggled to the safety of the shoreline, sobbing inconsolably.

Bent, burned, and broken, the shattered giant made himself bear witness to the brutal slaughter of his wife and the annihilation of his entire tribe of heroes that long night.

The human soul that once burned so brightly inside this legend drowned on that dry beach. Not physically but emotionally and spiritually and possibly forever. Because of his incompetence, everything and everyone Yuma had ever known and loved no longer existed.

The onslaught of familiar faces rushing by blinded him to everything else. He had failed his people with his ignorance in underestimating their fiercest enemy. Yuma had sworn to protect these hidden lands and their inhabitants forever. In his youth, the mighty warrior had taken a sacred oath to safeguard and preserve all living things within the invisible borders of this mysterious sanctuary known as the Bubble— in exchange for the magnificent gift of immortality that this unending responsibility demanded. He had cherished almost every day of this unimaginably long and adventurous life— until this precise tick in time.

Now, longevity itself seemed a curse.

The last of Mother Nature's immortals gathered himself

emotionally and rose to full height, ignoring the pain that tried to claw him back down as he shook his fists at the exploding sky.

"I am Yuma! Guardian of the Sacred Forest! I am accountable for this madness! Me! Yuma!" He pounded his chest. "I, and I alone, bear full burden for unleashing this ancient nightmare upon us again! I failed you all! But I swear to you, Blue Feather, and all victims of this slaughter—the last war against Wixx begins now! And it only ends when Wixx's neck is in my hands! So, it will be!"

Revenge flooded his darkest thoughts.

Why would that monster spare my life? To toy with me. How could Wixx humiliate me further? Why did she save me?

After hours of reflection, Yuma realized there were no choices left in his charmed life.

His tribe of immortals no longer existed. Wixx had discovered the ancient secret that the only way to kill immortals—was simply never granting them the time to self-heal.

Now he stood alone—vulnerable—without his army behind him to protect these timeless lands against the hordes to come. Yuma needed to be rescued for the first time in an extraordinarily long time. And he needed time to heal and plan.

But if help didn't arrive soon, Pepper Wixx's scorched earth policy would destroy this fragile garden and all the unspoiled lands that lie just beyond its cloaked borders—including the Upside world of the humans.

"We need help now if we are to survive," he confessed to Zip, Zash, and Zee.

Yuma closed his eyes, making a familiar grimace as he began his shamanistic chants, and the hummingbirds knew what to expect next. They flew away and hid in the treetops covering their heads with their wings.

Far below, Yuma seethed like a cauldron boiling over with centuries of pain and hope. Then, he roared as only a giant could roar, unleashing a ferocious bolt of pure, lucid anguish into an already shell-shocked sky.

"Aghhhhhhh!" he screamed.

The hypersonic blade of energy drove the partygoers to their knees as Yuma's psychic message ripped a hole through the walls of their protective Bubble. The force was so powerful that his desperate plea for help flew far beyond the borders of this unseen never-never land and launched itself into orbit.

This extraordinary Lucid Pulse lasted long enough to circle the globe twice, searching for any living giants—anywhere—still brave enough to ride to the rescue of this magical place.

And as with all great magic tricks—one never knows what to expect next—but everything was about to change forever in the most remarkable and unexpected ways—even for the magician.

-CHAPTER 2-

This Creepy Kid

Zack Goodnight swatted at the shiny gnats flitting about his head.

The nine-year-old orphan appeared frail and soulful, sitting alone in the empty lobby. And yet, there was a composed self-awareness about him to anyone lucky enough to notice.

A set of memorable eyes dominated a bud of a nose and tiny mouth. Standing only four and a half feet tall and weighing fifty-eight pounds, he was modest in most respects for his age—making that spellbinding gaze of his even more compelling. Lean in too closely, and you risked tumbling inside.

But that initial attraction faded once the potential adopters witnessed Zack flailing away at his imaginary demons. Most moved on to healthier options relatively quickly.

His nurses nicknamed the good-natured baby by his first words.

"Good night!" he chirped pleasantly from his crib one evening.

"Good night!" His caretakers giggled back.

He was nicknamed Good Night on the spot. Unfortunately for everyone inside the nursery, the jovial toddler continued to parrot 'Good night' and nothing else for the next two years, nonstop, day and night. No other words seemed to appeal to him.

As years ticked by, the unwanted child was relegated

to wandering the hallways of Briscoe like a lonely mascot in search of a team—adorable—but damaged goods to anyone who watched and listened.

"Good night."

Life can be unfair, especially to the young and disabled, and an uncaring world abandoned this unadoptable child on sight. Then, one stormy night, a sympathetic nurse with a penchant for doing the right thing forged a new identity for the orphan out of thin air.

"Every pup deserves their own handle, dog-gone-it," the part-time dog breeder said. "Especially you, bright eyes. So, you and I will make this right tonight."

Opening her files, she realized she'd burned through the alphabet twice in a record-setting year of infant abandonment.

"'Z' again," she sighed.

The sensitive nurse closed her eyes and listened to the advice of the storm winds brewing outside, then stitched her two choices together as nimbly as she stitched wounds on the graveyard shift.

"Zack Goodnight it is!"

She felt a rush of pride as she jotted down his legal name for the first time, and little John Doe #2376 became Zack Goodnight officially at the stroke of midnight. The thunderstorm raging outside rattled every window with the good news.

When Zack began communicating again at age six, he couldn't find anyone willing to listen to his bizarre descriptions of the universe any longer. Even the specialists grew weary of his repetitive gibberish. That's when he stopped speaking altogether.

Now, at nine, silent Zack Goodnight sat alone again on the same uncomfortable bench they always stuck him on whenever Dr. Briscoe summoned him to the lobby of the Briscoe Institute of Applied Emphasis.

He was waiting for his new parents to reemerge from the shuttered office across the hall. The wealthy couple wielded their influence like a baseball bat and demanded this last-minute emergency meeting with the orphanage's top executive, Doctor Ellsworth Briscoe, and the entire senior staff on a holiday evening.

It was growing late on the Fourth of July, and Zack wanted to get home in time to catch the fireworks in a few hours. These brand-new test parents had promised a fabulous view from their hilltop estate.

But that was over two hours ago, and Zack's legs ached from sitting on the unpadded bench for so long. Finally, his boredom took command, and his mind began searching for distractions to ease the discomfort.

Boy, I didn't think I'd be back inside this stinky old place so soon. Oh, look, they painted the library blue!

The hallways were empty except for shadows ghosting along the far walls. It was easy to believe that spirits prowled this renovated gothic facility. Ironically, the refurbished reformatory always smelled of fresh paint and modern disinfectants these days—a subtle effort to mask a century of sadness that still haunted the air.

And yet, over time, whenever they dumped Zack back on the doorstep like a bottle of spoiled milk, it was a reassuring homecoming of sorts to the boy. The Briscoe Institute of Applied Emphasis was the only nesting place he could remember.

Now Zack was back.

When the Pritchard's announced the last-minute road trip to celebrate the Fourth today, Zack expected a red, white, and blue surprise would be waiting at the other end from his new parents. At the least, a hotdog followed by a triple-decker cone.

But when he opened his eyes from the limo's back seat and saw they were driving through the twisted wrought-iron gates of Briscoe again, he realized he'd been ambushed.

"He sees bugs that aren't there, doctor. And other twisted things too! Unbelievable things!"

Zack realized over time that everyone felt the same—whether it was the doctors, the parents, or even other kids. Age didn't seem to matter when it came to fitting in.

Is being odd something so terrible?

"What's up with this kid? OCD? ADD? Autistic? He talks crazy talk—or he doesn't talk for months! He sees things in the air everywhere we go!"

There's nothing wrong with me! Zack wanted to scream. *I'm not the broken one. So don't try to fix me. The rest of you don't understand what you're missing.*

Zack giggled when he remembered their faces and how disturbing that sounded to the doctors whenever he shared his wisdom out loud—especially the psychiatrists.

But he knew he was right, and they were wrong. Simple as that.

"But I've seen them my whole life."

"Try to forget it. They're not there anymore, or they won't be soon. Now take the pills. Breathe in. Relax. You're doing just fine."

Their designer drugs dulled Zack's senses and drove him into deeper despair. Yet, despite their misdiagnoses, the boy continued to see his radiant pests, no matter how far down the chemical rabbit hole they tried to push him.

Zack's boredom evaporated when angry insults erupted from behind the closed doors.

Same as at home. Battles every day; nothing changes. Nothing ever does, Zack thought.

Without warning, Yuma's Lucid Pulse slammed into Zack with enough force to stagger ten giants.

The overpowering thought-wave blew the boy off the bench and flipped him onto the floor like a toy. It left Zack sprawled and gasping for air as the animated force-field enveloped him, enveloping his body in a dazzling cocoon of light. The shape-shifting cloud whispered its dire message before soaring back into the stratosphere in search of fresh giants.

"We must unite to save the light."

"Ow! What? Wait? What was that?"

His energized mind reeled with intersecting waves of sound and imagery that only his soul could fathom. And the scent of fresh pine replaced the chemical smell in the air with the elegant perfume of the deep forest.

"What happened? Did you guys hear that?"

Zack froze as a tendril of that sleek psychokinetic energy returned for a second opinion and lingered over him quizzically before dashing back to reconnect with the mother signal.

I know this is weird. But I knew this would happen... I've been waiting for this... my whole life.

Even in despair, Zack believed that something extraordinary would search him out one day to transport him out of his life of misery and back onto the light beam of his destiny.

I can feel it. I dream about it! I'm supposed to be here!

A furious onrush of insights meshing time and space surged through Zack's brain at light speeds. It was as if his developing mind required this complex superhuman jumpstart to illuminate his dangerous path forward.

Hidden whispers now beckoned within to return to his roots and rediscover his true self—wherever that journey might lead.

"We must unite to save the light." the spirit whispered.

I can still smell the whole forest on my hands. Maybe everybody's right? Maybe I am crazy. Am I lost in another dream?

The hinges blew off the door across the hallway, shattering any illusions of paradise.

"Get off the floor, you idiot!" Charlie Pritchard barked as he stepped over the boy and marched out of the orphanage—never acknowledging the quivering child except for the slur. There was no wink over his shoulder to reassure the frightened boy. None of his family bothered to equip Charlie Pritchard with those basic human accessories. Why change now?

He never smiles at me anymore, not even when I smile first.

Zack knew what to expect next. He adapted to living inside this spinning vortex of suck and rejection long ago. The emotional upheaval was nothing new—but it was always gut-wrenching and made him seasick.

When Shirley Pritchard stepped out of the office and saw Zack lying face down, she clutched the nearest arm to steady herself.

"Did Charlie strike him again?"

"No, no, ma'am."

Dr. Briscoe hung back in the safety of the shadows, lighting his pipe.

Just then, Zack noticed two orderlies, tagged Frick & Frack, hustling towards them. The staff only summoned these two rubber-soled goons whenever trouble was expected.

You'd think they'd know me better by now.

Zack slid back onto the bench, and Shirley sat beside him, folding his hands into hers, still timid of his touch.

"Zack darling," she began in tears. "You know that your father and I only want the very best for you? Do you understand that much, sweetheart?"

And here we go again. Zack thought.

He began miming her words silently, and she jerked her hands away and stood. Zack could deliver this same sad speech from memory by now—if he ever felt like talking again.

Charlie stumbled back through the ornate doors, struggling with all the boy's possessions on one awkward trip.

Was everything already packed?

Including my toys and stuffed animals?

We were never going out to see the fireworks tonight.

Stomping across the lobby, Charlie dumped everything in front of the surprised boy, spun on his heels, and walked out without a second look.

Go away faster! Zack thought. *Faster and forever!*

The oak doors followed Zack's wishes like bouncers in

an Irish pub and heaved the bum out.

"Whoop! Hey!"

The doors slammed shut in defiance, refusing further negotiations.

Facing another excruciating rejection, the brutal reality hit Zack like a lightning bolt.

I guess no one can love what they can't understand.

"It's only temporary," Shirley lied as she chased after her husband, and once outside, they ran for their car like they were fleeing a haunted house.

Twenty minutes later, Frick and Frack locked Zack inside the quarantine ward without fuss. This mandatory isolation was a strict protocol requirement for all orphans re-administered back into this closed commercial adoption system. And the medical staff were never surprised to discover Zack Goodnight back inside the airtight chamber again.

Eleven sets of parents had returned this troubled young boy to the Briscoe Institute eleven times in just nine short years of life—setting a heartbreaking, in-house record this holiday night.

Zack gazed around the empty squad bay as he changed into a fresh set of hospital PJs. He recognized the attending nurse, even with her back turned to him. She was an impressive woman in size and temperament, and everyone inside the Institute referred to her as 'Boss.'

"It's all right here, right in front of us, Boss."

The sound of his voice startled even the silence. As far as the records showed, this was the first time the patient had spoken in weeks. The shell-shocked nurse turned to face him.

"The world just can't see it, though," Zack gestured around the room. "But they will. Soon."

"What's that, darlin?" the nurse rolled in closer on her desk chair. "What do you see, Zack?"

He smiled as his eyes filled with light and wonder.

"Why everything, Boss? Everything."

-CHAPTER 3-

The Briscoe Institute versus Kate Tempest

Detention, anytime, anywhere, sucks. But on a national holiday? The Fourth of July, no less—even worse—especially when locked behind ten-foot-tall walls where even the slightest loss of freedom tasted bitter.

"Again? Come on, brainless!"

Kate Tempest stretched her leather jacket over her head and hid beneath it like a batwing. Her laptop froze again as her classmates snickered, watching her cheat in plain sight.

Since turning sixteen, rebellious Kate wore her hair ragged and longer on one side than the other, swinging down to her jawline—another rash decision she didn't regret. With a quick head flip to clear her gunsights, her piercing glare stopped three-hundred-pound orderlies in their tracks, and Kate's 'Don't go there, Bubba!' look could freeze meat on the bone.

Riveting and more than a little intimidating to most, she was unique, no doubt about it. Kate Tempest was a captivating original, whether you saw her angel or outlaw side.

She was a lone survivor caught in the confusing transformation between victim and victor—a born road warrior in pursuit of her own best self-defense and security.

Fool me once, your fault. Fool me twice, my fault.

Never again.

Like any victim, Kate craved a defensible landing spot after a lifetime of fighting or fleeing. She yearned for a cozy corner to snuggle down to make the personal transition from a cocoon into the armored butterfly she was born to be. And here at the fortified Briscoe Institute, she felt she had finally discovered that safe space.

Dr. Eugene Briscoe had single-handily transformed his ancestors' sprawling, gothic reformatory into this polished palace of profits.

He pitched his reinvented company as a cutting-edge medical facility combined with a children's psychological trauma center, creating—the Briscoe Institute of Applied Emphasis. The potential revenue streams seemed endless.

The doctor's pedigree and political connections brought him more influence and favors than his therapeutic skills deserved. But, despite his many faults, his reputation grew in pharmaceutical circles, as did the institute's fortunes, and eager investors swooped in early to scoop up the spoils.

From then on, the Briscoe Institute evolved like any well-fed organism, growing fatter and more complex with every lap around the sun. Dr. Briscoe added the profitable side business of re-adoption into his new corporate strategy to re-energize the symbiotic process.

Intake and outflow—just like a living entity.

"Our Future is Big Pharma! Big Pharma is us! We own the future!"

The rebranded Briscoe Institute of Applied Emphasis was impressive at every level of the organization. Boasting an onsite drug facility and a modernized orphanage with a daily curriculum taught by Ph. Ds, everything on the campus was now state-of-the-art in computer-equipped classrooms. It seemed a bold, win-win scenario for everyone involved, especially Dr. Briscoe's bank account.

Inside one of those polished classrooms, Kate Tempest struggled to finish her homework. Her overdue history project, the reason Dr. Prescott had sent her to detention in the first place, was still incomplete.

She whined and complained most of the day about how

unfair it was to miss the orphanage's yearly Fourth of July picnic this year instead of applying herself.

"I type on my phone faster than this sticky keyboard. I might as well use my toes."

Kate flipped her hair and checked the time above the chalkboard. She had only two minutes left before the class buzzer would squeal. At that point, Dr. Prescott would stride back in, and her holiday weekend would be crushed.

"This won't work. I'm never going to finish. Quick, Emily, give me your drive."

Her friend passed it under the desk, and Kate made the connection. The icon froze on her screen as Dr. Prescott walked in. The teacher stuck his fingers in his ears a split-second before the explosive school buzzer splintered the silence.

"Ohhh!"

"Geez!"

The students ducked and covered their heads as the sharp electronic yodel pulsed and blatted from the speakers—then repeated. Dr. Briscoe designed these ear-piercing harmonics to drag even the most drug-addled students screaming back into reality.

Kate didn't wince—she was that focused on getting Emily's homework transferred—but now, it was too late. She was out of digital runway.

May Day! May Day! I'm going down in flames.

Dr. Prescott sat at his desk and flipped his laptop open with an authoritative snap, and Kate's download saluted in sync.

"Yes!" she whispered, and her fist shot up. Smug in victory, she flashed a 'told you so!' grin at her friend Emily.

"You saved my hide again!" Kate signed in ASL and put her fist out to bump before remembering her friend didn't roll like that.

Emily Healy was a fifteen-year-old girl with Asperger's and a brilliant student despite her syndrome and other health problems. She was in detention because of her own silent

21

revolution against the tyrannical Dr. Prescott. The institute wasn't sure what to do with her yet. So, she remained under study, like every orphan. These unwanted children and teenagers weren't merely patients at the corporately owned Briscoe Institute. In fact, they were company assets of the most fragile kind.

Wards of the State—WOTS it read on all their paperwork.

It should have read—NWBA instead—not wanted by anyone.

Not even the state.

But Dr. Eugene Briscoe harvested these damaged souls like a grateful farmer.

Kate's first arrival was by ambulance to the Briscoe Institute four years ago when she was twelve. The police found her huddling underneath a freeway overpass, shivering in a nest of blood-stained rags, with no identity or memory of her former life. During those first tough years, she harbored a pathological distrust of all adults—men in particular. Whatever happened to this brutalized girl wasn't coming out any time soon.

Amnesia shielded her best memories, and she banished the rest of the horrors inside herself so deep that the monsters could never escape.

Never again.

Maybe that's why she began cutting herself—to exorcise those same demons as they festered. She wasn't saying. But she stopped years ago. She understood herself so much better now and covered her wrists with colorful wristbands and bracelets. Kate wasn't ashamed of the discolored blemishes anymore. She considered them battle scars; still, she didn't want to explain. It was her business.

Her last four years at the Briscoe Institute had been the most stable and comfortable years of her existence. Kate had grown into a teenager behind these walls and endured enough unwanted drug trials to make her suspicious of everyone's motives inside the institute she considered home.

Still, at Briscoe, she met other damaged teens whom she could relate with. Behind these ivy-covered walls, she knew what to expect from the shape of every prearranged day to come. And the next.

The only adventure Kate hungered for now, was looking forward to the superficial escapades all teenage girls enjoyed. Like long shopping trips to the mall and the institute's summer prom. She knew they'd have another lame rock band instead of someone extraordinary, like every year. Still, she'd never been asked before, and the upcoming celebration was just far enough in the future to fill her new dreams with swirling taffeta instead of nightmares.

There are only a couple of weeks left. I sure hope Josh asks me.

Dr. Prescott finished his checklist and stood, clearing his throat.

"Detention makeup homework assignments. Upload them now, or forever hold your peace, and face further detention."

Kate zapped her homework onto the server and winked at Emily, who blankly stared back. But, Kate saw the real sparks behind her friend's placid gaze and always noticed the corners of her mouth curl into a Mona Lisa smile whenever Emily heard a new joke or fresh jam.

P-I-C! Kate signed to Emily in ASL and whispered, "Partners-in-crime!"

There was a discreet software alert on Dr. Prescott's screen. He rechecked its results and peered at Kate over the rims of his glasses.

"Miss Tempest, will you rise, please?"

The air was sucked out of the classroom as if a tornado had swept in, aimed exclusively for a panicked Kate.

I forgot to change anything about Emily's homework! I didn't change a comma!

She knew better. This wasn't Kate's first rodeo.

What a rookie mistake!

Kate rose as ordered, ashamed by her recklessness, but no one cared except Prescott. The other students remained sullen and passive, either drugged or playing games on their laptops.

"Miss Tempest, you and Miss Healy have both inputted the same homework assignment into my system. Down to the punctuation marks in every sentence. Now, how do you suppose that happened? Hmm?"

He looked like an indignant owl behind his round specs.

"I... I don't know Dr. Prescott. A computer glitch, I guess," she chuckled, trying to deflect. "You're the Ph.D., you tell me, smart guy?"

Prescott snarled at her insubordination and stomped toward her.

"You cheated, Miss Tempest," he said. "You understand what that means? Four weeks of reassignment to the Re-Hash Team. Outdoor chores. Bootcamp style all over again."

"No! No, please!"

Kate's heart sank when she realized the summer prom was in sudden jeopardy if Prescott sent her back to Re-Hash for re-indoctrination. Her lovely daydreams would evaporate as soon as she opened her mouth.

"I did not cheat," Kate said.

"The plagiarism program on my computer never lies. People do. Correction. You do, Miss Tempest. With astonishing regularity."

Kate stared back, hopeless. Her only play left was utter BS.

"Emily cheated, sir."

Kate couldn't believe how easily those words slipped out.

Dr. Prescott turned to Emily.

"Miss Healy, did you cheat? I do not believe you have ever found the need with your IQ. Am I correct?"

There was a tense stand-off between the three.

"As I thought." Prescott grabbed Kate's shoulder, and she whacked his arm away, sending him off-balance.

"Hands off, bub!" Kate hissed.

He recoiled from her defensive stance and withdrew a few steps.

"Alright!" Kate said, ready to admit her guilt when Emily stepped forward.

"Yes," Emily said.

"What? Yes? Yes, what? Miss Healy? Do you understand the consequences of your reply?"

"Yes."

Kate couldn't believe her friend's self-sacrifice by diving onto this live grenade. But if anyone understood how much this upcoming dance meant to Kate, it was Emily who harbored no desire to go.

"I cheated," Emily said.

"Then you both cheated?"

"No. Just me. Kate did not know. I plucked her file."

Prescott turned to Kate.

"So, if I understand this situation correctly, you are allowing Miss Healy to take the fall and be sent down for reassignment to the Re-Hash Team for four weeks? Your best friend?"

"No, sir. Not me. That's all up to you, Doc," Kate tried to shift the blame back onto someone else again. "I'm not the one driving this school bus. You are."

Prescott squinted. He'd read her files—some of the information was quite impressive, yet much of it bleak.

"All twisted up inside, aren't you?" he grinned. "Like a nest of worms."

"Nope. Not me, Doc. My guts are just fine. I'm just scared all the time. No crime in being afraid of meat-mechanics like you in charge, is there?"

"Oh, fear not, my child. We'll come up with something to fix you, too. I'm sure there's a new chemical with your name on it waiting around the next corner."

Prescott stepped back, weighing his options about how to proceed with his dwindling Fourth of July evening.

I must get home to the cats before the fireworks go off, or they'll shred the curtains again, and there's so much paperwork in each of these ridiculous in-house transfers!

"Miss Healy, gather your belongings. You are being sent back down to the Re-Hash Team, ah, 1602. Let's go. Up and out. I only have so much time."

Emily followed orders, and when Kate stepped forward to retake the blame, Emily reached out and silenced her friend. Prescott urged her toward the door before turning broadside to fire one last volley at Kate.

"Congratulations, Miss Tempest. Our profiles predicted this kind of despicable behavior would surface in you one day, and here it is."

"What?"

"Our A.I. studies all concluded that as a certifiable narcissist, you would sacrifice any friend just to save yourself. One of the many dark psychological insights that have proven to be correct. You are predictably selfish to a fault. I wouldn't want you on any team of mine."

"No worries there, Doc. I swear."

He grabbed the laptop with its on-screen proof.

"Miss Healy must now endure four weeks of re-indoctrination so that you, Miss Tempest, may attend a three-hour dance party? Is that it? It's in your records. Yes, it says so right here. A silly dance. Really? How special it must be to have a friend like you?"

Kate lowered her head and hid behind her shield.

He's not wrong. What don't these geeks know?

But her guilt evaporated when she saw happy Emily signing in ASL. Emily's articulate fingers danced over the teacher's bald spot, babbling as excitedly as if she'd just won the lottery.

"P-I-C-F! 'Partners-in-crime-forever! 'School is out for summer, sister! I'll be spending every day outside until the end

26

of August! Yay! Sunshine again! Thank you, Katie! Good luck at the prom with you-know-who!"

Emily's brave sacrifice inspired Kate. The prom was only two weeks away. By then, everything would settle back to normal—wherever that new normal floated these days—and everything would be fine.

Kate flushed in optimism with the unexpected rush of fresh pine needles flooding the air.

-CHAPTER 4-

The Happy Trails Racing League

The spiderweb of dancing lights winked out above the Happy Trails Used Car Lot, leaving the five acres of asphalt as dark as the inside of a car salesman's bleak heart.

Hiding inside the surrounding shrubs, fifteen-year-old Wyatt Waylon Cooper flashed the 'Go' signal to his troops, and his last-ditch maneuver to save his summer launched like a flesh and blood video game before him. His small band of suburban guerrillas peeled out of hiding and swarmed across the vacant car lot.

Wow. Look at that! It's really on!

Wyatt Cooper was the unassuming kid everyone wanted to be. Natural. Relaxed. With no pretense about him. No bluff or guff. Just fun and intelligent. Tall for his age and lean, he moved with an awkward grace, though neither jock nor geek. He wasn't competing with anybody but himself.

Coop, as all his friends called him growing up, grew into a popular teen. At fifteen, he had lived exclusively with his grandmother since early childhood. Coop wanted a driver's license more than anything—the apex moment of becoming a natural teenager in his eyes. The only problem was his grandmother didn't own a car.

But he had stumbled upon one of the greatest secrets of all time just two weeks prior when he visited the Happy Trails car lot, pricing future rides.

Just imagine—my own wheels. I'm going to be the best race car driver that ever lived.

28

That's when Coop discovered an automotive secret that would change his life forever. This earth-shaking discovery was custom-made for a wheelless gearhead yearning for the freedom of the open road.

How long can I keep this top-secret stuff top-secret?

Coop had never experienced fear and paranoia like this before; now, he searched his phone for leaks every five minutes.

If they could pull the stunt off, this evening would be even more exhilarating than the first night they raided the car lot because tonight, they were bringing their dates along for the first time to thrill and impress.

Any foot-bound teenager knows how frustratingly impossible it is to thrill anyone on a date when you can only provide a skateboard or bike for transport. Parents worse. But tonight, everything would change. Tonight would be the payoff for all their secret efforts for the past two weeks. Coop wanted to astonish lovely Susan Leonard most of all.

It was already the Fourth of July, and the summer was running away as fast as a cat with firecrackers tied to its tail, and Coop still hadn't received so much as a simple peck on the cheek from Sue.

Not all summer long.

They held hands on their last two dates, but only briefly. That's when Coop shifted gears and decided to create a new impression. He just needed the perfect time and place to execute it.

Tonight is it!

He'd thought it through. Coop and his crew had everything prepped for The Big Reveal.

He took a deep breath and fumbled in the darkness for Sue's hand while leading her toward a classic '68 Mustang. The others followed, hunched over to avoid anyone spotting them from the street.

He turned to Jake, Dylan, Roland, and their girlfriends, Becky, Steph, and Jenna.

"Observe, guys." Coop pointed to the cars that lined the street next to the sidewalk. "No keys inside. All these cars for sale surrounding the lot have zero keys onboard. No batteries, no keys. Got it? It's an unmovable wall."

"Then what are we doing here, Coop? They could arrest us for trespassing. My dad's a lawyer. We could all get in real trouble."

"I know, I know. Coop whispered. "Until this second, nobody in town knew anything about this secret but us."

The co-conspirators exchanged winks.

"Now it's your turn. You lucky ladies are about to be let in on one of the biggest secrets ever." Coop beamed at Sue. "Prepare to be amazed."

Coop turned and pointed to the Mustang in the second row. He flicked the chrome handle, and the door swung open. "Incredible, right? And yes, ladies and gentlemen, the keys are inside!"

Coop's mischievous grin was contagious.

"Keys!" he yelled as he ran past a big finned Caddy.

A happy chase of discovery followed as the trespassers dashed across acres of free-range automobiles.

"Keys?"

"Yup, keys!"

"All the cars parked facing out along the sidewalk are locked up without the keys, so nobody steals them." Coop took a deep breath. "But all the cars behind have their keys inside! All of them!"

"What's fun about that?" Stephanie asked. "What good is it if we can't drive anywhere, right? Or did you think we'd all just dive into the back seat of someone else's stinky used car and make out on top of their scummy germs?"

"Ooooh!"

"Gag."

The guys saw nothing wrong with the idea

"Come on, Stephanie. We do it in your father's car in the driveway all the time. Same stink."

"Oh, shut up, Dylan!" She rolled her eyes.

"Patience, Steph. It's special—so much more than that. Trust me. Drum roll, please!" Coop requested, and his small band of brothers responded.

"Drrrrrrrrrrrrrrrrr!"

"Drrrrr," Amy joined in half-heartedly with the others.

"It is my honor, ladies, to announce that you are now founding members of the Happy Trails Racing League!"

"Ta-dah!"

"The what?"

"What's going on?"

Coop grinned and threw on a pair of slick racing shades.

"Gentlemen! Start your engines!"

He pumped his fist, and the other drivers tossed on sunglasses as they sprinted for their favorite muscle cars for an old-fashioned Le Man's start to their night. They fired up their eight-cylinder monsters in unison, and a thrilling roar of thunder exploded out of the engines, almost knocking over their startled spectators.

The drivers stepped out and opened the passenger doors in unison, allowing their dates to slide inside before closing the doors softly behind them as practiced.

With everyone onboard, Coop nodded again: the drivers slammed their doors shut, and the idling road racers revved three times before launching into reverse.

These inexperienced drivers exhibited precision and patience as the four cars backed out of their parking spots together, careful not to leave behind any rubber or scratches as incriminating evidence.

The finely tuned formation continued in reverse until they completed their wide arc and stopped. Now, they all faced one-hundred-and-eighty degrees from their original parking spaces, each muscle car still perfectly aligned.

Another nod from Coop, and the drivers shifted into first gear, accelerated forward without a slipped clutch, and after traveling two hundred feet, they halted simultaneously.

A murderer's row of the world's most dangerous muscle cars growled like a pack of predators along the rear property line of the Happy Trails Used Car Lot.

Coop rolled down the Mustang's window as his teammates cheered and revved their engines in victory.

"Ladies, the daring gentlemen of the Happy Trails Racing League salute you!"

Coop gestured beyond the sales stickers plastered on their windshields, and when their dates looked outside, they were astounded.

"What?" Sue laughed.

"We honor you by sharing our gift of free movies for the rest of the summer!"

Pop Corn's Magnificent Drive-In Movie Theatre sat a hundred yards below them at the rear of the car lot. Its twin oversized screens rose to such dramatic heights that aviation lights were required on top to warn away pilots. Each titanic movie screen soared over seventy feet tall and one hundred and twenty feet wide at the base—large enough to properly display any Hollywood blockbuster.

A barbed wire fence snaked across the sloping hillside separating the lots, but its prickly presence didn't intimidate the sounds of Tinseltown rushing up to entertain.

Inside their hijacked dream cars, the Happy Trails Racing League team all appreciated that they had created the perfect version of balcony seating at a Drive-In. From their lofty vantage point, they could watch either movie for free for the rest of the summer—if they didn't get caught first.

Coop's romantic gesture stole Sue's heart. He seemed reckless, but she found him fun, disarming, and dreamy at the same time. Tonight might be one of the most thrilling nights in her life.

Coop couldn't peel his eyes off Sue, even with the bright fireworks showering the sky.

On this special night, the Happy Trails Racing League transformed themselves into true action heroes inside an action-adventure movie of their own making, and their surprised dates purred back in contentment.

"This night couldn't be more legendary," Sue whispered.

She turned to Coop and liked who she saw shining back at her between the flashes of color.

Sue leaned in.

Coop couldn't tell whether she was leaning in or if he was falling forward like a fool; the weightless illusion was perfect. But when Sue removed his sunglasses, and their eyes met eyelash to eyelash, he knew he was staring into the face of someone special.

"You did all this... for me?"

"For us?" he grinned proudly.

Sue took his face and kissed him for the first time.

Her lips are so soft!

Coop melted into the groaning bucket seat, and Sue leaned in and kissed him again. But this time, her lips parted slightly, and the tip of her tongue touched his.

Shock!

Amazement!

Floored!

That sheer voltage from his first French Kiss popped his foot off the clutch and drove his other heel involuntarily onto the accelerator instead of the brake—launching their Mustang into orbit.

"Whoaaaa! Coop!"

"Hang on!"

-CHAPTER 5-

The Dreadful Event

The ceiling lights snapped on overhead as Dr. Eugene Briscoe burst into the quarantine ward alone.

"Where is he?"

A surprised Boss bolted to her feet, sending her chair twirling across the floor, startling Zack awake.

"Where's my boy? There he is!"

It embarrassed the veteran nurse her real boss had just caught her napping. But nothing seemed to faze the unflappable Dr. Briscoe these days, and she realized the good doctor was in another of his hyper-jovial moods. He ignored her as usual and shot straight for Zack.

Dark and attractive in the most unconventional ways, the polished doctor was standing beside Zack's bedside before the boy's sensitive eyes could adjust to the light.

The thin gentleman leaned in close enough that Zack could smell the wine and garlic still haunting his breath from a hasty holiday dinner date.

"Wake up, Goodnight! Welcome home, my boy!"

From the first day of the institute, Doctor Harlan Briscoe became famous for all kinds of unexpected surprises for his homeless wards. Occasionally, and usually after a bottle of evening red, the cerebral bachelor staggered home to visit the children for an injection of some unscripted happiness.

Unlike his granite-jawed ancestors, Dr. Briscoe wasn't chiseled out of emotionless stone and appeared to harbor genuine affection for most of his medically challenged

34

charges. It was as if he owned an exclusive petting zoo that only he could visit and profit from.

The melancholy doctor realized early that every unwanted child in his care endured a tragically broken backstory–regardless of whether they embraced it. And as a result, he memorized every personal detail whenever he engaged with them in small talk.

That's why Zack wasn't surprised when the grinning version of Dr. Briscoe rushed into the quarantine ward that Fourth of July evening, full of brown beans and celebratory flatulence.

"Welcome back home, Zackery! Happy Fourth of July! Hey, there is no reason to be depressed. I mean, all records are meant to be broken! Right? Now, you're a returning home champion, young man! Listen, I have a splendid idea! Let's get out of here and find us some wicked good fun."

Boss reminded him he was breaking all quarantine protocols. Still, she knew it was useless protesting when Briscoe had a full head of steam up, and she sat back and faked doing paperwork.

Before he knew it, Zack was dressed again. Once outside, Dr. Briscoe shoved the small boy aboard one of the Institute's three refurbished reform school buses. They crammed each bus full of excited orphans of all ages.

"Happy Fourth of July!" they cheered as the air brakes hissed and released, and they drove out through the open gates.

"Where are we going tonight, Dr. Briscoe?" a carefree kid named Ozzy called out.

"Unfortunately, all the fireworks displays have already started, Oz. So, who wants to go to the drive-in instead?"

"Yay!"

"Triple action features!" he promised. "We stay to the end credits!"

"Yay!"

And just like that, the nefarious Dr. Briscoe drove Zack

Goodnight out of his lethargy and right into the middle of an ongoing Fourth of July party.

Briscoe remained buoyant as he hopped out at the ticket booth. He paid old man Pop Corn in cash for the three busloads of screaming kids as fireworks filled the sky above the drive-in.

"You know you're rolling in late again, Doc. Full price and no money back! And you can't park these buses down in the front like you did last time. You got to take them up to the back. You and your rat pack can use the chairs outside the snack shop or on the lawn down front."

"Excellent. Say thank you, Pops!" Briscoe bowed.

"Thank you, Pops!" the kids chorused back.

"Now, shush! The shows have already started!" Pop declared.

Briscoe pushed a fingertip against his lips, and his pack followed their Pied Piper out of the buses without another sound. He led them underneath the two movie screens that towered above the playground and over to the rows of benches spread out beneath them. The giggling orphans and grim-faced counselors split up between the two big screen choices.

Kate Tempest and the others never minded being yanked out of their dorms to go on another magical mystery run or anywhere else the unpredictable Dr. Briscoe wanted. It always proved exciting and worthwhile.

She laid back on a patch of soft grass in front of the slides. Kate remembered her bunk blanket to wrap up in this time as she stared up at the monster screen. She was ready to dream or scream—it didn't matter. But then Kate noticed something peculiar.

"Wait a minute? Oooh! Gross, man! Check out how big this chick's nostrils are from this angle." Kate pointed up at the distorted on-screen image.

The orphans howled and made booger jokes, so no one noticed the sounds of the distant engines revving in the background.

Zack sat down next to Kate. They shared an unspoken

nod, and he laid down beside her in the grass and stared up. He giggled at the scale of the enormous nostrils, threatening to snort up its audience.

Kate smiled at the silent boy she'd only heard strange rumors about.

"What do you think, little guy? She must shoot out snot rockets bigger than our bus."

Zack chuckled again, and Kate was on a roll.

Hey! At least he's in on the jokes.

Back on the ridge behind the drive-in, the Happy Trails Racing League were making out inside their rumbling supercars when Coop and Sue unintentionally launched themselves into infamy. His distracted crew didn't even notice their liftoff.

The climactic car chase had begun on-screen, and Coop's engine roar matched the throaty movie star's Mustang in both pitch and fury.

"Not part of the plan! Not part of the plan!" Coop screamed as strands of snapping barbwire twanged across the hood like broken banjo strings.

Coop stomped on the brakes, but then his heel shoved the car's heavy floor mat over the accelerator, pinning the car's throttle wide open.

At that point, the Mustang roared into hyper-drive. It flew down through the back of the bowl-shaped drive-in's higher elevations—bucking like a bronco over every row it launched off.

Those moviegoers sitting outside their cars screamed as a real-life predator charged out of the darkness at them. They scattered like chickens in a barnyard, leaving a rooster tail of feathers and popcorn in the air behind them.

Down in the front, Zack swatted at his aggravating gnats. They seemed peskier than usual, forcing him to sit up. That's when he noticed the cries swelling behind them as something wicked roared their way.

"Stand up. Leave."

37

"What's that?" It surprised Kate to hear his voice." Do you have something to say, sweetie?"

"Run. Now."

He pointed, and Kate singled out the source of the chaos hurtling straight toward them.

Bouncing out of his driver's seat behind the wheel, Coop swerved between the obstacle course of parked cars, snapping speaker wires and shattering side windows, row after row.

"Just shut it off!"

"I tried! It's jammed! It won't slow down!"

Down below, Kate shot to her feet.

"Run!" she screamed before taking her best advice.

Dr. Briscoe spun from his phone, confused by the tidal wave of screams behind him—then shocked sober by the Mustang bearing down on everyone, and he dropped his cell phone and flask and bolted for safety.

"Look out!" Sue waved frantically inside the Mustang. "More kids! More kids! Left! Left! Right! Miss that one!" she screamed as her head pounded against the inside roof.

Zack stood motionless as the out-of-control muscle car swerved for him. He had waited a fraction of a heartbeat too long to save himself. Now he wasn't sure which way to dive. But in that last instant, Kate ran back and tackled the boy, tumbling them onto the harsh asphalt as the Mustang's grill filled her entire field of vision.

"Brace!" Coop yelled inside, cutting the steering wheel hard to the right over the last jump.

Kate and Zack hit the ground just as the car launched over the top of their heads—its popcorn-covered tires missing their scalps by inches.

Coop's last-second maneuver catapulted the Mustang into the air, where it soared over the occupied playground—before slamming sideways into the tubular support beams below.

The brutal collision knocked the movie screen off its foundation, and the monster favored one side now as if

38

crippled by a stroke.

Coop's door took the brunt of the impact as intended, but now the interior damage pinned him inside.

Sue kicked her door open and dragged Coop across the tilted bucket seats and onto the blacktop, where he passed out as soon as he landed.

Coop's memories swam in silent slow motion after that. He watched the silent, angry faces surging forward, hurling obscenities as they tried to punch and claw at him.

He could see bloodstained Sue in tears, backing them away. Then a man dressed formally, Dr. Briscoe, came rushing to their rescue, forcing everyone to submit to his authority.

"Stand back! I'm a doctor!" was the last thing Coop heard clearly inside the tunnel vision of his mind before he blacked out. But then he noticed the sounds of pandemonium rising in counterpoint to his heartbeat as everything became bright and wailed in closer.

"What? Oh no. Sue?" Coop sat up, shivering.

His eyes stayed riveted on hers as they both welled up seeing the other alive. Then, when he refocused through the dribble of blood, he saw the ruined Mustang sticking out of the side of the bloated whale like a harpoon.

"Nothing seems broken. Can you stand up?" Sue asked.

She coaxed Coop onto his feet as the paramedics rolled in, and Dr. Briscoe briefed them about everyone's condition.

The scale of property damage produced by only a single car across the breadth of Pop Corn's once Magnificent Drive-In Theatre was staggering.

Old Pop Corn kept hyperventilating into an empty popcorn bag. He swore so proficiently between breaths that his R-rated language singed the ears of many innocent PG moviegoers standing nearby.

"How many people did I...?" Coop choked on the word. "Kill?"

"None!" Sue answered with a smile. "Not a one. Nobody got hurt."

"What?"

"I know! It's a miracle! A real-life miracle. A couple of twisted ankles, but that's it so far. You were exceptional, Coop. Honest. Your driving saved lives."

She tried to reassure him as an army of police, and first responders closed in.

"It could have been so much worse," she promised too soon.

"It was supposed to be so much more."

In hindsight, Coop regretted this entire night and his foolish plans to reinvent himself.

Suddenly, the base buckled without a groan, and the compromised movie screen swung down like a giant flyswatter on a hinge aimed exclusively at the scattering ants below.

Everyone screamed as the overbearing shadow gobbled up the closest first.

It was too late for anyone to react, but Kate tried to run with Zack in her arms. That's when Zack thrust his fist over his head and screamed at the falling screen.

"Stop! Now!"

When Kate dared open her eye's seconds later, they were blinded by the dazzling aviation lights from on top of the movie screen staring directly into her face. Those rotating blue lights rippled across Zack's extended fingertips as if in communication, and the tilted colossus remained frozen in place, just inches short of crushing everyone to death. And the unbelieving crowd watched the miracle unfold—civilians, paramedics, and police alike.

The silver screen leaned at an impossible angle just a few feet above the asphalt—seemingly compelled to stop against gravity's laws by the strength of one child's incredible willpower.

Kate trembled with fear and anger at her actions.

How dare she not drop Zack and run for her life when her survival instincts kicked in?

What are you, nuts girl? You know our rules! You take care of us first! Her inner voice scolded.

Dr. Briscoe couldn't rationalize what he had just witnessed as everyone ran past him to safety. Nevertheless, his scientific mind remained institutionally skeptical of any excuses other than the most prominent and logical whenever confronted with random events like this.

Was it a fluke? Luck? Timing? Coincidence?

Is the human mind capable of superhuman explosions of power in life-or-death situations like this? Like a mother lifting a car off her pinned child in an accident. I know it is scientifically possible. It's documented.

But I believe I just saw Zack Goodnight stop that screen from falling with only the power of his mind.

Briscoe's mind raced ahead of the problem, searching for any answers that might include future profit potential.

What happened tonight?

But before questions could be satisfied, Wyatt Waylon Cooper had to deal with the law as they cuffed and rattled off his Miranda Rights to him on the fly.

"You have the right to remain silent...."

Dr. Briscoe ran behind, pleading the wounded teen's case to anyone who would listen while informing the authorities that the innocent teen had saved lives with his talents behind the wheel.

The shaken counselors gathered their orphans and herded them back onboard their school buses for an early return to the institute.

Stephanie, Sue's best friend, forced her way through the thinning crowd to get beside her friend as they watched Coop driven away in the back of a squad car.

"Sue? Sue? Are you alright? What? What happened?"

There was a long pause before she could find an answer.

"I... I kissed him," she said. "That's all. It was just... a kiss."

-CHAPTER 6-

A Very Dangerous Creature

Yuma thrust the meteorite into the flames of his two-thousand-degree forge, triggering any hitchhikers onboard to spit back with sparks of interstellar outrage.

The basement of his massive timber and boulder-framed lodge displayed the giant's mastery of all the metal, glass, and woodworking skills he'd acquired over the centuries. He applied those ancient trade secrets to constructing this sprawling, one-of-a-kind structure that he and Blue Feather had called home for the last three hundred years.

The growling giant no longer resembled the pitiful, crispy critter of only a few days prior as he hammered the molten meteor into submission inside his underground foundry. Once on the brink of death, the impressive First Nation warrior appeared healthy and filled with manic energy.

Even in advanced age, Yuma was an impressive man and rejuvenated, if not completely healed, from his most hideous wounds. Whereas before, he could barely lift his head, now he appeared ten decades younger. He held the dense meteorite out before him as if weightless. In only days, his immortal body had repaired his crippling injuries. Even the thick scars on his hands and face had faded into pale ghosts.

A silver buzz cut replaced his scorched mane of white hair, which remained his only vanity as it grew longer every day. His skin continuously itched as it stitched itself back together, one cell at a time from the inside. He resisted the urge to scratch by slaving like a madman over his sweat-drenched anvil.

Tales of Yuma's uncommon valor against foreign invaders stretched back across the centuries on all continents. Yet his extraordinary accomplishments remained hidden from anyone in modern times. But the sense-memory of this roaming giant lay firmly embedded within the gene pool of most indigenous cultures around the globe, no matter the tribe. He continued to stalk their collective nightmares from the shadows.

Any lasting memorials to his legendary victories were lost to time now except for stone-age petroglyphs chiseled across the mountaintops of South America or painted inside undiscovered caverns in the American southwest. There was no written account of Yuma's life story or legend in any existing libraries worldwide—except one.

The common belief shared across the ages was that even a careless mention of one of his sacred names might cause the winds of retribution to shift and blow hot again. So, whenever the weak called upon him amid their whimpering's of despair—those innocents all cried out for the same anonymous deity to return and save their tribes.

To some, they knew him *as The One Who Walks Between—to* others—t*he Earth-Shaker.* But no matter what name they whispered under their breath, Yuma was the only unconquerable hero in all their impoverished hopes and dreams. He was the steadfast champion of the underdog, no matter the tribe or how hopeless their circumstances were, and the only avenging agent capable of standing and delivering justice to his scattered people.

Yuma the Tree was no wispy, fictional god of legends and folklore, but a living, flesh and blood immortal cut from a distinct branch of humankind's evolution. A veritable titan among giants and born with a warrior's heart and a savant's dazzling mind, like all the unknown ancients that predated him.

No human had seen him in over a hundred years. But

true believers knew that if Yuma was ever spotted walking amongst the modern tribes, then the tides of wickedness had turned against humanity again. After that, our feeble world would falter under its blind stupidity and fall victim to another thousand-year abyss of unending darkness.

That eternal spiral of damnation and revelation would repeat endlessly for humankind, like a wheel within a wheel, until the one heralded as 'The Light in the Dark' appeared before the modern world—illuminating the truth inside our mindless chaos, like a lighthouse in a storm.

Yuma drew upon his anger for sustenance and grew stronger and younger with every hammer blow, but inside, he continued to hemorrhage spiritually.

He was a lost and lonely mess at his core—teetering on the brink of insanity and driven senseless by his overpowering hatred for Pepper Wixx—a hate that festered inside him like an incurable disease that even his super-cells couldn't defeat.

Less than a millennium ago, millions of giants roamed the planet. As far as Yuma could tell, he might be the only one left standing. And the unrelenting survivor's guilt he lived with every day drove him closer to the edge of madness.

I do not see my reflection staring back from the water any longer. I wonder if Blue Feather would recognize me?

Yuma continued hammering at an industrial pace—reshaping the metal like a hydraulic piston, folding hundreds of shimmering layers together into an indestructible blade of impressive length.

Under his mighty blows, the repurposed ingot slowly developed into a better version of itself—a staggering twelve-foot-long sword. He quenched the sizzling weapon in a trough of oil and water as the super-heated coolant exploded into clouds of steam and fire—as the sky steel hardened at the molecular level.

Yuma dried the blade, eyeing its deadly edge geometry for imperfections. Once satisfied on the grinding wheel, he poured acid along the length, revealing a series of recurring lightning bolts woven inside the fabric of the finely honed metal, reconfirming Yuma's mastery of all earthly materials.

He held the elegant sword before him, squinting down its length and searching for any blemishes that might tarnish its surface. But there were none. He tested its menace by shaving off only the tips of his forearm hair.

"You will bite. I loathe necromancers more than anything, but I love how their European blades slice through the flesh, and I cannot wait to feed Wixx a taste of her own bile."

Yuma delighted in his deadly craftsmanship, with an unsettling twinkle haunting his eyes.

Once satisfied, he stacked the long sword against a cluster of twenty other colossal blades of equal quality, each representing another lost warrior. Finally, Yuma acid-etched those weapons with the same lightning bolt symbol and then engraved each weapon with the name of the individual warrior who had wielded them in life.

Blue Feather.

Cheenoo.

Toth.

And all the others in his decimated army. Yuma's goal was to recreate a hundred battle swords in honor of his fallen tribe.

Like an ancient robot with an unlimited power supply, the Native American giant grabbed another volleyball-sized meteorite and stabbed it into the blast furnace. The pinwheeling sparks reminded him of that horrifying night only days ago and the shrieking fireballs that were his family.

"All I need is a little more time to prepare and a little more help. That is all I need. That is all I am asking of you." Yuma stared up, as if expecting an answer through the skylight above.

He willed every sword into existence as his mind and body fed on nothing but hatred and revenge—shattering imaginary skulls with every hammer blow.

With no sleep, the unstable Time Guardian grew more dangerous by the minute as he hammered without rest throughout all the days and nights that followed.

Ultimately, Yuma couldn't abide the haunting silence any longer, and his pent-up fury exploded in moral outrage— launching another Lucid Pulse skyward.

"We must unite to save the light! Or we will all die!"

Yuma's rage tore out of the protective Bubble and flew into the stratosphere, searching for help—but it was a rarified kind of help that didn't seem to exist anymore.

-CHAPTER 7-

Substance Over Style

Kate Tempest's budding confidence was feeling bruised.

Josh Blunt still hadn't asked her to go to the prom, and that special date was approaching fast. But she felt confident enough to choose a gown for the most memorable night of her life even before he asked.

She knew the perfect dress she wanted to wear. She'd seen it on late-night TV.

The beautiful actress wore it at some awards show in 2013 and tripped up the steps to receive her statue, and Kate fell in love with the actress and her elegant dress the instant they hit the stairs together.

The young performer looked like a hip version of a fairy-tale princess as she went sprawling across the world stage. Only to rise like a lovely phoenix and accept her award with grace, dignity, and self-deprecating laughs that drew a standing ovation.

Just my kind of style sister.

Dr. Briscoe footed the bill for every child old enough to choose the gown or suit of their choice. With a fiscal limit of two hundred and fifty dollars per kid—this was part of his carrot-on-a-stick philosophy of mental therapy—for every risk—there was a bigger reward.

Kate needed to find photos of that vintage dress for reference, but using her restricted laptop was a long, problematic process to accessing the outside world. She sat cross-legged on her pink bunk bed with a new accomplice, Pavarty Wong, helping her in the emergency.

When provoked, fourteen-year-old Pavarty's tongue could flay a teenager's ego like a bullwhip. Tiny Pavarty's best strategy for self-defense was always to be funnier than anybody else in the room—or at least the most fun. And because of that, she was about as discreet as a bad case of flatulence in church. If she thought it—it popped out.

In stark contrast, there was a sublime sophistication about her. Shorter than most and with a lovely, oval face, she made up for her stature with a natural elegance and grace. Even wearing low-top sneakers, hand-me-down jeans, and a simple white shirt, she made everything look upscale by adding splashes of her artistic sensibilities.

The doctors said she needed to slow down her over-anxious mind and relax in everything she did and thought. And Pavarty discovered she could achieve those goals without their drugs whenever she hung around the grounded Kate.

"You heard the amazing news, right? There's going to be a lottery to see who goes shopping for the prom first. Including a free lunch at the... wait for it... the redesigned Food Court! Can you believe it?"

Pavarty flushed as if she'd already won.

"Perfecto! Shop and dine! I'm in!"

Uncharacteristically, Kate shared her fragile dreams with this new, untested companion while safeguarding her unspoken past.

"We can eat a gazillion different things there! Any flavor combination you can think of from all over the world! But only after we try on every dress first."

"It's going to be fantastic, right?" Kate sighed, lost in her expectations. "Everything shiny and beautiful and new and innocent."

"Speak for yourself, pilgrim," Pav giggled, disgusting Kate.

"Ugh. No, Pav! It's not even about boys. I just want to

dance the night away and create the most perfect bubble in time. One that's all mine—nobody else's. Where everything and anything is possible. That way, those memories will last forever, no matter what else happens in my miserable life. I'll always have that magical night to cherish."

Pav teared up. She had heard the rumors about Emily Healy's recent self-sacrifice, and Pavarty realized that even she would return to Rehash to preserve that special night for her new idol.

Pav understood the prom's underlying significance in refloating Kate's emotional boat.

"Listen, sister, is there any way we can rig this lottery so we both get to go shopping at the mall together?" Pavarty said. "They call that a win-win."

They conspired with belly laughs reserved for best friends, but when Kate glanced out her dorm window on the top floor, she was startled by a sudden flurry of movement.

"Are those freaky raccoons back up here again?" Pav joked as she caught her friend's frightened glare, and then she gasped herself.

"Holy pretzel!"

They saw Zack Goodnight in his PJs standing outside their window, straddling the roofline. He swatted above his head, rocking dangerously from side to side on the highest pinnacle of the six-story rooftop.

Zack fled outdoors because of the summer heat, and the sticky air inside the dorm was too humid to breathe. Besides, he believed he heard something extraordinary flying by in the night again. He could smell the fresh pine needles flooding his nostrils once more as translucent wisps of energized color rippled out of the sky and swirled around his body, reinforcing its repeated message.

We must unite to save the light? But how could I know that? Where do these new feelings come from?

This dizzying interaction with external forces beyond his own unsettling visitations was unlike anything Zack had experienced, as the Lucid Pulse homed in on his open mind and struck him between the headlights with its ultimate message.

"Or we will all die!"

Zack lost his balance on contact and collapsed. He slid helplessly down the steep roofline until his bare heels caught the rain gutter at the last second, pitching him forward into a violent sit-up. But it was enough to stop his forward momentum, and he plopped back onto his rear.

"Ow!"

Kate jumped out before Zack could register what had happened.

She snagged his collar and yanked him back inside to safety, where they tumbled onto the floor. They sprawled underneath the open window, panting for air as Pavarty rushed over.

"Are you two crazy? I heard this one's wacky as a loon, but you, Kate?"

"You have to stop pulling these crazy stunts, Zack!" Kate scolded the hyperventilating child.

"Sorry."

"I've got to stop doing this. Too close a call again!" Kate said.

But that brutal rush of fear and adrenaline was fleeting and replaced with the soothing tides of relief and pride as she regained her senses.

"Great Caesar's ghost! Have a little self-respect for your own life, girl! Who do you think you are, Wonder Woman?"

Famous for being street-smart and world-wary, Kate had inexplicably risked her life twice now for this same bewildering boy.

I can't be this kid's only keeper. No one could survive it.

Zack stood and padded away on bare feet.

"That's it, bud? No thanks, no nothing?"

"Thank you, Kate," Zack replied as he disappeared into his room.

Kate's head popped up like a surprised jack-in-the-box, and she grinned.

What a gift to hear his tiny voice again.

He had said nothing meaningful to her, even after the dreadful event at the drive-in. He explained briefly, in as few words as possible, that his magical gnats and a large Bobokafayz named Garth had warned him to turn around at the incoming danger.

After that, not another peep came out of Zack. Even with hours of extensive new workups headed by Dr. Briscoe and his team of experts, this silent young boy remained the undecipherable mystery he had always been.

The one thing that had changed since he saved her life, and Kate returned the favor—Zack didn't wander far from her sight now.

"Why Zack... you are quite welcome, young man!"

Pavarty mimed her frustration about Kate's new protective obsession, and Kate replied in sign language that everything was fine and she would be right back as she tiptoed after him.

Zack walked into his private bedroom alone. It was a converted broom closet, large enough for a bed and a small footlocker of toys but otherwise bare and windowless. He slept alone because no one in the regular dorms could stand his constant twitching after a few days.

Zack dove underneath his bunk and spread out like a human starfish, absorbing any chill from the cool cement floor.

Kate watched from the doorway as his pajama top shot out from underneath the bed.

"What are you doing, Zack?" Kate asked, stepping into the room.

Zack's pajama bottoms came sailing out next.

"Are you stripping down naked under there, Zacks?" she giggled.

"Too hot," he said, with discomfort shading his usual

51

monotone.

"Too hot. That's exactly right, young man."

Kate couldn't help herself as she grew even more fascinated by this intriguing little boy.

She felt his tiny body levitating right out of her arms when she held him tight during the collapse that night. Something powerful had surged through his veins when he stopped that toppling movie screen from crushing them all. The power coursing through his small body felt elemental in its authority, like lightning and gravity.

Unless it was some crazy mind trick in the middle of a disaster.

Kate sat on his bed, and Zack watched from underneath as the mattress groaned toward his nose.

"Why are you sitting on my bed?"

"Well, first off, I thought, it's just too darn hot to stand any longer."

"I know."

Kate grinned and continued.

"And so, then I thought I'd like to talk to somebody about it, and I chose you."

There was silence for a moment until a soft... "Thank you," crept out from underneath the bed.

"You are welcome, Zack. Hey Zack? How hot is it?" Kate tried a fresh approach.

"I don't know?"

"Why Zack, it's so hot today... that I actually saw a chicken lay a fried egg."

It took a beat before the sweetest little boy's giggles spilled out from underneath the bed. The happy vibrations inside the sweltering room suddenly felt magical, like sleigh bells in July, and Kate was delighted by their purity.

And belly laughs too? It doesn't get better than that.

A sense of genuine warmth and well-being enveloped them both.

"You like that one? Good Zack, that's good. Hey Zack, ask

me how hot it is today?" Kate pressed for more interaction.

After a moment, Zack repeated her line.

"How hot is it today, Kate?"

Kate's crooked smile crept wider.

"Why Zack, it's so darn hot... that trees are whistling for dogs to come over. Now think about it. Get it? Not too PG, right?"

There was a beat while Zack pondered the words, and then another burst of untamed giggles bubbled out of the sullen child.

"Get it?"

"I got it."

He prodded her now. "How hot is it, Kate?"

"Why, Zack... it's so dang hot... that birds have to use potholders today to pull the worms up out of the ground."

Zack slid out from underneath the bunk halfway, giggling at his new friend—his first ever.

"How hot is it, Kate?"

Kate had to dig for more material.

"Why Zack, it's so hot today... so gosh darn hot... that ahh..." she scanned his toys for inspiration. "That I saw Optimus Prime Transform himself into... an air conditioner!"

"Air conditioner?" Zack snickered and swatted the surrounding air.

"You okay, Zack?"

Kate tried not to seem concerned by his physical reactions.

"Why it's so dumb hot... that it's... plain stupid hot," Zack wrote his first lousy joke, and Kate rolled on the bed laughing. Not at Zack's joke as much as the gratifying connection that she had forged with the lonely little guy.

She understood that sharing kind words with this unique boy was a privilege to be cherished. There was an automatic synergy established between them that needed no further explanation. Kate didn't want to burst the lovely bubble they'd created together, but the curfew was nearing, and she still had big plans to cook up with Pavarty about their upcoming mall trip.

"I tell you what, Zack... you understand what a promise is? Right?"

"Yes. It's unbreakable," he said, gazing back from the floor.

"Well, I promise you that if you ever want or just need to talk to anybody... I want you to come and talk to me, okay? I will always be there to listen. Alright? I promise to be there to listen. And I also promise that I will never tell anybody what we discussed unless you want me to. Deal? That's my solemn oath to you."

Kate shot out her hand, and Zack noticed her tiny scars for the first time.

"Anything?" he asked.

"Absolutely anything."

"People always say that, but when I talk, they all look at me funny," Zack whispered. "I never like those looks. They make me feel stupid and silly."

"I have never liked those kinds of looks from closed-minded freaks."

"Me, either."

"Seems like a waste of brainpower."

"Yup."

"Zack, I pinkie-swear-promise that you can tell me anything you want, and I won't tell another soul, and nothing can make me go back on that pledge." She kissed her pinkie and twisted it into his in a finger knot.

"Even if I talk about the Tic-Tacs, Zornoids, Great Garths, and Bobokafayz?"

She cocked her head at the strange names but smiled.

Computer games keep getting weirder and weirder, Kate thought, as if she was already an out-of-touch elder at fifteen.

"Zornoid and Great Garth away, Zacky boy! Anytime. But right now, I've got to get back to my room, and I suggest you put your britches back on and hop up onto that bunk for bed count, okay? After that, you can crawl back underneath and sleep on the cold floor all night if you like. Deal? I'll be just down the hall if you need me."

She smiled down like a proud new sister.

This poor little guy needs a champion.

Zack crawled onto his bed in his skivvies and called out one last time.

"How hot is it, Kate?"

"Well, Zack, little buddy... it's so darn hot that... I hear all the penguins in Antarctica are riding camels these days!"

Zack's belly laughs erupted out of his room, and Kate's mood soared. She gave a proud thumbs-up to a stupefied Pavarty as they stood back in shock, listening to his continuing chuckles.

"Camels in Antarctica." Zack chuckled again.

Those delightful giggles made Kate as proud as if she'd discovered a lost continent the experts had dismissed as legend.

The heck with all these doctors. I'll heal this little guy myself!

Her overinflated teenage bravado ballooned beyond all proportions.

"Watch out, world. It looks like I'm a natural-born healer."

-CHAPTER 8-

Reflections of the Fallen

Yuma soared up the trunk of the enormous sequoia effortlessly, like a natural-born tree surfer. Balancing upright onboard a polished wooden platform, he shot past branches as large as adult trees as he zoomed to the top. The homemade elevator's launch was always as gut-wrenching as his inspired rigging made it appear.

He built these self-powered, portable systems throughout the Sacred Forest using only native resources like counterbalanced boulders, hand-carved pulleys, and miles of intricate rope work. And Yuma only gained these superior engineering skills after centuries of deep thought, close-up examinations of spiderweb construction, and sheer laziness—the mother of all inventions.

The savvy giant had grown weary after centuries of back-breaking labor and hauling his heavy body up the skyscraper-sized sentinels daily. But he became inspired after realizing he merely had to tickle gravity in the right direction to provide all the fun in heavy lifting.

He celebrated Mother Nature's generosity by harnessing all the superpowers she provided so graciously—gravity, wind, water, earth, wood, stone, and fire—by using them to their best advantage. As a result, Yuma could soar to the tip of any redwood on nothing more than a whim and without a hitch to his breath.

The graceful platform slowed as it reached the top pulley and snuggled against the belly of the fogbank that nested among the treetops.

Peering down through the mist revealed a gasp-inducing, five-hundred-foot plunge to the forest floor below, and everything living at this breathtaking altitude swayed with just the rumor of wind.

Yuma tilted his head back and squinted at the faint outline of the Bubble shimmering overhead, searching for any damage he might have caused to the transparent membrane by his violent outbursts, but he saw none.

"This is good."

The mystical superstructure was another of Mother Nature's most ambitious achievements—the ability to hide worlds within worlds and within plain sight.

She cast her spell over these enchanted lands thousands of years before as humanity multiplied beyond all reason and swarmed across her natural world like a plague.

Human beings were born as curious and inspiring experiments at best. But they were also greedy, ravenous monsters at their worst. Their species slaughtered and consumed every animal and resource before them like spoiled children at a birthday party, never surrendering to the reality that all parties had to end.

Even their modern science remained ignorant of the Bubble's exceptional existence until Yuma's recent outbursts. His powerful Lucid Pulse sent sensors flickering onboard spy satellites orbiting overhead. Still, the paranormal transmissions didn't register on typical wavelengths and were dismissed by the smartest as mere background noise. And so, Mother Nature continued to blind the twenty-first century with its own arrogance precisely as she designed it.

Poor humans, nothing would change for humanity if everything remained the same. There were so many more beautiful secrets about the living planet than homo sapiens could even imagine, let alone fully conceptualize, and yet, their time for discovery was running out.

Yuma grappled with the fact that something

remarkable was on a collision course with human destiny again. A world-shaking challenge was hurtling towards them, and a time of great change was coming to their cosmic evolution—if—his interpretations of the emerald tablets were correct.

But even an immortal, drawing upon a well of limitless knowledge, couldn't conjure what shape that future transformation would come to them in or when it would appear. But it needed to happen soon, before it was too late.

Once the elevator docked, Yuma secured a braking rope, lifted out one of the meteor swords, and balanced on the nearest limb.

He pulled a pair of welder's goggles from his medicine bag and snapped them over his eyes. Like everything he built, he'd reinvented these gizmo-goggles several times after decades of constant tinkering. Tiny brass gears twirled multi-colored lenses over his eyes, snapping into place with a head nod. Yuma wouldn't admit to needing glasses at his rebellious best, but this homemade solution would suffice.

His oversized goggles made for a disturbing, bug-eyed look, but generations of eagle chicks imprinted on his predatory glare and considered him family.

That's when Yuma spotted a tiny orb of light darting between the trees and grew excited for the first time in weeks. He'd caught sight of this energized ball flitting around the forest using his specialized lenses, but only in the deepest parts of the rainforest. Now he watched with fascination as that same intriguing wisp hovered below.

"Do not be afraid, small visitor. I will not harm you. Wait, where did you go?"

It wasn't Zip, Zash, and Zee. He was sure of it. The glowing hummingbirds had flown away earlier in their search for insects.

"Ah, there you are."

This excited sparkle was something entirely new in Yuma's comprehensive knowledge of the forest. Once he realized his teeny visitor had vanished again, he turned back to lashing the twelve-foot weapons to the center spires of the tallest redwoods, with every sword tip pointing skyward.

No matter the design, each distinctive blade shared the same extraordinary lightning bolt finish—one gleaming masterpiece for every murdered friend.

Even partially installed, the growing memorial dazzled the eye as the morning sun rose, illuminating the morning sky in streaks of gold. Then, the wind came with the sun and lifted the blackbirds to the treetops, where Yuma requested they celebrate this moment in their songs and spread the sad news to the world's indigenous tribes—now broken and scattered like dust in the wind.

Yuma scowled through his lenses as he stared across the lake at the loathsome invaders, observing Dark Hollows from a predator's perspective.

The greasy little town bustled with early morning life as buzzards circled above in search of their next morsel.

From a distance, the jagged rooftops appeared covered in snow drifts in the middle of summer. But upon closer inspection by eye and nose, the centuries of constant bombardment of buzzard guano gave that false alpine illusion its real stink.

The hastily rebuilt town appeared as busy as it was vile these heady days of post-war reconstruction. The victorious citizens seemed secure enough in their defenses to go about their daily business, reassured because giants no longer existed.

"They do not view me as a threat. Not after watching so many immortals die. But they underestimate me for the last time."

Through his ever-shifting lenses, Yuma scanned past the two massive catapults on the beach, scorched to charcoal and abandoned to the waves.

"We were fools ever to trust them. Why did we let their pestilence grow? Why did we not obliterate them from those shores when we still had the chance? Peace. Ha! Treaties. Meaningless rubbish. There is no peace with evil. Here is where I draw the line."

The battle tactician in Yuma realized it was only a matter of time before Wixx and her hordes would lash out with overwhelming forces from across the infested lake and scourge these lands of their most precious secrets.

"They are coming—sooner than later. And I will stand ready and free. Alone, if that is the way."

The giant nodded, and the lenses danced again. He glassed the murderous town in a zoomed-in close-up and watched with contempt as the clustered businesses and factories spewed plumes of ash into the air while the entire population choked on a perfect sunny day.

The numerous mines and ore processing facilities, lead smelters, lumber mills, and even the wood-fired bakery in town all contributed to the toxic air quality of the southern shores. The prevailing winds from the north pinned the ginger haze against the shoreline for a reason.

Dialing into greater magnification, Yuma recognized individual citizens as they wheezed along the streets, some with facemasks covering their beaks, but most with none.

"Where is Wixx?" Yuma roared, startling himself.

The giant's thunderous voice exploded across the lake, and he watched with amusement as the bewildered townsfolk stumbled in confusion.

"I am still alive! Tell that to your witch! We have unfinished business!"

Something flashed next to his head, and Yuma flinched. *Watch out!*

His confused lenses kept sifting through all focus points until only the shadiest lenses clicked into position, and he jerked back instinctively as the brilliant twinkle buzzed by his ear. Yuma kept scanning the treetops until his lenses discovered the rare orb hiding behind a plume of evergreen needles.

"You again? Well, hello, my shy friend. This is the clearest I have seen you."

Yuma welcomed the surprising distraction to his work schedule and dialed back his anger.

"I apologize if my ugliness upset you. I am not your enemy. Where do you live in the forest? What clever creature be you, little one?"

The orb blinked out without responding.

"What could this be? It is neither fairy nor sprite. Neither lightning bug nor butterfly."

Yuma remained bewildered as he went back to work. He labored through the night until the next dawn revealed he had finished his crown of swords.

Once completed, the concentric spirals of over a hundred battle swords blazed as a single triumphant beacon of courage and hope.

"For as long as they exist, the citizens of Dark Hollows will never forget my warriors. Now they will see their names and faces reflected on their walls forever."

Yuma sighed and took a satisfying pull from his canteen. With his first goal achieved, he relaxed for a few minutes as the redwoods swayed in the winds sent to soothe an ailing giant.

The legendary shaman tried to recenter his beleaguered mind and purify his soul in the rhythmic reflections of the fallen. But the Time Warrior had more than beauty and honor on his mind.

"If I do not survive, the Sacred Forest will fall. I will never let that happen."

With eyes closed and his brow furrowed, he pondered his next move like a chess master—steeling his resolve against the inevitable assault of the pawns.

Finally, he could meditate no longer, and Yuma unleashed a familiar ululating war cry across the lake.

"Ayyyy ya!"

He chuckled as he watched the homicidal residents of

Dark Hollows run for their lives like in the good old days.

-CHAPTER 9-

Stranger in a Strange Land

A low-level sonic boom ripped across the campus, causing everyone to panic in terror and seek cover.

The overpowering wall of sound ping-ponged between buildings as Zack nosedived back through the same window he toppled through the night before, sprinted straight for Kate's room, and dove underneath her bunk, trembling like the walls.

The children screamed in the hallways as the shrill, punishing alarms blasted away, only adding to the chaotic confusion indoors.

"I'm sorry. I was just trying to answer that cry." Zack kept apologizing to Kate as if he had committed a crime.

The fact was that the mysterious detonation was Zack's bungled attempt at producing his first Lucid Pulse—something unattainable unless a giant.

"It's okay, Zack! What happened? Are you alright?"

Kate tried to focus on the frightened little boy instead of evacuating. As everyone ran for the exits, Kate took a deep breath and crawled underneath her bed, only to be hit with a face full of cobwebs.

"Eck! Answer me, little man, okay? Are you alright? What was that boom? Are you hurt?"

Zack shook his head no.

"I didn't do anything."

"What happened? Did you see something?"

"No."

Kate continued operating on untapped instincts to

63

shield the frightened child from further trauma as she swatted away the spiders.

"Are you sure you're alright?"

"I don't know. I don't know. I don't know anything. I was just trying to answer that sad cry I keep hearing," Zack muttered.

"What cry? Whose sad cry?"

"I don't know. I'm sorry, Katie. I went back out on the roof again."

"I know. It's okay. It's okay, Zack. Hey, listen. It's still so hot tonight. How hot is it?"

"I don't care. I've got a terrible headache."

Zack was too confused to think or make jokes and snuggled even closer to his protector just as Pavarty dashed into the room like her hair was already on fire.

"Kate! Kate?"

Kate's head slid out from underneath the bed. "What happened, Pav? Was it a bomb? A gas explosion? What?"

"I don't know, sister! But run! Run for your life now!" Pavarty shrieked over the piercing alarms as she scooped up her friends and shoved them out the shuddering door. "This place could collapse any second!"

The panicked orphans spilled outside onto the manicured grounds as guards ran out of their barracks, some hopping on one foot, still getting dressed—yet everyone froze when they saw it.

"What?"

"Hey."

"That can't be."

Kate and Zack stared back into the face of the impossible again.

An overturned school bus sat in the same spot the driver parked it in only ten minutes before, rubber side down. But after the big boom, all six tires now pointed skyward, while two buses parked on either side remained untouched.

Kate gasped in disbelief as Zack buried his face in her

side.

"What's going on here, man?"

That's when the fuel dripped onto the hot engine block. There was an enormous huff of ignition, and the children shrieked as the bus exploded.

Kate spun from the heat blast, shielding Zack as an orange and black fireball forced everyone back from the flames. Once it died, the curious rushed back in to witness the spectacle of their belly-up bus frying like a turtle in its own shell.

"This is twisted. I'm still dreaming, right?"

"Did a tornado snake through here?"

The bravest guards rushed in to save the buses as Dr. Briscoe skidded to a stop in his golf cart and hopped out just as the first extinguishers hit the flames. Still hungover and hastily dressed in robe and slippers, Dr. Briscoe could only stare in wobbly disbelief.

The rattled scientist felt as confused as everyone else on campus and couldn't comprehend what he saw. A sixteen-ton, thirty-nine-foot school bus was lying on its roof as if a giant hand had reached out of the night and flipped it over like a Hot Wheel.

Dr. Briscoe scanned the crowd, looking for guilty smirks among the awestruck children. But all he saw were shell-shocked expressions painted in all the shades of fear until his gaze tumbled into Zack's enormous eyes.

Wait. Could it be?

He studied the little boy's shivering demeanor and how tightly he hugged Kate.

Is that even possible? Is there something about this child we should study closer than the others?

Absolutely. The shark tank inside the scientist answered in unison. *Without question.*

Briscoe's entrepreneurial instincts overrode all other impulses whenever the smell of cash filled the water. And indeed, there was an ocean of money to be made by studying this remarkable child. Then, in a flash of insight, the new prophet foresaw the future of Biotech laid out before him like a golden road map.

The next day inside the cafeteria, Coop's surprise appearance on campus was already the number one topic in the orphan's heavily moderated chatrooms.

'Coop McQueen Has Finally Landed—Guess Where?' Read the newest meme with a repeating GIF of Coop in action behind the wheel of the Mustang and the people and popcorn flying into the air over and over again.

Most were convinced Coop was behind that insane flaming bus stunt the night before.

"I heard he plans to jump a Mustang over the Grand Canyon next year! He's that friggin good!"

"Somebody actually saw him doing wheelies with that same bus when they brought him in. No lie. Wheelies!"

"I heard he flipped it like a grilled cheese sandwich just to prove he could before they locked him up."

"Yeah. He's like some stunt-driving double in the movies, like in India or Pakistan or someplace exotic."

Their collective imaginations took flight as everyone on campus created their own versions of Coop. With no extra effort or pretense on his part, the notorious underage speed demon, and founding father of the Happy Trails Racing League, was immediately elevated to legendary status in the eyes of the entire Briscoe nerd herd.

Coop's cool-under-fire reputation preceded him, and this gaggle of misfits and daydreamers would forever claim him as one of their own.

So far, not so bad, Coop thought, glancing around at the friendly faces smiling back.

He sat alone at a corner table with his back against the wall and a detached look on his face as the entire cafeteria gossiped and giggled about him.

I feel like the new monkey in Dr. Briscoe's Mystery Zoo.

Dr. Eugene Briscoe had become enormously influential in Coop's life now. He proved to be the crucial witness at Coop's pretrial hearing when he testified in support of the teenage troublemaker.

The persuasive and noteworthy behavioralist convinced the judge, including the boy's guardian, his skeptical grandmother, that young Coop deserved a better chance at rehabilitation before throwing him into the wolves' den of the penal system.

"You've raised a great kid. I can make him even a better man if you just give me a chance, and all your legal troubles will disappear overnight, and months from now, he'll walk back in through your front door—because you'll still own your own home." He promised Coop's grandmother with authority.

"Why waste this precious young man's life when I can save him and, in his suffering, he can help save so many other young lives in the future? Off the taxpayers' backs." Briscoe pleaded with the court and anyone else that mattered.

"Make this problem go away, doctor." Came back the official response, as everyone washed their hands of the legal headache.

"My pleasure." The good doctor bowed. "I am only here to serve."

Once abandoned by the system and surrendered by his fragile grandmother to an unknown future inside Briscoe, Coop spiraled into a deep depression, even as his legal problems faded.

It took several soul-shattering nights alone in quarantine to make peace with his worst nightmares before the comforting thoughts resurfaced. That's when he realized how deliberately his grandmother had instilled her sense of resolve and self-worth in him.

Your willpower is your super strength, sweetheart. Never forget that fact, no matter what comes flying your way. It will never let you down.

It wasn't long before Coop understood that this new

corporate reality was a far healthier lifestyle choice for the next couple of years of incarceration compared to the harsh alternative of juvenile hall followed by prison.

I'll turn myself into a chameleon and just blend in here.

That was the plan, anyway.

If Dr. Briscoe hadn't rescued Coop, the endless lawsuits would have crippled the mini-celebrity for the rest of his life. But with everything settled, according to Dr. Briscoe and his legal team, Coop would walk away as a free man with a clean record in just thirty-six months. If he kept his nose clean, stayed intelligent, lucky, and followed the Doctor's directives without complaint.

This bacon burger tastes like heaven compared to the ground dog chow back in Juvey.

His tastebuds returned to life with the abundant choices overflowing on his tray.

So far, this place seems more like a spa for the Adams Family than an orphanage. They even have free juice and muffins in the hallways. Free video games. And there sure seem to be plenty of girls walking around.

Sitting alone with his thoughts, he caught sight of another of those flickers of celebrity recognition he got used to during the press coverage when Kate glanced over at him and did an awkward double-take.

He grinned and waved back, but she flipped her hair and scanned past him, barely acknowledging his existence. She was searching for bigger prey. Then, with her target firmly in sight, she shot straight for Josh Blunt, and Zack followed behind as an afterthought.

Kate cornered her dreamy date sitting at the crowded math table, and she tip-toed up behind him as his friends watched with growing amusement.

Beautiful Josh Blunt, sixteen years old, was a mathematical prodigy with the refined looks of a movie star from cinema's golden age.

Blessed with mile-long lashes shading a pair of blue

suede eyes, this handsome teenager turned heads in every room he entered. But his constant state of bewildering self-reflection offset any positive advantages his foxy exterior afforded him.

His relentless mind refused to surrender to any form of relaxation. Whenever seated, both his knees continually bounced like dueling pistons. Even in deep slumber submerged in the Dreampool, Josh's overactive imagination cramped most nights, forcing him awake and back onto his feet.

Only one person could break through that surface tension to rescue Josh whenever he sank to new lows, and that was his best friend and perennial lifeguard, Emiliano Guzman.

They had come through the foster system together from birth. Then, unfortunately, or fortuitously, depending on how they regarded their continuing friendship, they found themselves represented by the same corrupt adoption lawyer. He arranged for their dual incarceration into the Briscoe system for no other reason than a handsome payday. Double the kids, double the bucks, double the fun.

Kate's shadow slithered over Josh's shoulder like a cobra before snatching the juice drink off his tray with a sudden strike. But Josh didn't startle or move, and she took a long sip while considering her next move before replacing it.

"Ah! Thank you, Josh. I had something stuck in the back of my throat." She faked a tortured cough. "You should have heard me in the hall. I was croaking like a bullfrog at a Miley Cyrus concert."

Josh hardly acknowledged her presence, let alone her joke, already running new algorithms in his head.

"Uh, do you need a doctor or a paramedic or something?"

"No, Josh, just a sip and, oh, one more thing." Kate leaned in and pecked him on the cheek.

"There. I'm all better," she whispered inches away, and Josh's eyes glowed before filling with dread. It seemed Kate had hit the clear button on his internal calculator.

"Joshy?" Kate turned on the juice. "Like we talked before... are you still considering going to the prom this year?"

She waited for a response that never came as Josh's eyes clouded over, and he kick-started his calculations.

"Maybe. It might be something to do, I guess." He considered the proposition before drifting off to another whirlwind.

"Well?"

Kate waited patiently for an invitation that was never coming unless she took charge of her destiny.

"Josh... how about you and me... how about we go to the prom together?"

His friends giggled at Josh's legendary ineptitude. Even half-drugged, the jealous nerds realized their good-looking friend was utterly clueless.

Emiliano threw out the first spitball.

"Listen, dork, when the prettiest girl in the entire school invites you on a date... you accept! Do you understand *that* equation, Prince of all night moves?"

Everyone snickered and jabbed elbows.

Emiliano's smile stretched as wide as his rubber bands would allow. His brand-new plastic braces gleamed with saliva bubbles whenever he spoke fast, building up quite a frothy lather in the corners when overexcited.

"Why, thank you, Emil. That's a mighty sweet compliment, mi amigo," Kate gushed and blew him a kiss. "That's kind of beautiful."

"No. You are."

Kate enjoyed receiving these small bouquets of charm these days, and she tousled Emil's hair before sharing a warm smile with the rest of the dorks. She noticed their faces—made up of all shapes, colors, and zits—blushing like crimson Chinese lanterns whenever she was around. And she cherished that warm glow of mutual appreciation and respect they showed her.

"The most beautiful girl in school," Josh sighed.

"Why, thank you, Josh."

"No. I meant... the most beautiful girl in school?"

He had somehow cycled the words into another equation to solve.

Josh pondered the mathematical ramifications of Emil's subjective description. Then he articulated it again as if posing the deepest of all philosophical questions as everyone leaned in.

"Are you really the prettiest girl in the entire school? What are those odds?"

Kate's last name came immediately to mind as lightning bolts flashed behind the storm clouds rising in her eyes.

"Are... you... serious?"

Frustrated, Kate grabbed the next boy walking by, which happened to be Coop. She seized him by the back of the neck, spun him over backward like in the movies, and kissed him without hesitation.

They both gasped for air after she finished making her point, and Coop fought to maintain his balance with his tray as she supported him in her arms.

Kate cocked an eyebrow Josh's way, expecting some reaction or signs of jealousy, but he was a dead battery.

The nerds cheered silently, their arms raised in mock triumph without using their voices so they wouldn't annoy the staff, and Coop felt like the winner in a mimed sweepstake he never entered.

"Lucky duck."

"Lucky dork, you mean."

"Can you even imagine?"

"Oh yeah."

In that moment, Kate realized she was wasting her time on gorgeous Josh when so many other slimy jellyfish were left in the sea.

"That figures. This is on me," she admitted out loud.

She had worshiped the handsome teen from afar

without getting close enough to realize he was a solitary, damaged, over-thinker with a highly polished exterior. And there wasn't a lot of room left for anyone else inside.

I guess we all have our burdens to bear, pretty boy.

Without a glimmer of disappointment, she turned back to Coop, still arched over.

A bird in the hand, right?

"You? Good kisser." She spoke face to face for the first time.

"Thank you?"

"Do you want to go to the prom with me?"

"Sure. Why not?" Coop chirped, unwinding himself from her embrace and standing back up. "Otherwise, I was just headed for the trash

"What's your name, wise guy? Wait? Don't tell me. I know you."

"Call me, Coop," he answered. "What do they call you?"

"Try Kate."

She paused for a moment and refocused on his face.

"Oh yeah. Hey! Wait. You almost killed my friends and me!"

"I get that all the time. You'd be surprised."

Kate winced when she saw Coop still bore deep bruises on the left side of his neck and arm from the brutal impact.

"Sorry about that night. Something magical... ah... almost turned tragic."

"Yeah, I know that feeling. Well, stunt driver, you kiss cute and taste good to boot! So... you have booked a major date with me... officially, the prettiest girl at Briscoe. Just ask these fine gentlemen."

She reserved her last dart for Josh.

"See you on the other side of summertime, Joshy boy! You had your chance. Bye-bye, fellas!"

Kate wiggled her fingers as she danced away to the beat of her own drummer.

"And I'll see *you* prom night, Coop. If not before," she

called back. "I'll even help you pick out a tux?"

"Uh, okay, I guess. Thanks, Kate?"

"Lucky you!" she fired a killer smile at him over her shoulder.

"You are one lucky felon, Coop McQueen," Emiliano grinned, absorbing his new friend into their tribe.

"Just call me Coop."

The uber dorks giggled and jabbed each other as they watched Kate disappear around the corner, leaving them captivated even in her absence—especially Coop.

Well, things are certainly looking up around here!

Forget the mime sweepstakes. Coop felt like he had just won the Indianapolis 500 when no one was looking.

-CHAPTER 10-

A Clear Lucid Pulse

Yuma was doing close-up chart research in the master den of his sprawling lodge late that night and still sporting the gizmo-goggles when Zack's first intentional Lucid Pulse blew in and hit him full-on in the chest.

"Ahh!" the giant doubled over at the startling revelation as it blindsided him.

It was a brilliant mass of concealed energy unlike any he'd witnessed, cloaked inside hidden waves of amplified reality that brought the startled giant to his feet.

This emphatic reply to his plea for help made the hair stand on his neck as the radiating disc found him within the Bubble and enveloped him in compassion.

The sign! At last!

Yuma had waited for this unique signal for so long now that he'd given up hope—like waiting for an answer to a love letter that would never come.

Only a giant could produce such a bold, Lucid Pulse that is healthy and pure, he thought. *And only a giant among giants could do that.*

I have felt nothing like it before.

This Pulse is different—beyond description—almost frightening in its intensity.

Zip, Zash, and Zee body surfed away on the invisible wave as it splashed around the circular walls of the redwood lodge without penetrating the wood.

"Our reinforcements are moving, boys!" Yuma called

out. "They're on their way!"

The ancient Time Warrior felt as giddy as a child as he raced across the room to his curved, stream-fed aquarium, hoping for a better glimpse of the vanishing pulse.

How many lifetimes had he waited for such a clear yet mystical sign that announced itself boldly? A message of hope that verified that he and his fellow Time Warriors were never the last of their kind.

And now this perfect concentric signal has changed everything.

It was difficult for Yuma to believe that the intense mental signal was as strong as it appeared. Yet this first dramatic step into a new reality was a dream come true.

"A Pulse," Yuma grinned. "A precise Lucid Pulse like no other."

Inside his giant aquarium, strands of its psychic energy still rippled back and forth, trapped within, and dazzling fish in rainbow shards of spectral light.

With his brass goggles dialed into the correct spectrum, Yuma witnessed the lingering visual traces of the Lucid Pulse as it continued exploring the dense medium of water.

"What a powerful thing! Look at the variations in the color shifts!"

Yuma's childish grin exploded into laughter as he flipped his goggles onto his forehead and closed his eyes.

Internally, he drew from his own quiver of supernatural powers. He released a long hissing breath, and with a determined flinch of his head, Yuma sent another Lucid Pulse hurling up into the orbit in response.

Zip, Zash, and Zee flipped out of the way just in time, but the close proximity to the overpowering psychic blast sent the fish inside the freshwater tank flying. The trout and salmon evacuated first and launched themselves out of the tank and onto the floor into immediate distress as they gasped for their lives.

"Oh, no. Not again! Harley! Help me!" Yuma yelled. "I

must remind an idiot never to do this indoors again!"

An enormous Great Dane bounded confidently into the room, but the pony-sized hound slammed on the brakes as soon as his toes hit the chilly water.

"Please, boy. Help me get these floppers back inside the stream again, Harley!" Yuma begged in perfect dog-speak.

The confused hound voiced his complaints loudly at the desperate giant before picking up the nearest fish, standing on his massive rear haunches, and plopping it back into the aquarium unhurt.

"Did you feel it? They are coming, Harley. Help is on the way, boy!" Yuma gushed proudly to his best friend.

Yuma didn't know if his Lucid Pulse was strong enough to reach any of those new giants in the upside world. His powerful signal that horrible night was fueled by such an explosion of rage and unbearable anguish that it frightened even him in its fury. Yet, he hadn't achieved another pulse that monumental since.

It might not reach them for days, he thought. *Not at these great distances yet. But soon. They are coming my way!* He rewarded himself with the sweet taste of honey-colored hope.

Yuma prayed that the next Lucid Pulse would come from another giant standing face-to-face with him to see whose abilities were the strongest. He desperately missed his wife and comrades in arms and their wild conversations. The thought of other Time Warriors filling his ears with tales of their own exotic exploits was a thrilling luxury he could only fantasize about in the comforting waters of the Dreampool.

Yuma rechecked the star charts he was studying. Then, he cross-referenced that last pulse's date and time with another inscription etched into a beautiful transparent green tablet.

That's when he discovered a new glint on the crystal's pristine surface he had never seen before today.

"The sacred numbers align. If I am correct, the third glorious change of humankind's existence has begun."

Yuma sat down stunned and stroked Harley's brow, making the great battle dog seem puppylike compared to his hand.

"Our reinforcements are coming, boy. Help is headed our way. And maybe, if we are lucky, so much more."

He smiled at the beast, and Harley licked his fingers.

"I know it has been sad and boring living with only me. Well, I hope you are ready for some rowdy companionship again, my good friend. Soon we will have a great gathering of giants again. And then, together, we will save this world once more. The way it was meant to be."

-CHAPTER 11-

The Great Middlin Mall

The idling school bus cooked like a baked potato in the scorching sun.

Inside the sweatbox of the driver's metal security cage, Sgt. P.T. Crowley waited impatiently for his next round of passengers to board the reinforced security bus.

"Time to roll, people! Mush, mush! Let's move it!"

His starched uniform reeked of perspiration, coffee, cigars, and cheap drugstore cologne. Once those distinctive fragrances mingled with the stench of rancid mall food and stagnant diesel fumes, the noxious atmosphere inside the cabin would gag a pig.

The orphans nicknamed the cranky driver 'Petty' years ago. Yet even today, Sgt. Petty exceeded his notorious reputation by intentionally gunning the engine and blasting exhaust fumes into the children's faces to intimidate and speed up the security team outside.

"Knock it off, Sergeant, or I'm calling H.R.!" One wand-bearers coughed.

Ten excited orphans stood choking in line at the rear, waiting to pass through security for their first magical trip to the mall as Petty's uniform blossomed with new flowers.

"This freaking bus a/c works like you do, Norm. Sporadically."

He pounded and kicked the dash.

"Relax, Sergeant. Open a window." Norm replied

78

without looking up from his phone.

Petty's shift partner, Norm Prescott, learned to adapt to Petty's nonstop whining after years of riding shotgun with the outspoken loudmouth. Instead of listening to his inane jabber, he won every shift by bringing his noise-canceling earbuds with him whenever assigned together.

"It's one of those little freaks of nature right out there who blew up the only bus we had with a working a/c, and everybody knows it? And now I've got to drive these weirdos all the way to the mall and back in this summer heat without a working a/c? For what? Reward them, but no overtime or hazard pay for me? Briscoe's lost his mind, just like these psychos! Not like the old days around here, boy, I promise you that, Norm. Back in the good days, we skull-thumped these morons back into shape."

Dr. Briscoe stood on the veranda of his private Victorian mansion and waved goodbye to the children from across the campus. Hungover after another investment party, Dr. Briscoe presided over the noisy loading process from afar, clutching a fresh Bloody Mary and wearing his robe.

A man's soft voice drifted out from behind the French doors of Briscoe's home office.

"How prudent is this move, sir?"

Briscoe smiled and continued waving to the children, pointing to each as if kin—but his predatory shark grin turned deadly in response to any challenge of his authority.

Here was the true face behind the mask that was Dr. Eugene Briscoe. Unseen by all except those unfortunate enough to work for him. Here lurked the monster within the manor.

The timid silhouette in the doorway cleared his throat and raised his volume from the shadows.

"Surely, sir, after all the unwanted media attention and trouble with some of these notable orphans in public already..." Briscoe cut him off with an irritated wave of his drink, spilling ice and tomato juice on his satin slippers.

"Enough! I won't tell you how to be more of a conniving jackal than you already are, Mr. Bland, if you promise never to tell me how to do my job. Deal?"

Briscoe sneered as the pale man stepped out of the shadows and into the sunlight.

His name was Harlan Bland. Diminutive and unremarkable in every way, he was the go-to facilitator for some of the wealthiest scoundrels in the country. He covered up their notorious scandals and illegal maneuvers discreetly and without a trace of evidence left behind. As a result, they referred to him in their upper crust mythology as 'The Shadow Man.'

"You watched the security tapes with us, sir. This child you are releasing into the public eye is the same boy who stopped a movie screen with the sheer power of his mind. And the other troublemaker, Cooper, caused the entire disaster. And it was Goodnight who flipped the school bus over."

"All those claims are nonsense. Nothing's proven. Listen to your babble. I'm a practitioner of twenty-first-century science, not backward superstitious rubbish from the dark ages."

"Sir, with all due respect, when reviewing the surveillance footage with your security staff, we isolated Goodnight's solo movements on the roof when the bus was manipulated. You saw it yourself. There seems a direct, plausible link."

"Ridiculous, Bland. That's not evidence. There were a couple of unlikely coincidences and nothing more. Serendipity at best. Without further study, we can't be sure about any of this yet, and I refuse to draw any silly conclusions involving anything as shaky as psychic energy blasts and controlled telekinesis."

"But sir... in your best interests..."

"Listen, Bland, if I want to have this fragile child on my side, in the rare chance he has any demonstrable powers at all, then I don't need to oppress him now. Do I? Not after what he's been through. When I make a promise to these kids, I keep it, and that's how I stay in control of them. Carrot before the whip works miracles. I've proven it over and over. I've proven it with you."

"Yes, sir." Bland nodded—their brief eye contact hinting at some personal debt going back years.

"You understand the importance of this assignment, Harlan? Continue to impress me by being invisible at your job."

Harlan Bland possessed an extraordinary talent—a unique skill the elite paid for handsomely—the art of being somewhere without being there at all.

"You are correct in one regard. I cannot afford further notoriety if something embarrassing occurs. That is why I hired you, to prevent it from happening again, or I'd go myself. But my last outing was more than a few of our stockholders could bear."

"Indeed, sir. My point exactly. Why are we exposing our recent newsmakers to the public again? It could lead to our undoing."

"I will always act in my patient's best interests above profits. Always. I've taken an oath."

Harlan marveled at how effortlessly Mr. Hyde could slip back into Dr. Jekyll to suit Briscoe's needs.

"Of course, sir."

"These are a group of highly perceptive teenagers, so ensure you maintain a complete overview of everyone without being observed. But principally, keep tabs on young Goodnight. I don't want him out of your sight, but I need him blind to the reality that this institute is spying on him. I need to keep his trust intact. You have my authority to step in and do whatever is necessary to keep everyone safe and return them to me undamaged. Now vanish."

"Understood, doctor. As always, sir."

Harlan bowed and disappeared.

Still waiting inside the blistering bus, Petty felt miserable and didn't want to make this last city run.

"Trying to make these mental sad-sacks feel 'special' about their useless existence. Face it, Norm, these kids are just a bunch of future candle makers or serial killers. Pick one."

Petty realized the last foot-long chili dog at the mall was a bad idea, and the thought of enduring another trip inside that noisy, smelly food court nauseated him.

"This is all nonsense. I'm a trained and bonded security officer—not a babysitter!"

Norm ignored him and scanned his phone for baseball scores, ignoring the flatulence.

Kate Tempest was first aboard as she bounded up the steps at the rear security door with a whoop, and she chose her favorite seat.

"Hooo! What have you guys been doing in here? This ride stinks, y'all!"

She opened the windows between the security mesh to let the odors out and the hot air in.

Outside, nine lucky passengers waited to be cleared for final boarding by the wand-bearing detail. The guard's hand frisked for burner phones, tablets, or any other personal paraphernalia before the long trip into the city could proceed.

Zack shadowed Kate up the stairs and sat behind her. He was only tagging along because Dr. Briscoe noticed their codependence on each other lately. He thought it essential to keep their new bond intact, to maintain the fragile boy's psyche, and to keep him verbally active before the intensive testing began.

Coop boarded next, followed by Tim Finn, a tall, seventeen-year-old street hustler and thrasher with a reckless attitude that matched his bruises.

"Man, it's stinkin' hot in here!"

Pavarty Wong squealed herself onboard in two giant leaps, making Kate laugh as she patted the seat beside her.

As far as they were concerned, destiny must have

thrown them together onto the same bus, because they never figured out how to fix the lottery. In fact, there was never a valid lottery for any bus assignments. Nothing as random as chance existed inside the institute unless it was Dr. Briscoe's idea. He alone chose who would travel to the mall and in what order.

Lennon Dupree boarded next, an eleven-year-old found abandoned in the deep forest as a baby. Lennon was an insecure child who danced wherever she went. She even danced down the aisle. Too young for a prom like Zack, Dr. Briscoe had promised Lennon the chance to buy her favorite ballerina tutu for her birthday after her last painful round of tests.

Josh Blunt followed in a mathematical trance, and his bud Emiliano bounded right after him, all smiles.

Then Ozzy' the Fish' Waterson climbed onboard. Oz was a lifelong institutional couch-potato, a committed movie nerd, and an insatiable reader built like a retired linebacker—all soft and gooey in the middle with broad shoulders the size of cannon balls.

And the last orphan to hop onboard was spunky Jesse Largent. She was a willowy fourteen-year-old skateboarder who had ping-ponged between the suburbs and foster homes from birth, just like the other sad stories.

With the doctor's handpicked passengers onboard, the rear security door hissed and locked, Petty ground the gears, and everyone cheered as they pulled out the main gate.

The reformed school bus followed behind an escort van carrying two male and two female counselors to chaperone the over-excited kids once inside the dressing rooms.

After only a few minutes on the road, Tim Finn became agitated, sitting across from fidgety Zack. He jumped out of his seat, acting like the little boy's swatting was infectious.

"What's this simp even doing on board with us? Does he have bedbugs or something? We are supposed to be going shopping for a prom, right? Not a 'Paw Patrol Party.'"

The gangly seventeen-year-old from the streets of Middlin carried a scar from every face plant he'd ever made, and that was saying a lot. His curly hair exploded out of a stained knit cap that appeared to be a permanent lifestyle choice, and his left eye squinted more than the right after colliding with the last concrete barrier he thrashed.

"Hey! Watch your mouth, zit!" Kate swung back hard.

Tim blushed and turned to face her, pimples and all, but Kate was having none of his guff, and she jumped into the aisle.

"What's it to you anyway, Finn? This kid has every right to get outside the walls, just like you do, bully!"

"He's a frigging deformed schizoid baby! Just look at him!"

Petty pounded his fist against the metal cage door up front.

"Sit down back there, or so help me, I'll turn this bus around, and nobody goes shopping nowhere!"

Kate wouldn't back down and took another step forward. Tim retreated and swung into another row of seats further back, stretching his legs out into the aisle with false bravado. She continued to stare him down until he broke eye contact.

Tim might have been older and streetwise, but Kate's ferocious glare was far too intimidating for an awkward, insecure boy to comprehend. But the profound pain he saw lurking behind her wounded gaze humbled him.

No better guardian than a victim, he realized for the first time as a young man.

"It was just a stupid joke," he whispered.

"Who's the joke, now? That kind of macho B.S. is not happening around me anymore, bud. Never again," Kate promised. "You're so much better than that, man. Remember that."

Everyone fell silent in that uncomfortable moment, but finally, Oz couldn't contain himself.

"Whoa! Serious burn, people!" He shouted between cupped hands. "Han Solo fired first!" he shouted.

"She sure did!" Pavarty grinned at her new intergalactic hero.

Soon R2D2 beeps, and 'Pew! Pew!" sounds ricocheted around the bus, and Tim, a massive Star Wars geek, didn't appreciate the comparison.

"I'm not Gweedo."

Kate was immediately sympathetic and tried to divert everyone's attention.

"Hey, Tim? Where do you think we'll shop first? You've been there before?"

"How should I know?"

Tim saw nothing but snarky grins staring back at him while his cheeks burned bright red. He never knew who his real folks were, but he figured that whoever he belonged to, they probably hot-flushed the same ridiculous shade of crimson—a lifelong embarrassment both times.

"Come on, Tim, you old mall pirate, you know that place like the skid marks on your Vans, don't you?" Kate kicked his scuffed sneakers, prodding a reluctant smirk. "You bragged you'd shredded that place a million times."

Tim warmed to Kate's less threatening demeanor and attempted to save face.

"Yeah. I used to get booted out of that joint for grinding down the edge of that enormous fountain of theirs. The place has got a humongous Clancy's out front. We might stop in there first, for sure. Plenty of delicate ladies' stuff on level five."

"Heavenly!" Ozzy chirped. "Going up!"

"Oh, stop it."

"Perfecto!" Kate responded in a high comedy falsetto.

Everyone laughed, including Tim, as the mood brightened into excitement again, and Kate rushed up to the driver's cage and banged back on it—startling the guards.

"Lord of mercy!" Petty jumped behind the wheel. "Don't do that!"

85

"Officer Petty! To the mall, sir! And be quick about it, my good man!"

"You call me Sergeant, brat!"

"Okay, Sgt. Brat! Floor it!"

"Shut up and sit back down!"

The passengers made fun of the cantankerous guard locked inside his protective cage like he was transporting gangsters, and Kate swung back into her seat next to Zack, laughing.

"We're going to the mall! We're going to the mall!" She sing-songed as everyone sang along.

Their adlibbed mini-musical drove Petty and Norm batty, even with his earbuds on high. But the security detail was under strict orders from Dr. Briscoe not to intimidate these children in any way and allow them the privilege and joy of having this positive experience. That left the guards with only their professionalism to endure the rest of the long trip.

More than an hour later, the escort van pulled into the mall, and the counselors hustled out just as the bus pulled into its special parking section.

As the teens jumped off, they pulled up short at the sight of the new Middlin Mall.

"Whoa!"

"Holy Moly!"

"Wow! Talk about super-sized."

"It looks like Oz!" Kate sighed, as obsessed as everyone.

The brilliant architects had designed this fantasy-based machine to separate every dollar from every shopper, regardless of age.

One end sported a children's amusement park, including a Ferris wheel and double merry-go-round. On the other end was an elegant stretch of gilded and domed storefronts. The entire indoor/outdoor mega-mall stretched for over a mile, surrounded by a prairie of cars where buffalo used to roam.

"It's the most beautiful place that I've ever seen," Zack

gushed.

"Sure is, sweetie," Kate agreed. It felt like they woke up inside the same dreamscape.

But fantasy constantly collides with reality, and the results at the apex can be jarring.

Their hands shot to their ears as the roar of amplified voices rattled them—every voice reverberating against the reflective glass environment that was the Middlin Mall.

There was a holiday sale, and noisy shoppers rushed from store to store, level to level, underneath a massive stained-glass ceiling that stretched for blocks in either direction.

The counselors separated the herd into two packs—six boys—four girls—and they each wandered off in different directions with their precious shopping lists.

Zack even peeled off with the boys, allowing Kate to experience her dream shopping spree without an anchor.

And Harlan Bland had been hovering above them all the entire time. He was lurking in the shadows long before their arrival. Now, he perched high overhead on the upper level where he could take in everything in a single sweep—like a sniper in his God Spot.

No one below suspected they were under tight surveillance except by regular security.

Even the Shadow couldn't comprehend the intense scrutiny his notorious presence had stirred up in the mall—because he was also being surveilled from on high.

The Briscoe boys preoccupied themselves with their shopping lists, and no one noticed when Zack peeled away. The unleashed guys were more interested in vulgar jokes and busting chops than babysitting.

"Are you kidding me, Josh? Orange striped pants? That's just plain gross, man, unless you're selling hot dogs on a stick in the food court!"

They laughed and clowned around as the exhausted Briscoe counselors slumped into some plush chairs in the middle of the store. Bone-tired, they escaped their escort duties by diving into their cell phones.

Tim discovered a full-scale skater mannequin with a couple of actual boards beside it on display. He pulled the boards down and started doing ollies and gigaflops between the clothes racks, showing off for the others.

Wandering alone into the center of the grand mall, Zack found the vast indoor complex an intimidating, alien world of sights and smells. He had never been inside such a massive artificial structure before,

Too many frantic things were happening simultaneously indoors, creating visual confusion about what he was seeing. This new reality rushing by was far more complex than anything he'd experienced as hundreds of people shot past him with rapid, unpredictable movements.

And Zack stiffened when he saw the clouds of other people's gnats swirling overhead. He could see thousands of glowing gnats of every shape and color gathering above the crowds. And these invisible bugs appeared radically different from his personal collection of irritants.

These dazzling specks formed a single cloud above the upper walkways before whipping themselves into a menacing tornado. The intense funnel cloud whirled over the top of one specific person—a tiny man standing motionless amid the sea of confusion on the upper levels.

Zack watched in bewilderment as the whirling cloud changed from brilliantly translucent to an angry crimson twister.

Zack had seen something like this before.

Remember Kansas?

I remember the screams.

Is this real?

As real as that day with the cows in the hay fields.

Zack's vivid fears circled back to haunt him once more.

They swallowed those two people alive.

Zack could still hear the muffled screams some nights

as the brutal farmer and his abusive wife left the ground howling—as whatever it was, hurled them into a clear blue Kansas sky, never to be seen or heard from again.

Zack had to do something this time. He couldn't allow these terrifying monsters to murder an innocent man—one that had done him no wrong.

Harlan Bland stood oblivious to any threat to his life. Without possessing Zack's extraordinary vision, he couldn't fathom that a cyclone of death spiraled overhead.

But he could see Zack below, staring right at him and pointing straight up.

Zack closed his eyes, took a deep breath, and screamed at the top of his lungs.

"Noooooooooooo! Runnnnnn!"

The mall fell quiet in a growing silence as the boy's screams bounced against the glass canyons.

That intense silence exploded into panic as Kate pushed back through the rattled crowds to reach Zack's side.

The little boy stood trembling and pointed at the infamous Shadow, now frozen on the upper level, and gaping back.

Zack's horrified expression calcified Bland and shook him to his foundation, and he shivered as if chilled to the bone. No one had ever exposed the great undercover detective on any of his surveillance missions before—not once. But now, Bland stood motionless, trapped by the boy's petrifying glare.

Zack knew he shouldn't have screamed in public, but he couldn't allow that innocent man to die. But now, the invisible crimson cloud turned its collective rage toward him.

They spiraled down into his face and enveloped him in a furious, glowing swarm, swallowing him whole—as everyone else watching Zack saw him swatting at the empty air and spinning around as if on fire.

Kate tried to grab Zack's whirling arms, but he was moving too fast. That's when Coop knelt, and with a nod between them, he and Kate ducked and seized Zack's arms as he continued to scream.

"Get them off me! They're going to eat me!"

Zack's eyes suddenly rolled back, and he collapsed in a heap.

He looked at me... as if I was about to die today. Harlan recognized that horrified expression from experience as he bolted for the nearest exit. The Shadow Man vanished as if he'd never been there, leaving the amateurs behind to clean up this unmitigated disaster.

A big guard named Sledge, the counselor in charge of Briscoe's security team, tried to keep the crowds at bay with the help of mall security.

"Come on, people! It's all handled! Just a minor seizure! Move along. Keep shopping."

The other counselors rushed in, winded and reassembled, with the orphans still clutching their shopping bags.

"Thanks, folks, for your concern. Now please, move away! Give us some air!"

That's when Sledge snatched Zack up off the floor too aggressively for Coop's taste, and the teen jumped forward and seized the guard's arm.

"Hey! Knock off the rough stuff, man!" Coop ordered.

Kate was a split second behind him.

"Watch it, Sledge, or I'll report you!"

Sledge shook off Coop's grip, resisting the urge to do more damage.

"Stay back, you troublemakers, or you'll both be the ones on report and back in Rehash."

With no warning, a brilliant Lucid Pulse exploded from Zack's body, and the boy's eyes snapped back open, and he screamed.

"Noooooo!"

The invisible force field shot out through the crowds in a sleek blast of pure intent. Most of its victims never saw or felt the impact of the positive twinkling energy as its invisible colors rippled through them. But the enormous sonic boom that followed a split-second later shattered every window inside the glass cathedral, sending everyone into an uncontrollable panic.

Storefront windows exploded into waterfalls as millions of beads of tempered glass tumbled down the escalators like jewels in the rapids, and the crowds shrieked for the exits.

Still gripped by fear, Officer Sledge trembled over Zack's body like he was disarming a ticking time bomb. "What's going on here, sonny boy?" Sledge stammered, too frightened to move. "What just happened?"

The shaken counselors shared a frightened look. Sledge gave the final nod, and they each pulled out a dummy pen and injected the children with Dr. Briscoe's newest emergency sedative. It was an untested nerve agent conceived of only days before as his last resort against any future out-of-control scenarios.

"Ow!"

"Hey, man!"

Briscoe named the new designer drug 'Goodnight' after realizing that he had to stay ahead of the curve if he ever needed to overpower this passionate little boy. And the new drug's effectiveness proved immediate as ten orphans crumpled unconscious in the middle of a disaster.

-CHAPTER 12-

Only a Giant

Yuma perched on the crown of the towering sequoia, scanning the enchanted lands below like an eagle searching for prey.

The legendary redwood soared six hundred feet above the forest floor before tickling the clouds with its spongy greenery to nourish the new saplings sprouting sixty stories below.

Yuma only spoke with this two-thousand-year-old lifeform in the sweetest of whispers and nicknamed her 'Mother' long ago.

The new crown of swords surrounded him in their brilliance and re-energized the lonely warrior with encouragement and memories from every angle.

Even under the waning moonlight, the swords shimmered every night now with blue fire. They scattered their bold message of hope and defiance throughout the expanse of the Bubble, like beacons of truth.

The giant had waited in this same tree every day since that last Lucid Pulse cut through his lodge the night of the dancing fish.

Yuma focused on the simple. If he prepared and was lucky—he might glimpse the next invisible pulse rippling through the forest using a new combination of lenses he'd invented. Then, he might determine the direction the giant or giants were coming from.

92

If only they would send another signal.

Yuma nodded, and the gizmo-goggles snapped over his eyes as he scanned above and below for any recent disturbances.

The familiar trio of hummingbirds appeared overhead, hovering like a halo of miniature angels at these heavenly altitudes. They buzzed around the ancient giant whenever they weren't chasing insects or devouring new nectars down below. Yuma had saved their fragile species from extinction, and every hummingbird remembered their guardian's courageous actions and always paid him their most profound respects.

"Zip, Zash, Zee? Anything suspicious about?" He quizzed his iridescent color guard.

"Hopefully, you will pick up on that next pulse before I do. If another ever arrives."

Considering the recent bout of good news, Yuma tried to remain positive. Still, he found patience the most challenging of virtues as he watched the shadows drift across the floor, bearing no good news.

Our reinforcements must be drawing closer. But not close enough to be here where we need them.

The giant tried to calm himself in the prevailing winds.

A dog's deep bark echoed far beneath, interrupting his thoughts.

Peering over the edge, he saw Harley smiling up at him from the broad base of the redwood. A massive pack of misfits and underdogs surrounded him. Whatever their shape or size, they were all waiting for Yuma to return to earth, and their happy tails swept the leaves into confetti.

An immortal giant required a veritable colossus of a dog as his best friend, companion, and protector, and Harley lived up to those overwhelming challenges in every regard. Although not a giant of Yuma's scale, he was twice the size of any contemporary Great Dane or Bull Mastiff and wiser than most holy men.

They adopted each other by fate over six hundred years before while fighting on opposing sides of the conquistadors' invasions of the Americas. That's when destiny made a complete U-turn and flung these two legends together in the back seat of life.

'Bruto the Terrible,' as his sadistic Spanish handlers called the fiercest of all their battle dogs, had grown weary of his abusive masters until the taste and smell of terrified human flesh sickened him.

Following another savage flogging for refusing to devour children in front of their parents, Bruto turned on his Spanish masters in a rage and slaughtered the entire detachment.

He killed them individually, using the same lethal skills they beat into him since puppyhood, then chewed through his chains before bolting into the jungle to recover his lost freedom.

Besides the dead, the only evidence he left behind was his chains and a few broken teeth.

Giant and beast collided at the junction of a dead-end jungle canyon—seeking escape from their common enemy.

Stunned by the sudden impact, they found themselves cornered by the same deadly foe closing in on two sides. Both winded fighters recognized the warrior in the other and agreed to stand together for something nobler than dying alone. They chose to defend the other to the end—no matter the odds or consequences. And although outnumbered, they fought their way out of every ambush—no matter the odds—fifty to two at some points.

They attacked standing side-by-side and back-to-back, saving hundreds of tribes from annihilation, and allowing entire families to escape into the safety of the mountains or jungles.

That's when the relentless invaders sent out hunter/killer teams to track down these two inhuman monstrosities and destroy them. The Spanish crown committed hundreds of disposable soldiers to the pursuit and offered handsome land grants and rich rewards for the deaths of these marauding savages.

With a royal bounty on their heads, the exhausted fugitives had no choice but to escape the ever-tightening noose. So, they outran the invaders and fled toward something neither Yuma nor Harley had ever experienced—the reality of personal freedom.

The unlikely pair dashed through the jungles, swamps, and across vast deserts, creating new legends as they sprinted north. They were searching for the golden lands with the snowcapped mountains Yuma remembered so vividly from his childhood wanderings.

Only to discover Mother Earth treasured their unparalleled bravery as her avengers long before they believed she existed. And she manipulated man and dog through a gauntlet of tests and misadventures that led them to their ultimate destiny as her Guardians of the Sacred Forest.

Not long after escaping, the fierce battle-hound, Bruto the Terrible, chose his free-dog name. He was no longer 'Bruto the Terrible' inside. Those days were over forever. No one owned him anymore. No one could, ever again.

He named himself—Harley—because when enunciated in dogspeak or spoken phonetically in humanspeak—Harley meant the same rumble of freedom in most languages.

"Harley, my friend! Good to see you back!" Yuma called down in perfectly accented dogspeak. "Who's hungry?"

The homesick pups understood every word as they yipped and howled in delight.

Dogs are such delightful creatures! Yuma grinned. *And yet they should never sing. Especially Harley.*

The giant swung down into his handmade elevator. He un-lashed the rope; waved to Zip, Zash, and Zee; and plummeted six-hundred feet in a gut-wrenching, nose-dive.

The pack cringed back, fearing another disastrous crash landing by the howling, bug-eyed madman. It had happened twice before, but the giant wind-surfed down without consequence as the affection-starved pups swarmed in for a happy pat on the head when he touched down.

Harley's pack of lost mutts had returned from their seasonal wanderings, either looking for new homes or searching for their old ones. Unfortunately, most weren't successful in that quest. As a result, some were turning feral, which was never healthy for the pack. They all needed some proper alpha Pappy love and homemade food to center them and put their scavenging days behind.

No animal was turned away. Gratitude and benevolence were the most admired traits living underneath the Bubble. And Yuma was renowned for having plenty of both.

He led the hungry pack down the stone steps by the waterfalls and into the massive root cellar at the rear of his sprawling compound. Yuma designed it expressly for this purpose—to feed his army.

The giant had expanded this oversized subterranean root cellar for centuries until the camouflaged bunker darted off in several directions, like the interior of a molehill large enough to drive a tank through.

He pulled several eels from his stream-fed cooler in his underground kitchen and plopped them onto a cutting board as the three hummingbirds caught up.

"Fresh eel steaks for supper?" he asked in dogspeak, brandishing his cleaver.

"Yes!"

"Please!"

"Medium rare!" bayed a spoiled Basset Hound from the suburbs,

The hungry dogs waited as Yuma chopped and filleted the meat into thick, juicy steaks before throwing them onto a hot grill to heat the meat and warm some bellies.

He fed every dog until they belched—passed-wind—or both—full tanks for everyone.

After supper, the well-fed pups collapsed, bloated and

content once again, with most curling up wherever they dropped, and the snoring competition began.

In that sublime moment of relaxation, Yuma was unprepared when Zack's Lucid Pulse blasted into his invisible world head-on.

The boy's defensive pulse had penetrated the protective coordinates of the Bubble so precisely—it seemed almost GPS guided. The pure thought wave pierced the thickest timbers of Yuma's lodge before striking him in the center of his soul, and he staggered and gasped for air.

Harley and the pack howled as their fur lit up with sparks. Every dog bristled with strands of static electricity rippling around like colored Saint Elmo's Fire, and the entire pack shimmered with frequencies never experienced in the magical forest before.

As Yuma expected, the hummingbirds, Zip, Zash, and Zee, flared even brighter within the luminescent power burst—as if their brilliant feathers were turbo-charged by the psychic blast.

Yuma's heart regained its rhythm, and he dropped everything and dashed outdoors to catch sight of the retreating wave.

Only the greatest of giants could produce such focused energy of pure resolve!

He jumped into the nearest elevator and slashed the tie-down with his knife. The counterweight dropped and shot him straight back into the sky again.

With a head flick, his geared goggles snapped down, and he scanned the forest, trying to capture another glimpse of this magical energy source before it diffused. If he could do that, he could forecast the general direction his reinforcements were traveling from.

That's when he caught sight of a wisp of the invisible shimmer winking back at him through his lenses.

"There it is! There you are! I see you!"

The retreating Lucid Pulse glowed along its leading

edge, forming a concentric ripple of translucent rainbow-colored energy, leaving foamy contrails of sonic pops and sparkles behind.

Only then did Yuma notice the screams erupting from Dark Hollows. Zack's powerful pulse had plowed into them first before racing across the lake to find Yuma—and those without souls always trembled in the presence of such an overpowering, positive life force.

Yuma pushed the goggles back onto his forehead with a huge smile plastered on his leathery face.

"I believe they are traveling from the south by the direction of the final slipstream."

Zip, Zash, and Zee tumbled happily above his head, regaining their normal luminosity.

"That is wonderful news, Triple Z. Our giants are moving north and closer still."

But his next realization was the sucker punch he never saw coming.

"But... wait..."

Yuma's joy faded to black as he slammed his eyes shut.

"My reinforcements are trying to rescue me by traveling from the south. That is a grave, tactical mistake. Now they will march straight through Dark Hollows. It is the only way in."

All his optimism dissolved.

"They kill giants over there."

-CHAPTER 13-

Ghost Exit

Immediately after Zack's incredible sonic blast, Officer Petty started cramming tissues up his nose to staunch the constant trickle of blood.

Frantic screams for help began crackling over his radio.

"Emergency! Code Red! Get that bus back here now!"

Petty hadn't been feeling well and stayed onboard the parked bus, listening to his brand of tinny music while the others shopped. He was busy preening away in the side mirror using tiny vanity scissors to trim some protruding nose hairs and humming along when...

KABOOM!

Every window exploded inward, showering Petty in safety glass. The concussive blast forced his grooming scissors straight up one nostril, almost slicing his nose off.

That wounded hole began spurting blood like a rusty water faucet. Then another panicked voice started screaming over the static-filled walkie-talkie.

"Code red! Code red, man! Evac! Get over here, Crowley! On the double! Now!"

Outside the mall, the Briscoe guards reassembled as a shaken team. They loaded the ten unconscious teenagers back into the caged bus and quickly strapped each child into their seats.

With that awkward task complete, the two male counselors jumped back into their escort van as the two certified RNs remained on board the bus with Petty and Norm to tend to the unconscious children.

With the panicked crowds still swirling everywhere, their sudden departure appeared to be a regular part of any emergency response to a disaster—nothing more sinister than that.

Onboard the fleeing security bus, the hot wind now rushed in through the blown-out windows as a carpet of constantly shifting glass marbles whirred back and forth underneath the children's feet, sounding like a giant rain stick.

Petty kept trying to shift gears and steer the enormous vehicle with one hand—while tending to his bloody nose with the other—and doing both poorly.

Shotgun Norm cared for the unconscious children in the back of the bus, and the two female counselors, Shelly and Greta Scott, took charge. The Scott twins were registered nurses, and they monitored and rechecked the sedated children's vitals.

"I told them snobs upstairs! I told Briscoe himself! I warned you all! Freaky, spooky kids like these with raging hormones don't get transported unless we put them under with some big red pill! I told you all that yesterday, and I told you all that today!"

Petty continued to spit blood and scold them, which made his nose bleed more.

"If these weirdoes need to go shopping, let them shop groggy! Or shop online like I do. That's what they'd be doing if they were out in the actual world, anyway!"

He shook his head in disgust.

"I watch TV, I'm informed!" bragged the man, who watched only two cable channels. "You all saw what that freaky kid did to that bus! One just like this! Everybody knows it! There are tapes! And now look at what that brat's done to the great Middlin Mall! He just blew it all to smithereens! That's a national landmark, for Pete's sake!"

Even though he had predicted it, Petty couldn't believe what was happening now.

"This is not on me. No, sir, no way! I warned you all! You are all going to lose your jobs over this one! You bet! Every one of you!" he promised.

Four ambulances went screaming by, heading in the opposite direction. Shelly broke down, sobbing at the scale of the catastrophe they had just endured.

"P.T.! Pullover," Shelly pleaded. "Come on, Petty, pullover! I'm getting carsick!"

Shelly lurched for the locked door, rattling it and huffing to keep everything down as Petty stared back from behind his driver's cage, devoid of compassion.

"Aw, crapola... the weakness of the entire human species in all its glory! And my name is Sergeant Crowley to you, Missy. Whoever you are!"

"Pull over now!" Norm barked at his obstinate partner.

Petty blanched at Norm's uncharacteristic intensity and dropped his bloody tissues before grabbing the steering wheel with both hands to muscle the groaning behemoth over to the side of the road.

This deserted stretch of two-lane blacktop began blossoming with more emergency lights than flowers in a botanical garden. They bloomed in every shape and color as police cars and ambulances screamed past the bus to reach the ongoing calamity back at the mall. The guards watched in admiration as every agency voluntarily dashed back into the face of whatever unknown danger awaited them, as real-life first responders do daily.

Shelly only made it down two steps off the back of the bus before she pitched over, and projectile vomited the entire contents of the colorful mall food in one gut-wrenching geyser. Greta followed to help her twin, and a queasy Norm hopped off as well as they both tried to calm the gagging Shelly without puking themselves.

The growing cavalcade of sirens continued to wail by, one after another, while inside the idling school bus, Petty wasn't feeling well himself.

101

Not even a little bit.

Thick rivulets of sweat flowed into the blood dripping from his nose, staining his uniform as his stomach heaved and growled in distress.

"You don't hear me whining about my personal problems, do you? Never. Like no sissy girl."

Petty spotted the first ambulance speeding back towards them in the shattered rear-view mirror. They were returning with the first of the many casualties. Every rescue vehicle would soon head back north to the nearest trauma hospital, still twenty-five miles away in Crestline.

"Hey! Let's get going, people! Hey!" Petty screamed through the blown-out windows, blaring the air horn.

"If we don't get out of here in front of these sirens going back to town right now, we'll get pulled over on the side of this road for hours, waiting for them to pass! Hop aboard! We gotta go! We gotta go now!" Petty commanded.

The escort van pulled a quick U-turn and skidded in behind the idling bus as Sledge and the other supervisor came running to Shelly's aid.

"The hell with you, buttercups! That's it!" Petty squawked like an angry parrot through his bloody beak. He punched the button on his dash, and the rear hydraulic bus door swung closed behind him and locked.

"See you, greenhorns, back at the ranch! This cowboy don't need GPS to find my way home! No reason to hurry, neither! You hipster idiots won't have jobs once I have my words with Briscoe!"

Petty shoved a tissue up his nose and the bus into gear and roared back onto the highway, intentionally spewing a cloud of diesel and gravel onto his coworkers and far ahead of the approaching ambulance.

Every orphan onboard the swerving bus remained as unconscious as a busload of hammers. Their heads bobbed back and forth without stirring.

Petty felt better inside the soothing cocoon of this

uncommon silence. With the lush night wind rushing in and not having to pretend to talk or care about anybody else for a change, except himself—well, that suited his disposition just fine.

"And I'm right about all those ambulances coming along, too. You'll see!"

Dr. Briscoe will understand everything. That doctor understands me better than me.

Petty laughed at the sight of the silhouetted guards, still coughing and swearing in his wake.

Officer Sledge tried to raise him on the radio and cell phone, but Petty had already snapped off both at first contact.

"Come on, Betsy girl," Petty patted his shattered dashboard as the air gusted freely through the windowless bus. "Let's me and you get back to the Institute while all these freaks are still nighty-night, so they can't do no more damage. Like the original heroes we are."

Petty winced as a fresh wave of chest pain washed over him, driving his heel harder into the accelerator.

Twenty minutes later, the security van caught up to the speeding bus, but Petty wouldn't let them pass him and kept swerving, cutting them off—so the van backed off and tucked in behind, giving him plenty of tantrum room to throw his snit as they followed at a discreet distance.

Old Petty couldn't have cared less that they caught back up, but there was no way he would ever allow these young pups to pass him on the Interstate and file their reports first.

I will not abide that!

The small convoy was still an hour away from the Institute when the strange opaque fog bank drifted in from the north and abducted them, changing everyone's life forever.

Petty doubled over behind the wheel, and the unsteady driver lost sight of the road inside the swirling mist.

What's this? What's all this?

They hurtled through the core of the whirling mists, forming a glowing tunnel that surrounded and expanded before them in all directions. It was as if the sparkling clouds were attracted to the bus itself—excluding everything else as it glided effortlessly over the countryside. The billowing cloud bank chased and danced around the oversized vehicle in a swirling vortex of blushing colors like some enamored lover.

But the unexpected sparkles blinded Petty, who overreacted and steered the bus off the main road.

With nothing but blind luck on their side—or maybe something a lot more interesting than that—the runaway bus plunged thirty feet through the air and down onto an abandoned logging road buried beneath a centuries-worth of overgrown weeds. The plush overgrowth cushioned the deadly impact as the armored bus bounced several times and kept going.

This was a secret turnoff to a dark destination that few realized existed until a split second ago.

There was never a cutoff out here before? Was there? Petty's mind sought familiar landmarks rushing by. *I've driven this road a thousand times and never seen it."*

The obsessed fog bank streaked after the runaway bus, leaving only wisps of a tail above as it chased its prey down into the steep, foreboding canyons leading nowhere.

Petty's fevered mind raced to catch up to his dangerous circumstances as they bounced out of control and down onto a steep backcountry road.

Overgrown tree branches pummeled the hurtling trespasser, drumming continuously against the bus's aluminum skin and permanently dimpling its hide like a golf ball.

By then, it was far too late to turn around as gravity and inertia took hold, as it always does once the math gets involved.

The sloping pass dropped away like a bad dream, twisting and coiling itself around in the shadows like a hungry snake. In some places, the undeveloped road narrowed to nothing more than a goat path, making it impossible to steer the extended bus around its abrupt turns without using some radical maneuvers.

Above, on the main highway, the counselor's chase van plowed through the last vestiges of the disappearing fogbank without ever realizing anything was amiss as they drove past the ghost exit.

None of the guards riding inside the escort van questioned the bus's disappearance up ahead until they arrived back at Briscoe Institute an hour later. That's when they discovered the cranky driver with his extraordinary cargo never returned, and the heads began to roll.

Another limb thrust gouged the headlights out of their chrome sockets, and Petty jumped on the brakes with both feet as they burst through the outer layers of the twinkling fogbank. Now, the panicked driver could finally see the roadway again. But it wasn't good news.

They were speeding downhill along the spine of a descending ridgeline of an abandoned logging road with steep ravines falling off on either side and zero margins for error.

Careening out of the fogbank, the sedated teens snapped awake from their drug-enforced stupors as if on command. Only to discover they were locked aboard a hurtling nightmare with a dying man behind the wheel, trapped on the road to nowhere.

Petty downshifted, tearing up already overstressed gears as he forced the behemoth to fishtail around that next tight corner, only to contend with another switchback right after that.

"Geez! I'm up, Grandma!" Coop yelled as he thrashed around in his seat and opened his eyes.

The others startled awake—each jolted back into a brand-new reality with tree limbs drumming against the sides.

"Hey! Slow down, jerk-weed!" Tim cried out.

The vehicle side-swiped the next inside turn and crumpled the starboard ceiling on contact.

"Quit it, old man!" Tim unbuckled and stood up. "You

ripped a hole in the roof!"

With his skateboarder's balance, he made his way through the careening bus and began pounding on the cage that separated the inmates from the guards.

"You're going to kill us, Petty! Slow down, old man!"

"No, brakes left! I'm all used up! I'd buckle back up if I were you, kid."

The six tires howled as one, threatening to explode off their glowing rims.

"Just turn it off, man! Turn off the engine!" Kate shouted from the rear.

"Not again?" Coop was experiencing an extreme case of Déjà vu.

"Then I won't be able to steer it, will I?" Petty roared as if answering an idiot. "It's got power-steering, dumbbell!"

"Downshift!" Coop yelled.

"Downshift! Now!" Kate screamed.

"I am, I am! Shut up! I've lost all the lower gears!"

Petty's face drooped on one side, and his head nodded to his chest as Tim banged the cage.

"Petty! Petty! Wake up and steer, man! Steer!" Coop shouted in panic.

As the stroke ravaged his brain, it contorted his face in palsy, and when Petty lifted his head again, it was the face of a sad, melted monster.

"Haven't you ever heard the song, boy?"

Petty's speech slurred as his head rolled back on his neck, and Tim noticed the emergency dash lights reflecting off the guard's single gold tooth.

"Don't you know you gotta go through hell before you ever get to heaven," Petty sing-songed the lyrics of a familiar old tune—and those were his last clear thoughts.

Incredibly, the old-school guard had somehow navigated the massive school bus to the bottom of the steepest ravines and onto the sloping valley floor as his last official act before passing out behind the wheel while traveling sixty miles an hour.

The driverless bus plowed straight through a wide stream and slammed onto a sloping sandbar in the center, launching the enormous vehicle skyward.

The screaming passengers lurched violently against their seatbelts on take-off, yet all stayed strapped into their seats. But unfortunately, the unbuckled bodies of Tim and Petty collided with the bus's roof with a painful, double thud.

Coop thought the illusion of temporary safety seemed a moot point—because they were all about to die within the nanoseconds that existed between the gravity of the here and now.

Just then, a sudden flash of searing blue light lit up the cabin's interior, and that's when the horrified youngsters realized the falling school bus had stopped and was still floating gently above the tree line in the sky.

Their hair drifted above their heads, like astronauts living inside the International Space Station. New gowns waltzed out of shopping bags and into the air with the tuxes.

The near-vertical bus lingered high above the rushing stream, making a massive exclamation point as the multi-ton beast refused to fall back to earth. Even though its brave engine continued to roar and the four rear wheels still sought traction midair.

The rider's weightless state remained perfect as the magical moments ticked by, and the bus floated and bobbed in the air like a heavy-metal whale taking a nap at sea.

The kids spun around in their skyward-facing seats to stare up and down at each other in disbelief, searching for the magical culprit among them.

But they all knew who it was.

"Of course, it's you!"

"It's Zack!"

"Cool, Zack!"

"Not me," he said.

Kate stared at the little boy, searching for any sign

of intent. But Zack just giggled innocently and seemed as genuinely surprised as the rest of the orphans at their Zero-G surprise.

"This is fun!"

"What is going on here, man?" Ozzy moaned, tumbling to reestablish any kind of body control in weightlessness. "This is so weird!"

"It's amazing!" Kate yelled.

"They call that enchanted!"

The always adventurous Coop had a great new idea. He released his seatbelt, floated into the center of the aisle, and started performing aerial somersaults up and down the length of the long bus.

"I always wanted to do this! Once in a lifetime!" he yelled. "I'm Peter Pan!"

The others unsnapped their belts and floated into the fun, including Lennon, who pirouetted up between them like a ballerina in Zero-G.

And as they continued playing weightless tag, flying from end to end, the enormous bus slowly drifted back down towards the streambed below.

The suspension groaned with the re-introduction of gravity as the damaged bus relaxed its tortured spine, and the undercarriage sizzled down into the chilly waters with a sigh.

That was when everyone's spiky hair flopped back down onto their heads—now earthbound again.

They couldn't stop grinning at each other.

"Okay. So, whoever just did that? Do it again!" Ozzy pleaded, and everyone cheered.

-CHAPTER 14-

Sudden Skill Set

The hijacked orphans found themselves safely back on solid ground after their shared flight of fantasy drifting above the treetops. Back on earth, their new formalwear lay scattered around the cabin like a bouquet of deflated balloons.

Unfortunately, it was then that the group also discovered they were all trapped inside the belly of the security bus with no way of escape.

The thick metal mesh welded over the blown-out windows was pry-proof and prevented simple escape, and only the driver inside his protective cage could operate the hydraulic doors by design in the old reform school days.

Petty was convulsing inside his driver's cage, but the security door remained locked, and no one could budge it to administer to the stricken guard.

"Hey, I know! Why don't you use some of that magic talent? Anyone?" Emiliano asked.

"Come on, Zack. Hint! Hint! Admit it. If you can hold up a school bus in midair with your mind, what's a little metal door? It should prove no problem at all. Right? It only makes sense! Just a small mental nudge!"

"I didn't do anything."

"Then who did that?"

"Come on, Zack! Blast it open! We all know it's you."

"I second that motion!" Ozzy added. "Go ahead. Use the Force again, kid!"

No one moved.

Kate stared at Zack, who gazed back at her as if nothing was left to be discussed.

The group grew even more concerned as the guard thrashed inside the metal cage and moaned.

"Come on, mutants. We can't just stand here and watch him die. What about just the lock? Just open the door lock with a little brain zap, right, Zack?" Emiliano pleaded to the unknown superpower holder.

"Maybe it wasn't any of us. Maybe it was this place?" Pavarty's mind raced for mystical answers to explain what had just happened to them as the mysterious fog swirled around them. "I mean, we just floated!"

"If we don't open this door, we don't get out, folks! Simple math, hey Josh?." Emiliano pointed to the steel mesh over the blown-out windows.

"There's no other way out except through the front gate or through that hydraulic rear door at the rear, which only opens from the cage," Josh added.

"If we can get through this cage door somehow, then we can climb out the windshield," Coop stated.

"But if we don't get out, do you guys understand what happens after that?" Ozzy asked. "All of us locked up in this same cage?"

"What?" Lennon shivered at the thought.

"No food. No water."

"What? Starvation?"

"Worse."

"What?"

"A fate worse than death. Cannibalism! Boo*waaaaa!*" Ozzy roared.

"Stop it!"

"You're a bunch of wimps!" Tim scoffed. "Zack! Silent Zack! Get over here!"

Tim Finn assumed an uneasy authority, being the oldest of the bunch, as Zack made his way forward, still swatting at his invisible gnats in the fog.

"Okay, Dumbo..." Tim started, but Kate's laser glare changed his usual snotty approach.

"Right. Listen, my man. I need your skinny little arms, not some booga-booga magic spell from you. Okay? Can you reach under those bars and grab the keys off Petty's belt?" Tim tried to be gentle. "Mine won't fit. See? Too many muscles."

He displayed his torn-up forearms from multiple attempts.

The lingering fog enveloped the bus again as the teens became shrouded within the glowing mist. Their faces materialized in and out of the dense fog like swirling specters urging him on.

"Do it, Zack," Jesse pleaded, as did Coop, Oz, and the rest. "Go on."

"I've gotta whiz something terrible, my man!" Oz added, causing a ripple effect of groans from everyone.

"Oh, man. Now I gotta go!"

"Go ahead, Zack," Kate encouraged, feeling the sudden uncomfortable urge herself now. "We all need your help now, okay? See if you can reach the keys. Just try? For me?"

Zack said nothing for a full minute. He just stared at each of them as they waited for his response.

There was none.

Then he dropped into the fogbank without a word and spread out on the floor. He stretched out his arm through the tiny breach between the security bars and the bed and reached in as far as he could.

"That a boy," Tim praised.

"Go, Zack," Coop encouraged him. "You can do it, kiddo."

Zack's fingers tiptoed across the minefield of broken glass. Even with his small digits extended, he couldn't quite touch Petty's gun belt.

Zack's arms were thin but far too short for snagging the keys.

That's when Tim spotted Petty's revolver on the floor. The handgun had toppled out of the guard's holster in

Zero-G. It appeared to be a couple of inches closer than the actual keys if they attacked it from a different angle.

"Get the gun instead, Zack," Tim smiled, nodding in the affirmative as if he were encouraging an idiot.

"What?" What for?" Kate demanded.

"Blow the lock clean off!" Ozzy shouted and began firing imaginary bullets out of his fingertips. "Pew! Pew! Pew!"

Zack looked to Kate for permission, and she nodded her approval, although grudgingly.

The boy took a breath and sunk back down to the floor. He squeezed his shoulder against the security door even tighter this time and reached out just as far as he could stretch his fingertips.

Zack's heart was pounding against his ribcage. His fingernails were just flicking against the ivory handle of the gun when Petty rammed himself against the metal cage, screaming in agony.

"I need my dress shoes, Ma! You gotta get my good ones out of the closet for my funeral!"

"No!" Zack froze in terror.

"Geez!"

Everyone cartwheeled away from the contorted face— but that left Zack staring eyeball to eyeball with the dying guard.

"Did you hear me? They're for my funeral! Ma?" Petty shrieked as his eyes rolled back into their sockets, and he collapsed onto the cage floor, unconscious again.

"Whoa. dude!" Ozzy bolted away.

Somehow the big teen found himself in the bus's rear when, only an instant before, he'd been up in front with the others. He'd never moved faster in his entire life. It was almost time travel.

Petty's body stopped convulsing and settled.

"Hey, Zack? Is he dead yet?" Ozzy asked.

"Calm down, everybody. Petty's not dead."

"Pretty close," Tim cracked.

"Not yet! Now, stop it. He's still breathing," Kate tried comforting the younger kids as she redirected her attention back to her frightened little buddy.

"Petty will never hurt you. Not alive or dead. I promise you, Zack. Trust me?"

The frightened boy nodded and swatted at his irritating gnats.

"He just startled us; that's all, sweetie. He's hurt terribly. It's up to us now to get him some help and get ourselves out of a real pickle," she explained.

"Pickle?" he giggled unexpectedly. "We're in a pickle?"

"That's right. If you want to get us out of this big, ugly metal pickle, please reach back inside and pull that gun out unless you'd rather try for the keys on his belt one more time?"

Gun it is! Zack chose without hesitation.

With Kate's encouragement, the little boy rested on the floor again. Then, summoning his courage from an untapped well of resolve, he reached back through the narrow opening with his arm extended.

I can't believe it. This little guy is doing exactly what I asked him to do just because I asked him to.

Their new connection still stunned Kate. Silent Zack's sudden reemergence from the institutional-sized dark hole he had fallen into so long ago amazed her and everyone else trapped inside this pickle jar.

Bits of jagged glass bit into his forearm again as his fingertips scratched against the smooth ivory handle of the revolver, trying to gain some traction.

Petty gurgled and threatened to move again, but Zack didn't hesitate this time. He stretched out just as far as he could without popping his shoulder out of its socket—and with that last bit of exertion, he snagged two fingers around the handle—and it was his.

He grabbed the revolver and froze for an instant, half-expecting Petty to snap back up at the waist and demand it back.

113

The little boy slid the firearm out from underneath the security cage, and Tim stepped forward and snatched the weapon away like it was his.

"Alright, stand back, toddlers." Tim snarled low and slow, in a ridiculous impression of a Hollywood tough guy.

The awkward teen cocked the hammer with some difficulty and aimed the weapon down at the locked door point-blank like a true make-believe macho man.

"All hat—no ranch," Pavarty said.

"Now, hold on there, sport!" Jesse challenged him.

Usually quiet and reserved, Jess regarded the street huckster with the practiced disdain of a veteran cop.

Like Kate, Jesse had survived a rough and tumble life on the streets alone.

"You're telling me that the only stupid escape plan you have is to blast a cap off inside here?" she pushed his wandering gun hand away.

"Got any better ideas for getting out, Little Miss Poseur from Awesome-Town?"

"No. Not yet. Don't you?"

Tim scoffed that a teenage girl could ever be an absolute ripper at heart like him.

It's in my blood, man!

But Tim had seen that Jesse could out-shred him any day of the week.

That Largent's got some deep talent.

He secretly admired her skills but hid them to shield his bruised ego.

Jesse continued with her aggressive stance.

"Well, face plant? Speak up! Look around for a split second. You might notice that you are about to fire a copper bullet down at a thick metal lock while trapped inside a huge aluminum tin can full of metal bars and steel cages!"

Jesse was ready to explode like a hollow point herself at his vapid stupidity.

"So?"

114

"So. And oh yeah! One more thing. What information are you missing in that last brain fart? Surprise! Us! Us Tim! Ten of us are trapped inside this same tin drum, you fool! And we aren't bulletproof! You've never heard the term *ricochet* before?"

Tim tried to maintain the illusion of his Alpha status within this newly established pack, but it wasn't working.

"Sure, I know that word. I know all about ricochets, dimples. And I was just going to say that before you cut me off."

He turned to the others and gestured with the loaded gun.

"You know, everybody, like get back... like duck back down behind, you know, something solid."

"You've never fired a real gun off before in your life, have you, Finn?" Jesse had this part-time carny square in her sights.

"Of course I have. I'm not suburb scum like you!" He blustered.

"Twenty-twos don't count."

"I've shot a real gun."

"How many times?

"Three... four... times."

"Where? When?" she challenged.

"Well... County Fair, mostly at the adult shooting range. And then, once, I shot Jay's shotgun out at his farm. But... I kind of mangled his cat, so that was enough of that. I didn't mean to do it. It just zigged when it should have zagged."

Jesse turned to the group and begged for sanity with a simple roll of her eyes.

"And this broken potato chip is the leader we're putting in charge of the dip, people? Really?"

"Aw, quiet down and duck behind Ozzy if you're all worried about getting hit. Hell, all nine of you could hide behind that moose! You should be safe back there."

"Bite me, Ruffles!"

Tim raised the gun and aimed at the lock again when Zack reached out of the fog and stopped his hand.

115

"What?" Tim flinched at the cold contact.

This kid even feels weird, Tim thought after he jumped back.

Kind of tingly-like.

He didn't understand what the timid little boy wanted, but the child was still gripping his gun hand and wouldn't release it.

"Let go, kid."

Ozzy figured it out first.

"He just risked his life for Kate. Not for you, stud."

Kate smiled and realized Oz was right, and she took the gun away from Tim, and Zack dropped his protest.

"Thank you, Zack," she tousled his hair, snapped open the revolver with one hand, and noted the five rounds inside.

"Well. We've got five chances," she said.

"What? Now you're going to fire it. Suddenly it's a great idea because you're a woman?"

She snapped the cylinder closed with an experienced flick of her wrist.

"Look, kid. I've hunted cape buffalo in Botswana and tigers in Tangiers. So, I believe I can blow this lock off safer than you."

"Liar! You've never been out of this state. I saw your files online. Miss Pathological Liar! That's you! You lie so much they named a mental illness after just you! Kate-Atonic!"

"I'm firing on the count of three, everyone. Everybody duck down and get tucked up behind something solid," she ordered as she re-cocked the hammer.

"Not behind me!" Ozzy yelled as he fell to all fours.

Kate moved off to the side for a more glancing angled shot and leveled the short barrel revolver closer to the lock, reconsidering the bullet's trajectory and its ricochets like a billiard shot.

"Now, stay down."

"Kate. Kate, this is still a stupid idea." Jesse stood her ground. However, she ducked when she realized Kate was deadly serious.

"It's our only shot, Jess. Get it?" she smirked at her awkward attempt at a joke. "Stand back, everybody."

They all scattered to the rear in a mad rush.

"What? You never heard of a ricochet before, idiot?" Tim taunted her.

"One!" she started.

"Hey! I'm the oldest one here! I say what goes!" Tim protested.

"Two!" Kate continued her countdown and readjusted her angle.

"I should be the one shooting the gun! I'm the man!"

"Three!"

Tim ducked.

Kate didn't. She fired.

Kaboom!

The interior of the bus rang like a bell hit by cannon fire. The pieces of the calved bullet ricocheted around the cabin's interior in three pieces before embedding in the wall directly above Tim's head.

"Hey!"

"Help!" Ozzy cried, his head shaking like a bobblehead on a bumpy road from the volume of the amplified explosion.

Even Kate dropped the gun and covered her ears after firing. The gun smoke added another disturbing layer of confusion to the already tense atmosphere inside the bus.

Kate reached out and gave the invisible door a pull.

They heard the gate groaning open in the fog before they ever saw it. Still, that beautiful squawk promised their immediate freedom.

Ozzy freaked first and bolted over the top of everyone as the rest of the orphans scampered behind him in a panic through the broken windshield, following the path of least resistance.

Even Kate, Coop, and Tim climbed out before realizing they had left Zack alone, back on the bus with the stricken driver.

They found the little guy still inside and tending to Petty by wiping the older man's brow with a tissue now covered in streaks of black hair dye.

Kate kneeled beside Zack, and he gazed up at her.

"Is he going to die?"

Kate grinned back and steeled her resolve to tell him the truth.

"Not right now. Not if we can help it. Right?"

"Right."

Zack smiled back, but Tim looked terrified as he stared down at the stricken guard.

"Listen, call 911 or Triple-AAA or something, man! I don't have the chops for this level of the game. What do we even do here to help this old dude? Somebody else has got to help him."

Whenever life became too real, too fast—the true Tim Finn surfaced and didn't want to play leader anymore.

"Who has a phone? Anybody? Are you kidding me? No contraband phones. No Burners? Come on!" Tim pleaded, feeling less than useless in the middle of this ongoing disaster.

"They confiscated them all when we boarded!"

"Wait? Where's Petty's?" Kate started searching the older man's pockets.

"Yes!" Kate freaked out when she found the phone, and she held it up in triumph when Tim snatched it away and dialed 911 just as fast as he could punch the three keys.

But there was no dial tone or signal to receive at the bottom of the hollows. They might as well have been trying to use their shoes from the surface of the moon.

"No signal."

Kate was disappointed, but she tried to remain positive. She began thinking like a survivor again and not a victim.

"Alright... we need to get ourselves higher on one of these mountaintops to get a clear signal out. After that, we just have to improvise, adapt, and overcome! Like the Marines."

"What's a Marine?"

"A survivor."

She knew she was right. It was the best survival move they could make.

"Yeah, well, there's just a slight kink in that equation." Tim nodded down to Petty, still unconscious and appearing frail.

"We can't just leave him. Can we?"

"Alright. You're right. Then you all stay down here, and I guess I'll go for a little force march. I'll climb up alone. Eh, well... up there, someplace, and I'll be back in, like, maybe in a couple of hours."

Kate volunteered, but inside, the thought of climbing that spooky hillside alone in the dark petrified her.

"Okay, then. Well, hopefully, I'll see you on the dance floor soon, good kisser," she took a deep breath and started out alone.

"Wait," Zack ran after and grabbed her hand, not letting her move further away. "We stay together. You promised," Zack reminded her.

I'm loving this kid, Kate thought.

Coop knelt beside the little boy.

"Listen, everybody—Zack's right. We shouldn't be splitting up at night. So, let's stay together, at least until sunrise. You know they're going to start searching for us right away."

"Yeah! All-points bulletin! So, they can arrest us and punish us all for blowing up the mall." Oz declared.

Zack darted off into the darkness, startling everyone.

"Don't take it so personally, weirdo! I didn't say it was you! Who knows what that even was?"

Then Zack reemerged from the woods, pulling two straight branches behind him.

"Those saplings are too green to make a signal fire with, moron," Tim mocked the young boy's firewood choice, and Kate picked up a rock and chucked it.

"Ow!" He skipped away and shut his mouth for a few minutes.

Zack scampered back onto the bus, snatched Petty's uniform jacket off the back of the seat, and hopped out.   He slipped the stripped-down poles into the sleeves, one apiece, into each armhole, with the arms extended out.

The other kids didn't understand what Zack was doing as they watched him in their confused silence and mocked him in whispers.

"Is he making a scarecrow?" Lennon asked.

"A kite?"

Then Zack zipped up the front of the coat, enclosing the top half of the two poles.

"Hold on! I saw this on a survival show!" Ozzy yelled, impressed with the young cipher's efforts. "Zack's making Petty a homemade stretcher!"

"Oh, I get it."

Ozzy and Tim hopped back onto the bus and grabbed a yellow rain slicker they found stashed onboard. They used it to finish the other half of the improvised transport.

"Look! It works! A battle-stretcher!" Oz beamed as if it were all his idea. "There's nothing wrong with a little institutional binge-watching, is there? Now admit it! That's a great survival hack, people!"

Kate couldn't believe Zack's hidden skill set in constructing their new emergency stretcher. He had just saved the day, although Oz was still busy gobbling up all the credit.

She wondered what was happening behind those beautiful, wounded eyes as Zack smiled, watching his emergency stretcher in action. And that bright look of joy in his clear eyes was all that counted as far as Kate was concerned. There were so many other things to be worried about right now, but this special little boy would not be one of them.

"Coop has to be right. Help must be on its way by now. We just have to wait until daybreak and hope and pray that

Petty doesn't croak tonight in the middle of these woods."

"Is that all?"

Tim slipped back on board the bus as everyone else huddled together to make plans.

That's when he discovered what he was hunting for.

He secretly pocketed Petty's forgotten revolver with no one the wiser.

-CHAPTER 15-

Archie

The forest was alive with a sinister, electric curiosity that first night lost underneath the enchanted Bubble.

Primitive shadows with large nocturnal glowing eyes, unknown to the upside world, prowled these woods like predatory silhouettes—continuously on the hunt for easy prey.

The smallest of the hideous creatures darted back into the shadows upon seeing the hissing, red fireball floating on the trail toward them as the lost orphans struggled downhill. A couple of road flares discovered in the glove box provided their only illumination.

Jesse held the flare high above the group as she took point, using her natural height and balance to her advantage.

"We should have stayed back at the bus, not started a midnight stroll with fireworks in the middle of a tinder-dry forest!" Ozzy complained the loudest.

"But I thought I saw lights," Kate kept explaining as they crept further downhill. "Somebody might be living down here that can help us."

"Yeah, it sure looks like it," Tim shot back. "Oh, look! I think I see a tennis court!" he pointed.

"Really?"

"Get serious."

The night creatures scampered across the treetops, giggling at the sight of the latest group of unsuspecting trespassers stumbling toward them.

122

Coop and Tim struggled to navigate the steep grade down through the slanted forest with the unconscious Sgt. Petty still providing the deadweight on Zack's improvised stretcher.

"I'm sorry, everybody. I swear I saw lights right down here," Kate apologized as she tried to help everyone stay balanced on the tricky ridge.

"We should have stayed back by the bus!" Ozzy whined. He was out of breath and stumbling in the dark behind everyone else. "Everybody knows that! Get lost? Sit tight! No reason to move unless you're being chased!"

Kate felt guilty because she knew he was right. She should have gone ahead to check the lights out, but she was too frightened and proud to ask for help. Besides, Zack wouldn't leave her side, no matter what.

"I know, Ozzy. I'm sorry. You're right. We should have stayed put, but I swear I thought I saw someone's flashlights moving around down here," Kate explained.

She was losing faith in her survival skills and her lung capacity as she let out a tremendous sigh.

"I saw something. Bright and moving, I swear. Right down there."

Coop stumbled over a jagged rock, skinning his knee, and surefooted, Tim stumbled over the same one. They almost dumped Petty off the stretcher as they fought to steady him.

"Alright! Alright! I'm calling an audible! That's it. We'll camp here!" an exhausted Coop decided for everyone without taking a vote.

He fell onto his wounded knee, panting while controlling the stretcher. He and Tim lowered Petty to the ground as gently as possible, but the unconscious man let out a painful yowl.

"Owooohhhhh!"

"Really? We're stopping here, in the middle of the trail?" Kate whined, disappointed at the group's decision to quit.

"We've only made... what? A mile? Maybe a little more

123

from the bus. I can't go on, and I don't see anybody else here capable enough to carry this stretcher back up this elevator shaft. Do you want to try it? Please be my guest?" he offered as he tried to catch up to his breath.

Kate wanted to protest, but she knew he was right, and she felt relieved that someone else was helping her decide their fate now.

We should have never left the bus. I was wrong about that choice. But what did I see? I saw lights—glowing—moving around.

Something was down here.

"Maybe it was only fireflies?" She realized as lightning bugs began floating through the darkness.

This must be how Zack feels. Kate thought as she began swatting at the low-flying bugs. *Imagine living like this twenty-four hours a day? Poor kid.*

When Kate turned, she was shocked to see Zack bolt off again—as if maybe she had offended him with her thoughtless pantomime. But Zack reappeared minutes later with enough dry wood to start a campfire and a proud smile brightening his face.

That snapped Kate out of her self-doubt when she saw the little boy so happy and in his element in the deep woods.

The other citified teenagers watched with varying degrees of fascination as Zack stripped and bundled the smaller kindling together and then built a perfect little teepee of wood for a fire.

"Got a light, Jess?" Kate asked.

Jesse stared back, confused for a beat, the guilty closet smoker smelling a trap.

"Uh, no, Kate. You know I don't do that anymore," Jess deadpanned.

Kate chuckled and pointed up at Jess's diminishing flare.

"Relax, sis."

Embarrassed, Jesse lowered the burning torch to the wood—instant flames.

"Listen, everybody, Oz was right," Kate began.

"Oz is always right!" The big kid agreed.

"We should have stayed put back on the bus. But don't worry, okay? I left a marked trail for any rescuers to follow this trek downhill. Still, maybe we should hike back up to the bus? It's only a mile, or so Coop thinks. I was just so worried about getting Petty some medical help tonight."

Kate began doubting every decision.

"I'm sorry I let you down."

"Led us down!" Oz corrected.

"Let's rest here for a bit, and then we'll climb back up to the bus."

"Back uphill? With him?" Coop heaved. "Not likely. Not this year or anytime soon."

Tim still couldn't form words.

She admired how Coop and Tim had pitched in without hesitation to help everyone.

Coop is a great guy.

Tim isn't so bad, either.

Whatever their personal challenges, Kate appreciated they were both here.

An hour later and quiet tears wet some cheeks as it grew later, and the forest grew darker and damper.

"Shouldn't the police have come for us by now?" Pavarty complained. "Someone? Anyone? With searchlights and barking dogs and helicopters? Like on the News?"

"Listen, Pav; helicopters can't fly in the fog. They need visibility. It might take them a little longer to find us than we thought, that's all," Kate explained. "I know. Let's build up this fire so big that there's no way they can miss it when they get close, fog or not! Okay? Everybody up!"

The sluggish teens stirred from their frozen circle.

"Let's make a fire ring out of some rocks and gather lots more dry firewood. Okay? Tons of it. No one will ignore our bonfire."

Everyone stood up, used to following her directions.

Kate smiled at Zack.

"Sound like a plan, Stan?"

"My name is not Stan?" Zack responded.

"Well, I thought it was because you were just—standing around?"

Zack giggled, and Kate felt better as he ran off searching for wood.

"Everybody, stay close, stay smart, and don't leave this immediate area."

It didn't take long before they had a massive bonfire roaring.

Petty was still unconscious but lying close enough to the fire to absorb its warmth, and he seemed to rest comfortably.

Pavarty couldn't keep her darkest fears from crawling up her spine like spiders as the flames drew her soul closer.

"What if nobody ever comes looking for us? What if they don't care we're gone?"

"No, the odds are very high that someone will rescue us within the first twenty-four hours—once reported." Josh had run the standard statistics repeatedly.

"I'll take that bet!" Ozzy chuckled with his outstretched mitt. "We could be lost out here for days."

"Done!" Emiliano chipped in.

They shook on it.

"Don't you ever get sick of losing to us, Ozzy?" Emiliano asked. "Josh is never wrong, and neither am I! And you have never won a single bet in your entire life!"

"Not True! Bet ya!" Oz protested, doubling down on the wrong side again.

"Not even one time." Emiliano couldn't be persuaded otherwise.

"Shouldn't we try calling the police again?" Lennon asked, tucked up underneath Pavarty's wing.

At only twelve, she was the youngest of the teenagers, except for Zack. This timid little girl had been abandoned at birth in a forest much like this one more than a decade before.

A solitary Forest Ranger riding the backcountry on horseback found the shivering pink bundle in the middle of a downpour. There were no other tracks on the rain-soaked logging road leading either way.

"Did you fall out of the sky, little one?"

Now whenever she heard thunder, Lennon remembered his smiling face with the bushy mustache as he sheltered her from the storm underneath his warm poncho.

And then his face disappeared from her life as well.

Now, the sad young girl lived in constant fear of being abandoned. She'd already been returned to Briscoe twice before.

"Do I have to live down here forever now?" Lennon worried out loud.

"No way, child. I am not living in any damp woods, and you're with me! Right?" Pavarty hugged her tighter.

"Right," Lennon snuggled.

Kate flipped open the old-style phone and gave it to Lennon to hold.

"Here, kid. You check every few minutes and see if we have any kind of signal, then shut it right back off, okay?"

Kate seemed to blossom under this sudden duress, and she was proud of her city gal, Pavarty, for stepping up and coping with their weird situation so well.

"Now listen, Lennon. You'll be the one who's in charge when we call for help, okay? We can't waste the battery, though. Understand? Protect that battery life and get us some help, girlfriend," Kate prodded her with an elbow. Lennon felt in charge of her fate and less insecure with Kate's and Pavarty's sisterly attention.

"Come on, Kate! We can't use our only phone for a nightlight! Use your brainpan!" Tim stepped in to confront her again, but Coop stood, grabbed him by the elbow, and spun him around in the opposite direction with a restrained shove.

"Come on, Timmy boy, let's you and me and the Zanies here gather some more firewood. We'll take our time to simmer down and back off."

Kate smiled at Coop as he passed by, and everyone else stood up and joined the search.

With the others occupied, Zack snuck away again, searching for a quiet space to think.

What is going on?

What are these new feelings I feel inside me now?

The voices?

The smells.

And why do I feel so at home in this strange place?

He ambled absently along the familiar streambed as if he recognized it when he discovered a rich tangle of old driftwood washed up on a bend. That's when he heard the first rustle of the brush.

Zack swatted at his gnats as he turned around to see what the noise might be.

"Kate?"

Leaves started exploding into the air behind him as a gigantic rushing shadow devoured him first.

"Hey! No!" Zack backpedaled as fast as he could, but the monstrous creature landed on top—driving the little boy down hard into the mud with a breath-stealing thud.

"Ooof!"

He lay there dazed for a moment.

"Harley!" A young, unfamiliar voice floated in from somewhere else as Zack's vision tunneled.

"Harley! Here, boy!" The youthful voice drifted further off, and Zack's world went black.

He was startled awake a few seconds later when a long, wet tongue started lapping his face from chin to forehead, like an ice cream cone.

Yuck!

That's when Zack realized a huge, dappled Great Dane still pinned him to the ground. The giant dog seemed to grin down at him as if he'd just found the best new play toy imaginable.

Harley began whipping his enormous tail so fast that it made sharp swishing noises like Zorro's blade as it cut through the air.

"Harley." Zack heard that strange boy's voice growing closer—but no one was standing there.

"I said to find him, not fetch him like a stick. Now get your dirty paws off him."

The unseen voice seemed to come from the fabric of the night sky as Zack began to see the dark ripples of an apparition coalescing above his head. It was the glowing silhouette of a young boy about his age, hovering just above him.

"What? Who are you?" Zack jumped up as soon as Harley stepped off.

The smiling specter floated to the ground, revealing a memorable gap in-between his front teeth.

"Well, that was some strange fun, I can tell you that!" the apparition giggled as he took full shape. "That's my first time."

"Uh, yeah. Mine too."

The smiling apparition made sure he had all his pieces.

"Wow. Who, who are you?"

"Why, I'm Archie, Zack." The bright-faced boy replied. He stood about Zack's height and sported a pair of dirty bib overalls over a torn flannel.

"I mean... what are you?" Zack clarified.

"Why, I'm your Forever-Friend, Zack. Kind of like one of your invisible bugs, only lots bigger!" The boy's jade-green eyes glinted with truth.

"Those bugs aren't my friends," Zack replied.

"Oh, yes, they are—more than you know. And now so is Harley," Archie confirmed as the happy Great Dane barked.

Zack felt off balance, which seemed to be his constant state lately.

How does this strange kid even know what I can see? I've never met him before.

Sure, he saw the gnats. Zack saw so much more

129

than anyone could ever believe. But Zack had never seen a human being materialize out of thin air before. Let alone a shimmering, talking one.

"Why do you look so... familiar to me?" Zack asked.

The radiant boy grinned.

"Maybe because we've both known each other forever? That just might be how the whole thing works."

"I don't think so?" Zack answered.

"Then maybe not," the boy's gap grin grew wider. "Either way, I have other gifts to help you move ahead in your quest."

The boy produced two mason jars crammed with enough lightning bugs to illuminate the surroundings in a halo of soft light.

"Neat," Zack said, impressed. "Thank you."

"We wish you nothing but a safe passage, Zack. What you're after is waiting for you just across the lake."

"I'm looking for firewood."

Archie chuckled.

"That too. Harley will guide you the rest of the way when the time is right. Trust him."

Archie bowed at the waist and faded away as he lifted his arms and rose higher into the sky.

"This is so much more fun than the other place!"

"Wait! We who? What's this all about? Hey! Don't forget your dog!" Zack yelled.

"His name is Harley. He's your dog now, or you are his human now. Forever. It works best like that, too. You'll see. Follow him wherever he goes. He will never guide you in the wrong direction or let you down."

Harley smiled and licked Zack's face again, and by the time the drool was dry, Archie had disappeared back into the night.

Zack searched everywhere, using his new firefly jars to illuminate the area, but found nothing.

Zack was no longer standing alone. He had a brand-new

best friend by his side.

"Whoa." was all Zack could muster, standing next to the battle-scarred behemoth with the tender brown eyes.

"Woof!" Harley concurred.

-CHAPTER 16-

Real Help

Zack returned to the bonfire with Harley trotting beside him like a shadow.

The magnificent dog howled with delight when he spotted the other lost kids and bounded ahead of Zack as the startled orphans screamed and scattered in the bushes.

"Whoa! Whoa! Whoa!"

"Hey, hey!" Ozzy ducked behind Jesse.

Coop stood in front of Kate, who shoved him aside, sending him off balance into Tim.

Kate didn't depend on anyone else's gallantry or chivalry in standing her ground against any threat.

Thank you very much.

Besides, she had seen Zack's wide smile illuminated by the firefly jars and spotted the hound's happy tail as they approached.

Harley galloped up to everyone and sniffed them, from head to toe, before sitting next to Zack as if something had always fastened him there.

Resting on his haunches, the majestic dog still towered several inches above Zack's head.

If one knows what to look for, one can always spot a dog's sunny smile—and Harley was positively beaming. The happy old battle dog had always wanted a little boy to call his own, and now he had one to treasure.

Everyone was stunned at the size of the scarred beast.

"Is that a Shetland pony?" City girl Pavarty couldn't

132

grasp what she was seeing.

"Found yourself a new protector there?" Kate chuckled as she approached the boy and his affectionate new friend.

"The way I understood it... he's got me," Zack answered.

The young boy was still pondering the meaning of Archie's puzzling words.

"You got a talking dog?" Ozzy peeped out of hiding.

"No. That other boy said it to me," Zack replied.

"What, boy? You found someone out there, Zack?" Kate's heart surged at the news, and the others gathered around.

"Well. Not exactly. His name is Archie, and he appeared, and then he... disappeared."

"You mean you lost him?"

"No. Archie just vanished."

Zack had grown weary of explaining the strange alternative universe he lived in to the unseeing world of the walking blind.

"Just disappeared like that, huh?" Emiliano snapped his fingers.

"No. A lot slower than that," Zack answered.

"Where did you ever find these beautiful jars, Zack?" Even Kate seemed confused.

"Why, he's a real-life Boy Scout! He handmade them right out of the sand," Pavarty joked.

"No, I didn't. Archie gave them to me."

"Wait. You're saying that an invisible boy gave you two real jars? Full of living bugs?" Emiliano scratched his head and pondered the science behind the possibilities of that scenario. "That doesn't quite compute, little dude? Make no sense at all, does it?" he questioned the others.

"It's impossible to commingle physical and ethereal constructs," Josh concurred. "Everyone knows that."

"Nothing is impossible," Zack said assuredly. It seemed he held the wisdom of the ages within his tiny frame.

Kate reached down and took one of the canning jars to inspect it.

It was a hand-blown green glass jar. A ring of clear crystals surrounded the outer edges and top in a circle of amplifying lenses, magnifying the natural biological light from within and scattering the light beams. Kate shook it to agitate the fireflies trapped inside. Their soft glow lit up the darkness.

"This is a wonderful gift, whatever realm it came from. From now on, whatever Zack says goes, folks." She grinned before firing an intimidating glare at the rest of the dubious pack.

"We didn't know we needed a stretcher, but Zack built us one. We needed a source of dependable light—now we have a source of dependable light, thanks to Zack. So, we should all be thankful and stop grilling him right now. He's ahead in this outdoor game."

Zack appreciated being around Kate. He'd never had a proper friend before.

Not a Forever Friends, either.

Or a dog.

But the institutionalized lad also understood that Kate couldn't possibly say she believed or understood anything about him, either.

How could she? It's impossible. Nobody normal can ever understand all that I see if their eyes don't work that way. It's not their fault.

"You're inviting insanity upon yourself!" Briscoe had warned him repeatedly in their closed-door sessions.

He was beginning to believe that the good doctor was telling the truth.

"Where is everybody? When is somebody going to show up and help us? Help!" Lennon cried out.

Her tiny voice echoed around the hollows when they heard a distant reply from another glen.

"Hello? Hello? Did somebody cry for help?" a woman's voice called back in the night.

The teens shrieked and cheered at the contact, but

Harley stood up protectively in front of Zack.

A twig snapped nearby, and Harley lowered his head, ready for mortal combat. The fur along his spine bristled like body armor, making the battle-hardened hound appear several times larger than his already intimidating size.

"Harley, wait!"

Zack held back the snarling beast with only his words as the brawny dog clawed the ground, ready to attack. That's when the silhouette of a young woman stepped out of the darkness, and her appearance threw everyone off balance.

"Hello! Must I repeat myself? Did someone cry out for help? Or is this another prank played by my brothers? Hello?"

The young woman appeared to be in her late twenties, but it was difficult to tell in the firelight. She had a pronounced hitch to her stride, and it seemed she might have over-applied her makeup in places. Curiously, she was wearing a pair of old-fashioned riding breeches, tall black boots, and clutching a riding crop as she limped out of the shadows as if from a midnight fox hunt gone terribly wrong.

"Well, well, well. So, what do we have here?" She seemed surprised and oddly delighted about her discovery.

"We got us more ghosts, sis?"

A man's deep voice startled everyone as helmet lights snapped on, and two enormous men stepped out of the shadows behind her.

"I don't like them, ghost kids."

"Relax, Berk. No ghosts here. But it looks like they could use a little Pepper," the woman answered.

"What the whaa?" Oz choked as he ducked behind Jesse again. "They're fricken cannibals, guys!"

The men's faces remained hidden beneath the brims of their floppy felt hats, with their metal mining helmets plopped on top of those. But from what the teens could see was unsettling and disturbing from any angle. It was hard to get an accurate fix on these two imposing silhouettes hiding behind the glare of their headlamps as they towered over everyone like twin Bigfoots at a Munchkin convention.

"I'm sorry for the fright, children. I spotted your bonfire a while back and thought you were another gaggle of trespassers, but then I heard that pitiful little cry for help, and I reconsidered. I thought maybe somebody was in real trouble. And it looks like I was right." The young woman crossed closer to the fire. "Do you need our help?"

"Yes! Yes!" Kate squealed and ran forward with outstretched arms, but was rebuffed with a gesture.

"Do tell. Well, hello, all. My name is Shelby. Shelby Tann. It looks like your little outing has turned serious," she gestured to Petty lying by the fire.

"Oh, god, yes! Thank you, thank you!" Kate exclaimed and leaned in for a warm hug, but Shelby spun away.

"What happened to you? What are you children doing way out here at this time of night?"

"We're from the Briscoe Institute. Our bus got stranded when our driver got sick. My name is Kate. Kate Tempest. This is Zack and Coop, Jesse, Lennon, Pavarty, Emiliano, Josh, Tim, and Ozzy."

"Well, I am very pleased to meet all of you. My name is Shelby. This is my stepbrother Berk, and this is Moody, the baby of the family."

"You sure these aren't just more ghosts, sis? What about that pale little one over there?" Moody whispered, unconvinced.

"Are there real ghosts out here?" Lennon shivered as she peered around.

"Hell yes," he answered.

"Hush up, Moody. You're only scaring these poor children," Shelby snapped.

"What are you folks even doing out at this hour? Ghost-busting?" Coop grew suspicious.

"Well, it's all quite fortunate, I guess. First, I quarreled with my mother tonight, so I went for a moonlight ride to cool down. Then it seemed even my horse grew prickly with me, threw me off. Luckily, my big brothers grew concerned and came out looking for me after some time. So, it seems we all got lucky tonight. Because then we found you."

Shelby's grin creased her face with a little joy in it.

"See! I was right! I saw your flashlights moving around," Kate nudged Coop. "We are so lucky to meet you!"

It relieved Kate to see a flesh and blood adult again and to cede any authority back onto their mature shoulders, no matter who and why they showed up.

"Wait a minute. I heard something on the news about a missing busload of orphan children from the Briscoe Institute out on old Highway Forty-nine before I rode out tonight."

"Yes! That's us!"

"Hot dog, we're saved!"

"Hey! If they mentioned us on TV, then we're already famous! Instant celebrities! That's how it works!" Ozzy said. "I'm gonna be an influencer!"

"Maybe we'll get adopted."

"Well, this is a real-life miracle, isn't it?" Shelby squealed. "And you kids couldn't have... materialized at a better time in so many ways."

"Well, timing is everything!" Kate swung but failed to connect her high-five with the uncomfortable woman.

"In more ways than you'll ever know, child. It's almost like magic."

Shelby's insincere grin was more than her brothers could bear, and they snickered behind her like giant hyenas.

"What's so funny, guys?" Coop challenged their rudeness.

"Excuse their manners. My mother, Pepper, and I run the local DHCHS in town. So that's what I meant when I said you could use some Pepper."

"The what?" Kate asked.

"Why the Dark Hollows Children's Home Society?"

"You run an orphanage?"

"Yes, we do. What luck! Can you believe it? And,

what a headline it will make online—Lost orphans found by Assistant Manager Shelby Tann from the DHCHS while out on a moonlight ride. It will make an incredible internet story and raise even more donations for our lives' work. Another lost orphan story told with a delightful Hollywood ending."

"So, you have heard of the Briscoe Institute? It's a pretty secretive place."

"Of course, darling, who hasn't in our field? We are very close competitors of a sort. But enough about business. Let's get your driver some medical help and get you all back to civilization, pronto."

"I can't believe it. We're saved!"

"But it is still quite a hike. We will all have to walk. My horse is probably sleeping back in the stables by now, and my brothers came out looking for me on foot."

The surrounding forest was still alive with agitated movements along the highway of branches.

"Muy malo?" Emiliano whispered, sensing the wicked vibe in the flurry of activity above.

"Pay them critters, no mind. Nothing will harm you in our care. Now let's find you a new home base."

Shelby reached out to move Zack along, and Harley stepped in between and nudged her out of the way with his wet snout.

"Oooh. Bad dog."

The suspicious dog kept his eyes trained on the strange lady and her even stranger brothers—and he grumbled as if he already knew their secrets—because he did.

"I hate to be the one to tell you this, young man, but I'm afraid dogs aren't allowed inside the city limits of Dark Hollows. That's a hard and fast law."

"Why?"

"Because there's a horrible curse of rabies and a distemper down here. Every single dog ends up catching the virus and goes foaming at the mouth mad, and then those monsters tear into us. The diseases come from the vampire bats' roosting in the endless caves and mines down here. I'm sorry, child, but we banned all canines from our town generations ago."

"Well, I won't leave him behind," Zack stated flatly, and Harley agreed.

Shelby measured the stoic little boy with some professional disdain at first—sizing him up as a future adoption prospect.

She sensed something different bubbling just below the surface of this peculiar child's aura as she stared deeper into his eyes, and it confused her at first.

Here's an odd duck. I haven't seen a lost soul like this before. Mother might love the essence of this one.

Shelby tempered her standard approach with the boy.

"Well. We'll just have to bend the rules for you tonight, won't we? It is an emergency, after all. How does that sound, young man? A new rule just for you!" she quizzed Zack, eager to please the rare boy now.

"Yes, ma'am," Zack answered.

If Harley doesn't trust her, then I don't trust her either, Zack thought.

"Please, children, follow my brothers." Shelby nudged everyone along.

Berk and Moody picked up the stretcher with Petty aboard, and everyone began the long trek into town.

"Hey! Whoo-hoo! Officially rescued gang!" Emiliano grinned. "You lose the bet again, Ozzy! Whaa, whaaa, whaaa!"

"Oh, man!"

Zack was easing through the darkness on a parallel path through the woods. His firefly jars lit the way as Coop hung back with Kate at the end of the procession.

"What the heck is this all about?" Coop asked.

"What?" Kate didn't understand the problem.

"You don't feel it? Like, I don't know... something is not right here, like in a big, weird, hair-stand-up-on-the-back-of-your-neck kind of way. Does she really run an adoption agency? With her mother? Where did they even come from? And why? It's almost two in the morning. These are some strange-looking people, Kate. My instincts are screaming to run off in the opposite direction. Not yours?"

"No way, Coop. Make sense. They're just country folk living out here, and now they're trying to help. Working at an orphanage is just too weird for anyone to make up off the top of their heads. Who would ever say such a thing out loud if it wasn't true? No one. Like ever."

The branches above their heads creaked and bowed down toward them under the weight of added observers.

"Geez, duck!"

Coop flinched, but Kate didn't as the treetops hummed with a frustrated chatter and then snapped back up as the predators lost hope for an easy late-night snack.

Kate lived in a perpetual state of hyper-situational awareness, but after this frightening night, she gladly lowered her usual defenses when she caught sight of the distant lake town.

"Once we were lost, and now we are found!" she sang as she pointed to the tiny oasis dozing on the moonlit shoreline below them.

"Whoever even heard of this place before?" Coop was still skeptical as they descended the ever-flattening trail. "I never saw this enormous lake on any of my roadmaps, and I've studied them all, planning my future road trips."

The dense, rotting woods receded around them, and the weary travelers moved onto the level, open land. The moonlight revealed endless fields of tombstones fanning out before them in every direction throughout the staggered hills of oak and ash. Vultures by the hundreds slept on the twisted branches of the polluted forest.

"Are you kidding me? Who designed this place? Chuckie?"

"It looks like a lot of your kin ended up dying around here, Shelby. Was there a historical battle or a plague that happened down here?" Coop asked.

"Something like that."

Coop noticed that most of the dates on the soot-stained markers weren't that ancient, and a lot were new.

"Recently?"

"Of a sort," she replied, limping ahead.

"Miss Shelby? Did you hurt your leg when you fell off your horse?" Lennon asked.

"No," she huffed and picked up the pace.

Something about this place stinks beyond the air! Coop thought.

Traveling along the meandering road, they began seeing black cast-iron pipes sprouting up among the fields of headstones like ebony-colored mushrooms.

Each crooked pipe–standing between three and five feet tall—belched black and yellow smoke from somewhere deep underground. The permanent toxic clouds shrouded the entire countryside in a constant plume of smoke, suffocating this side of the lake in constantly drifting waves of soot and ash.

"Eee-yew, this place smells like rotten eggs!" Pavarty grimaced and covered her nose, as did the others.

"Ugh!"

"It smells like one big cow fart!" Ozzy said.

"A herd of diarrhetic cow farts!" Emiliano corrected.

"Ozzie's old grandmother's farts!" Tim taunted Ozzy.

"Nuh-uh?" Ozzy pouted. "She's dead by now, anyway. She doesn't fart no more, man."

Kate yelled from the back of the group, "Hey Shelby? What's up with all these weird smokestacks?"

"Yeah, but let's not mention the world's largest unknown cemetery," Coop cracked.

Shelby stopped and gestured with her riding crop for the orphans to keep moving along past her in an orderly fashion.

"Our ancestors sank those stacks, back in the day, to relieve the ground pressure that's building up underneath ever since our coal mines caught fire more than a century ago."

"Wait? This same fire has been burning underground for over a hundred years?"

Kate couldn't believe that was even possible.

"Yes. And it will burn for another hundred or more, too," Shelby added. "It's an anthracite fire. There's enough coal spread throughout all these hills and valleys for it to burn underground forever. A thick vein of that coal rose to the surface at the city dump back in those days. It caught fire like a fuse and began burning its way down through all the mines below ever since."

"It smells as god-awful as this butt-ugly place looks," Tim fake gagged.

Shelby took immediate offense at the easily thrown slurs.

"We are simply doing our best with what we have down here, sport. There might be a life lesson in that for you spoiled Briscoe orphans. Suppose you all just learn to hold your stuck-up little noses closed with your fingertips long enough so that you can criticize my hometown later—once we've fed and clothed you orphans with our generosity." Shelby limped away.

"Can't wait."

"This place and these people are so freaking weird," Ozzy whispered to Tim as they continued hiking through the nightmarish landscape.

"Don't panic, son. If anyone gives us any trouble—I appropriated some real big city Deliverance protection against any yahoos out here."

"What do you mean?"

"How much you give me to see?"

"I only got twelve bucks left from the mall."

"Give me two."

Tim winked and opened his denim jacket, flashing the ivory handle of Petty's revolver stashed in his waistband.

"What? No way. You get caught with that cap gun, son, and you'll get us all sent back to Juvey for permanent! Just touching that thing is an instant felony for any of us, and you know it!"

A vulture's startling screech from the tree line made everyone duck and cringe.

"Now, tell me you aren't glad I'm packing this heat, bad boy?" Tim challenged.

Oz could only respond with a frightened sigh as they drew closer to the sleepy village known as Dark Hollows.

"Yeah, sure, dude. Whatever. My fuses are already totally blown, man. What else could possibly go wrong? Just everything?"

-CHAPTER 17 –

Dark Hollows

Beguiled by the rising moon, the small town's silhouette resembled a crocodile dozing on some exotic beach more than it did a sleepy lakefront village. When seen from almost any angle, there was something predatory about its overall reptilian profile.

The stragglers picked up their pace as they walked down the muddy road that ended in the town square. The lost orphans were returned to the safe harbor of human civilization once more.

Or so it appeared.

"Welcome to Dark Hollows, children." Shelby forced another ragged smile as she urged her brothers to carry Petty away on the stretcher.

"Where are they taking him?" Kate followed.

"He'll be just fine, don't worry another minute about him. My brothers are taking him straight to the doctor. If he needs any further help, they'll call an ambulance from there. Now let's get you all settled down for the night. I believe it will delight my mother to see every single one of you. And you will all get me off a very nasty hook."

"Nobody in their right mind is ever going to be happy at this hour, lady," Tim said.

"She might just surprise you. Mother is a famous night owl like me. She'll be more than happy to see you. You'll see."

A few dozen dark buildings made up the formal downtown area, yet there wasn't a working streetlight glowing in the entire dingy township. No porch lights burned in any of the clustered shanties, with not even a dog bark to sound the alarm.

This madly disorganized industrial side of town was an insane mixture of timber mills, coal mines, smelters, salt mines, and all the administration and supply buildings that came with the demands.

Any new inhabitants had to build their temporary homes on stilts out over the water because all flat land had already been claimed centuries before.

Shelby held her riding crop up and halted the exhausted parade before a grand three-story home. It sat isolated from the rest of the industrial area in a protected glen of live oak trees that overlooked the lakefront.

In front, a sign read- Dark Hollows Children's Home Society- Established Sept 15th, 1950.

"See. Just as I told you!" Shelby led them up the manicured driveway.

"Holy moly! She wasn't lying!"

The colonial-style brick structure wasn't what anyone would expect to find in the deep forest. Instead, the house appeared to be a proper three-story home from a bygone era. Smothered in vines, it was the picture-perfect version of a stately country home, including the grand circular driveway.

"Wow means wow."

"Is this really an orphanage-orphanage, or did Elvis die in the bathroom here?" Ozzy asked.

"Silly boy. It sure is. And it beats the rice and beans right out of spooky old Briscoe's fancy bouillabaisse' now, doesn't it?" Shelby bragged.

"By parsecs, lady!"

"And look at that lake view."

"Wait until you see the portraits of our famous clients inside. All your favorite superstars deal with my mother. From all around the world."

Shelby hobbled up the steps onto the formal porch and

attempted to open the front door, but it didn't budge. She remembered her mother angrily locking it behind her after their fight, and she felt embarrassed both times.

"I'm sorry. I never take along my keys when I go out riding. No pockets, you see."

She knocked again, but there was no response, so she knocked again and then once more.

"Alright! Who is it?" a woman's voice barked on the other side of the door.

"It's Shelby, ma! Open up. I forgot my keys! I have a wonderful surprise for you!"

"What surprise? You were supposed to be flying out to the coast to pick up that last batch of kids for my coronation!" came back the surly reply. "Now, I don't want to see that ugly face of yours again until you do as you're told! We have a pipeline to keep full!"

Shelby grew alarmed.

"Shhh! Not now, mother! Hush up! I explained to you I couldn't travel today! Now just listen, I have some VIP guests here with me who would be thrilled to meet you!"

"Guests?" the woman's voice recoiled back behind the door. "What guests? Curses! At this hour, Shelby? It could only be... wait! You just wait a minute!" the woman's stressed-out voice seemed to tunnel away.

A flurry of rushed activity downstairs was followed by the sounds of someone running up the stairs and onto the second and third floors. Lights snapped on, then off, and it took a good five minutes before the front door unbolted from the inside and creaked open.

The flat shadow of Shelby's mother transformed into a three-dimensional shape as she took a cautious step onto the front porch. She remained in silhouette and shrouded from ambient light as she deliberately slammed the door behind her, startling everyone.

"What's all this? Why, this isn't what I was expecting at all!" the old woman exclaimed. "What a big, wonderful surprise. Who do we have here, Shelby?" the matronly figure unexpectedly purred. Her stern demeanor flipped on command while she steadied herself with a silver-tipped cane.

"These are the missing children from the Briscoe Institute mother. The ones we heard about last night on the news before our little row?"

"Really? Briscoe, you say?" replied the silhouette. "The lost orphans. Yes, I remember."

"All ten of them."

"Ten? How on earth did you ever succeed in cap...?" the older woman stopped herself as she stepped out of the shadows and into the rising moonlight.

She was a sturdy-looking woman, standing about five foot seven. Her broad shoulders stooped forward with a bent back, and her hair displayed every gradation of gray within a messy tangle of curls swept back into a long twisting ponytail.

"Children, this is my world-famous mother about whom I was bragging. The humanitarian of every year... the great...."

The older woman cut her off with a dismissive hand.

"Pepper Wixx is the name." She drew out that last syllable in a hiss. "And lost children are just my game. I am so pleased to meet you all. You might have heard of me?" She feigned shyness while thrusting her gnarled hand out like a crooked politician.

So here stood the notorious Pepper Wixx in all her stooped glory. How was it possible that this old woman was Yuma's mortal enemy?

The physical reality of the actual flesh and blood Pepper Wixx appeared to be about as terrifying at first glance as someone's sweet great Nana selling Hippy beads at the county fair. But looks are always deceiving, especially under the Bubble, because this mad sorceress had just discovered the only way to kill over a hundred immortal giants in a single night.

Harley recognized her as the murderer she was

147

immediately, as he grumbled under his breath, still undercover.

Luckily, they had never crossed paths before, and the great battle hound didn't want to draw any further scrutiny from this most powerful of sorcerers to short-circuit Yuma's ultimate plans. Still, he couldn't help himself as his sworn enemy stood only feet away, and her evil presence fouled all his senses.

The exhausted teens never felt the powerful witch's dark spells washing over them. Pepper Wixx possessed the subtle but powerful ability to cast a mystical thrall over anyone upon first meeting. This was only one of many deceptive tricks she kept in her bag of spells. She could change people's perceptions of how they saw her—shifting between what she physically looked like, sounded like, and even smelled like— whenever she felt the need for camouflage. Whether in the upside world—or down here with her own kind. It took only a blink of an eye for her to change personas.

It was only one of a thousand survival hacks that she had learned from an old wizard named Icthius back in her days in Salem, Massachusetts before she fled the witch trials. She had renamed this new trick- 'the Knack.'

If notes or photos of her were ever compared for legal reasons, they would all describe an entirely different being from the one lurking behind her manufactured veil. And that rang especially true for miserable Shelby—who never knew which mother she would serve on any day.

"Great to meet you," Kate gushed. "I'm Kate, this is Zack, Pavarty, Coop, Jesse, Tim, Josh, Emiliano, Lennon and Ozzie. Your daughter said...?" Pepper cut her off.

"Foster daughter," she corrected. "We could never even give her away when she was young." Then she added with a dark chuckle, "But she might as well be from my womb. We're so much alike. Aren't we, darling?"

Shelby registered every verbal jab thrown her way with an eye twitch. After years of indentured servitude, she

148

wondered why she hadn't formed a thicker scar tissue by now.

It shouldn't sting every time she pinches me with her sarcastic words, but it still does.

"Yes, Mother, we are two peas in the proverbial pod," Shelby forced her reply before changing the subject. "Their driver was injured in the bus accident, and I had Berk and Moody rush him off to the doctor for help."

"Which Doc?"

"Doctor Robards."

"Better than Doc Cleaver, I guess. He's too quick to judge and hack."

Wixx turned her attention back to the rescued children huddling in front of her. She seemed to grow taller in their presence—more regal and overbearing.

"Well, excuse my hideous manners, children. You would think I was born a lowlife like your horrible Doctor Briscoe," the woman sneered.

"Hey! That's not nice!" Lennon yelped in defense of the only decent man she knew.

"And neither is he, child, trust me. I will never lie to you as he does every minute he's awake. Just remember Briscoe is an over-calculating deal-breaker and not a tenth the chemist or deal-broker I am."

Pepper pulled her daughter aside as she gestured for the others to enter her elegantly appointed home.

"You scared the wits out of me with this late-night surprise, darling. I thought you'd gone rogue and brought the authorities down on me."

"Mother, really? Never. But just look at them. Aren't you happy now that I didn't go?"

"Ten? That's quite a haul, all at once, I must say. Not quite a baker's dozen, but I am quite impressed." She patted her daughter's blushing cheek as they all entered.

As the lights snapped on, the teenagers saw that Pepper Wixx and company had set up a modern administrative office on one side of the expansive home's ground floor, with a formal waiting room in the large foyer. Several desks inside the office were stacked high with photos, files, and other identity paperwork and ringed by racks of official-looking rubber stamps.

The stub of a deserted cigar burned in an ashtray under a desk lamp as if someone had just been working there.

As they moved further inside, they realized that the rest of the main floor had been transformed by Wixx into a makeshift children's dormitory, excluding the kitchen and formal dining room. Temporary cots were scattered everywhere.

Hand-painted signs hung in between the collections of celebrity portraits lining the walls. And the repeated overriding commandment emphasized this prestigious orphanage's main philosophy on every wall.

Silence is Golden!

"I apologize for this embarrassing mess. But unfortunately, we run out of space so often these days, and we must indulge these huge overflows between catastrophes somehow," Pepper explained.

They painted the different rooms bright pink or pale blue, with inflatable mattresses serving as temporary beds along with the cots—each littered with either toys or snacks scattered around as if abandoned in flight.

Enormous portraits spanning decades of celebrities and sports heroes gave this temporary home the look of an Adoption Hall of Fame.

Wixx appeared in most of the superstar portraits along with her famous clients, The Movie Star, The Baseball Player, The Senator, The Soccer Star— as if the subjects were now all part of some extended royal family. Most held captions from tabloid newspapers and the internet engraved onto brass plaques beneath them.

'Little Miss Christmas Carol finds a famous home on Christmas Eve.'

'Happy Chanukah, Handsome Teddy Bear Benjamin.'

'The Betty Allison Twins Tour the World with their famous mother.'

"Hold it!" Oz chirped to a stop. "Now I get it! So you are that Pepper Wixx?" he finally recognized the famous name from all the late-night television ads. "You're the Celebrity Stork to the Stars?"

Pepper winked. "Guilty as charged, young man."

"And you run a famous bakery too? From down here?"

"Oops. Guilty again. I guess another smart fanboy has found me out, Shelby. So now you can see why I hide my celebrity down here, pumpkin. It's hard to get away and feel safe nowadays being a celebrity in that nasty upside world—a lot of trolls to contend with, as you probably know. So, I stay out of the spotlight unless needed for sales and let all my other humanitarian work speak for itself," Wixx confided as modestly as she could muster.

"So, where did all these other orphans go?" Coop asked, looking around.

"Thankfully, we have what we call 'the Sunny House' tonight. I've placed the last of our new litter of orphans into the homes of the rich and famous just this week."

"Anybody we know?"

"Everybody, you know. But I'm not allowed to say. Confidentiality agreements and all."

"I wish someone famous would adopt me," Pavarty sighed.

Wixx gave the young girl a quick up and down and made her professional assessment.

"You're not too bad a package, child. A little squat, but you have a suitable set of teeth. I think we could probably set you up with, say, a prominent dentist's family."

"Really?"

"Sure. With a new change of clothes. Doctors all seem to be foreign these days; they should love your... exotic looks. We'll talk more about that later, child. Now listen, everyone... I do not have the time to clean up after messy children. As you can see, I already have a monumental job on my hands, and with no reliable staff—I put the stress on the *mental*. And I still have to prepare myself for an extraordinary celebration the townsfolk are throwing in my honor this weekend."

"Congratulations."

She stared at each child, making eye contact and using the Knack to her full advantage.

"That being said. You can all sleep down here on somebody else's messy beds tonight. Or? Someone might persuade me to allow you all to come next door and spend just the one night in my private country lodge."

"Really?"

"Please."

"No way!"

"Where I just might rustle you up some hot chocolate before we go off to bed on clean sheets."

"Hot chocolate!" Oz's hands shot up along with the others.

"Clean sheets."

"I just want to sleep." Emiliano yawned and leaned on Josh's shoulder.

"Follow me then. Oh, and Shelby, please notify the proper authorities. And do contact Dr. Briscoe and his staff and inform them that these children are all safe and now under Dr. Pepper Wixx's personal care at the DHCHS. That should be enough for the authorities to call off their search and quash any more worries."

"Yes, ma'am," Shelby turned away, dismissed like a servant.

"Oh, and Shelby?"

"Yes, mother?"

"Magnificent timing, darling! Truly magnificent improvisational work tonight!" Pepper gestured at the fresh crop of kids.

Shelby returned the conspiratorial smile, acknowledging her evil deed.

Exactly like my mother, she thought.

Once outside the colonial children's home, Pepper steered the teens down the driveway and through the trees next door, separating her large properties.

"Now, you must all promise not to make any mess for Granny Pepper to pick up. I have limos full of celebrity guests coming in this weekend to stay here, followed by a huge celebration. So, I demand that you all keep everything tidy tonight," Pepper stated. "This is not my first rodeo. You must obey, or there will be serious consequences. Do we understand each other?"

"Yes, ma'am."

"We get it."

"We'll keep it clean as a whistle. Whatever that means—because whistles are usually full of spit and saliva—but we promise, nevertheless." Oz crossed his heart.

"Alright then, here we are. Welcome to my home, boys and girls. Just remember—in my homes—silence is golden."

It was like stepping back in time compared to the elegant but straightforward colonial-style children's home sitting next door. The sharp-peaked rooflines of this old-world-inspired lodge towered seven stories tall. Thick coils of vines held together the ancient structure—so that the twisted lodge appeared to be heaving for air trapped inside a living straight-jacket.

"This place looks like it eats humans alive," Ozzy gulped.

He finally realized it was the lake breeze rippling across the face of the leaves, causing the uncanny illusion of struggle.

There wasn't a single straight line anywhere in the gabled structure. It seemed built without a proper plan, plumb-bob, or even a blueprint—simply plopped down here straight out of someone's twisted imagination.

"Hold on. Let me get this straight. You run a world-famous orphanage and own a dodgy, run-down resort next door? Here? In the middle of nowhere?" Tim grew agitated by their spooky surroundings, as was Coop, who scanned the

153

haunted structure with frightened awe.

"Not only that. Don't forget Pepper's soon-to-be world-famous bakery, man!" Oz jumped to her defense. "No, B.S. Tim! Pepper is a born world-shaker. She's getting nationally famous online, on cable and network TV! You cannot tell me you've never heard of 'Granny Pepper's Perfectly Peppered Pickle Pepper Bread?' 'Buy a loaf, and a free loaf feeds a starving child somewhere!'! I can even rap you the jingle!"

"Spare us, Oz."

Wixx crossed over to Tim, readjusting the Knack so that her identity flowed convincingly into her more familiar commercial image on television.

"Tell me, skeptical Tim, what does everyone crave at the end of a long, exhausting trail? I already know that answer. Do you, young man?"

"Uh, no?" he answered. "Who cares? What's that got to do with anything?"

"Why, at the end of a long trail, everyone yearns for the same thing anywhere in the world, boy. A fresh loaf of bread and a clean fluffy place to lay their tired heads down at night. It's that simple, Timmy. You're in my most special place. Here is the one special spot I know I'm in the safest place on earth where I can finally sink my toes into my own piece of the earth after a life of constant pilgrimages worldwide, making other broken families happy and whole again."

"Aw. That's nice. I want to put down roots someday."

"Me too, by being adopted by somebody world famous! Jet-Set roots!"

"With a cup of hot chocolate!" Lennon chirped.

"I second that motion!" Oz added.

"Yes, children," Wixx cooed back, accepting the prod. Still, she kept her attention pinned on Tim, sensing the troublemaker lurking within the sensitive boy.

Poor specimen. Only a three on the adoption scale of qualities, at best.

She couldn't resist rating all children on her cynical

adoption scale of one to ten.

He's far too old, too ugly, with no actual market value if he isn't strong enough for forced labor—there's no money in that.

"Relax, Timmy. You are just like everybody else down here. No better, no worse. You have left the nasty upside world of judgment behind and won yourself the chance to rest up at the end of the trail down here for a few days. Not so bad. Better than a sharp stick in the eye, as we say in the forest."

"Relax, Timmy. We've landed in the lap of luxury, dork!" Ozzy boasted. "Look around! Score!"

"Now, back in the old days, we called my place a Country Inn, then maybe a Hunting Lodge back in the fifties. But today, we call it a B&B in the hospitality business world. A proper Bed & Breakfast," Wixx informed the children.

"Do you serve breakfast in the bed?"

"We surely do," she winked.

"It's official then. Honestly, this is like the best-lost road trip ever!" Oz bragged.

"Hey!" Lennon yelled for everyone's attention. "Quick! Everybody get over here! It's a miracle! I've got two complete bars!"

Lennon held the glowing phone up above her head to improve the signal.

"Two bars!"

She punched in 911 when Pepper limped over and snatched it away.

"Please let me see that, child. I've got a knack."

Pepper fidgeted with the phone until it blinked out in her hands.

"Oh, no. So sorry, sweetie, we don't have any reliable cell service down here. None that lasts anyway," Pepper promised.

Lennon grabbed the phone from the old lady, upset that the pampered battery was dead, as Kate tried calming the others down.

"It's okay. No worries. We're already safe here. So, relax, no big deal."

"Don't you have a charger?"

"We will get you all the help you could ever need come first light," Pepper promised. "Now, let's all get inside and out of the chill. Let's see, one, two, three..." She began counting heads, including Harley's, who growled as she passed.

"Ten piglets in a blanket and a big mean mutt to boot. Sounds yum. I'll rustle us up some hot chocolate with a big dollop of whipped cream on top. Let's go."

Pepper whirled around and headed back inside as some children held back with Kate and Coop.

Kate took the phone from Lennon and rechecked it— drained.

"We had a quarter charge just a second ago," Lennon said. "I babied it. I promise."

Tim stewed but for only a second.

"I knew it! But you know what? Good! Who needs to be rescued right now?"

"Petty does!" Kate protested as everyone began moving inside.

"The doctor's tending to him as you speak," Wixx startled them as she stepped back out. "Don't worry, another hair on that shaggy little head about your bus driver. You all did a splendid job of getting him down here in one piece. Now he's not your concern any longer. The professionals are in charge, child, as it should be. Now let's get all of your rooms sorted out."

Tim and Coop held back with Kate as the younger kids filed indoors, their patient's mentality kicking back instinctively—see a line—be a line.

"Come on, Kate? Who cares about Petty? I mean, really?" Tim sneered.

"He saved our lives! He saved your life, fool!"

"He got us to the bottom of the hill. I'll give him that much, but something else saved our lives. Luck. Whatever? Why do you want to get yanked back into the Institute tonight?" Tim challenged. "Because I sure don't. For all I care, they can take a week or two before they ever come back to claim us like unwanted baggage. Let's just enjoy this freedom while we have it, Kate. School's out for summer, man!"

"Listen to me, Finn. I don't want to risk not getting to go to the pro..." Kate felt immediately flustered that she'd almost let the dreaded word 'Prom' slip out of her mouth.

How shallow am I?

She flipped to a different answer.

"I don't want to mess up my standing in the Program. The Institute is my only real home. Yours, too, unless you want to go back to jail. I just want all of us to get back to Briscoe. Including Petty. I feel responsible."

"Whoa. Slow down, slick. You aren't talking about me now, are you? Because only me handles me!"

Tim was having none of this, and he readjusted the pistol hidden inside his waistband.

"I'm in charge of my own life now, for once!"

Kate stepped closer.

.   "I've learned the hard way that I am responsible for anyone and everyone standing around me. That's the only way the world works when it works at all. Maybe that's something you still need to learn. People struggle and suffer daily on this planet more than you, man."

"That's their problem!"

Kate had spoken her piece. She followed everyone inside the lodge against her own better judgment.

I don't care what anybody else says. I'm getting us all home safe. She swore to herself.

Coop didn't have to say a word to Tim. Instead, he arched his eyebrows and shot the skateboarder a big thumbs-up.

"What does that even mean, car geek?" Tim shrugged but followed.

That left Zack outside, where he hung back with Harley as Wixx hovered in the doorway, beckoning them both indoors with her cane.

157

"Come on, boys, let's go. It's way past everyone's bedtime by hours."

Harley growled, and Zack hesitated, but when Kate returned and held out her hand, Zack followed her inside.

As Zack squeezed past the old woman in the doorway, he paused and drew near enough to peer into her clouded eyes.

Wixx's trusty Knack wasn't working on the young boy, and he could see her for who she truly was inside. The shock went far beyond disturbing.

It terrified him to see that Pepper Wixx possessed her own private strain of virulent black gnats trapped inside her head and not existing just on the outside, like his.

Zack had never witnessed that internal stinging horror show before.

I didn't know they could find a way inside my head too!

The boy froze in the doorway.

He watched as Wixx's black gnats collided with his white ones. Both boy and witch absently swatted at the invisible bugs as if inflicted with the same mental disorder.

He sees them too! Wixx realized.

That means he's already insane or on his way.

Too bad he's infected like the rest of the swine down here!

That means he's useless to me now.

Without a hint of warning, Harley suddenly erupted in a soul-shattering howl.

Awoooooooo!

The hound's enormous volume staggered Pepper, and every citizen living in Dark Hollows woke up angry at the exact same moment.

-CHAPTER 18-

The Infinite Library

Yuma remained impatient as he made himself climb back into bed. He kept waiting for another signal confirming that a giant or, better yet, several giants would soon arrive on his doorstep.

But he wasn't confident in when, or what shape, that following message might arrive in. Every unusual sound or smell took on an entirely new meaning—highlighted by his urgency to decipher everything at once.

The weary giant reached out with his powerful mind, using every trick in his arsenal of over-amplified senses—seeing, smelling, hearing, tasting, feeling. As a result, he constantly misinterpreted the winds, and its interwoven gossip, as fact.

Yuma's mind longed to be slammed with another Lucid Pulse, like a shrunken belly craves a tremendous amount of food it could never contain.

Still, he knew there might be other, more subtle cues to pay attention to if his reinforcements were traveling in stealth mode, with the brave Harley leading the way. And because of those immediate mental distractions, Yuma misinterpreted his battle hound's horrible howls, echoing in pain when he first heard them.

"Oh, no. What have I done?"

The soulful voice of Harley's agonizing howls launched Yuma from his bed on the run. He snatched his lance, Thunapa, as another series of distant warbling groans made the giant's soul cringe, and he dashed outside with the three glowing Z's in hot pursuit.

Those faraway cries reminded Yuma of the night of the hundred fireballs.

"Not again."

Flashbacks of his burning army hurtling out over the savage lake by catapult haunted him with the sonic rebounds of their tortured screams.

Yuma knew he had failed once more.

Now I have killed my noble Harley on a fool's errand. Why did I not go myself?"

But then, Yuma realized the following howls weren't the defeated yowls of anyone's victim or even cries of pain. On the contrary, there were no dire tones in the canine's sour ballad as it roused Dark Hollows from slumber.

"That dog cannot sing." Yuma grinned in admiration at his comrade's bravery.

Harley had been merely warming his vocal cords, searching for just the right key to launch his long-distance message back home to Yuma.

His magnificently off-key operetta, with all its embedded information, was the magical song that Yuma had been waiting for as he carefully deciphered the dogspeak.

"Yes, Harley! Yes! Ten of them?"

Yuma's smile flashed so wide that centuries of wrinkles disappeared from his face as he realized just how wrong his elevated human senses could still fool him.

"My proud battle hound has found my giants. Bellow, boy! Bellow! Proclaim to those trespassers whose land this is!"

The pack of sleeping dogs inside the lodge startled at Harley's bravery, with each animal howling their support— sending respect back to their fearless leader.

Harley was voluntarily in the heart of a ruthless land that any sensible dog would fear to tread.

Yuma's grin widened as lights bloomed across the irritated southern shoreline, and Harley continued his yodeling.

"This means my re-enforcements are here. They are inside Dark Hollows now. I wonder what happens next?"

Yuma's usual stoicism flushed with hope, and he danced for a moment in the ways of his people, for he had absorbed all tribes' wisdom and teachings through the years.

It had taken Yuma centuries to gather his specialized army, giant by giant, man and woman, as equals. Some were mere brutes when he discovered them–monsters on the hoof– others were brilliant architects, world builders, athletes, and soldiers—everyone from different continents and cultures. And then Yuma educated and trained these immortal titans in the brutal secrets of protecting Mother Earth's deepest secrets by honing their individual combat skills into a single, sacred fist that could hammer any enemy into submission.

But the night his glorious army disappeared beneath the smoky waters, Yuma discovered the unplumbed depths of individual loneliness that he never knew existed.

"Until tonight, I believed I was the last of the giants." He confided to Zip, Zash, and Zee. "And yet… it seems I am not."

The sacred texts promised that a glorious day would come in the distant future when the great Time Warrior would be released from all command responsibilities.

"Has my relief finally come?"

Yuma knew that when the prophesied day arrived, he would be relieved from any sense of duty and unburdened of the earthly shackles of responsibility for the rest of his immortal life. Mother Nature would grant him total freedom and send him onto whatever path to enlightenment he chose. And once unburdened from his sacred duties, Yuma the Tree could resume his spiritual quest for the ultimate illumination, still to come to an immortal being craving more insight while wandering the open plains on other worlds. He grew misty-eyed at the possibilities.

"There are still so many unanswered questions. So many more adventures to have as my retirement draws near."

Who are my replacements? He wondered. *And where do they come from? And why did it take them so long to find me and come to my aid?*

His mind raced ahead of events as the pack of baying hounds continued to harmonize with Harley.

"I hope they come trained and armed. There is far too much to teach an untested Time Warrior. And we have so little time left before the coronation of Wixx." He worried out loud to the hovering hummingbirds.

The rare joyful moment fled the scene as his next wave of thoughts attacked

"And the only way to baptize a true warrior is trial by combat."

He grew up knowing that as a fact.

"We've run out of time."

Yuma headed indoors, searching for his library, lost somewhere inside another curved wing of his sprawling lodge.

The timeless, giant-made world existed almost entirely underground on the north side of the lake. His enemies could never pinpoint the exact location from the water, not even with binoculars.

The enormous, ground-hugging home existed in harmony with the towering grove like an earthbound iceberg, where seven/eighths of the structure existed far underground without disturbing a single living root system above.

Yuma had designed his magnificent lodge for peaceful coexistence within its natural setting without the possibility of intrusion. The sprawling organic structure conformed to the glens' fern-covered hills as if Mother Nature had designed it herself.

And whenever an immortal giant stomachs one place long enough, that same antsy titan spreads out in search of some custom-made, epic-sized creature comforts no one had ever had the time to think of before. And Yuma had done that here in spades.

This luxurious and nature-friendly lodge could swallow

several city blocks within its monumental boundaries, including the subway system below. The grand lodge once housed an army of over a hundred First Nations giants. But make no mistake; they had never treated this elegant space as a barracks or a clubhouse.

Yuma had built this entire structure for his wife as her home. And then came the additions.

Blue Feather's immaculate taste still haunted every inch of the elegant interior, with her lively spirit living around every turn. With its long sweeping hallways of curved redwood, the refined space shot off in every direction in long graceful arcs. Each handcrafted corridor displayed fine art and artistry from around the world.

Yuma had used amber in constructing the windows and skylights instead of glass. That intentional choice bathed every room and corridor underground in a distinct golden glow.

The motion-sensitive lights snapped on when he located his formal library down another winding hallway. That single electric miracle always made the giant giggle as he ran past, appreciating the modern tech-wizardry for what it was—cold magic.

Wandering between the endless book stacks that towered high over his enormous head, he squeezed past generation after generation of modern computers that monitored the upside world on a minute-to-minute basis.

Underneath a tremendous amber dome, Yuma's spiraling monument of a library contained the most essential and profound works of science, mathematics, literature, art, and philosophy ever written. His vast collection was so exhaustive that even the fabled Library of Alexandria never had the immaculate fortune to possess such a stockpile of recaptured knowledge from all cultures, especially those no one knew existed.

Yuma had rescued and plundered these precious lost works to preserve them in this Infinite Library, an ideal space for recapturing knowledge he had planned in his youth.

Finally finding what he was searching for, the excited giant pulled down a delicate emerald tablet along with two other dusty crystal slabs from opposing shelves. He laid them beside each other on his reading table and examined each.

When angled in just the proper orientation, they clicked together like a complicated interlocking puzzle, forming an uninterrupted passage of elegant script written in an unknown language centuries apart.

These sacred texts, composed over multiple generations, were more ancient by the tens of thousands of years than any other written human records discovered to date.

Using his gizmo-goggles and some extra lighting tricks, Yuma teased the almost invisible antediluvian scripture back to life, using his remarkable skills at homemade scientific hi-tech magic.

"The Illuminators." He read.

Yuma held warm feelings and admiration for the ancient authors of these sacred texts.

He began whispering their strange, esoteric language aloud with a familiar reverence. The warrior shaman was using a lilting sound that wasn't quite human but soulful in intent as it danced and clicked off his tongue like prehistoric music.

That's when he located the most important passages he had been searching for in the hand-carved crystal.

Yuma read the elevated words aloud and with great reverence.

"The Wait."
"The Earn."
"The See."
"The Be."

-CHAPTER 19-

Pepper's Five-Star B&B

"Pipe down!" Pepper Wixx shrieked at the top of her lungs, and the children ran out of the B&B to catch the baying hound's intimidating performance.

Only then, with a proper audience to applaud, did Harley consent to conclude his boisterous serenade and heed the angry catcalls.

"Who let a damn dog get back into town?"

"Hey! Scat! Get out of here, Pooper Scooper!"

"Begone, mutt!"

His irritated critics made the stubborn Harley double down, and he bayed a few more defiant notes before concluding his encoded message with a massive belch before licking his wet chops in triumph.

He could always taste a successful performance.

The admirable beast felt satisfied and gave Zack a lavish tongue bath to finish his bows, as his distant backup choir across the lake soon calmed.

"Dogs? Again?"

"Who let another stinking mongrel wander back here?"

A strange assortment of townspeople began wandering the streets in their nightclothes—everyone outraged and searching for the canine culprit.

"We don't allow no stinking mongrels!" a woman's shrill voice cried out.

"That's illegal... illegal for a damn good reason, right?"

Someone picked up an axe, and other crude weapons

appeared.

"I said, who brought a dog down here? Was it you again, Morgan?" One man accused another, starting a scuffle in the shadows.

"I invited him!" Pepper growled, and everyone froze in place.

It was hard to tell if it was out of genuine fear or respect for the older woman—but no one spoke after that. Instead, the once surly townsfolk sulked back to their shanties without uttering another word.

Flashlights and lanterns snuffed out, and soon the town fell back into a disturbing silence that matched the uncomfortable ambiance of the graveyards surrounding them.

"Alright! Everybody else, and I mean every single one of you brats, inside! And get that pre-rabid mutt off my streets! Now!"

Pepper wasn't asking, and all the intimidated orphans, including Zack, rushed back indoors with his belligerent protector bringing up the rear.

Once inside Pepper's B&B, the teenagers couldn't believe the bizarre surprises waiting for them around every corner. The imposing log entryway opened into a soaring U-shaped lobby that rose to the exposed rafters seven stories overhead.

The walls were covered in vertical herb racks, hanging mushroom gardens, bottle art filled with unimaginable concoctions, weird stuffed animals of every description, and a strange assortment of ancient tribal weapons, including primitive European war art.

Pepper surveyed the teenagers' gawking reactions to her collection, never apologizing for her lack of taste by acknowledging their snickers.

"I'm a confessed hoarder. Or eclectic! You choose. But either way, I'm as guilty as they come!" Pepper cackled. "Now, let's get you all up to your rooms, and I'll whip up that world-famous hot chocolate with a big dollop of whipped creme on top! How's that sound?"

"Great!" they answered as one.

Pepper assigned each child to their room, using her cane to point out the levels.

"Does this troublemaker have to sleep with you, angel eyes?" Pepper quizzed Zack, hoping for a different answer than she knew she would receive.

Harley growled, and the woman took a bold step forward, lifting her cane in her fist.

"How dare you? You're in my home now. I remember some old stories about an ugly cur your size. So, watch your step in my home, pup!"

Zack and Harley gulped, yet Pepper chuckled at their reactions, never suspecting the bold hound's ulterior motives or this boy's fate.

"C'mon along, child, with a dog as big as a mule, you'll need a stall to yourselves. Up there. Top floor. And you muck it out if he soils it."

Minutes later, the excited kids came rushing into Kate and Pav's room, exhausted but still energized by their ongoing adrenaline-fueled adventures.

"Have you looked around yet? There's so much weird stuff in here."

"When's the last time anyone had real homemade hot chocolate?"

"Like never."

"This place is so cool," Lennon squealed. "It's so much prettier than Briscoe. Like a fairy tale come to life."

"Completely twisted and rotten is more like it," Tim offered. "But then, I attract twisted."

"And rotten."

"Yeah." He smirked.

"No joke there. But don't get used to this place. We still have to go back. So don't forget that, right?" Kate warned.

"Well, thank you, Miss Buzzkill," Pavarty snapped. Her rebellious friend's sudden lack of adventure shocked her.

"No. It's really simple, Pav. And, unfortunately, we don't

have a choice, do we?"

"Wrong again!" Tim said.

"Wait, wait. Slow down, Kate. I'm with Tim, which is ludicrous, I know, but he's right. Why rush back to Briscoe, girl? Same old, same old, every day." Pavarty gestured to the ruffled trappings in the upscale room. "I mean, look at this place. If we stay with Pepper, we might get adopted by real-life movie stars or doctors and stop being lab rats."

"Yay! See!" Tim grunted like a proud pack leader to the others. He tried to high-five—but Coop deflected it.

"I think they're both right, Kate," Coop said. "We'll be back in custody in plenty of time for more of the same."

Coop's new reality of round-the-clock incarceration had reduced him.

"I can feel it inside, too. That need to be free for at least a little while longer," he admitted.

"Listen. If we don't get Petty some real help tonight, he could die in some backcountry hospital while we're all sitting around here drinking hot chocolate!" Kate's eyes teared. "And I don't want that on my conscience. Never again. Do you want it on yours? Or yours?" she pointed between them.

"It's not up to us now, Kate," Coop sighed. "Let the adults be in charge again. That's what they're here for! Right? They've already brought Petty to the doctor. Aren't you tired of worrying? Aren't you sick of trying to protect everyone all the time? Just try relaxing," Coop's voice softened. "Let's enjoy ourselves while we still can play outside the walls."

"But..."

"No buts," Coop stated with a weary, condescending attitude, and she was going to fight back when Zack stepped between and curled Kate's hand into his.

"I don't want to go back to Briscoe yet, Kate," Zack said, ending any argument.

The other teens nodded, and Kate relented.

"It is what it is. Right?" Tim said.

"Well, if we're staying here overnight, then everybody

get out of my face," Kate demanded as she sniffed and wiped away tears. "I'm going to pass out. I'm exhausted."

"Night, Kate."

"Good night!"

"Good night, Zack," Kate blew a small kiss. "I'll be right here if you need me."

"Good night. Kate."

The kids wandered back to their respective rooms to wait for that special cup of hot chocolate to arrive with the ding of the elevator bell, but most fell asleep as soon as their heads touched the down pillows.

Ozzy stayed awake as his stomach rumbled in anticipation of the sweet treat. And as he waited in the fancy room by himself, he noticed something moving underneath the shiny comforter at the foot of his bed.

It petrified him.

He froze.

It froze.

He moved.

It moved.

Oz gathered his courage and whipped back the blankets, only to reveal his nervous foot was the jiggling monster. He fell back onto the mattress with a thud of relief.

"You are such a nerd."

He had just relaxed when Pepper limped into his room, startling him upright.

"Geez, lady!"

"Oh, dear! Calm down, son. You will give yourself a full-on heart attack, being this jumpy."

The old woman handed him the oversized cup with a mountain of whipped cream floating on top.

"Here. Relax, Hoss."

"Oz.".

"Drink up, Oz, and then get yourself a good night's sleep. Just don't let the dragons steal your slumber in the Dreampool tonight." She winked as she turned to limp back out to the elevator.

"What? The what-pool?"

Pepper stopped and turned.

"Why the Dreampool, darling? Have you never heard it called that before? Where do you come from? The moon? Why it's where all living things go when they dream together at night? You'll recognize it when you see it now. Sleep tight. I have some exciting plans lined up for everyone tomorrow. Lucky for you, you're in the right place at just the right time, my sweet ogre."

"Ogre? I've never been called that before. Shrek once or twice, but...."

"Drink up. Sweet thing. I meant it in the very best way."

Oz shrugged off the insult and savored the perfect cup of hot chocolate like it was his last. Kate and the others slept beside theirs as the elevator creaked back down to the main floor on its final run.

Tim fell asleep with Petty's gun tucked underneath the pillow and his fingers cradling the handle.

Zack stayed awake the longest, unable to sleep because he kept hearing what he took to be drunken singing. Finally, after straining to listen for a while, he realized it might be someone sobbing in the basement that was ghosting up through the upper floor's ventilation grill.

When Zack ultimately nodded off, Harley laid his head down on his paws but stayed alert by the boy's bedside all night, hyper-vigilant to any sound and ready to take on whatever tried to separate them.

But there was no way of protecting this precious boy from his bad dreams once he drifted off as Zack plunged into the depths of the Dreampool.

After a few peaceful moments in the soothing abyss of deep REM sleep, the dead babies began swimming out of his nightmares. They tried to pull him back down, as Zack sank even deeper and started drowning in his sleep again.

-CHAPTER 20-

A Fractured Fairy Tale

The depths of the Dreampool are unlimited and inexhaustible within the ever-shifting universe of space-time.

Boundless in every direction—no living species has ever touched its outer dimensions or discovered its inner core.

The Dreampool is the first sacred location that consciousness plunges into when the universe creates life—and the very last place that same interior soul visits before it flies back out at death.

It is a familiar yet unorthodox space of great mystical insights and unparalleled beauty.

The only portal into the Dreampool lies protected within the folds of every bio-electric mind—coveted there as if the brain was cradling pure biological gold.

All original ideas and breakthroughs in mental constructs are conceived communally within the shared space of the electro-organic Dreampool. That's why all our brilliant human innovations and technical accomplishments discovered throughout the ages have always come in multiple, intuitive bursts of harmonizing waves—Rembrandt-Caravaggio. Edison-Tesla. Einstein-Planck. Lennon-McCartney, etc.

For reasons still unknown to all but the Elders, every species on Earth desperately needs to escape the gravity of daily life and withdraw for a short time to cope with its startling complexities. And every creature accomplishes this by abandoning their physical reality for at least a few precious hours every night to recharge their spiritual batteries in the Dreampool's soothing but energizing waters.

Once submerged inside this passive womb, the individual's mind uses the interior vastness to tap directly into the subconscious. Under no constraints, our open minds frolic like dolphins at sea.

But these are also the same stormy psychic waters that spawn nightmares the size of hurricanes—or tornadoes of drowning babies.

Zack dove deeper into the Dreampool to outrun the wide-eyed infants. Finally, he swam past the sleeping souls of his newfound friends. That's when he caught sight of an unknown hand, stretching up from the swirling gloom of someone else's nightmare roiling up from below.

The shriveled hand shot out of the inky blackness, twirling a coffin-shaped crystal several inches above the palm, hypnotizing him with its swirling, mystical precision.

The nightmarish arm kept stretching and popping each joint unnaturally, growing thinner and more terrifying as it jerked closer.

In the next flash, Zack became merely a spectator inside someone else's bizarre dreams. He watched as a happy little three-year-old sat playing alone on his front porch in the country, bouncing a striped ball.

A sudden shadow engulfed the startled toddler, and Zack watched in horror as those same shriveled hands—the ones that spun the floating coffin crystal—clamped down over the toddler's mouth, muffling his terrified screams.

The child's mother continued hanging the laundry on the clothesline, humming to herself only a few yards away. She didn't notice the abandoned ball when it rolled in and lightly tapped her shoe. By the time she looked down, it was already too late. The only evidence of her son's disappearance was the roar of a powerful car engine and the dusty rooster tail it left behind in exchange for her precious little boy.

As Zack escaped that ensnarling nightmare, other bad

dreams unfurled their long tentacles and dragged him back down to bear tragic witness inside them, too.

These dark, violent visions were instinctively drawn to his bright heart. Even in the deepest recesses of the Dreampool—Zack's luminescent presence promised a shiny lure of hope in an underwater void filled with dark despair.

He witnessed shadow creatures snatching newborns right out of their cribs while safely tucked into bed at home. And he watched helplessly as a pair of identical twins were lured into an idling Rolls Royce using the same hypnotizing lure of the twirling crystals.

"Want to take a ride and spin my magic crystals?" Zack heard a distorted underwater voice beckon the children inside.

Within the blink of an eye, there were so many dreaming children clinging to Zack's legs that he plunged even deeper into the Dreampool. He didn't believe he would ever reach the surface again, and the instinctual fight for his own survival became his new nightmare.

Bang! Putt! Putt! Bang!

Tiny explosions tapping his eardrums startled Zack out of his worst nightmare. He was still trying to clear his head when he heard another minor explosion. He hopped out of bed and threw back the curtains in the room.

The tangled vines strangling the outside of the building with its grape-scented flowers had wrapped around and blinded these upper-level windows long ago.

He could see the morning sunshine peeking through the interlocking vines, but it was like staring through a tattered mask. Still, he could make out Pepper's noisy bakery truck, with her smiling logo on the side, backfiring and sputtering away on the same rutted shoreline road they had hiked into town on only a few hours before.

Zack and Harley sprinted down to Kate's room and woke her first, and she ran to see, but a solid wall of greenery blocked her view from both windows.

The news spread quickly between the floors as Kate

ran downstairs for more information, just as Pepper limped towards her with a tray full of freshly squeezed orange juice. When they met halfway, the old woman groaned and set the heavy tray on a side table.

"Early riser! Good news. Wonderful news. Your driver has made it through the night and is now off to the hospital. And we have informed our delivery driver to rush him straight to the ER."

"Wait, Petty's only going to the hospital now? On a bakery truck?" Kate's hand shot to her forehead. "What about calling an ambulance last night, like you promised?"

"Wow! That ex-cop is getting delivered with the fresh donuts. Something poetic about that," Ozzy cracked, but no one laughed.

"Listen to me, dear. It proved far more efficient to evacuate him this morning than waiting for help to arrive all the way down here, sweetie. They don't make ambulances to make it down these rugged mountain roads like my dependable delivery trucks can. "

She pointed to an advertising calendar on the wall displaying several sturdy examples of her fleet with their off-road wheels.

"What about a medivac? A helicopter?"

"The fog never lifted enough—besides, no need for that horrible expense and danger. Don't worry. Your driver was sitting up and gabbing his head off this morning, so I expect he will be just fine. He said for you children to behave yourselves and make him proud, and he said he would be back himself to pick you up or send someone you trusted to do it. Seemed like a nice man."

"Petty?"

"Is she talking about the same guy?"

"Yay!"

"Why, yay, idiot?" Tim shot back. "I don't want to go back anywhere right now."

"Well, I have placed another call to Dr. Briscoe on our

spotty landline, and if we can work things out legally, I might have some... inspiring surprises for you all shortly." Pepper winked.

It felt like Pepper already had the deed done, and the orphans couldn't help but grow optimistic as the prospect of great news seemed possible for a change.

"Now, who wants to eat a real down-home country breakfast to put the flush back on those cheeks?" she asked, clapping her hands together.

The more Zack watched her unique gestures, the more the boy thought he recognized those gnarled, wrinkled hands from his nightmare of only minutes before.

"Let's start your morning off with some fresh-squeezed OJ!" Pepper grabbed the tray and offered a glass to everyone, like the proper B&B hostess she was.

"Yes, ma'am!" Ozzy replied, downed his in one gulp, and then forced his way past the rest, trying to be the first in a line that hadn't yet formed.

When Pepper Wixx threw open the doors to the formal dining room, the children gasped at the grand banquet displayed before them.

The long community dining table held every kind of breakfast food imaginable, like fresh blueberry pancakes and golden waffles the size of dinner plates. Fresh honey, jams, and syrups sat waiting to be slathered over fresh-baked scones and biscuits—still steaming hot from the oven. Homemade sausages and candied bacon were stacked toward the ceiling, with different preparations of eggs and cheeses following close behind. A halo of bowls of hot & cold cereals and fruit cocktails surrounded all of it, along with fresh homemade donuts.

"Look at this treasure trove!" Oz said. "Granny Pepper's Picture-Perfect Bed and Breakfast! I give it five stars! No! Ten stars!" Ozzy dove head-first without being invited.

"Eat up, children. You are only young once. Trust me."

Every kid was too busy filling their plates to notice that Wixx's eyes narrowed to slits behind her colorful specs—

mentally grading them like a Livestock Trader.

"And once is all you ever get," she whispered.

An hour later, Pepper had to shoo them away like a gaggle of fat geese.

A few offered half-hearted squawks about doing the dishes—but most flopped down exhausted into the lobby's overstuffed chairs and began a belching and tooting contest.

"Wow. I have never tasted anything that fantastic in my entire life! And believe me. I've tried!"

Ozzy's exclamation was loud enough for the proud Pepper to hear, and she grinned. Oz was food drunk, and he released an enormous belch that warbled like a sick walrus for several seconds.

"Beyond my wildest dreams."

"Well, thank you, children. My pleasure. It's what I do best. You can see my blue ribbons upstairs. Now go on, get outside, have yourselves some fun, and get that nasty gas out of your systems. You all need some summer blush on your pale skins to make your new pictures more... palatable."

"Pictures? What pictures?

"Why inside my newest adoption catalog, darling? We are going to find you all proper superstar homes. Top Shelf."

"No way?"

"Way!"

"Really?"

"Yes. I promise. But mind me, watch out."

Her tone turned serious, and the kids picked up on it. Again, the Knack worked wonders on them as she gently refocused on each child individually.

"The townsfolk living here are still very upset about that dog's impression of an alarm clock this morning."

"We're sorry. He's not even ours. We've never seen him before," Kate tried to explain their innocence by throwing Harley under the bus.

"And it is especially irritating when dogs aren't allowed in our town by law. And Shelby knew that. No one found that ruckus cute or funny. They thought it was another horrible rabies attack that traumatized this town."

Wixx glared at the large mutt, and Harley grumbled, then barked back.

"Dogs. What a useless burden. All they do is eat, soil, and sleep—repeat. But listen, do me a favor, and don't any of you bother going into town and riling everybody up again. There is a perfect spot down by the lake for you to play and swim all day. It's a sandy beach, not half a mile up that road. You, noisy troublemakers, can make it all your own. Nobody has gone up there since I attained the property. So go swimming to your heart's content. Your holiday starts right now!"

"What?"

"Yes! Ditch day!"

Pepper Wixx had magically sanctioned their surprise summer vacation.

"I've got mountains of work to keep up my reputation at ten stars," she winked at Oz. "And I must prepare for my Coronation Party at the Fair. I'm getting crowned Queen of the County, don't you know?"

"Congratulations."

"Hey, look, everybody. A real Queen has served us!"

Pepper curtsied and seemed as giddy as a schoolgirl at the thought.

I've waited such a long time for this special night.

"You children get back here when the sun's straight up in the sky, and I'll have a small lunch ready for you," she promised with another wink.

"This is all too good to be true."

"No meetings with doctors, no medical exams, and no summer school?

The teenagers flew away like the uncaged birds they were.

Some hadn't tasted unbound physical freedom in years, and they didn't know how to begin and what to do first.

The girls fluttered away behind Kate like butterflies, and not long after, they located the sandy beach Wixx had been bragging about. Although it appeared overcast with a thin layer of smog, it was otherwise a beautiful spot with a magnificent view of the imposing cliffs leading around to the lush northern shore.

The boys hung out with Coop as they trekked north along the tumble of rocks that defined the lake's craggy shoreline. Tim tried to stay in front, balancing on top of every boulder as if he was leading this pack. And although Coop wanted to stay close to Kate, he remained with the other guys while shadowing her location.

Zack hung back with the guys, skipping stones across the lake's calm surface while unintentionally sending Harley bounding out to retrieve them.

Unseen by all, a menacing surface ripple formed here and there. Still, those subtle hints of danger lurking just offshore went unnoticed by the boys as most of the nocturnal eels slept the day away, far below.

Playing fetch with rocks became boring fast, so the boys drifted off, seeking other adventures without including Zack and his new companion. No one missed them when Harley and Zack peeled away in the opposite direction and began heading up the coast to explore the cliffs.

On his own again, Zack noticed a series of bright flashes tickling the skyline on the other side of the lake. Amplified sunlight somehow glinted off the tallest redwoods as if Mother Nature had dipped her crown in gold.

What is that? Zack wondered.

He drifted towards the sparkling beacons with Harley bounding in front, more than happy to lead the way back to his home turf.

Meanwhile, the girls abandoned the beach once the boys showed up, and they discovered a small rustic flour mill sitting on the edge of the woods just outside of town.

Its quaint wooden waterwheel was spinning, driven by the small stream rushing by, and the ancient stone structure appeared stolen from a different epoch.

"This is right out of a fairy tale," Lennon gushed, and she spun and danced around the glen in delight.

"Hardly that," Jesse said. Nothing here impressed her as she lit up a smuggled cigarette butt. "These people live down here like they're stuck back in the Middle Ages. Like the eighties or something."

"Come on, girl. You saw that Martha Stewart-sized breakfast spread. No one is hurting down here, child, and certainly not Ms. Pepper Wixx! She's a rich old witch, I can tell you that, and as hip as you can get. Why she owns an orphanage, a successful B&B, her own bakery, and she stars in ads on national TV. So, forgive me if you see that as a backward girl. I see nothing but that old woman's mega success as a big mega positive for us."

Pavarty could dominate any conversation without being invited in.

"Still, it feels like we've all shot through a wormhole in time or something, doesn't it? Something doesn't feel right. This place makes my skin crawl." Jess remained skeptical about most everything, but never more so than here.

Jess glanced down and noticed the subtle hints of Kate's self-destructive past peeking out from beneath her bracelets, and Kate caught her looking.

"You still...?" Jess cocked a curious eyebrow at the pale scars.

"Nope. Not since I grew up a little and realized—funny thing, I wasn't hurting others by hurting myself. Just poor me. That was enough of that. Bing! Illumination! If you're lucky, a light goes on."

The older girl's honesty moved Jess, and she took a long drag, exposing her recent attempts on her forearm.

"Thank you," she exhaled and coughed, brushing away a tiny tear. "I have to quit these damn cancer sticks, too."

"How are you dealing with your depression without your meds? Are you okay?" Kate asked.

"So far. I've got good days and bad, just like everybody else. But I've got a new scale I go by now. Green, orange, red. Green Day- I'm floating on top of the water. Orange Day- I'm just treading water. Red Day- I'm full-on drowning."

She paused, reading her interior monitors, and smiled.

"But... I'm feeling all forest green today. So, who knows? If I go full-blown red scale, I'll pull out my trusty claws and fight for my life."

Jess reached behind her, pulled out a cat-head-shaped hair clip she always wore in self-defense, and chuckled.

Innocent appearing at first, she slipped the large clip over her fingers. Jess showed them that the cute cat ears were now re-enforcing her knuckles with two sharp metal points like a pair of brass knuckles—ÔoÔ.

"Nobody's victim." Jess arched her eyebrow. "Ever."

"Especially on a red day," Kate winked with a knowing laugh.

"Oh, oh! You are officially a badass, girl!" Pavarty was never easy to impress. "I like this girl!"

Kate agreed.

Back at the polluted beach, the boys discovered a gigantic eel carcass washed up on the shore among the scattered litter. It measured over seven feet long, and they each took turns prodding the dead body with sticks as it flopped back and forth in the shallow tide—blood still oozing from its horrific wounds as the clouds of black flies fed.

"How fast did this thing have to be traveling to beach himself way up here, like this? Look! He left skid marks in the sand."

"Now I got skid marks, too," Oz needlessly confessed.

"By the size of those bite marks, something humongous must have been chasing him, man. This bad boy was swimming for his life."

"These bites are bigger than him! What else lives in freshwater that's larger than this beast? The Loch Ness Monster? Tahoe Tessie?"

"A Velociraptor?"

"They can't swim!"

"How do you know?"

"Tiny forearms."

"Oh yeah."

The amount of physical damage to the eel's tortured carcass was impressive.

"Looks like more than one thing got him, too," Coop said.

"Yeah. Look at all those random bite marks. Different size teeth."

"Cannibal Bay!" Ozzy pronounced in his best, deep movie trailer voice. "In a backward world where if they can't mate with it—they eat it—will you be the monster's next lover—or their next snack? 'Cannibal Bay Summer'—Coming to a Theater or Beach near you!"

Ozzie sang the theme from Jaws.

"Dunnn dunn... dunn dunn... dunn dunn!"

They all laughed but quickly sloshed out of the bloody water as they sought refuge further up the beach.

"This place is deranged," Coop said, and no one disagreed. "Why haven't we ever heard about this place before? It's not on any maps I know."

"Me either. But that's exactly why I like it here, man! Completely off the grid!" Tim grinned, always the odd man out. "Forgotten like us. It's already trashed and overlooked. So then, what's the harm in doing a little more thrashing?"

He chucked his juice bottle into the lake, where it sank.

"Figures."

"Your actions say a lot about you, bud."

"Bite me! All of you!" he laughed. "Look around. This place is all used up and run out of time. Even the vultures can't wait for it to die. Aha, but look. Over there, across the bay.

The promise of Eden. Not like the rest of the world at all. Just a faraway dream. Embrace the filth, amigo. This is our actual future here. Not over there. Nothing can stay green forever. So why not learn to wallow in the filth now? Become the King of the junk pile."

Emiliano rolled his eyes.

"Los despropósitos!"

"What's that mean? Spit that out in English, amigo," Tim said.

"Nonsense!" Emiliano snapped back. "You know nothing."

Emiliano wanted to be an engineer more than anything else in the world. He could already picture in his mind what everyone's future would look like because he was going to be the one to help invent it.

"Only fools can't see the shape of the good things to come."

"So now I'm a fool?"

"Let's go find the girls. Better company than hanging out with the garbage," Coop said, walking away from Tim without permission.

The younger guys leaped at the chance to leave the insulting skateboarder behind and follow Coop away as a feeling of dread corrupted the sunny beach on a perfectly fine morning.

An hour later, and Zack still wasn't missed.

He and his grand dog were halfway through their hike around the lake's western shoreline. Harley was leading him home—forging a path through the dense underbrush where none existed.

The further boy and his gigantic companion moved away from Dark Hollows, the greener the Sacred Forest grew. Until the emerald world became so intense, there were moments when no other color existed except for the occasional splashes of contrasting bird colors.

Zack and Harley traveled north through overlapping thickets of thorny berries—squeezing themselves between walls of towering oleander as the ground-hugging mists grew thicker all around them.

Their non-existent path narrowed to nothing, slowing their progress until they came to a halt when they spotted two foreboding shadows looming up before them in the distant haze.

The menacing silhouettes were massive in scale and towered at least five stories above the forest floor. They were unnatural in their cone-shaped appearance—obviously human-made—but why?

Zack could hear a low droning. A sub-harmonic hum was being generated from somewhere just ahead of them in the same direction.

Are these machines?

Harley grumbled an answer under his breath. The hound was trying to communicate his deepest regrets with only his sad eyes to work with since Zack didn't understand dogspeak. But Zack had already sensed the sudden heaviness in his friend's heart and yet couldn't fathom the depths of the dog's emotions.

They shared the unknown pain for another moment before Harley lowered his head and plodded toward the intimidating shadows.

Harley stared straight ahead as he crossed between the imposing sentinels straddling the trail without looking off to either side. Instead, he moved towards the promise of the sunlight glowing ahead and never looked back.

Left behind, Zack drew a deep breath before he dared to follow.

The air was thick with clouds of buzzing flies, and that noisy swarm of pestilence embraced the little boy, far outnumbering his overprotective gnats.

Only when he walked into the clearing could Zack see what the black flies were worshipping in such vast numbers.

Someone had stacked two towering pyramids of dog collars on either side of the trail as a deadly warning. Here lies the boundary between good and evil—man and beast—sense and madness.

Each gruesome pylon of death grew taller daily, using only dog collars to build upon these murderous abominations to hate. Hatred splattered every color in the rainbow with blood and maggots.

"What...?" Zack gagged at the stench of the rancid piles of leather and nylon.

These sinister, rotting pyramids existed for intimidation. Both fifty-foot monstrosities were started decades ago to warn away all canines never to trespass into these deadly woods or face the inhuman consequences.

How many lost pups did it take to build these piles so high?

For how many years had these massacres gone on?

Are there even bigger piles someplace else?

Zack had so many unanswered questions—and yet he knew from that moment on that he would never forget the hideous symbols of animal torture and death he witnessed on that horrible day.

He followed silently behind Harley for a long while until they both discovered it was impossible to chase the rugged shoreline northward any further. Instead, they had to turn inland into the deeper folds of the impenetrable forest.

Although scratched and bleeding, Zack's growing curiosity and Harley's constant nudging drove them forward.

He saw a great waterfall tumbling off the spectacular pinnacles of a batwing-shaped mountain to the north and couldn't tell from his perspective where that enormous plume of water landed. But he could hear its roar growing louder as it cascaded down somewhere not that far up ahead and disappeared into the fortress of green.

Zack felt like a trespasser on holy ground as Harley led him deeper into the very heart of the sacred Redwood Forest.

Here, the greatest and oldest of the secret giants

revealed themselves in all their enduring grandeur to the star-struck lad. Each majestic sequoia was taller than the next as he gazed up in amazement and wonder.

Any of these immortal sentinels was impressive enough to make a simple giant feel insignificant in their magnificent presence, which was the point, after all, let alone a tiny child.

"Whoa."

Boy and dog kept trekking through the lush groves of redwood. They circled clockwise through the forest when Zack spotted the mouth of a large overgrown cavern, swallowing up their path—sending the rough trail underground.

With forested cliffs soaring up on all sides in a box canyon, the only way to continue their journey north was to enter the cave.

That left them with two choices. Keep moving ahead, maintaining their present course, heading north into the cavern, or begin the long retreat south, retracing their steps back to Dark Hollows.

Zack checked the sun's position overhead; it wasn't close to noon yet.

"No reason to go back early. Right, boy? Further?"

Harley barked back in agreement, trotted up to the mouth of the smoky cavern, and waited. Zack took another deep breath and hiked down into the cave with Harley leading the way.

Once underground in the darkness, they found themselves inside a high vaulted grotto. Then, the cave floor fell away into a sloping, slimy blackness.

"Yuck! Does every place down here stink?"

The festering cavern entrance smelled of smoke, rot, and decay, birthing plagues and diseases not even contemplated by humans yet.

But a soft, lilting sound drifting on the foul air baffled them and drew their curiosity deeper. It sounded like whispering and yet melodic. Zack felt anything might lurk around the next corner, but he kept moving forward.

The boy stifled his gag reflex and stepped into the squishy darkness. That's when something swooped out of the blackness, peeling away a two-inch curl of skin from the back of his neck.

"Ow!" Zack yelped and ducked. When he brought his hand back, it was covered in red.

Harley roared to his defense as thousands of vampire bats swooped down from the ceilings in a single massive attack.

They trapped the boy and dog inside a shrieking cyclone of leathery wings and claws.

Harley defended Zack without pausing. He was munching his way through the swirling ring of bat flesh and enforcing a clear corridor for them both to escape back toward the light.

Once outside, the angry bats chasing them swirled around when hit by direct sunlight, and they spun back into the cooling solace of the Cave of Whispers.

Only seconds ago, the fanged vampires were attacking their victims without mercy—and in the next instant, they were all hanging upside down inside their stinky cavern, like clumps of rotten fruit.

"Wow. Didn't you expect that? So, what do we do now, boy?"

Zack and Harley caught their breaths as the battle hound realized they needed time to regroup.

Further south, Ozzy and Tim discovered a lightning-fast stream off the lakeside road. It hid a natural water slide that rushed between evenly spaced boulders, ending in a deep, natural pool.

"Why not, man? No crazy mutant eels surf in shallow waters! Right?"

"Right!" they convinced each other.

They peeled off their clothes, down to their skivvies, and jumped into the rushing water. Splashing and playing around, they began busting each other's chops and having a great time as they floated effortlessly between the rocks.

Everything was calm and peaceful, and they were just giving each other grief when the girls came shrieking out of the bushes, screaming like it was the world's end.

"Whaaaat?"

"Nooooo!"

Panicked, Ozzy and Tim bolted for the shore and snatched up their clothes, afraid to be found dead and half-naked together.

It wasn't until they were half-dressed that they realized it was just a joke as the girls surrounded them, giggling, pointing, and taunting again.

That's when everyone noticed the growing wet stain on Ozzie's crotch.

"Get a grip on yourself, Ozzy!"

"I'm not doing anything!" Oz shrieked in horror when he realized the embarrassing dark blue stain his wet underwear was making underneath his dry jeans.

But Ozzy was more than happy to take any verbal abuse. It thrilled him to be safe and alive, and he howled back, "But I am extremely... *relieved!*"

The sick jokes didn't stop for fifteen minutes. Everyone pantomimed through tears, mimicking the startled faces, teasing, and counter-teasing until they couldn't laugh anymore.

They needed to breathe, and Ozzy required an actual pant washing, after all.

The group was exhausted from the release of so much pent-up silliness. Their faces hurt from grinning, and fugitive snickers still escaped from resting faces. That's when Ozzy heard the distant dinner bell, summoning them back to the southern shore.

"Listen to that? Just like on an old TV rerun on Netflix!" Ozzy chirped.

"What? Like, 'the Avengers'?"

"No, man. More like 'The Walton's.'"

"Oh yeah! Good night, John-Boy, I love you, John-Boy, good night!"

"How quaint!" Pavarty chirped. She appreciated this open countryside compared to the congested city.

"Wait? Good night. Where's Zack?" Kate was immediately upset.

"Haven't seen him?"

Coop glanced around and then noticed the sun's position overhead.

"Guess it's lunchtime, folks!"

Ozzy stretched his unused quads for the sprint back.

"Has anybody seen Zack?" Kate asked again.

"He heard the same bell. He's probably already back there with that big, nasty dog."

"Alright, people! What about a beach party down here tonight?" Tim said. "If we don't get shipped back to Briscoe first. But I saw some bottles of something wicked this way comes in that old biddies' kitchen that needs serious investigating. And she's got some sick herbs growing out back—if you know what I mean?" Tim grinned like the Joker in a stacked deck.

"Knock it off," Kate said. "You will not destroy everything we've got going for us back at Briscoe so you can get high."

"Why not? They do it legally to me every day."

"You know the Institute will find out, idiot! They're going to do drug tests on all of us as soon as we get back! Do you want to be sent back down to Rehash and re-scrubbed all over again?"

"Like your best friend, Emily? Shouldn't you already be in Rehash yourself? Some kind of friend you are," Tim teased.

Kate was furious at the truth—remembering Emily's fine sacrifice—and now selfishly frightened that this entire off-road adventure would screw up her comfortable lifestyle back at Briscoe and lose the prom as well. The Briscoe Institute was the only stable home she had ever known. She couldn't lose that now, too.

Tim inched closer to rub it in.

"It's as simple as the nose on your smug face. You've already given up, Katie. They've won you over with their miracle placebos. But I haven't. I'm still me, no matter what they do to me. No matter what chemicals, they shoot into me without my permission. And what are they going to do, Kate? Lock me up inside a prison and shoot me full of illegal drugs? Because I might imbibe in something civilian? I already live inside a prison, just like you. But I know it. And you don't. Or you pretend not to!"

"Make some sense out of this! You're on probation! You're ready to be released with a clean record in just months. So, you've got to hold on," Kate said.

"Who cares? I could handle prison now if I had to. It's my life. I'm plenty tough enough. I got street-cred. Not like cowards like you," Tim raged on in a hormone-fueled tear.

"I am going to devour every second I have left of this freedom—no permission needed from you or anyone else here, sis! Hell, I may not go back. Maybe I'll go on the run! Make the law chase after me. I'm almost a legal adult. I can do what I want with my life."

Kate was unimpressed and furious, but she had no arguments left in her.

"Your future, your choice." And she turned away.

"I'll see what happens next. I still haven't decided my future yet," Tim boasted. He felt the revolver's secret power tucked behind his wet shirt, bolstering his ego.

"There are an awful lot of hollows out here. Nobody would ever find me if I wanted to stay lost—become an outlaw!"

Coop noticed the gun handle straining against Tim's damp shirt.

"Come on, Tim, let's get something wonderful to eat and laugh some more." Coop put his arm around the older teen's

189

shoulder and led him away from the others.

"You know Timmy-boy, and I think I can speak for everybody here. We all like you so much better when you just shut up and bray like a donkey."

"Who cares what you think?" Tim scoffed and shrugged off his arm. "I've already got my driver's license. What about you, loser?"

-CHAPTER 21-

Pepper's Sorrows

Pepper Wixx had outdone herself again. She'd smothered the long dining table in another incredible feast. Yet, somehow, she made feeding these finicky children appear effortless—reproducing all their personal favorites as if she could read minds.

The orphans' choices were endless. There was roast beef, pastrami, turkey, ham, and four-inch-thick peanut butter & jelly sandwiches. All stacked high on beautiful platters alongside grilled burgers, hot dogs, cheesesteaks, and other more exotic-looking lunch meats.

French fries and homemade potato chips competed against each other in separate colorful baskets with platters of tacos and enchiladas alongside. In addition, there were individual pizzas, cups of fruit and nuts, and cold bottles of soda pop, juice, and milk in every conceivable color.

The overabundance of food simply overwhelmed the table.

"Do you always eat like this? Like... like the Queen of Hearts?" Ozzy dashed for the table as the others filtered in.

"Indeed I do!" Pepper answered with a proud, regal air. "I am to be crowned a real-life Queen, after all."

"You've got to watch it. You're going to give away the kingdom if you keep feeding everybody this well, Granny Pepper," Pavarty advised.

The old woman cackled and ushered Pav to a seat at the head of the table.

191

"Nonsense, child. Eat up, child. It's just what I do. People like to do what they're good at."

"Well, I think you're a genius at this, Granny Pepper! Please adopt me?"

"Me too?"

The hungry pack of teens took it all at face value, except for Coop. Tim and Jess.

"This hotel is enormous. The upkeep must be huge. So why aren't there any other guests here now? It's the middle of summer on a lake." He quizzed between amazing bites.

"Our official tourist season doesn't begin down here until this weekend with a very special... uh... well, let's just call it a Harvest Fair being held in town. With the moon's full eclipse, we should have hundreds of celebrities in town by Saturday night."

"Lunar eclipses are common," Josh interjected.

"So are celebrities," Coop responded.

"Not of this caliber, darling. And so, to celebrate our undying culture down here in the hollows, we hold a big traditional hoe-down, old-world style celebration to remind ourselves of our humble beginnings."

"Yeah, and at whose expense?"

Pepper noted the skepticism and turned up the Knack.

"We have an orchestra and a free pot-luck dinner for everybody in town. And the community will name me the new Queen of the Harvest Festival that night for all my... social work." she giggled like a nervous schoolgirl. "I've been cooking for weeks to prepare to fill all those bellies with free samples of my specialties. Use them as guinea pigs for my new product lines. It all starts down here. It's going to be an unforgettable night." Pepper swooned in anticipation of the upcoming events.

"Congratulations, Queen Wixx!" Lennon curtsied.

"Why, thank you, my petite lady-in-waiting."

"Any word from the authorities back at Briscoe?" Kate asked. "Have you seen Zack?"

"Oh, don't bring that up now!" the children around the table whined.

Pepper's demeanor changed as she read into their fears before answering.

"Great things are percolating for you all. I won't spoil it yet. So let's leave it at that, not to build your hopes up too high. Everything's being handled quite amicably. And I'm sure that boy and dog will be along shortly, hon. Now eat up."

The excited orphans returned into vacation mode while downing frosty mugs of root beer in chugging contests.

Pepper poured herself an ale into an ancient stein. She studied the children as they demolished the magnificent spread.

"That's it. Eat up, children. Any new prospective parents will want quality meat on those sturdy young bones so they can buy you pretty, new things to wear. The rich are so much better informed than us, you know. Better than anybody if you listen to them speak. You can't sell garbage to people with an elevated taste without putting a good sparkle and spit-shine to it first."

"Except on a doughnut," Oz said. "Don't be spit-shining the doughnuts or Bundt cakes."

She walked by Ozzy, admiring him like a farmer sized up a prized pig, and she reached out, squeezing his cheek and biceps.

"Now, this fine hulk knows how to make a farmer's wife swoon!" she purred.

Ozzy grinned uneasily but kept chewing, never realizing that Pepper spoke about his immediate future.

He'll make someone a fine farmhand soon.

"Is that your fairy tale windmill?" Lennon asked.

"She means the old mill down by the stream," Kate added.

Pepper paused and took another sip before answering, dabbing her lips.

"Why, yes? Well, you have run hellbent all over my

193

property, haven't you?"

"This place is so beautiful."

"We want to see everything."

"That mill is off-limits to everyone. No public tours yet. So please, stay off that piece of property," Pepper warned.

"Must be for all the health code violations?" Emiliano teased.

"What's that? Nonsense!" Pepper shot back. "I have immaculate quality control!"

"We saw pigeons flying out of it, lady!"

"And squirrels, too," Josh added. "Uh, but they weren't the flying kind."

Pepper's eyes narrowed

"It's where I mill the limited-edition artisan flour for my bakery whenever I need it. But it's presently under renovation to meet my growing demands to go nationwide. So now, stay off that property. And I'm not kidding around, either. Don't you mess with my business," the deadly entrepreneur warned.

She took another pull from her stein.

Should I lock them up now or fatten them for a few more hours?

Tim surveyed the dining room as he downed a second helping of everything. He recognized the vaulted building as if he had seen it all in a dream before. The over-generous feast, the rustic lodge setting in all its twisted grandeur, held an ageless wonder and reckless familiarity about it.

"Where else have you, rascals, wandered off to where you shouldn't have?" Pepper asked.

"Just the sandy beach you told us about," Kate added. "It was beautiful."

"It's polluted," Coop countered.

"The waterslide was too, wasn't it, nature boys?" Jesse teased.

"It was once Tim and Ozzy got through with it!" Pavarty cracked, and they all laughed.

"I didn't do anything! Ozzy did!" Tim moaned.

Oz blushed but laughed.

"Who lives in the cave?" Came a voice from behind.

Everyone choked on their giggles and whipped around in their seats.

Zack stood in the front doorway, scratched and bleeding, as Harley stood guard beside him with his own checklist of bat and briar wounds.

Pepper limped toward him, drying her hands on her apron.

"What was that child?"

"Who lives inside the whispering caves?" Zack asked.

"There you are!" Kate brightened. She had looked all over for the little boy but decided not to panic for once, knowing his untapped skills outdoors.

Still—here he is—and now he's bleeding.

Kate ran over to embrace him.

"I wondered where you went. But I thought you might like some space. Are you okay, little guy? You're all cut up!"

She hadn't even missed him until now.

"I'm very okay, Kate," Zack answered brightly.

"You made it to the Cave of Whispers? Well, you wandered even further than these trespassing rascals did."

Pepper's eyes grew darker, and Harley stepped forward, blocking any closer advance.

"You must stay away from that abandoned cave, boy. For those whispers lead to nothing but lingering misery and death," Pepper warned. "All of you must promise me you will stay far away from that horrible place. Those caverns are filled with rabid bats. That's why we don't allow dogs here. And these hills are perforated with toxic mercury pits and abandoned mineshafts that lead straight down to the firestorms below underneath every step along the way."

Pepper turned and stared directly into Zack's eyes, trying to hypnotize him as she floated in closer with her words. She was firing the Knack on all cylinders, but it still wasn't working.

"You wouldn't be the first idiot to fall into oblivion over there," she promised with a smile.

But she could feel that her unique talent wasn't working on the young boy, and she spun around to the rest of the group to concentrate on them.

"Now, don't take advantage of my kindness and see it as a weakness. I am here to help all of you. That is what I do. I am a savior, not a monster." Pepper defended herself against an accusation that no one had made. "That's why they are going to make me a Queen."

"And it looks like you do alright for yourself too, Queenie." Tim was still casing the joint when Pepper caught his greedy gaze.

"Make no mistake; we have a jail in town, young man. We will not condone any hooliganism of any sort in our town. Law and order every time."

She knew this lower-class type of Uman road trash and despised them all.

No profit to be made with any of them.

"Where did all the bloody dog collars come from? And who lives on the other side of the lake?" Unfortunately, Zack wasn't through asking his questions, and Pepper wasn't ready to answer him.

"Is that why you're so quiet, little one? You're always thinking up these weird thought bombs to drop on the grownups?"

"No. That's Josh, lady." Emiliano said and pointed to his over-calculating bud.

Pepper responded to all their smirks and wisecracks with a steely glare. "No wonder this feeble bunch hasn't been adopted out yet."

"Ouch!"

"That's nasty," Jess said.

"Who is it? Across the lake." Zack pushed.

"Be careful what you ask for, young man."

Pepper took another pull on her stein as she turned to

the others, avoiding Zack's stare.

"You saw proof of that old hermit's bloody work. He eats dogs. That's all, child. He's a monster from another place and another time. We had ourselves a happy Independence holiday celebration once we legally got rid of that homeless madman back on the Fourth."

"Then how could Zack see him if you got rid of him?" Kate asked.

"I meant driven away. Evicted."

"I didn't see him," Zack said.

"Mamma Mia, here we go with the invisible people again."

"First, I saw a flickering glow up in the trees across the lake. After that, I found the stacks of dead dog collars, and then we heard the whispers inside the cave, and we went in," Zack said.

"Just the two of you made it out of those horrid caverns. Alive? With whose help?" Pepper demanded.

"I had Harley beside me. I didn't need any other help."

"Why, that's quite an accomplishment, young man." That unexpected revelation shocked Pepper. "I've known experienced miners that have never returned once they entered those toxic pits."

"Is it the hermit who whispers inside the cave?" Zack asked again.

"No matter. We stranded that psychopath for a good reason and exiled him forever. He's trapped like a giant rat in a maze of his own making, and there's no longer room for his kind over here. There'll be no running away from his final fate once I get through with him!" Pepper's eyes burned with hatred as the children leaned in.

"What did he do that was so bad?"

"Back in the day, if anyone got within arms-reach of that rabid monster, whether man or beast, it didn't matter—they never lived to tell the tale. That old savage killed thousands of his own people. Women and children alike. Cut out their beating hearts and devoured them. He has started wars that have never ended!"

"That's impossible—one man. Thousands killed? Then he's a serial killer, lady. Why isn't it on the news? Why isn't he in jail forever?" Coop wanted answers he didn't have.

"Yeah! Those are ridiculously serious war crimes you're accusing someone of, lady," Emiliano said.

"Never you mind about him any longer. He's been taken care of. The will of the people neutralizes him with a little nudge from me." Pepper dismissed everything as she tried to change the subject by refocusing the Knack back into her more famous Granny image.

"What do you mean, neutralized?" Zack pushed for more answers.

"Banished. There's no escape for that beast. He's cornered! He has mountains holding him down on all three sides." She pointed out the bay window. "Unsurmountable waterfalls cut off any escape on three sides, and neither permits him any access back into our hollows. That's why you must never attempt to travel there."

"Then how'd you get him over there?" Coop quizzed.

"He went by air," Pepper smiled.

"Huh?"

"Doesn't matter, kid!" she chuckled. "He's too old and injured to crawl beyond his camp now. I hope he dies a slow, painful death, thousands of times over, for all I care," Pepper said and spat between her fingers twice.

The children sat spellbound by the emotional tale.

"Why couldn't he just swim back over here then? Or build a raft?" Ozzy asked.

"Remember the beach? That eel was as big enough to capsize any raft," Coop arched an eyebrow, and they all remembered the size of the carcass savaged on the beach.

"We're going to need a bigger boat!" Oz teased with another 'Jaws' reference, but no one felt like laughing.

Pepper was through having this discussion. She began

slamming the china around on the table, causing a sudden irrational mess among the splendor.

"Why are you so angry? What did he ever do to you?" Zack asked.

"Murdered, my boys! That's what he did! He killed my husband and my three natural-born sons! Murdered them all!" Pepper broke down in tears as she limped away, sobbing.

"Whoa! That goes beyond heavy, man." Ozzy felt horrible for the old woman.

"Never judge a book by its cover, fools," Jess whispered.

No one knew how to react or what to say next.

What had seemed so confusing and scary about Pepper Wixx only moments before now seemed to make sense. Her twisted backstory made this frightening and powerful woman appear to be what she was—a bereaved home-spun mother and widow. A grieving old woman still longing for her missing children and making up for it by becoming an adoption specialist to the world.

"Stork to the Stars."

"No wonder she's always so kind and generous," Lennon said, tears rimming her eyes. "She just wants her babies back."

"Nice going, Wacky Zacky!" Tim attempted to shove the boy aside, but Harley grabbed Tim's hand in his mouth and held it there—waiting for Tim's next stupid move before applying any serious pressure.

Coop was in Tim's face before Kate could get there this time.

"You leave this little boy alone, or you and I will have a genuine problem that you and I presently do not have. Understood, bud?" Coop warned.

Tim backed off, intimidated by the seriousness of the younger boy but still not satisfied.

"Sure, Coop! He's all yours! Screw all of this! Alright, kiddies, now who wants to head back to the beach before our special Independence Day ends and this sick dance party is over because of a bunch of inconsiderate cry-babies?"

Zack held back as the others quickly headed outdoors to recapture any sense of natural fun before the day ended.

"Do you want to come along with us?" Kate invited Zack.

"No. I'm tired, Kate." He begged off. "I'm going to get washed and take a nap."

"I can help."

"It's okay. I'll see you later."

The first part of Zack and Harley's alternative scheme went into action just as soon as everyone left the building, and his scavenger hunt began.

Pepper's sad sobs in the kitchen had turned to distracted humming as Zack snatched an old hickory cane from an umbrella stand and picked up a few discarded socks underneath the lobby chairs. Then he began assembling the other things he needed, stealing an apple, a rusty spool of wire, several candles, rags, and a box of wooden matches. He shoved them all into his pockets and a small backpack as he snuck out the back door with his faithful shadow trotting beside him like a getaway driver.

Zack understood now that they were both on the same mission as they headed out into the unknown, and Harley led the way.

What was the purpose behind this defiant adventure— and to what ends? Young Zack still didn't have a clue. But he knew that he was drawing closer to the heart of this glorious adventure. He could feel it beating in his chest.

-CHAPTER 22-

Enlightened

Swirling clouds of angry vampire bats engulfed Zack and Harley again, crushing them within their claustrophobic biomass.

But instead of turning at the challenge and running outside, Zack and Harley had forged a new battle plan.

They charged straight through the bat storm, with Zack taking point and attacking from the front with his flaming torch.

He was wielding it like a baseball bat, and the wire-wrapped socks and candle wax flared with every flick of the wrist and flashed even brighter on impact. Like a rookie ballplayer trying to impress, young Zack swung at every nasty pitch that came howling his way, connecting with most and dinging a few.

Harley defended their rear as they sprinted down into the next chamber that led deeper underground.

Only the bravest bats followed, and Harley made quick work of the most aggressive of the rampaging mutants. The mighty battle hound tore them apart as easily as he would crush a plush toy—each bat emitting a satisfying final squeak.

What seemed a savage, unprovoked assault seconds before had transformed into nothing more sinister than a deadly game of Frisbee—with a giant canine who enjoyed flying.

After a few more minutes, the last rabid attackers fled for their lives.

Zack and Harley realized that the lilting, whispering sounds had grown louder in the abrupt absence of any other sounds except their ragged breathing.

It was a soft, pulsating vibration that seemed human and yet not human at all—musical notes with a soul—but without a recognizable voice.

"Is it just the wind moaning through the caves?" Zack wondered out loud.

Or is it something else? His mind echoed.

Whatever the source, it sounded closer now, coming from somewhere up ahead.

They continued traveling deeper underground when they discovered an unnatural cavern opening up before them. Boy and dog stood underneath a ceiling of arched stones, with a waterfall roaring down from the center of a solid granite ceiling.

I wonder if this is the bottom of those great falls above?

Is this the source of the whispers?

Zack saw that a sloping stone ledge, as large as a Los Angeles offramp, existed on the far side of the deep chasm that separated them. Three dark tunnels teased their existence, flickering behind the turbulent veils of constantly moving whitewater.

Someone reckless—and yet bold enough to challenge Mother Nature herself—had attempted to bore these massive tunnels straight through a mountain of solid granite.

Harley navigated casually across the monumental boulder field at the base of the underground falls like he was headed home for a warm meal and nap. Dark whirlpools formed and eddied between the car-sized boulders as Harley used his immense size to full advantage to leap effortlessly between them. But he stopped halfway, shook himself dry, and waited to provide lifeguard support.

Zack realized this was just the beginning of some epic ordeal designed to turn back the weak, the frivolous, and the greedy. Finding himself stuck on a boulder in the middle of the raging waters, Zack knew he had to keep moving or drown. He tried to retrace his dog's wet footprints across the boulder field, finding traction with every smart step by following Harley's example. He slipped twice but recovered both times, and his homemade torch snuffed out the second time, plunging them into complete darkness.

Zack held onto Harley's tail in the pitch-black as the large hound led him up behind the waterfall by touch and sense memory alone.

As their eyes adjusted to the dark, they could make out the three ominous shadows of the openings looming over them. Each massive borehole appeared more neglected than the next, either flooded, collapsed, or on fire. These impressive artificial structures were of such magnitude it was impossible not to believe that someone once tried to swallow the earth whole.

There was no going back. They needed to choose the correct tunnel to proceed through this threshold as Zack struggled in the darkness to rebuild his torch from scratch.

"Welcome to the Temple of the Three Windows," Archie's familiar voice rang out from nowhere.

"Which way do we go now?" Zack seemed unfazed by Archie's sudden disembodied presence as he continued reconstructing his waterlogged torch from the fresh reserves of socks stuffed in the backpack. He rewired them and covered the surface with melted candle wax. This added fuel source would feed the flame they would need to travel any deeper underground.

The improvised torch lit on the first try, and the boy's self-confidence grew bright along with it.

Archie materialized beside him, standing shoulder to shoulder as if he'd been waiting on the wet ledge the entire time.

"Which way?" Zack asked again.

"If you ask me, it depends on what you're searching for. Doesn't it?" Archie smiled.

Zack grew frustrated. He just wanted answers.

"I'm not sure what I'm looking for. I'm not sure of anything except what I can see. So, what path should I take then? There are only three choices. Four if we go back. And none look good. Which one would you choose if you were looking for the right path?" Zack quizzed the specter.

"Try the center path," Archie suggested. "Extremes cuts on either side of the main jewel only damage the purity of the stone's original intentions. Go the wrong way, and you'll never get close to the heart and soul of the real gem. My Pap taught me that," he bragged.

"I don't even know what that means?"

"Try this way." Archie pointed straight ahead to the middle tunnel.

A barrier of spiderwebs covered the entrance to the enormous center tunnel and the web of roosting spiders scattered in every direction at the shocking intrusions of firelight as Zack ripped holes through their sticky universe.

"Yuck! Are you crazy?" Zack was horrified. "Why am I listening to you? Why should I even trust you?"

"Don't have a clue, chum. I don't have any idea at all! I sure wouldn't trust me! And I know me!" Archie snatched the torch from Zack's hand and scampered up the sloping debris field before disappearing through a small opening near the caved-in ceiling.

He dropped unseen to the other side and ran away laughing, leaving Zack and Harley behind with nothing but his taunting echoes to follow in the pitch-blackness.

That's when they heard a deeper rumble growing behind them. Stone against stone began gnashing together somewhere overhead as boy and dog turned to see an enormous slab of solid granite begin to slide down from above, threatening to seal them inside this collapsed tomb forever.

If they didn't run now, they could never travel back this way again.

Zack bolted out, but when Harley didn't follow and

stayed inside, it left Zack with a chilling and world-changing choice.

Go back now—or go on?

There would be no going anywhere in the next few seconds. That is when Zack realized what he had to do.

He turned around and ducked back inside the collapsing tunnel just before the thick door slammed shut behind him. The sounds of the noisy waterfall were silenced forever by the massive stone.

"Archie! Wait for us!" His voice chased Archie down the tunnel, and Zack and Harley dove through the same ragged opening on good faith alone.

They tumbled down on the other side of the debris field, chasing after the diminishing torchlight the best they could.

When they finally caught up to Archie, he had stopped inches short of falling off a sheer vertical cliff that plummeted hundreds of feet below them into the fire.

From where Zack stood, the only way to navigate across the open shaft was a sooty rope bridge abandoned long ago. Its warped and splintered planks appeared as pliable as a handful of potato chips.

"Come on, Zack!" Archie teased as he danced across the creaking structure, and it bowed even beneath his spectral presence.

"You can do it if I can. See? Easy-peasy!" Archie bragged.

Zack stood mesmerized as he stared down into the raging pits of the deep.

The constant updraft of soot and ash corrupted everything it touched.

"Is it worth it? Or not?" Archie cocked his head. "You're already here."

"I don't know?" Zack hesitated. "How do I know anything? I'm nine!"

"What do you feel, Zack? Inside? Right now? Inside your boldest heart?"

"I don't know what I feel. Hot!"

Zack was honest to a fault.

"Yup. I bet you are. But in all your life, until now... isn't this the best you've ever felt? About yourself? About anything?" Archie smiled as if he already knew the answer.

Zack hesitated before he spoke.

"I feel smarter. And I feel like... like I've got to keep going forward. Because if I don't... I will fall behind."

"Or just fall." Archie nodded down at the fires.

Zack clenched his jaw.

I do feel different inside.

Stronger.

But why? Zack pondered.

"Then, onward, it is. A hop, a skip, and a jump, and you're over!" Archie promised.

Zack stepped onto the ancient rope bridge, and the swaying boards groaned under the strain of his thirty-five-pound load.

The web of frayed ropes began whining and snapping as if losing their faith in their own integrity. And Zack sprung to the other side just as the last plank split down the middle.

Zack experienced a massive rush of relief. He felt like a real-life action hero for the first time in his life.

"Yes!"

He'd never felt this proud and triumphant about anything before.

"Congratulations, Zack!" Archie grinned.

But now Harley was stranded alone on the other side of the open pit. The muscular mastiff weighed well over three hundred pounds and understood his physical limitations more than most.

Gravity had been trying to drag him down for centuries.

He pawed at the dusty planks, testing them for support. His faint, unheard whines confirmed his tentativeness with only the weak strands of rope to rely on, with several planks missing now.

"Come on, Harley!" Zack called. "You can do it, boy! You

can do anything!"

The weary hound crept onto the shifting rope bridge as gently as he could, but when the slats started snapping again— he launched.

The massive dog flew through the air like a seasoned aerialist.

"*A-rooooooo!*" Harley exclaimed midflight.

Zack and Archie grabbed him as he landed on them on the edge.

"Good boy! Great jump!" Zack hopped up unharmed.

They watched as the twisting rope bridge settled back down over the shaft—ripped and fractured—it would make traveling back across even more treacherous the next time.

But they were no longer headed in that direction—and they all understood that with a simple nod between them.

That was the past. There was no going back now.

The strange trio struggled downward through another series of collapsed tunnels until they discovered an abandoned industrial complex built deep underground inside a vast, vaulted manufactured chamber as the central hub of all mining operations.

Ancient ore cart tracks and giant cranes crisscrossed this subterranean world in a convoluted roller-coaster of mine-car tracks heading in every direction. The multi-layered tracks flowed in and out of a complex honeycomb of tunnels on several levels. The sheer scale of this unfathomable human operation was mind-boggling.

Did people live like this?

Archie lit an old oil lantern he found waiting at the back of an abandoned ore cart and jumped aboard.

"Well, Zack Goodnight. Do you want to see who you really are?" Archie flashed his familiar gap-toothed smile.

"What?"

"Do you want to see who you've always been? On the inside?"

He lit the second lantern that hung at the front of his

cart.

Zack was unsure what to expect next from this rascal.

"Don't you want to see what you're made of? Who you're going to become? Then please, don't let me stand in your way! Climb aboard! And become the creator of your own destiny!" Archie said. "Board!"

Harley leaped into the first cart without hesitation, and Zack realized he had no other choice.

Zack snuffed out his homemade torch and tucked it into the metal cart as he climbed in and crouched down next to his dog inside the heavy, rusty mine cart.

Archie giggled, released the hand brake to the iron mule, and they rolled forward into their grand adventure together.

"So, do you want to see what it's all about, boy? What makes you tick inside? Well, hold on, Zack! It's going to be a bumpy ride," Archie warned.

The tandem ore carts made a sudden, gut-wrenching turn and a startling Zero-G drop. It was like plunging off the top of a mountaintop underground. And as they spiraled down, the tilted carts picked up enormous speed.

They careened around unlit, sharp corners–with Harley's jowls flapping so furiously in the rushing wind–they provided an aerodynamic lift to his massive head. The hound had to force his noggin down to avoid clobbering the tunnel's bumpy ceiling above.

Hunkered beside his dog, Zack began seeing tiny explosions of color along the tunnel walls. The colors were morphing into light waves of so many varied frequencies he'd never seen before that he couldn't keep up with them, and everything streaked past him in fast-moving blurs of upended time.

His future seemed to collide with his past. Things made little sense—some things did.

He witnessed underground calamities on an unimaginable scale.

Monster-sized miners and humans alike, all trapped underground by rampaging firestorms.

The molten walls flew past Zack's unique gaze, informing him in a bright splash of colors and images meant only for him as they rushed by. The unending carnage of ancient battlefields exploded from a dozen different futures until Zack's mind collapsed under the pressure, and he voluntarily dove into the safety of the Dreampool—seeking temporary emotional solace in its calming depths away from the searing, brutal confusion still rushing by above.

Everything went black for the boy as he sank into the inky lagoon in shock—when a disturbing movement startled him in the darkness. Something above was reaching down—reaching for him.

There was a powerful flash of pink.

Light.

Air.

Then he saw her sweet face.

His mother.

That's her!

And then another sense-memory of her first expressions of joy flashed by.

It is my mother. It is her.

He knew in his heart that he was seeing his actual mother. Not a dream. And for only the second time in his life.

This is her!

Someone had robbed this magical connection between them in the first seconds of his life. That's when they tore him out of her arms in the delivery room and rushed him out the door.

But now, his mind's-eye was blessed with her kind face again.

He recognized her youthful radiance the instant he first saw her.

How beautiful.

The physical resemblance was striking—especially

their shared trait of luminous, oversized eyes.

Even in the Dreampool, he could never quite conjure her face—until now—until here.

This is my mom!

What a gift.

He would never forget her again. That precious memory burned in cell deep forever.

And she loved me. I could tell.

He saw her for the last time, beaming down at her new baby boy with all the pride of a new baby's mother.

Then she was gone.

Strange souls began haunting him with their concerned faces peering down from his mysterious past—then more flashes of light were followed by earth-shaking explosions.

A blue sky filled with boiling clouds inside his dreamscape—as if he was standing back alone in the cornfields again.

The sky is still full of screams.

Zack's momentary state of bliss exploded as tornadoes of unhappy masks came swirling in beside him, and they swept him up into the spiraling storm years of loss and regret.

Tormented with memories of abandonment and inadequacy—enduring bullies—the daily abuse for being different took a steep emotional toll over the years as he relived all of them once more.

I can never be what everyone wants me to be.

These horrible, damaged feelings were the hidden wounds that hemorrhaged daily and burned the most—the ones he tried to bury the deepest. The ones that left scars forever.

There have been so many in my life that didn't need me in theirs, he realized

His tattered personal life flashed before him like an unending tapestry of misery and death. Only then did the young boy understand his recurring abandonment, with no further illumination needed.

But those damaging images faltered—replaced with unfamiliar tableaus of death and destruction of others trapped underground.

Apocalyptic mine shaft disasters throughout the ages collapsed around him, and he screamed as each catastrophic vision became even more devastating than the next as the haunted tracks spiraled him downward without pause.

Zack witnessed miners and enslaved people in chains buried alive underneath millions of tons of earth in man-caused cataclysm after cataclysm as the ancient stone rebelled against the greedy human invasion.

He watched as survivors, trapped underground for weeks, began clawing for air—succumbing to madness without equal as their last puff of precious oxygen ran out.

"I... can't... breathe!" The victim choked.

"Stop!" Zack howled in sympathy, gulping down mouthfuls of air like a fish out of water. His eyes stayed shut against the horrible emotional assault whipping past him in the cart.

As they plunged even deeper, the physical appearance of the flames began changing. Soon, flickering fields of blue lava replaced the towering firestorms of orange and yellow.

Underneath here, the molten liquid of blue flowed only in one direction—uphill—defying gravity's edict as the sapphire flames burned eternally in reverse.

Archie pulled hard on the handbrake, and they rode a carpet of sparks to a screeching halt among the glowing blue flows.

Zack opened his eyes, hopped out of the cart, and vomited onto the tracks as the waves of blue lava swept toward him.

Then, unexpectantly, the reverse flames formed a series of concentric circles surrounding Zack, completing a lost symbol.

Isn't lava hot? Zack's unsettled mind searched for any logic to grab onto.

The information overload was so much more than Zack could bear. He felt mentally incompetent, just like all the psychiatrists had always proclaimed him to be.

His tortured brain was stretched so far beyond its natural limits it had to snap back into shape just to keep him human.

He threw up again.

"Oh, settle down. Get ahold of yourself, Zack. That's just motion sickness you're feeling. There's so much more that lies ahead for you." Archie's once sincere smile seemed sinister now.

Zack looked up with tears.

Why can't I just turn around? He wondered to himself.

Why can't you just learn to be like everybody else?

"No!" Archie replied as if sharing Zack's private thoughts.

"Why not?" Zack demanded, his exhausted voice filled with emotion.

"Your future lies ahead of you, not behind you, Zack. That's how the future works, chum!"

Archie reached out for Zack's hand to help him back into the cart, but Zack hesitated, pulling away. He only relented with Harley's gentle nudging, and when he climbed back aboard, his dog quickly licked his tears of regret away

"Board!" Archie's voice boomed throughout the haunting tunnels.

He released the handbrake, and they rolled forward through the flowing fields of blue lava. Soon, they began picking up more speed when the cart spun around one-hundred-and-eighty-degrees and started rolling uphill backward onto an entirely distinct style of unworn tracks. The strange, ornate rails arched over, and they fell back into a death-defying free dive into the darkness, where gravity demanded her unbreakable laws be paid in full.

Zack felt woozy again as the dual carts bottomed out and then hurtled faster and faster along a long straightaway, pinning them into their seats.

His mind began reeling in more bright flashes and dark insights with back-lit horrors as the elegant blue lava burned in reverse.

Zack saw everything at once—as he never could before.

It's as if I can see inside of everything!

He understood now that his tragically flawed life was always meant to be lonely—but that didn't mean forever. Next came the other chapters of his life he'd always dreamed about without ever realizing their meaning.

"Further?" Archie asked above the onrushing winds on the ancient tracks.

"Yes!" Zack replied, turning back into the wind to face whatever fate offered him head-on.

"Further!"

-CHAPTER 23-

Welcome to Ribbit Resorts

Once Kate realized everyone had lost sight of Zack again, she panicked.

"Hasn't anyone seen him?"

The others playing in the stream all shook their heads.

"He's probably still crashing back at Pepper's."

"No. I saw him and his new attack donkey crossing down by the lake again a while ago," Oz said.

"You don't think he's headed back to those caverns, do you?" Jesse asked, trusting her instincts. "That's where I'd be going if someone ordered me not to. Just saying."

"I bet you're right, Jess," Kate nodded.

Both girls hopped off the boulders to track down the lost kid when they were startled by a powerful car engine revving behind them on the old lakeside road.

Stork to the Stars, Pepper Wixx rolled up behind them in a vintage Rolls Royce with a tiny chauffeur seated behind the wheel. One of her fabled delivery red trucks swung around her limo, gave a familiar air horn toot, and roared out of the valley on another delivery run.

Coop glimpsed inside the back as it rolled past, but the delivery van appeared empty, which was odd.

Pepper gestured for her limo driver to stop beside the children and rolled down the back window of the silver Phantom.

"Well, look what we have here, Beaumont. The calvary I was seeking."

"Whoa! Look at that car."

"Check it out!"

"Classy wheels, Pepper!"

"Why, thank you, children. After all these years of self-neglect, I needed a break from driving cross-country in my old van, and I finally rewarded myself with this luxury vehicle. It and Beaumont suit me so, don't you think?" She fished for compliments.

"Why not? You're going to be a Queen, after all. You deserve it!" Ozzy sucked up to his all-time favorite chef.

"Well, thank you, son. This is only my first Rolls when I should have had dozens by now..." She caught herself and adjusted the Knack. "But that's another story and someone else's problem now." Her lips curled back to normal.

"You look like the Queen of the Ball!" Ozzy sucked harder.

"Indeed, I am. And they are going to crown me so tomorrow night. But right now, your future Queen needs a last-minute rescue, and I was hoping you could all help me out of a bind?"

"Of course, Pepper. But listen, I'm sorry, but we're missing Zack again." Kate confessed.

"Again? And his big ugly dog, too, I suppose?"

Pepper's complexation flushed, and she redirected her attention to the flashes of light flickering across the lake—taunting her night and day with their insolence by verifying Yuma's impossible survival.

You are within hours of never existing again, you heathen!

Pepper regained her focus by camouflaging her emotions behind the wispy tendrils of the Knack.

"No worries, child. This adventure should only take a few minutes at most. We won't be gone long. Besides, that ugly hound will take good care of that feeble-minded child," Pepper offered. "Loyalty. That's the only thing they're good for."

"Zack's far from feeble-minded," Kate said.

"Listen to how absurd you sound, child. It's almost

215

funny. Now one of us speaking has developed a professional eye for the inflicted flesh after years of painful experiences and research, while one hasn't. Guess which one you are, my dear?"

"There's nothing wrong with him. He's just wired differently than us. Nothing wrong with that. He's NexGen."

"What? We'll deal with him later, I promise. Now, who is the fastest among you?"

Everyone's hand shot up but Kate's.

Pepper lifted her cane out the window and aimed it like a sniper rifle at the nearest tree line.

"Right over there is a great big surprise waiting for you just behind that stand of yellow trees. Run, and we'll race you over there!" Pepper tapped Beaumont's shoulder with the cane. "Go. Boy! Go!"

Beaumont gunned the Rolls around into a powerful fishtail, and a cross-country race was officially on.

The teens sprinted across the wide-open field for the stand of Aspens, with the fleet-footed Emiliano leading the way and the limo spitting up dust devils in its wake. When Emil skidded to a stop, the rest piled up behind him at the edge of a steep embankment, almost toppling everyone off after several awkward collisions.

"Look."

Thirty feet below them sat a deep, natural pond hidden behind the circular berm. And floating within this secret lagoon swam hundreds of plump contented bullfrogs zapping flies and croaking like they owned the place. They sprawled everywhere, sunning themselves on the oversized lily pads in sheer amphibian bliss.

If Bullfrogs designed a world-class luxury spa for themselves, this would be it.

"Welcome to Ribbit Resorts," Pepper cackled softly out the window, then raised a gloved finger to her lips as she coasted to a stop behind them.

"Shh, hush-puppies. Remember—silence is golden." Pepper whispered. "Now, whoever brings me the most bullfrogs, pound for pound, will get to special order any dessert of their choosing tonight, made by me."

"What? Do you mean those things? Frogs?"

Beaumont was shockingly shorter than he appeared behind the wheel of the limo once he hopped down from his extra seat cushions. He began handing out empty burlap sacks from the trunk as if he'd done this chore a thousand times before.

"You want us to fill up these bags with live frogs?" Kate felt queasy at the slimy thought.

"Better than dead ones, don't you think?!" Pepper laughed and then explained as she refocused the Knack to make her jokes land better.

"They are for the Fair, hon, but not for the faint of heart. Surely, you've all heard of the 'World Famous Jumping Frogs of Calaveras County,' right? Everybody from around these parts has. It's an American classic!" Pepper challenged.

"No," said Tim.

"Mark Twain!" Pavarty shot back.

"Exactly, my bright doctor's daughter," Pepper honed in on her.

Pav squealed at hearing those unbelievable words put together by the famous woman.

"Oh, that's right," Kate remembered the short story about the legendary frog-jumping contest.

"So, they're for a jumping contest?"

"Well, it's something like that... kind of rodeo for the kids. It's become a tradition at all our festivals." Pepper seemed proud of her quaint hometown traditions.

"Any dessert we could ever want? Like full-on Willy Wonka style?" Oz asked.

"Wonka is a rank amateur when compared to my skills."

Ozzy began nodding in the affirmative at each of his competitors as they lined up abreast, giving them each an equal opportunity at the challenge ahead.

"Get ready..."

"Game on, boys and girls!"

"Get set."

"Go!" Ozzy screamed and barreled down the hill.

The others tumbled behind him, squealing at the giant tidal wave of green pond water following Oz's massive cannonball impact. Their unexpected ambush sent the lethargic amphibians into a state of total panic.

The small pond magically became the center of a frog-jumping universe. They shattered new world records as ten- and fifteen-pound bullfrogs soared through the air in every direction. So many airborne bullfrogs landed back inside the curved basin that the kids simply had to open their hands to catch one.

The citified orphans snagged and bagged as many frogs as they could catch. They were naturals—like they'd been doing it in the backcountry all their lives.

Even Pepper Wixx had to chuckle at the squeals of unbridled joy erupting from the gullets of these delighted Uman pollywogs.

A half-hour later found the pond-drenched crowd trying to hoist their squirming gunny sacks into the back of the Rolls Royce. But it was almost impossible without help. The soaking canvas bags held up to a hundred-and-ten pounds of potatoes, and now each weighed that, if not more, with its living load. It required everyone's effort, including tiny Beaumont's, to get their spoils loaded inside.

"Thank you, thank you," Pepper praised her gang of frog rustlers. "The tradition lives on, thanks to you all. Now follow me home, and we'll do the final tally and reward the winner!"

"Wait! What about Zack?"

"Come on, Kate. This will only take a second." Oz pleaded. "He's probably already there."

Once back inside Pepper's Lodge, they unloaded the heavy sacks onto carts and wheeled each wriggling load indoors.

Pepper led the wet kids into her industrial-sized kitchen

for the official count and up to a set of commercial scales hanging above her large triple sink.

The frog rodeo started immediately as desperate amphibians jumped and attempted a mass escape. Still, when Pepper tallied up the eventual results—Ozzy had won the count by a landslide.

He cheated, of course. Competitive to a fault, Ozzy had stashed several extra giants down his pants and shirt to help tip the scales in his favor. Ozzy wasn't about to lose this food fight to anyone.

"If you wouldn't cheat for a custom dessert by the great Granny Pepper, then you don't deserve to win it!" That was his opinion when everyone groaned at the inflated tally.

"Now, what can I whip up for your favorite dessert delight, my grand-prize winner? That will be my last gift before I return to my proper chores?" Pepper leaned in and pinched his cheek.

"Just imagine this, okay, Pepper? Picture a ten-layered, chocolate-swirled raspberry cream cake, smothered in pink strawberry frosting, with chocolate caramel swirls and coconut M&M's sprinkled throughout, and every layer is a distinct flavor and color!"

He grinned as if he'd just won the food lottery.

"Ooh-ooh! And throw in some candied bacon bits all over the top, too, if you don't mind?" Oz added.

"Of course not. You're still a growing boy. Your wish is my command. And that good news I mentioned to you kids before? Well, everything keeps blossoming in all the right directions from what I've been hearing from my clients about you all if you know what I mean?" She winked. "So, continue to behave yourselves. You never know when something magical will happen to your life in my business. Now behave yourselves! Silence is golden around here."

The thought of any good news coming their way thrilled the kids. Pepper dismissed them with a flick of her wrist, which set everyone free to run outside and play again until sundown.

They all bolted except for Ozzy, who kept adding to his custom cake order until Pepper disappeared into another part of her large kitchen.

"We've got to find Zack before dark!" Kate said to Jesse once they cleared the doorway. Although not invited, Coop chased after them as the other orphans scattered to the winds in search of their own misadventures.

Once Ozzy joined the others, it left no one inside to witness what happened next.

Born paranoid, Pepper Wixx ensured she was alone before lifting a huge burlap bag full of frogs over her head with one arm effortlessly before dumping its living contents into a cauldron of boiling water on top of her industrial-sized stove.

The word croak took on a shocking new meaning inside her kitchen that afternoon.

Hundreds of terrified frogs screamed, shriveled, and drowned inside the bubbling broth.

The bemused witch emptied every gunny sack into the oversized pots until she had boiled every frog alive.

That's when the soles of her shoes trembled against the hardwood floors as she lost contact with the earth, and Pepper Wixx floated several feet into the air and hovered there.

"My frog broth needs a touch of acid."

She twirled through the air, reveling in her newest secret achievement—complete Transvectional Flight. And she used those burgeoning skills to search for a particular herb hiding among her hanging gardens.

"I must continue to practice these exercises, so my grand entrance as the new Queen of the Damned is the most talked-about ever. Flying freely above everyone without a broom, just like in my dreams. Just like in the legends."

She giggled, picturing the shocked, jealous faces below her when she revealed these frightening new capabilities to her less powerful subjects and enemies.

"Bear witness, my fellow pagans. Not one of you can

stand in my way now. No committees nor Uman's will ever be able to look down their noses at me again—without trembling in fear."

-CHAPTER 24-

Creeps

Zack's eyes flooded with a decade's worth of unspent tears as his once-banished memories rushed back to taunt him. Waves of soul-crushing sadness and regret threatened to drown him in his past sorrows as he and his dog hurtled through the darkness, crammed inside the runaway bucket.

"I can't catch my breath!"

Zack saw everything about his past, present, and future illuminated along the crumbling walls of the ancient mineshafts—with every tragic moment projected in deep abstract blurs of meaning. Bright flashes of melancholy colors and long-forgotten molten memories streaked past without remorse.

Abandonment.

Loss.

Abuse.

The constant bullying.

Here was a child's life—*wasted*—with no understanding, love, or hope in any corner of it.

Solitary.

Alone.

Happiness is a place I've never visited.

In that moment of perfect illumination, he realized that any enlightenment he gained inside these mystical caverns wasn't coming from somewhere outside himself—or from supernatural forces lying in wait around the next curve in the track.

222

It came instead from the bottomless pit of pain and sorrow that ate through his abandoned soul like acid every day, forming an open wound that would never heal.

Life ripped Zack from the protective cocoon that shields most childhoods from the realities of a brutal world too early—only to emerge in a nightmare he didn't deserve or create.

But here, in this extraordinary land, Zack finally understood something for the first time.

"I have nothing and no one to count on... for the rest of my life... but myself."

Those pangs of overpowering loneliness ravaged his mind and suffocated all his dreams for a normal life in the future.

Zack recognized now, with absolute certainty, that his unique destiny had brought him to this point in time and place for one extraordinary reason.

I am one. Forever.

He was singular. No one else existed in the universe like him.

But wizened beyond his years by the continuous neglect and abandonment, Zack Goodnight also appreciated that he was more fortunate than most among the suffering and lonely souls on the planet.

The Ying needs the Yang to counterbalance the turbulent universe, and Zack realized happily that the only pure, unconditional love that had ever existed for him, except for his brief snippet of time with his mother, was sitting right next to him—drooling buckets of saliva all over the place, in the here and now.

Harley the Magnificent was his new best friend—and that love would never fade or go away.

The colossal hound leaned closer against his new boy, feeling the bond, and bracing him against every turn. And he did it without a whimper of self-doubt or hesitation as they hurtled headlong into another cavern in their rusty bucket of bolts.

Now this is love.

And bravery.

And that is enough for now.

Harley barked as if reading Zack's happy thoughts, and Zack grinned back, not understanding dogspeak yet—which proved unfortunate.

Look Out! Harley howled seconds before the rails vanished in front of them.

The underground world fell silent for a few seconds of hang time, allowing Zack enough time to turn and ask.

"What are you doing, Archie?"

Then impact.

Blackness exploded into concussive stars inside an even deeper shade of nothing as Zack drifted in and out of consciousness to the sound of the ore carts ricocheting down the gullet of a hungry abyss.

It could have been two minutes or two weeks. There was no way of marking the passage of time in the unlit void.

The hideous darkness erased everything positive as fresh images of death and chaos re-flooded his mind and sucked Zack down into the most terrifying depths of the Dreampool.

"Zack! Wake up, boy!" A familiar voice dove into the gloom to break through the spell he was drowning in.

"We gotta go, boy!" the muffled voice yelled down through dark ripples. "Wake up!"

Zack winced in pain as he turned around and swam back to the surface of his consciousness.

"Ow!" he yelped once awake. "My arm! What happened?"

"Yeah, well, the short version is we plumb ran out of track, son. We took a bit of a wrong turn and a tumble I didn't count on."

Archie's face drifted back into focus, as did the radiant face of a relieved Harley.

"I think I broke it?" Zack picked up his injured left arm

and rested it between his shirt and pants for support. Harley moved to protect his wounded side. "I need a minute to..."

"No! We don't have the time." Archie cut him off. "Get up and move, move, move. They're a-comin' for us, boy?"

Zack could see that Archie was terrified.

"Who's coming?" Zack asked.

"You don't want to meet them. Trust me, friend. Let's go-go-go!"

Archie was trying to help Zack to his feet when they heard an annoying clicking sound irritating the silence. They had crushed one of their lanterns in the accident, but the second still sputtered and relit when turned upright, casting flickering shadows against the walls and ceiling.

Zack looked around to re-orient himself in the pale light and spotted where their ore cart had flown off the tracks. Those dangling rails broke off thirty feet over their heads in midair—incomplete—like an unfinished thought. Or was it always designed to obliterate any idiots foolish enough to travel on these unforgiving rails?

Either way—gravity always rules—unless you're Blue Lava.

After flying off the tracks, they crashed onto the cavern floor with a tremendous thud and tumbled toward an open fissure along with the carts. The funnel-shaped abyss waited fifty feet below with open jaws—ready to swallow any joy riders fool-hardy enough to take this engineering leap of faith to nowhere. Here was the perfect solution to guide every greedy victim to their own destruction without further fuss.

Harley pulled the tumbling Zack closer to his body during the fall and shielded him as they slid down the natural chute toward the hungry opening. That's when Harley reached out with his muscular legs, stopping them from skidding any further by his sheer willpower alone when backed up by a set of oversized claws.

They only stopped moving inches short of a painful, permanent death below.

"Whoa. Wow! Thank you, boy!" Zack heaved.

Harley licked his chops and smiled as he nudged Zack safely back to the rim.

Once they looked around, they realized somebody had designed this deadly exit to nowhere for this exact purpose. There were a few bones scattered about.

"Looks like we all got hoodwinked." Archie shrugged.

"We?"

The unsettling clicks grew louder and sharper as the sounds became distinct, like hundreds of ice picks striking the same chalkboard together.

Archie's eyes widened in terror.

"No, no, no. We have got to go, son! You've got to get up! Now, now, now!"

But Zack leaned forward out of raw curiosity and stared down into the abyss to see what was causing the disturbance inside the void.

The dark crystalline field surrounding Zack began glowing a soft pearly white as the boy moved around the crater, searching for an answer to the mystery sound. Each crystal shimmered brighter as Zack stepped closer to examine them, and flickers of intense ignition sparked inside the heart of every piece of obsidian he touched.

"Whoa. What's going on here?"

An elaborate light show began radiating across the crystalized field, lighting up the darkness. The dancing lights mimicked even the subtlest of Zack's movements, producing a surreal counterpoint to his shadow.

To say it impressed Archie would be an understatement. Neither he nor Harley cast such shadows, and he launched a knowing giggle into his hands to stifle the joy he felt in the presence of such magic. But that temporary distraction fled as the clicking sound grew bolder and closer.

"Bats? Are more bats flying up?" Zack asked. "We know how to handle bats, don't we, Harley?" Zack bragged. He found his extinguished cane and twirled it over his head.

"Bat meets bat"! Zack wrote the second joke of his life.

Zack had nothing physical to brag about leading a non-athletic life so far, but he knew how to swing this hickory stick like a champion now, even with a bad wing.

"Oh, this is worse than bats, boyo. So much worse. That stick's no match against them! Now, run! Run!" Archie bolted, snatching up the lantern on the way.

Zack and Harley launched after him on instinct now.

The loud clicks echoing up from below transformed into squeals and growls as both boys and the dog ran to the other side of the cavern's cantilevered floor. They discovered an elevated wooden stairwell towering straight up into the impenetrable darkness above them. The miners had erected it to conquer the cavern's sheer granite face, and it provided their only escape.

"Climb! Now!" Archie ordered.

The noisy creatures vomited out of the earth in a neon-colored gush of gnashing teeth and whipping tails as they scrambled over the top of each other in a frenzy to escape the massive sinkhole. These reptilian, day-glow terrors swarmed out of the abyss by the hundreds, chasing the fresh scent of Umans for their unique musk of upworld flesh.

"What are those things?" Zack shrieked as he looked back over his shoulder.

"Creeps! I call them Creeps! Because they give me the creeps!" Archie screamed and scampered up the first flight of wooden stairs with their lantern without stopping to look back.

Zack couldn't climb fast enough with just one working arm, so he threw the cane down and struggled to use his injured arm as well.

Harley knew Zack needed more time than they had to escape. So, the massive dog spun around to face the advancing swarm of Creeps head-on.

He would defend Zack's shaky retreat at all costs, and Harley wedged his body between the stairwell and the granite wall to form a permanent roadblock with teeth. He would make his last stand here if need be.

The Creep's repulsive physical appearance wasn't just horrific to the eye but shattering to the mind and spirit as well.

Nothing like this monster can exist! Can it? Zack tried to rationalize his first glimpse of the scurrying horde.

The fleshy creatures were the size of wolverines—except more vicious and belligerent, if possible. A raptor's muscular hindquarters propelled their scaly bodies, and they brandished long, metallic claws, both front and back, on four legs.

Each Creep wielded a thick pink tail that ended in a stinger at the tip as part of its deadly arsenal. They whipped these toxic appendages around like a gang of bullying scorpions trying to impress each other.

But the most disturbing feature about these vile creatures was their heads—their faces, to be exact.

These demented-looking beasts appeared to harbor deformed human-shaped faces, and their pulpy pink features sprouted a thin fishing pole nose—dangling a bioluminescent lure off the end, directly in front of their horror-inducing mouths.

Their oddly shaped jaws held needle-sharp teeth that resembled those of the horrifying Angler Fish. Combined with the fleshy head and bulging eyes of a human corpse along with the scaly body of a tiny Komodo Dragon, it was impossible for a human to comprehend its physical existence with a rational mind.

These predatory packs were evil incarnate—as if something had gone violently wrong at the point of creation.

Ancient myths described these horrifying creatures as once part of a remote tribe of underground-dwelling human beings. However, this damaged and inbred species soon became overwhelmed by their wicked tastes and depravities for human flesh. Cut off from the rest of humankind, they became cannibals. And in the process, they voluntarily infected their children's children with the same damning curse as their everlasting punishment took on this dreadful new shape. Losing all cognitive language and free thought over the centuries, the new repulsive species couldn't even remember their own creation story anymore.

Half Uman—half monster—or the other way around? Either way, these soulless hunters of the deep craved fresh human flesh whenever they could find the tasty species exploring underground. And these sneaky Creeps could change color and skin texture at will, making the invisible maneaters even more frightening. Their chameleon-like abilities provided the perfect stealth mode of ambush or retreat.

But these dazzling beasts weren't hiding from anyone when they charged straight for Harley in probing sets of twos and threes.

The reflections from their provocative battle colors illuminated Harley's face with their ever-shifting neon colors as they drew nearer and backed off. But they slowed their hissing advance entirely when they caught sight of Harley's massive frame and ferocity. They crept toward him, tongues darting between four-inch fangs—leery at first around this formidable new foe. They flashed neon war signals across their bioluminescent bodies and snapped their stingers around like bullwhips, stirring up a frenzy behind them.

When the first line of Creeps grew bolder, they charged as a unified line, and Harley braced himself against the creaking stairwell. He blocked all entry. Nothing was going anywhere near Zack without going over the top of him first—and that wasn't about to happen.

The battle-hound stood his ground against the gnashing teeth and flashing stripes without backup—as, above him, Zack struggled to climb the crumbling stairway after Archie.

Zack's arm was causing him terrible pain, and his panic and guilt added to the claustrophobic burden inside this slow-motion nightmare. But he continued scrambling up the decrepit stairway as if his best friend's life depended on it—because it did.

Only when Zack was safely above the threat would Harley abandon his post, follow his joy up the stairs, and rescue his own life. Zack understood that unspoken commitment as he fought harder to climb higher.

Below, Harley made quick work of the first wave of attackers. After that skirmish, ambush hunting—not face-to-face combat—suited the Creeps' adaptive hunting style better as they fanned out before the giant dog.

Their rapid-burst stingers zapped Harley dozens of times, and they ripped the flesh on his legs with their syringe-like teeth. Still, Harley would never surrender his position no matter the numbers, and he held fast. Not a single Creep made it past him as he decimated any that tried.

After what seemed like forever, the bloodied hound heard Zack's feeble whistle floating down from somewhere high above like a feather of hope.

At that point, the greatest battle hound that ever lived turned his back on the hissing mob and loped two stories up the crumbling wooden stairway in just five bounds. And with the final impact of his massive hind legs, he intentionally collapsed the rotten stairway behind him, leaving only an avalanche of dusty planks and sawdust in his wake.

The angry color shifters hissed as they scattered below, with no way up.

"Harley, you're bleeding!" Zack inspected the most severe bites and plucked each stinger out. He tried to address the wounds as best he could with only one working hand as the unflappable Harley lapped away the salt glistening the boy's cheeks from his tears. It was a joyous reunion on the dark landing, and Harley seemed unfazed by the deadly ambush, and Zack almost drowned in the dog's affection.

Harley lived only in the present, like every dog.

When a single, twenty-four-hour day equals an entire

week in a dog's lifespan—time is seen as a precious gift in their species. Luckily for Harley, time wasn't the issue anymore. But the noble hound never took a day in his charmed life for granted, and, as a result, Harley was constantly delighted by the richness of the bounty that came his way every day from that simple philosophy.

"Hey!" Archie called down. "We still gotta a long way to go, folks! We're burning lamplight!"

"I'm trying!" Zack answered.

They struggled against the exposed granite face on the rickety stairway until they discovered a message chiseled into the stone wall before them. In huge, jack-hammered letters, it proclaimed that they had arrived at—The Top Shelf—The First Level.

"We made it."

The young explorers collapsed among the charred equipment and twisted debris of the Top Shelf Mine disaster. They panted from their harrowing climb and close brush at being on the wrong end of the food chain, and an unexpected breeze gusted through the upper chambers, keeping the smoke at bay while replenishing their lungs with some badly needed fresh air.

Archie kicked around in the soot and debris with the toe of his boot and discovered another abandoned lantern. He shook it—heard sloshing inside and lit it with his dying one. Then he began rummaging around in the pile as if he knew what he was looking for and came up with a charred, rusty lunch pail. Archie unscrewed the fork and the spoon that held the metal lid in place and popped it open. He gave the abandoned contents a sniff.

"Not too bad."

He offered Zack and Harley a whiff, and both jolted back as if snake-bit.

"Whooo!"

Archie took a tentative bite.

"Want some? They're homemade corn dodgers. They

might taste nasty, but they're made to last forever! Like a brick!"

Zack took a small bite and spat it out.

"Eww. How old is that thing?"

"Older than you! Well, everything's a matter of taste! Isn't it?" Archie shrugged as he crunched away on the bone-hard crust, and Zack pulled a squished apple out of his pants pocket.

"Want some applesauce to go along with it?" Zack cracked another original joke.

Both boys laughed.

"So, wait. Can you eat too? Even though, you know, you float through the sky?"

Archie checked himself out, eager to see.

"Oh yeah. Look at that. Yup! Seems so. Everything's stuck so far."

Harley lapped at a small stream trickling downhill, and Zack grabbed a nugget of quartz to chuck down at the noisy Creeps still hissing below.

But when he held the clear crystal up, it flared bright yellow in his hand, and he dropped it like it was on fire.

"Whoa! What?" Zack startled and checked his fingertips for burns.

Archie smiled.

"Did it hurt?" he asked.

"No," Zack said. "Wait. Did I do that? Or you?"

"You, mate. And downstairs too. Remember?"

"Not me. You're the magic floating kid."

But inside, Zack knew the truth. Like everything else, he felt a stirring inside.

"I know I didn't do it," Archie answered. "Did you do it, Harley?"

Harley always appreciated being spoken to in Uman and shook his head and moaned back, 'No.'

Zack reached down and picked up another chunk of quartz, and nothing happened. He glanced over at Archie and

Harley with an almost disappointed shrug.

That's when a bolt of mini lightning ignited inside the crystal's translucent core, blazing to life in a shimmering bright blue glow.

"That's weird, isn't it?" Zack held it up for Archie and Harley to see. "It's not hot at all. But I thought it was yell...?"

And before he even finished speaking, the crystal glowed bright yellow—in sync with the speed of his thoughts and not his mouth.

"That's pretty darn cool," Zack smiled, enthralled by this new talent.

"Make it green!" Archie suggested, and with a simple nod from Zack, green it became.   Archie scooped up a quartz crystal and held it in his open hand.

"Make mine glow red," Archie challenged.

Zack simply had to think about it to make the color change.

"Purple, white, orange, puce!" Arch challenged.

"Puce? What color is puce?"

"That's a matter of opinion!"

Both boys kept playing with the colors, temporarily forgetting their dire predicament underground, and laughed at every ridiculous color choice.

"Tartan." Archie challenged.

Zack cocked a playful eyebrow and shrugged his shoulders. "What's that?"

"Plaid," Archie giggled.

The multifaceted stone in Zack's hand instantly became plaid and then shifted to another blend of tartan, and others followed.

"Do my clan!"

"What's a clan?"

"A family, silly boy. Everybody's got a clan. Even you."

They laughed at every bizarre color scheme tumbling out of his untapped mind.

Following an errant reflection, Zack noticed a name

233

etched onto the scorched lunch pail—MacGregor.

"Hey. Look at that!" Archie pointed in the opposite direction.

That's when they noticed the thick veins of quartz embedded within the mine's rock walls were now glowing and almost pulsating. The veins shifted in sympathetic harmony with Zack's color choices and moods—plaids included.

"I feel like I'm inside the Cartoon Network."

Zack picked up a fist-sized quartz crystal from the stream, wiped it off, and held it before him.

There were snaps and soft pops inside the raw gem as microscopic lightning bolts discharged around the center of the crystal. The newborn light source began spinning and gained speed. It turned faster and faster, forming a miniature vortex of brilliant light emanating from the crystal's central core until the entire body of the jewel flared—lighting up the tunnel in its sharp glare.

"Wow!" Zack squinted at his handiwork. "I think I just invented a flashlight without batteries."

"What's a flashlight? That's a lighthouse, boy!" Archie corrected with a chuckle.

As Zack turned to show off the dazzling sun crystal to Archie, his proud grin disappeared.

He saw the ripples of hundreds of invisible Creeps crawling straight toward them. The silent army of camouflaged monsters infested the entire mineshaft from floor to ceiling, and the sudden glare of Zack's indoor sun blinded their light-sensitive eyes, freezing them in place.

But as soon as their leader hissed, the enormous army of Creeps uncloaked in front of Zack and started flashing their fluorescent combat colors at him.

These cunning predators had been sneaking up to ambush their unsuspecting victims the entire time. They had scaled the mine's sheer walls using their powerful titanium nails and arrived hungry and ready to eat.

As their night vision recovered, the Creeps regrouped.

When their battle colors flashed in sync, they pounced simultaneously as one fearsome beast.

"Run!" Archie screamed, but Zack and Harley were already gone.

But they couldn't outrun a snail across the jumbled floor, and the Creeps ran them down, overpowering them with their numbers, and brought boy and dog down hard from behind.

Zack had the wind knocked out as the gnashing monsters swarmed over them in a carpet of smothering Creeps. They began stinging with one end and biting with the other, filling them with toxins. These brilliant pack creatures had worked out their only chance was to overpower the thrashing giant with their combined weight.

Zack screamed in agony, believing he was about to die.

"Help! Somebody help me!"

But when he heard Harley's first howls of genuine pain—ever—Zack began fighting back like the young warrior he saw in his new world visions on the walls. Creeps began flying everywhere as he grabbed and threw their squealing bodies off his buried dog, his injured arm unnoticed.

"Stop! Get off!" Zack struggled to climb to his feet.

The veins of white quartzite embedded throughout the tunnel system pulsed in rapid heartbeats of scarlet energy, mirroring Zack's raging bloodstream.

"No! Stop it! Get off him!" he screamed, trying to reach Harley as the brutal Creeps kept snapping and dragging him back down.

The entire crystalline structure heaved in a sudden, sympathetic rage in rhythm with Zack's heart as boulders crashed down from the ceiling.

As Zack watched several Creeps bite Harley's exposed throat, everything snapped inside his tiny soul. His unvarnished willpower exploded out of his mind in an invisible blade of astonishing fury.

"Stop it, I said!"

Zack's Lucid Pulse detonated in every direction at once, and the interlocking veins of quartz exploded in harmony, launching the entire mountaintop skyward.

The boy's untapped defensive powers were now abundantly clear. There existed a mental authority within this unique child strong enough to shatter the matrix of an entire mountainside by the sheer force of his mind.

Only the inherent strength built into the enchanted Bubble could have contained such unexpected fury.

And the Top Shelf Mine—the deadly location that threatened to become the boy's tomb—ceased to exist.

-CHAPTER 25-

Reinforcements

Yuma snapped the gizmo-goggles on and poked fun at that elusive pink orb tumbling above his fingertips when Zack's Lucid blast hit him head-on.

The ballistic concussion from Zack's psychic discharge not only sheared away a small mountaintop but body-slammed the giant to the ground from the top of a redwood over five miles away, leaving Yuma breathless and blinded from his amplified lenses.

"I can't see." Yuma fought back to his feet.

Zack's formidable, almost point-blank Lucid Pulse had plowed straight through Yuma's heart—along with everything else standing within its incandescent radius. The defensive ring radiated throughout the forest in a swirling cataclysm of invisible colors, electrifying and illuminating every living thing it touched.

The astounded creatures of the Sacred Forest became vocal with the signal's elegant passage, and a delicate veil of falling leaves rained behind it, leaving the rest of the natural world shimmering but intact.

Yuma tore off the goggles and spun in the Pulse's direction.

"They are here!"

The sightless giant staggered towards the Pulse's origins, with Zip, Zash, and Zee trying to guide the way with their whispers. And as his vision cleared, he sprinted across a mammoth highway of interconnecting root systems to discover the source of the blast.

He finally discovered Zack's unconscious body bathed in dappled sunshine. From ground level up, the top layer of the Top Shelf Mountain had gone missing.

"Who is this? Where are my reinforcements?" Yuma was confused.

Zack remembered flashes of light as he slid in and out of consciousness for the rest of the day. Something gigantic had plucked him up and thrown him over a shoulder like a carcass.

He could feel the muscular shoulders moving underneath him—swaying with unnaturally long strides.

Harley hung off the opposite shoulder, his tongue hanging out. Zack remembered seeing his unconscious hero's lifeless body swinging from side to side and thinking—

Are we dead yet?

As Yuma carried the boy into the heart of the redwood groves, the crystal outcroppings scattered among the ferns shimmered as they passed, which only made the giant more curious about his find.

When Zack opened his eyes, he stared up at a tall, curved ceiling. A ribcage of living branches provided all the vertical support, and the rest of the room blended perfectly with the masterful woodwork surrounding it. Simple and elegant design. It felt natural and modern, yet as old as time.

Zip, Zash, and Zee hovered over Zack's head as he sat up. The soft downdraft from their wings tousled his hair.

I must have had way too many concussions today or something.

He was dwarfed on a bed of immense proportions and covered with quilts and handwoven blankets.

Zack reached up to find his forehead wounded, and when he felt his legs, he winced, seeing new stitches and bandages all over his body. Someone had placed his injured arm inside a makeshift sling lined with soft rabbit fur.

That's when he recalled the hideous rampage of the

Creeps. He shot up in bed, frightened as a field mouse, afraid to make a peep inside these spooky new surroundings.

Where am I?

Where's Harley?

And who is that?

On the other side of the dark bedroom, he saw the figure of an enormous man with his back turned toward him. The man was seated inside a cone of intense sunlight streaking down from a large skylight overhead. The giant sat hunched over, working intently on something before him, but he was too wide to see what it might be.

Even from behind, this gigantic man appeared First Nations in birthright. He wore neutral-colored, loose-fitting clothing and appeared almost godly in his presence, with his snow-white hair illuminated in a glowing halo of the backlight.

When Zack leaned off to the side, he saw the giant was stitching up the last of Harley's most serious battle wounds with a surgeon's precision. The unconcerned hound tended to his own injured front paw while stretched out on a makeshift operating table of crisp white sheets and state-of-the-art supplies.

While receiving over two hundred stitches, Harley's demeanor was pure Harley—no-fuss, no-muss—and on to the next glorious adventure.

Yuma felt the burn of the boy's gaze from behind, and he turned to face him. Unfortunately, he forgot he was still wearing his magnifying gizmo-goggles, and his bulging eyes appeared enormous as Zack gasped and ducked, shivering beneath the covers.

"Geez!"

The giant chuckled at his bumbling introduction.

"Well, we are off to a fine start. At least you are smart enough to be afraid of a bug-eyed monster when you see one. That is a positive sign. It would suggest you might possess some intact survival instincts, after all." Yuma peeled off his goggles and smiled when the boy was brave enough to peek back out.

"Boo!" Yuma blurted and chuckled.

Zack ducked back, but after a second, he caught the playful sparkle in the giant's weathered face, and the child's curiosity soon replaced any initial fears of the oversized shaman.

"Boo yourself!" Zack replied as he crawled from underneath the blankets.

Yuma's chuckle turned into a hearty belly laugh.

"Are you a real-life giant?" Zack asked.

Yuma patted his body, running his hands up and down his long legs and onto his head with some bemusement.

"Why look? I believe you are correct. I am real. And I am a giant. Or are you just a very tiny person?"

"Nope. You're a giant, alright."

"Are you a leprechaun, perhaps? I hear they are evil and yet small."

"Nope."

"Point of view, I guess. Are you a real little boy?"

"Something like that. I'm not sleeping now, right?"

"You are not."

"Where am I then?"

"On my bed."

"No. I mean, where?"

"Why, you are... here. The Sacred Forest, where you were always meant to be, I assume? My question is, who are you? And where are my reinforcements?" Yuma couldn't wait to hear the good news from this small messenger.

"I don't know?"

"What? I do not understand."

Yuma was confused, and he checked with Harley, who hopped off the operating table and onto the bed beside Zack.

"Where are the other giants? My reinforcements?"

"I don't know what you're talking about, Mr. Giant."

Yuma's additional concern was that someone had

ambushed his reinforcements back in Dark Hollows and substituted this trickster for cover.

"Are you still in shock, boy? Who sent you to me? Other giants must be nearby. I have never felt a Lucid Pulse that powerful before. The Elders must have given you a message for me. With the symbol? Maybe a sign? A tablet?"

Zack crawled across the bed and dangled his legs over the edge like he was on the lip of a patchwork canyon.

"Nope. Nobody sent me," he replied as he re-adjusted his arm in the sling. "Nobody cares where I go. It's all an accident that I'm even here. My name is Zack. What's your name?"

The giant leaned in.

"Most intelligent people never ask, tiny pilgrim."

"Pepper Wixx called you a murderer," Zack replied.

"Wixx?" Yuma let the familiar last name drag out in a hiss. "I bet she did." His nostrils flared as his senses went into full battle alert at just the mention of the witch.

"She said you killed her husband and her three sons."

"And so many more," Yuma promised.

"Why?"

"Why, indeed?" Yuma chuckled, remembering he was speaking to a youngling.

None of these events were unfolding to meet his expectations.

The signals.

The crystal tablets.

The timing.

All the signs were present.

Everything seems perfectly aligned for the Change.

But now, this extra burden.

He turned to Harley for an explanation. They conversed for a long time in dogspeak, arguing muzzle to muzzle—with soft growls and other articulated yipping tones and bared fangs—until Harley convinced Yuma that this little boy was indeed the prophesied reinforcement that they had been waiting for.

Their only reinforcement was dangling his legs over the edge of the bed—decades younger than expected and packed into a much smaller frame than a true giant.

"How can I raise a child? By myself? What foolishness is this when we need to be ready to go to war by tomorrow night?" Yuma pleaded to Harley, who could only shrug back. "No one special sent you here?"

"No. I told you. It's an accident. I saw the lights up in the trees across the lake," Zack explained. "Harley led me over here."

"Like that? How could you already know this dog's name unless you speak dogspeak? Do you speak dog?"

"No. Archie told me," Zack replied.

Yuma couldn't wrap his head around this new predicament. With his vast backlog of lifelong experiences, he had never been this bewildered by a series of random events before.

And they send me a child, no less.

"I'm just lucky you found me." Zack smiled.

"The first life lesson, boy—there is no such thing as chance or luck. There simply exists randomized order and fluctuating forms. No accidents—but arbitrary occurrences and indiscriminate singularities all wrapped together in overlapping and decaying orbits of probability. It's all predictable as well as wholly unpredictable. You just have to know where to look."

"What?"

"Trust me. It's complicated." Yuma responded to the child in the only way he knew how to convey the universe's grand inner workings, as he understood it so far.

"What's your name?" Zack asked, and after a long moment, the giant let out a long, frustrated sigh and answered.

"Yuma. You may call me Yuma. And your name?"

"Zack. Zackery Goodnight."

"Well... yes... I suppose it is. I have seen some

formulations with that reference... where was it?"

There was another bewildered silence.

"Who were you expecting today?" Zack asked, thinking he should push for more information about this new and confusing reality.

"Certainly not you, child," Yuma stated matter-of-factly. "By the time the Elders chose me, I was already a battle-hardened young man. How is a tiny human boy with no battle experience meant to become a Time Guardian without first becoming a warrior for the Earth? Tell me that. This places all of us in an impossible strategic situation."

Zack grew uneasy as the giant's anger rose.

"Relax, Yuma. I'm only nine. I'm not who anybody thinks I am."

"Exactly."

They sat silent, but there were so many unanswered questions that still needed answers.

"How old are you, Yuma?" Zack asked.

The giant turned and glared down.

"Older than some mountains but younger than the sea," he replied as he realized explaining his actual numerical age to a child was pointless.

"How old is that?" Zack asked, proving Yuma right.

"Old enough to know better," Yuma replied. "Why are you here?" Yuma flipped the blunt end of the questioning around to face Zack.

"I don't know. After seeing that stuff in the tunnels, I know that maybe I'm supposed to be here. But that makes no sense, just bad feelings and confusing pictures," Zack confessed.

"You survived passage through the Mirrors of the Soul and crossed through the fields of Blue Lava unharmed?" Yuma turned to Harley, impressed, and Harley barked in the affirmative. "The blue flames didn't burn you?"

"No. It's not even hot, really."

The shaman in Yuma grew more intrigued than ever,

but he still couldn't consider this child anything more than an unexpected drain in this time of great military need. This must be a sick practical joke visited on him by the Elders as some kind of loyalty test.

He grew angrier as desperation flared inside his warrior's chest, and he turned on the boy.

"Cheenoo, my best friend and one of the fiercest warriors that ever lived, was a giant who stood over eighteen feet tall. He was so fierce and fast he could sprint across the prairies and scoop up buffalos in the middle of a stampede, two at a time, and carry them away under each arm for a snack! What can you do to equal that, boy?"

"Nothing."

"Exactly."

Harley let out a short, attention-grabbing snort and twitched his eyebrows toward the open window.

Yuma followed the dog's gaze outside and realized a legendary mountaintop was now missing.

"Yes. I see your point, Harley." Yuma replied.

The child's unexpected arrival has already permanently altered the physical landscape of the Sacred Forest. What other damage might he do?

"Point taken." The impressed giant softened his tone, not letting his nerves fuel his instincts about the boy's miraculous appearance.

"Do you remember sending out that Lucid Pulse?" Yuma leaned in for a closer glimpse at the truth.

"No? What's that?"

"Of course not," he turned to Harley to scoff. "I did not think so."

"Wait. Was that when I passed out?"

Zack remembered the snarling pack of Creeps and their savage attacks upon Harley.

He knew that protective power was inside him. He had only triggered it a few times before.

Zack didn't know what it was when he first felt its

244

authority. He just nicknamed it the Thing.

It was that Thing continuously buzzing around inside his head—simmering just below the surface of his everyday life like an acute case of tinnitus that seemed to cause all his troubles with people.

I had to save Harley's life! He rationalized. *I had to use it.*

Like when I flipped the school bus over at Briscoe, he remembered. *I didn't know I could even do that until I tried it that night!*

Then the Mall Thing happened accidentally and...

As Yuma watched, Zack's inner dialogue swept across the boy's face like a summer storm, and the Time Warrior discovered the answers he had been searching for but never expected.

"You don't answer, but your eyes confirm everything," Yuma replied. "That extra push of feeling came directly from you? You are certain?"

"It was so bright for a second. Then, there was a silent explosion in my brain." Zack remembered the exact moment of detonation, saving Harley.

"You blew an entire mountaintop off, son," Yuma said in astonishment.

"Oh. Sorry, Yuma. But those Creeps were killing Harley, and I could never let that happen," Zack said. "No way. I'd blow up a thousand mountains for him if I had to."

Yuma knew Zack meant it, and the thought frightened him.

Zack harbored no further ill will against the nasty Creeps, but he was unapologetic about the outcome of their fatal encounter.

"I'd do anything to save Harley."

Yuma grinned and leaned back, taking the dangerous boy in and somewhat satisfied that at least he had a new weapon to call upon in his arsenal.

"Fine. It appears there might be the healthy seed of a warrior in you yet. Well, we will waste no more time teaching you about loyalty then. Agreed?"

Zack nodded.

"Good. One less thing to worry about."

Yuma liked this strange child—something was captivating about his good nature mixed with such rarified abilities.

And what other superpowers could he possess?

"Where's Archie? Archie!" Zack called out as if startled out of a dream. He glanced around, unsure what had happened to his invisible friend after the mountain blew up.

"Archie?" Yuma asked, confused. "There are only you and Harley? Was there someone else with you?"

"Yes. Archie. He's about my age, and he gave me Harley, and then he gave me some lightning bugs in some jars. He showed me how to get through the Cave of Whispers with Harley, and he helped us escape the Creeps and the Blue Lava and get me here safely. Well, most of the way..." Zack felt confused about everything.

"No, son. There is no other boy. I sent Harley alone to fetch my reinforcements and bring them back here. Giants. Or another Time Warrior like me. And all he delivered after all that planning and hoping...."

"Was me." Zack finished his sentence. "Sorry."

"There is no reason to apologize, son. Harley is the heart and soul of my pack, and I trust his instincts in all things strategic and of the heart implicitly. Under his watch, no one has ever trespassed on these sacred shores without his permission."

"Really?"

"Only giants... until now."

-CHAPTER 26-

Guess Who's Coming For Dinner?

Zack's Lucid Pulse destroyed the Top Shelf Mine with a brilliant disc of concentrated energy intense enough to radiate across Eel Lake as fast as a supersonic thought could fly.

The rancid cat-of-nine-tails, growing along the polluted southern shoreline, bowed in reverence as the shimmering life force sailed through their slender reeds, nourishing them in its passing and leaving them greener and healthier from the unexpected sustenance.

But the unfortunate beings existing inside Dark Hollows were another story, as the concentric rings of pure mental energy tore through the evil township with such tremendous abandon that its bright collisions with any resistance caused the immediate collapse of the opposing force. Zack's powerful pulse drove the residents onto their knees, squirming in agony as they curled into a ball against the savage auditory assault.

For those living on the dark side of the light spectrum, a Lucid Pulse as unadulterated as Zack's produced a cosmic shriek so acute that it sliced through their corrupted bodies like razor-sharp fingernails scraping across the chalkboard of their lifeless souls.

Kate, Jesse, and Coop couldn't believe their eyes as the terrified citizens collapsed all over town, wailing in pain and terror—while the outbound teens felt nothing. But then the slower sonic boom exploded, and they fell to their knees in shock.

"What the...?"

The confused teens ran back down the dirt road toward town, ready to help in the emergency, only to witness something even more disturbing. Everyone stood up and pointed across the lake, screaming as if Godzilla were swimming ashore.

"It's Yuma!"

"Run for your lives!"

"The headhunter's attacking again!"

The astonished orphans turned and gasped as a giant mushroom cloud of dirt and debris rained down on the far side of the lake, forming a perfect ballistic umbrella of destruction. Thousands of boulders the size of freight trains rained down into the calm lake waters, causing whitewater to explode into the sky in giant plumes.

Kate turned to Coop and Jess, shaken as the tenuous ground still trembling beneath their feet.

"Zack's over there somewhere. I can feel it," Kate said.

"What do we do? How can we get over there now?" Coop didn't have a simple answer.

"Let's find Pepper. She'll know." Jesse suggested.

The three confused teens rushed back into town and ran up the circular driveway. Finding the front door of the Children's Home locked, they all began pounding on the front door.

"Pepper? Pepper? Let us in!"

"Hold your darn horses." Came back the old woman's salty response.

It was several minutes before the front door creaked open, and a badly shaken Pepper Wixx peeked outside.

"What, what just happened?" Pepper saw the billowing dust clouds still raining acres of earth into the lake.

She turned on the Knack to face the frightened children, but she was keenly aware of the source of that horrible sound.

A giant's Lucid Pulse. No natural explosion in nature can reproduce such horrid feelings of dread. Not even the thunder.

"We think something must have trapped Zack over there, Pepper. We've got to find him," Kate pleaded.

"Let's gather a search party?" Coop said.

"Get in here, quick." Pepper gestured and bolted the door behind them. "It could be another natural gas leak!"

Once indoors, Kate, Jess, and Coop heard the staccato of hammering coming from somewhere upstairs.

"You have new orphans? I thought you were staying empty," Kate said.

"No. That's just silly. Shelby is cleaning up another mess she caused." Pepper spun the teens into her office as she yelled upstairs to her stepdaughter.

"Shelby! Quit it! Now!"

"Mother! For once, just let me finish something I start!" came back her irritated reply, followed by a few more passive-aggressive hammer bangs.

They heard the click of an energized solenoid inside the wall. Then the tiny residential elevator inside the multi-story Children's Home descended to the ground floor behind them and opened, revealing Shelby leaning against the wall inside and clutching a pink, bedazzled hammer. She seemed startled by the sight of the children.

"You could have said something, Mother."

"You watch that attitude, young lady. Now, call the sheriff, and inform him we have a lost orphan boy over by the mine explosion. Probably another gas leak. Have him send out a search party immediately."

"I need to go, too. I need to be with them when they search. Zack's a special little guy. But he's frightened. If he's too scared or wounded and hiding, I know he'll come out for me before any strangers," Kate said.

"Nonsense. That damaged child's not worth a dime more of your time, girl. You don't need another burden in your young life. You two pretties can still fetch a nice profit from a fine family. If you just follow my professional advice and keep your big mouths shut for a second," Pepper promised.

Kate exploded. "He's just a little boy, and he needs our help! What's wrong with you, lady?"

"Oh, much more than you could ever handle, dumpling," Pepper hissed back. "Now, get the others back here. You will all be staying here at the orphanage from now on instead of at my lodge. And all house rules apply now that you are officially under my care. Nothing is going to spoil my special day tomorrow."

Pepper leaned in for emphasis with her Knack cranked up to the full blast. "Understood?"

The old woman looked down and rubber-stamped two more forms in front of her, and slammed the files shut.

"Now, round up the others and get them back here to safety. Then upstairs to the second floor so Shelby can assign your beds. We'll contact law enforcement about the missing boy, and that'll be enough of that."

Kate noticed a small, muffled mewling drifting down from upstairs somewhere.

"What's that? Do you have cats?"

"Don't hesitate. Move! Who knows how many more explosions will come our way this time? Every mine is interconnected!"

Kate, Jesse, and Coop didn't need another invitation to leave, and they raced out the front door.

"You guys get the others back here," Kate ordered as she kept running.

"Where are you going?" Coop called.

"After Zack. That way."

Jesse jumped in. "Coop, help her. You two find Zack. I'll get the others back here. Then I'm going to poke around and see what's really going on around here when they don't think we're looking!"

Kate looked back and saw that Coop was still chasing after her, and it didn't make her sad.

"I'm sorry, Coop. You were right all along. Something stinks about this place, and it isn't just the foul air. It's all the lies!" She called back.

"Slow down! Wait! This is way too dangerous, Kate, don't you think? There could be toxic fumes still lingering over there!"

"Then stay behind, alright? No harm. But I don't believe another word that old witch says anymore!" Kate continued running.

"Well, see. I told you! Damn it! Neither do I! I never believed that old biddy!" Coop chased after Kate.

Could my life get any weirder? Coop stifled that thought, not fancying the answer that might come back to bite him.

Kate found Pavarty and Lennon as she sprinted past them. She ordered them back to Pepper's and told them to stay put. Then Coop spotted Josh and Emiliano as he ran past.

They were taking a break from snooping around the off-limits mill again like a couple of bored house detectives. And although both nerds had witnessed the massive explosion and the dramatic aftermath, they weren't concerned enough to give up their newfound freedom until Coop convinced them.

Back at the orphanage, Jesse started spying on the odd town across the railroad tracks from the concealment of the surrounding hedges when Pavarty and Lennon came running back down the old road.

Jesse pulled both giggling girls into the bushes just as the front door to the Children's Home opened, and they watched Pepper and Shelby arguing with each other as they exited.

Jess pulled her friends deeper into hiding as Pepper climbed into her waiting Rolls Royce after barking a few more orders, and Shelby limped back inside in a huff and slammed the front door.

They watched as the limo drove down the circular driveway toward them without noticing their prying eyes.

But as the Phantom slid past, they all caught a brief glimpse inside, and it looked like Pepper was levitating something dark but shiny over the palm of her gloved hand.

"I saw that in my dreams last night?" Jess whispered.

"Me too," Pav replied.

"Me three." Lennon nodded.

Jesse gestured for Pav and Lennon to remain silent as they snuck back up the driveway and onto the covered front porch.

Unknown to everyone else, Tim and Ozzy were sneaking around next door, trying to steal some of the old crone's secret herbs and sauces.

They stumbled upon what looked like a medicinal root cellar buried in the backyard of Pepper's lodge. It sat beside an enormous wishing well that separated her B&B from the Children's Home next door with all its swing sets and hammocks. A wall of vines smothered the crooked, tiny outbuilding like everything else it murdered in town.

The tilted roundhouse looked like someone had pounded it into the ground like a stake—plucked from another time and place and transplanted on a whim.

After a quick fidget with a pilfered butter knife, the old lock guarding the secrets of the root cellar yielded. It clicked open without resistance on Tim's command, and the rusty chains slid away.

"What can I say? I am the master of some serious skills, kid!" Tim shrugged as he nudged Ozzy aside to cross the dark threshold first.

Once inside the brick structure, they found an irregular stone stairwell that corkscrewed counterclockwise deep underground in an ever-tightening spiral.

"Stairway to heaven!" Tim rubbed his hands together in anticipation as they started down.

"Think you might have that backward, son?" Oz disagreed.

Jesse, Pavarty, and Lennon opened the orphanage door

and stepped inside. Shelby had stripped the messy beds and removed several bunks from the lower level.

They saw Shelby hunched over her desk and working the rubber stamps like a percussionist. She appeared frail and worn for such a young woman, and she glanced up bleary-eyed as the girls tip-toed in.

"Good. Come here. I've been up all night working on your cases. I'm just getting your paperwork in proper order."

"We don't have any paperwork."

"I sure don't."

"Don't worry. You do now... uh, Donna." Shelby handed Pav a piece of paper.

"Donna?"

"Now, get upstairs with the three of you. Your new clothes are lying on your assigned beds upstairs for you to try on for your pictures in the online catalog."

"Donna? Who's Donna? And what catalog?" Pavarty questioned.

"That's your new name. Get used to it. You all want to be stars, don't you? Stars change their real names all the time to increase their image," she teased. "And the catalog is the newest edition of our exclusive Stork to the Stars Adoption campaign."

"Really?"

"Second floor with you rejects now. I stenciled your new names above your beds so you can learn them," Shelby said, handing out more paperwork. "Memorize them because the old you's don't exist anymore."

The girls nodded and silently crept up the carpeted stairway like they were walking into an ambush, as every survivor instinct they'd gained in incarceration went onto full alert.

When the girls got up to the second landing, they discovered the entire second level was a single open squad bay full of children's bunk beds lining both walls from one end to the other and a double set of lockers down the middle.

"How many orphans does Pepper have?" Lennon asked.

"This place smells like a bus station," Jesse observed.

"Well, however many, it doesn't look like they stick around for very long. So that's one positive sign!" Pav allowed herself to feel 'glass-half-full,' optimistic about her adoption chances for once.

Shelby had made every bunk bed herself, and tiny animal decals adorned the headboards as seen in the celebrity portraits downstairs. Whoever painted these walls only pink or blue didn't seem to grasp the reality of the actual world of Umans at all.

As Jesse walked into the silent dorm, she felt a chill breath blow against the back of her neck. She reached to find it damp and thought her friends had caused it somehow, but Pav and Lennon stood several bunks away.

The slight wisp of air sent shivers down her spine on a hot day, and she checked her assigned space for the source of the cold draft.

When Jess caught sight of the large bay window that dominated the upstairs room, she saw it was shut tight. Except for a single tiny handprint smudging the surface of the clear glass, the view of the lake outside was unparalleled.

"Get real, people. Just look at this knock-off Gucci they expect me to wear," Pavarty howled. "Are they serious or just ignorant? I can't wear this thrift-store garbage. I've got a reputation to uphold," she protested. "Don't they understand pictures last forever online?"

Jesse picked up the pale green shift for the pictures and smirked at the odd choice as she held it before her.

These are definitely Shelby's hand-me-downs," Jesse cracked. But when she lowered the dress, she gasped.

Hundreds of squirming handprints smeared the clean bay window, where only seconds before, there was only one.

"Hey, girls. Hey, look. Is this just a trick of the light?" Jess pointed.

More and more dewy handprints began pressing

themselves up against the glass as Jess backed away in quiet horror, and the desperate squeaks intensified, pounding and rattling the entire building.

But Pavarty and Lennon didn't react. They didn't seem to see or hear anything.

Am I going nuts?

"Look at me!" Lennon chirped as she twirled around in her new dress, but she paused in front of a large purple door bristling with crude nails at the room's far end.

"Why is this pretty door hammered shut like this?" she quizzed the older girls.

Ozzy crept downstairs behind Tim, fearing he could be stuck inside this confining root cellar alone. He was happy to follow. Someone had built this diminishing nightmare to induce claustrophobia—while still allowing passage to this underworld.

Is this worth it? They both thought as the funnel narrowed.

A slight disturbance echoed up from somewhere below. It was hard to tell what made it.

"Was that the wind? Listen?"

"I didn't hear nothing."

"There it is again!"

Tim stopped short, and Oz bumped into him.

"What? Why'd you stop?"

Tim pointed to a pale light flickering far below.

"Let's go if we're going, brother. Otherwise, I'm gone like the wind." Oz pushed.

"Shhh!" Tim demanded silence, and the muffled cries responded to his echoes.

"What is that?" Oz squirmed as the tiny moans grew even more agonized.

Tim reached to his waistband to reassure himself that Petty's revolver was still aboard. Once satisfied, he continued descending the spiraling stairwell, with Ozzy close behind as they dropped towards a trembling light.

Emiliano and Josh flipped bones together in the dirt from a discarded pile they found by the mill. Each teenager's methodical mind searched for any hidden architecture.

"We should really get back, amigo. Coop seemed serious. And if he's scared, I'm petrified." Emiliano stood up.

"Why would so many animal bones be next to a grain mill?" Josh asked, assembling bits and pieces with methodical precision. "Lots of forests here. Do hunters use the grain to lure deer in, maybe?"

"Fee-Fi-Fo-Fum..." Emiliano answered.

"What's that? Fum what?" Josh cocked his head, not sure of the cultural reference.

"I smell the blood of an Englishman..." Emiliano continued. "Be they alive... or be they dead... I'll grind their bones to make my bread! 'Jack and the Beanstalk.'"

Josh sat still for a second.

"Can anyone make bread out of human bones?" Josh asked.

"Why do you say that?"

"Because if you ask me? This looks like a human skeleton," he responded. Only then could they both see the complete outline of the creature they had reassembled and Josh jumped to his feet.

Kate and Coop continued working their way around the shores of the lake in their search for Zack, calling out his name periodically.

"Zack! Zack!"

"How far away are we now from where that explosion went off? What do you think? Another mile?"

It was almost impossible to gauge the distance and location inside the towering green forest

"I don't think more than a mile, maybe two? It's so dense in here it's hard to tell. But it was up here around the red bluffs,

256

for sure," Coop said as they pushed on.

The geography of the land kept dictating where they could travel until they hit the impassable lakeshore cliffs.

"Should we keep going or head back?" Coop asked, no longer spotting any obvious path forward.

Kate spun on him.

"Of course, we go on!"

Her intensity shook him.

"I didn't mean to give up."

"What are you even doing here?"

"What? Trying to help find Zack, just like you!"

"Why? What do you want from him? From me?"

"What? Nothing."

Kate knew by his startled reaction that she had lived up to her surname again, and she tried to calm herself. She could see that Coop was off balance and uncharacteristically leery.

"What do you believe in?"

"Huh?"

"Down deep. What do you truly believe in?"

Coop hesitated to answer such a personal question. Instead, he struggled to find the proper response, even for himself.

It feels like I'm walking into an ambush.

"Ah. Look, if I knew I was going to take a test today, I would have studied a lot harder, alright? Can I get back to you on that point later? After I've thought about it a bit, so I don't sound as ridiculously full of B.S. as I already think I am?"

Kate stifled a short nose snort, and Coop startled at the funny nose fart and relaxed.

"Bless you!" he chuckled.

Kate smiled.

"Let's go this way, knucklehead." She didn't suggest as she recomposed herself and stepped off.

"Oh, now I'm guilty of being an admitted knucklehead, huh? Works out perfect for you."

Kate laughed out loud this time.

They traveled north through the mists together until they stumbled upon the two forbidding pyramids of blood-stained dog collars straddling the trail.

"Who? Who on earth could ever do such an evil, twisted thing? Is it that crazy hermit Pepper was warning us about?"

"This might not be the work of one hermit, Kate," Coop nodded back towards Dark Hollows.

"Not to be crude, but there's an entire town of dog haters right back that way that might mark their territory with their hind legs hiked up right here. I wouldn't be surprised."

"We have to find Zack right now. Even that monster dog of his isn't safe over here." Kate grew more determined.

They continued hiking north along the animal trail, which brought them into the deep recesses of the redwood forest when they stopped short. Blocking their progress sat the Cave of Whispers, with its perpetual swirls of smoke wafting out of its gaping maw.

Coop spotted Zack and Harley's footprints in the mud everywhere, heading in and out of the intimidating cavern several times.

"These are fresh. He's been in there and back out," Coop stood and pointed. "It looks like he and that dog had quite a dance party here. In and out."

"Listen? What's that?"

Kate stretched out her hearing and took a few steps closer, following the sound to the yawning caverns.

There was a faint whispering coming from somewhere inside.

"Zack! Hello!"

Coop stepped into the vast cavern and gave a loud whistle, and immediately a cyclone of vampire bats attacked them as one entity. They both screamed inside the sudden tornado of bat flesh and bolted back down the trail in a panic.

"Run! Run! They're vampire bats! Run!"

Jesse used her unique cat-shaped hairpin to pry out the last nail in the purple door.

It was reassuring to hear the busy staccato of Shelby's rubber stamps echoing downstairs, which meant she was still occupied while they snooped around.

The uncooperative door stuck along the painted frame and complained loudly when jerked open.

"Shhh!"

The purple portal swung open to reveal a hidden stairwell connecting the home's second and third floors. There was a small landing off to the side of the staff elevator that both mother and daughter used daily.

Jess heard a sudden scurry of movement behind the doors at the top of the dark stairway.

The purple doors had 'Silence is Golden' scribbled all over them in many small hands.

"Is Shelby still busy?" Jesse asked over her shoulder, concerned, as Pav checked and then ran back.

"Still drumming away solo. You go, girl. We got your back."

Jesse swallowed a gulp of air and stepped up onto the creaking stairway. She spotted flickers of shadows moving underneath the double doors as she advanced. When she reached the top, she also found these doors hammered shut.

Shelby's been busy with her pretty little pink hammer, Jesse thought as she pulled out her trusty hairpin again.

Tim and Ozzy took one last step down from the spiral stairway, where they discovered themselves inside a small, circular vaulted room. It was thirty feet around, buried sixty feet underground, and lit by a single brutish candle that flickered for its life in the corner.

In the center of the chamber sat a circle of abandoned baby highchairs.—over a dozen brands spanning the decades since its nineteenth-century invention.

An enormous ball of twine and scissors sat discarded off to one side as if recently in use. Except for the flickering candlelight, there were no other signs of life at the bottom of the pit.

Someone had bolted three iron signs along the walls. They all read the exact phrase repeated above in her Children's Home- 'Shhh! Silence is Golden.'

But it was the yellow warning signs that gave both boys instant gooseflesh.

'Iron Clad Rule Number 13," It read. 'All Tongues Must Be Tied Down To Lower Jawbone Before Final Abandonment!'

That bone-chilling message put the ball of twine and scissors into a new context. Especially when followed by Iron Clad Rule Number 14- "Make Every Last Wish End At The Wishing Well."

"What the hell's been going on down here?" Tim felt ill.

"Exactly that, brother."

That's when they heard the first small whimpers coming to life inside the frightening pit—but there was no one else alive inside this circular torture chamber but them.

"Look." Oz pointed.

They watched as a highchair began bucking back and forth like a toddler was still onboard. And then the chair beside it followed suit. Highchair after highchair began trembling and rocking back and forth, with the sounds of screaming, horrified babies filling the chamber. Their tortured wails chased Tim and Ozzy back up the stairs, with their hair standing up on end as the entire root cellar began auguring itself even deeper underground.

"Ahhhhh!"

"Up! Up!"

They ran up the crumbling stairway and dove out of the sinking structure just before the doorway splintered and disappeared below ground as the earth swallowed it whole.

Tim and Oz never stopped running as they swept past the haunted wishing well, where hundreds of lost spirits spewed out of the dank portal, seeking revenge, and the empty swing sets danced madly with the newest batch of spirits aboard.

Still upstairs inside the Children's Home, Jesse wrenched the last nail out of the last door. It swung open as Pavarty and Lennon stepped up the stairs onto the landing behind her to peer in.

Once inside the dark room, the girls froze at what they saw, cowering from them in the darkness.

"What is that?"

"What's moving over there?"

Timidly, a dozen small children of differing species began crawling out of the shadows toward them, exposing their otherworldliness and their apparent injuries, and other physical disadvantages in their distinct ways.

"Those monsters!" Jess hissed.

"No! They're just children," Pavarty corrected. "Babies."

"Not them! I meant Wixx and her ugly daughter!"

"You mean ugly stepdaughter, don't ya!" Shelby screeched behind them before yanking them all away from the door. It caused an avalanche as everyone tumbled down the stairway backward, landing in a heap at the bottom.

"Get back here! You're all mine!" Shelby raged as she clawed, trying to rise from the tangle. "My mother promised me!"

But the young girls shot back to their feet faster than Shelby could.

They dashed out the orphanage's front door just as Tim and Ozzy came out of hiding from the haunted backyard.

And that's when Emiliano and Josh came sprinting down the lakeside road, followed by a still-screaming Kate and Coop.

When they all collided in the middle of the street.

"Vampire bats! There are vampire bats!"

"These monsters are starving kids!"

"They're killing babies!"

"It's a town full of cannibals!"

Shelby stumbled out the front door, more broken than ever, shrieking in an overpowering dimensional voice.

"Stop them! Seize these Umans! They're mine!" she struggled to free a broken wand from her sweater pocket.

They spun at the roar of Pepper's Rolls Royce speeding towards them, with a mob of angry locals following close behind. The cornered teenagers formed a defensive circle in the middle of the street, not knowing what direction to run now.

Beaumont slid the Rolls to a stop, and Pepper Wixx stepped out from the rear of the moving car before it stopped— like the true Queen of the Damned, she was born to be.

Pepper hijacked their Uman emotions with just a single twirl of her cane—unleashing her most potent dose of the Knack yet and freezing them as if trapped in ice.

"Well, well, look who it is. Who wants to know what's on the dinner menu for tonight?"

The frozen teens tried to scream.

"We do! We do!" the angry crowd roared back.

That's when the Briscoe Ten got their first clear sight of the monsters who built Dark Hollows—and unsurprisingly—it wasn't good news.

-CHAPTER 27-

Inklings

The giant used his animated gizmo-goggles to peer deeper into the depths of Zack's eyes, searching for the source of their amazing capabilities.

"What do you see inside?" Zack whispered.

"Stars, boy. Stars."

Yuma took the boy's face and turned it gently from side to side, measuring the different light spectrums emitted from his wondrous orbs.

"The question is... what do you see?"

Yuma flicked his head back, and the goggles snapped to rest on his forehead.

"Everything," Zack shrugged.

"So... you can see these tiny Inklings hovering around your face wearing no specialized lenses? Every day? All the time?"

Zack nodded.

"The doctors all say I'm crazy. But they use different words they don't think I understand."

"I have never seen so many Inklings gathered in one place before. And they seem so much brighter around you," Yuma replied.

"Inklings? Do they actually have a name?" That idea stunned Zack.

"Well, not formally. I informally named these invisible phenomena Inklings eons ago. Just a nickname for a thing I had an inkling about but had never seen. I considered calling them Wonderments or Whimzees, but I have grown fond of Inklings.

"I see lots of... Inklings."

"Then it is official. Inklings they are. I am the one who discovered them; therefore, I believe I inherit the right to name them."

"I don't think you discovered anything, Yuma. I think they discovered you," Zack grinned, and the old man knew the boy was just about right.

"Do you know what they are? I often cannot find even one with my lenses and never in proper focus."

Yuma marveled at the hazy, unseen cloud of visual phenomena flittering around the boy's head.

Living Lights.

Yuma realized that Mother Earth was constantly creating unknown life forms that humans had no reason to know anything about. Distinct species only alluded to in a host of obscure ancient writings with vague hints leading to more unsolvable riddles.

"So, you can confirm that more of these Inklings exist?"

"Are you kidding? The skies are full of Inklings. Flocks of them. Night and day."

The promise of the boy's visual perception staggered the giant's imagination.

"Am I fooling myself by listening to you, child? Are you trying to trick me with more witchcraft sent from Wixx and her cronies?"

"Nope," Zack answered honestly.

Is this how the universe works at this new level of hyper-reality? Yuma thought. *Have we entered the new phase already? Have I missed vital signs in my ignorance?*

Yuma suddenly stood and sprinted out of the room.

"Are they as alive as we are!" Yuma yelled back as the startled child and dog gave chase through the thundering hallways.

"Yes!" Zack yelled. "They are! Nobody else can see them

but you and me, I guess!"

"That makes us part of a unique tribe, boy!" Yuma replied, followed by a hearty laugh as he swept into his Library of Lost Knowledge, and the lights snapped on among the endless stacks.

He re-located the interlocking crystal and jade tablets he had been studying earlier on the reading table.

Zack took a moment to catch his breath and gazed in wonder at this endless library, marveling at its scope and complexity.

"So many words," Zack said.

"Ah! So many open minds!" Yuma corrected. "So much knowledge.

Whether the texts or pictographs had been recorded on papyrus or typed online, analog or digital, Yuma had compiled every lost, treasured fragment of humankind's most precious thought over endless lifespans in search of his own personal illumination.

How long had Yuma lived here? Zack thought, looking around. *Over a hundred years? More?*

That's when Zack noticed the soft blue light flickering underneath a doorway down a connecting hallway.

"Here it is. I found it," Yuma whispered, breaking Zack's spell by pointing to the invisible text.

The boy noticed tears were now streaming down the giant's chiseled cheeks.

"The Wait... the Earn... the See... the Be," Yuma read reverently.

"What's the matter, Yuma?" Zack asked. "Are you really sad I'm here?"

"No. Nothing like that boy. The opposite. Everything is precisely as it should be," he sniffed and turned to face the brave youngster.

"Tell me what our world looks like, son. Tell me everything in your own words. How do you see it?"

Zack didn't know how or where to begin. No one ever

seemed to understand.

After gazing out through the library's window for a quiet spell, he concentrated on the falling waters of the waterfall cascading behind them into the forest.

"I can see it all, Yuma. Everything and everyone all at once."

Now that Zack had finally discovered someone willing to listen to him, how could he hope to explain it so that Yuma could fully understand?

"I would imagine seeing everything all at once can be more of a curse than a blessing," the giant said.

"I know. And I'm not sure if you really want to know the whole truth, Yuma," Zack whispered. "Nobody does. It's like one of my doctors warned me. What I see... is enough to drive anyone... insane."

-CHAPTER 28-

The Beginning of Everything.

The Time Warrior burst back through the massive doors to his bedroom, enraged and in tears. He slammed them shut and rammed the hand-forged locks together, barricading himself inside.

He seethed with powerful new emotions and felt off balance. A child had just turned his entire world upside down, and the burden of the new knowledge sent his once confident mind reeling.

Was up the new down, just like at the Threshold? What am I to believe?

How is any of this possible?

How can any of these things he says be true?

His sophisticated mind raged against the illogical, unsettling information as he paced, backed, and forth, trying to cope with the impossible world the boy had just described in excruciating detail.

"I know other unspoken life forms exist. But nothing like this. No one could ever know all that he told me. No one should know all he sees. What kind of evil sorcery is this child bringing with him to the shores of the Sacred Forest? It's more... so much more than anyone has ever conceived of. Ever. His new knowledge will cause insanity and fear if even a fraction of what this boy says is true."

He gazed outside his window and beseeched the sky for any sense of enlightenment. And then he saw it—the overpowering reminder of the boy's frightening powers—a

267

missing mountaintop.

"Even I cannot do that. If a small portion of what he says is true, then he will change the physical nature of this planet forever," Yuma whispered.

Now the mighty giant was fearful of just what might lurk on the other side of the locked double doors.

Only a child?

Hardly.

Or a monster in disguise?

A disruptor sent to destroy the modern world as we've always known it.

Yuma feared that if this boy ever released his sacred knowledge upon an unsuspecting world—it would have devastating and unintended consequences that would reverberate forever.

World religions would topple from within at the explosive conundrums of the boy's new truths.

What would happen to the planet's fragile psyche when everyone realized invisible entities lived right beside them during every moment of their fragile lives? Inklings were present when they worked and slept and bathed, including every tender and private moment. The complete intellectual and emotional comprehension of such a staggering loss of privacy could stagger and drive any culture insane, especially the superstitious.

Yuma had witnessed thousands of great civilizations crumble over so much less.

Zackery Goodnight's fresh revelations about life on this planet threatened to topple the entire civilized world of all codified thought—like the fragile house of cards or reality represented in its constant state of blind ignorance to all else.

The price of Yuma's recent illumination had scalded his scholarly mind and clouded his usual clear thinking.

This boy. This single child could be the end... or the beginning... of everything.

And that makes him the most dangerous human being on

the planet! Became Yuma's first dreadful insight.

Maybe even more than Wixx.

Like her, he will forever redefine the world in his own making! Became Yuma's second dark revelation.

He realized that the boy's earth-shattering claims about the true nature at the heart of our reality would destroy the fear-filled humans all over the planet who still hadn't learned to live with their own kind yet, after millions of years, let alone the news of spirits from another dimension in their daily lives.

This child will bring about more chaos and division than any human before him and collapse the known world with his blistering insights.

He might even start World Wars—or bring about another Dark Age.

"Yuma?" Zack's small voice called out from the hallway. "Yuma?"

The giant turned towards the muffled voice as the boy tried to open the heavy oak doors from the outside.

"Yuma? Are you in there?"

The giant seized his battle lance, snapping the tip of its crystal blade up in front of him as Zack continued rattling the doors.

"Hey! Yuma!" the voice drifted down the hallway. "Yumaaaaaa!"

And then it dawned on the giant. His choice was as obvious as the deadly weapon clutched between his tattooed fists.

That's when Yuma came to the most chilling revelation of the day.

"I must sacrifice this innocent youngling to protect the Sacred Forest and the entire human race. Because if I do not... he might destroy us first."

-CHAPTER 29-

Necromantics

Pepper Wixx's subtle manipulation of the Knack held her struggling pawns in check like the terrifying chess master she was. No matter how they screamed, they couldn't escape her dark countermoves as the rabid mob surrounded them.

Here stood the actual monster called Pepper Wixx. She ensured all the children could see her clearly for the first time.

Tomorrow night, her cult of adoration would crown her Queen of the Damned, and immediately after, she'd hand-deliver death to the doorstep of the last giant on earth as her first formal act.

I know he hides the Calamity Stone there. I can feel it vibrating under my feet. And I will destroy everything and anyone to possess it.

Tomorrow night it all ends.

"Party over! Out of time!" Wixx chirped to the frozen teens when she snapped out of her reverie. She twirled the hypnotic crystal above her open palm, its tumbling reflections astounding the eye.

"You children don't have to rush off anywhere just yet, do you?" Pepper toyed as the dark crystal spun round and round. "You simply can't miss my party tomorrow night. Berk, Moody, seize them." Pepper snapped her fingers like a Queen.

Her sons parted the crowd of lowlifes, and that's when the paralyzed teens got a close-up view of the hulking grim brothers in broad daylight without their hats covering their hideous faces.

Berk and Moody were quite an imposing pair to behold, for sure. But a pair of what was hard to pin down.

Whenever ogres are mentioned in storybook legends, these two hideous man-like beasts fit the bill to perfection. To say they were misshapen and hairy in unusual ways would be an understatement. And standing at full height, both furry monsters towered over seven feet tall.

The growing mob laughed at the shivering children as they tore off their human disguises and revealed their true selves.

Oz puked and then swallowed, Lennon, screamed backward, and Coop slammed his eyes shut but couldn't keep them closed as they watched the town's physical transformation turn into a nightmare only fever dreams can induce.

Pepper leaned in closer and sniffed around as she surveyed each hostage.

"I am going to find a brand-new parent exactly as I promised. Pepper Wixx never lies. One pair for every single one of you. But... probably... just not the same species you might expect!" Pepper cackled. "Alright! Who wants to be adopted by a fluffy new Mama Troll? You get used to the smell after a few months!" Pepper teased the horrified orphans. "Or do you kids prefer the reptilians instead?"

Kate kept struggling against her invisible restraints, trying to speak. Her mouth wouldn't work, and any sound coming out fed back in amplified reverse.

"Please! You don't have to do this! - ¡siht od ot evah t'nod uoy esaelP"

"Oh, I realize that, darling. I've known that all along," Wixx cooed into her ear. "For centuries. It's just what I do, you see. It's just what I do." She kissed Kate's forehead and then licked it with her lizard's tongue, savoring the taste of her next meal.

"Ugh! - ¡hgU" Kate squealed.

"Tell your noisy friends this for me, child..."

271

Pepper leaned in and whispered.

The others watched as Kate's eyes fluttered at the disturbing information spewing from the old woman's mouth. Teardrops raced down Kate's cheeks, fleeing the promised horrors to come.

"I demand a seamless, silent surrender of your willpower, or else everyone dies right now! Easy Peasy." Wixx demanded with a kiss and a wink at the others.

That's when the captured teens heard the first encouraging sounds of rescue.

Ahhhh-Ooooooga!

That blast from the past ended Pepper's meticulously planned afternoon on a horrible note.

"You did not come here a full day early without informing me?" Pepper howled at the horn.

Ahhhh-Ooooooga!

"You did! You, horrible piece of...!"

Ahhhh-Ooooooga!

Pepper spied the phantom caravan materializing out of thin air like a fleet of elongated ghost ships.

"How dare you! We aren't close to being ready for you over-pampered fools!" Pepper panicked.

The impressive limousines uncloaked one by one, revealing a sinister custom design to every spirit vehicle snaking through the forest.

Ahhhh-Ooooooga! The lead limousine belched again.

It was such a tasteless, counterintuitive choice for a luxury vehicle. But down here, inside the dark, forbidding context of this spooky place—it sounded menacing.

Pepper knew who blew that sad clown horn.

"Henrietta Hoodwinker is pulling a snap inspection on me, that troll! This is an ambush set up by her and her cronies to snatch away my last chance at the crown. Jealous old hag," Pepper growled. Her face flushed as she realized her closest rival for the Royal Crown had outmaneuvered her again as they rolled closer into town, hoping to catch her adversary flatfooted.

Pepper's eyes rolled back into her skull, displaying only the veins of her whites peering out at the world.

She blinked twice at the traffic light that had hung lifeless in the middle of the intersection for fifty years.

HALT! The cobwebbed light screamed in big, fire-breathing 3D letters.

The railroad crossing gates dinged down over a set of tracks that didn't exist anymore, and the line of spectral limos slowed and stopped, waiting for a ghost train to roar past.

Wixx smiled, savoring this minute of triumph, and called out to her stepdaughter.

"Shelby! Run! Fetch me my burgundy gown. And the fascinator that goes with it! And don't forget the clutch and pumps! Fast like a bunny!"

"Yes, Mum," Shelby said and limped quickly back towards the house.

"No. That'll take too long, Crip! Berk! Give your stepsister a ride. You both know better than to waste my time with your silly disabilities. What's the matter with you two?"

Shelby threw herself up onto the back of her colossal brother as if she'd ridden him a thousand times before. Just like the night they rode out and discovered the missing orphans. Ogre racing and betting was a going sport down in the hollows.

She galloped her brother over, hopped onto the porch, and dashed inside. A few seconds later, they both galloped back to their stepmother—a fluttering crimson dress in hand as the ground quaked underfoot.

Pepper stepped back inside her Rolls and pulled down the privacy shades. She removed a worn leather pouch lined with ceremonial Native American beads from her purse. It contained a handful of Yuma's distinctive spirit crystals.

Thank you, monster Yuma. Just when I needed a better weapon, poof! You showed up in my life like a bad dream, looking for a fight.

Wixx rolled her eyes and chanted in a mystic tongue, Taub, and a soft explosion of light thumped to life within the car.

When Pepper Wixx stepped back out of her Rolls— Pepper Wixx didn't look like Pepper Wixx anymore.

Her physical appearance had changed radically in those few seconds, and her final transformation was stunning.

Instead of appearing as an aging, hulking serial killer, there now stood an elegant woman of taste who carried her centuries of life effortlessly on her squared shoulders. Dressed in flowing chiffon, she bejeweled like royalty from another dimension.

A fascinator with colorful bird plumes adorned her silky hair.

Pepper's eyes rolled to white again, and the phantom traffic light blinked from red to green, urging every vehicle-

GO! GO! GO!

The railroad gates dinged once, and as the striped boards rose, they crumpled into sawdust at the exertion, and the royal procession rolled over their ashes to meet their new Queen.

Kate and the others believed that their rescue was at hand. So many expensive cars were driving in; this had to be their salvation. The orphans kept motioning for help within the weakening embrace of Pepper's distracted spell.

But as the convoy drew closer, it became apparent to even the most optimistic among them that any hope of rescue was a mirage in this twisted land.

Every limousine carried a witch, goblin, or ghoul inside, including unnamed species no sane human could ever imagine.

The stretched-out hearses represented the finest examples of automotive witchcraft above or below ground in either fractured universe. This was a decadent display of old-world, gas-guzzling, money-to-burn—Concours D' Elegance style snobbery at its best.

And then Henrietta Hoodwinker emerged from the rear of her unique Bentley with the golden caskets.

Executive Director of the Royal Academy of Necromancers and ex-Queen of the Damned herself, several times over, Henrietta kept trying for a graceful exit—all awkward six-foot-nine of her. Her father, Adamus Hoodwinker, had founded this town and was the first Darksider to discover gold under the Bubble.

Today, Henrietta Hoodwinker, at over four hundred years old, still behaved like the royal-blooded princess she was born to be. Her stylists had dressed her from head-to-toe, in brilliant swirls of tangerine crepe that amplified every one of her awkward, bony movements.

"The gall to wear orange to my coronation," Pepper fumed. "Like wearing white to a wedding!"

"There you are!" Henrietta squinted as she gave Wixx and her hostages a proper double-take. "It appears we caught you in the middle of something quite unsavory, Pepper, darling. I see events have spiraled out of your control once again?" Henrietta gestured to the struggling children.

Like a true Hoodwinker, Henrietta struck like a cobra whenever she sensed weakness. She was bred to make this kind of tasteless commoner appear weak and stupid in front of the Royal Council's eyes—even though most now held Pepper Wixx in some regard as a recent war hero.

"No trouble is ever too big if you're not afraid to smudge your overdone makeup, darling!" Pepper hissed back.

Pepper regretted her insolent tone as it rippled through the other dignitaries. She refocused her Knack to squash any insipid spitefulness.

Remember—it is time to outshine—not outfight.

Not yet.

"That was a joke, Henrietta, darling!" Pepper purred. "Love, love, love the orange dress! Georgina, Willy, Gavin! El Rodrigo! Polonius! How wonderful to see all of you! And what a surprise!" she flattered. "You've brought everyone a full day early, I see. What a wicked surprise on me!"

"What is going on here?" Henrietta gestured again to the terrified Umans. The ogres held them high above their heads as the villagers genuflected in front of their royal court, like the serfs they were born to be.

"Them?" Pepper shot a malicious glare back over her shoulder, so concentrated that the intimidated teens froze.

She turned back to Henrietta and cleared her thoughts along with her throat.

"Haven't you heard, dear? Of course, you wouldn't have. It's a big surprise. I am holding a surprise raffle tomorrow night. These fine Uman specimens and a few more I've rounded up will be awarded as door prizes at the end of the party. And only for the price of a single crystal donated to my Children's Home Charity!"

"What a... novel idea."

The line of horror elite continued exiting their custom limos, revealing themselves in all their hideous, black-tie glory as the town filled up.

The pushy dignitary from Oosk Village forced his way in front of everyone else and bowed.

"Darling Pepper, I believe this is the most prestigious gathering of Necromancers in all the world. This is quite a record to set. And all to celebrate you and your well-deserved coronation, Pepper darling! You are our brave new national hero!"

"Why, thank you, Wink. I just did what any patriotic idiot shou..."

Pepper never finished—because that's when the first gunshot rang out.

-CHAPTER 30-

Staring Down a Giant

After searching the hallways for Yuma proved fruitless, Zack rediscovered the only hint of life inside this sprawling, underground structure: the massive library door with the flickering blue light spilling out underneath.

Zack planted himself in front of the glowing doorway with a moral dilemma.

Do I open it?

Or do I leave it alone?

He took a few deep breaths and reached out to test his resolve when Archie materialized, standing next to him.

"Whoa!" Zack jumped off balance, and Harley barked and bounded over to Zack. "You have to stop zapping in and out like that, Archie! You'll give us a heart attack."

"Pretty nifty trick, though, huh, pal?" Archie grinned back.

"Man."

"Better than a sideshow mermaid with three legs. I saw her once, you know?"

Zack refocused his interest on the door.

"Uh-uh. I wouldn't open that if I were you." Arch nodded at the handle, turning clockwise in Zack's hand.

Then the latch popped open.

Zack froze.

"Why wait? I think there's a secret inside here. I can feel it. Can't you? Why shouldn't I open it? It's not locked. Nobody's here to care."

Zack discovered the nerve to challenge someone's authority for the first time.

He had already broken the seal on the creaking door, and the electrifying mysteries buzzing inside beckoned him.

"It's simple, chum. You're a guest in someone else's home. And nobody gave you permission to open it." Archie admonished. "It would be vulgar to take advantage of that fact."

Zack thought about it for a moment before releasing the tension on the handle, and he pulled the door closed.

He turned, shaking his head at the quirky kid with the gap-toothed smile.

"Poof, here you go again! How do you even travel like that? In and out! In and out!" Zack demanded more information from the happy country boy.

"Just happens when I least expect it. This is all new to me, Zack. It seems I'm just zipping along for the ride, like you."

Archie darted around, emboldening Zack. It made Zack happy just to see him. He felt less alone, like having Harley by his side. He'd never been part of a team before.

"So, where are you zipping in from?" Zack asked.

"Anywhere and everywhere, but especially here because wherever I find myself, there I am... right here," Archie gestured. "And you, sir?"

Zack chuckled.

"The same, I guess. Nowhere. But where are you really from?" Zack insisted.

"These parts. Right around here," Archie nodded. "What about you?"

"I don't know. I don't have a place. The Briscoe Institute, I guess. No place like an actual home, I remember. But then... I find myself, and here I am... right here!" Zack giggled at his own joke, and Archie chuckled.

"Likewise."

"What's behind this door?" Zack quizzed, still intrigued by the shimmering lights dancing at their feet.

Archie stopped laughing and spun Zack away from the bright room.

"Grief. Nothing but sadness and grief," he promised.

Archie led Zack away into the hallway, where they startled at a colossal shadow looming across the wall.

Yuma was ready to slaughter Zack when he walked around the next corner. His crystal-tipped lance, Thunupa, shook in his fists as the frightened giant stood ready to strike within the next heartbeat, but the interior clash between his raging emotions blinded him to tears.

Why not?

Because I cannot kill an innocent child!" His enlightened mind challenged the darker voices.

"Run!" Archie screamed, and Zack launched down the hallway like he'd been training.

Harley collided with Yuma and ripped the crystal lance from the giant's hands before spitting it out like a discarded toothpick.

As he sprinted down the tunnel of hallways, Zack heard Harley mount a ferocious attack against his best friend. Zack didn't dare slow down. Instead, an intuitive blast of 'fight or flight' lifted his heels and moved him faster than he ever thought possible.

He sprinted down corridor after curving corridor until he stopped at the intersection of several grand hallways that met in one of the central hubs around the base of a mammoth indoor redwood.

"Which way leads out? I've been running in circles!"

Zack sprinted back to the room with the blue light flickering beneath the doorway, and he threw it open, hoping to find an exit for the outside world. But the dazzling wall of light blinded his sensitive eyes.

He found himself inside a tall, mirrored room as his sight adjusted to the shimmering lights, and he could see that the blue room wasn't an exit at all—but a living, multidimensional memorial to Yuma's deceased wife, Blue

Feather.

Her art and self-portraits adorned the gallery's illuminated walls, and a life-sized 3D hologram of Blue Feather rotated in perpetuity in the center of the magical space.

This was the eternal shrine that Yuma had dedicated to his beloved Blue Feather, and Zack understood now just how wrong it was for him to be here among these magical memories.

This was beyond a private place. He was the unwanted trespasser inside a sacred personal space.

The boy could hear the distant battle between man and beast still raging. And his heart sank once he listened to it and realized he must turn around and return to face the mad giant head-on himself.

That's why I am here. I saw my death on the walls. I don't die that way.

He couldn't leave Harley behind to fight the great Yuma alone.

I will never abandon him.

There must be something I can do to help.

Zack wiped away his tears and turned to face his worst fears head-on, just as he had done in the mines.

His walk back turned into a trot as his surroundings grew familiar again, and he ran towards the savage fight.

Zack returned to witness Harley the Magnificent run up the curving walls. The great battle-hound gained enough traction to launch himself straight at Yuma's elevated head.

The collision between man and beast was enormous, sending both crashing onto the floor, smashing every stick of elegant furniture in their way.

Harley caught sight of Zack and sprung to his feet before the enraged giant could rise, leaping in front of the frightened boy to defend him.

Zack held up the only weapon he could find out in front of him. He held an oversized whiskbroom clenched in his good hand, with his limp arm still tucked away in the rabbit sling.

Yuma leaped back to his feet and snarled with a giant's full fury, deafening the ear and physically rattling the art hanging along the halls.

Yuma had wounds ripped open, up and down his forearms and hands, with a severe gash slashed across his cheekbone—now bleeding from fang and claw.

Zack stood horrified by the sheer physical efficiency inflicted by the massive battle hound.

Will he ever turn on me?

I sure hope not. I'd disappear in one bite!

Harley was panting but ready for more action, even though many of his stitches had popped open—stitches sewn shut by Yuma only hours before.

"You show up to your first battle carrying a broomstick, boy? Are you planning on sweeping me under the rug of history like all the others?"

Yuma reached down to retrieve his abandoned lance, and Harley lurched forward, ready to attack once more, when the winded warrior threw up a protective hand and barked back in perfect dogspeak-

"Stop it! Enough! I yield! I understand!"

Harley idled his snarling as Yuma watched Zack step out of the shadows again. He shivered at the sight of the wounded legend but was still brave enough to face off against a giant holding nothing more deadly than a handful of straw.

The always dangerous Time Warrior couldn't help but stifle a snicker at the quixotic sight.

Harley growled as he took another step forward to cover Zack from any further attack. No one understood this warrior's strategic capabilities clearer than his best friend. And Harley knew from experience how quick and deadly Yuma could turn as he growled another warning to back off.

"Enough orders!" Yuma roared back in dogspeak.

A few more yips and barks between the old comrades followed, and their grumbling argument seemed to end at a draw, with both still uneasy and growling at each other under their breaths.

That's when Yuma turned his attention back to Zack, yet the boy wasn't sure he was ready to listen when his instincts still told him to run.

"After... a heated discussion... well... let us just say that if my friend Harley will fight me... as ferocious as that... to protect you... from me? Well, if I was a wiser man, I should think I should pause now, shouldn't I? Take a breath."

Zack didn't know what to think about anything at this point. Here was another 'first'—staring down a veritable giant in a life-and-death standoff.

"If I trust Harley with his big heart and pure soul, as truly I do... well, I must assume that means I must be wrong about you, as he insists."

Harley sighed and sat down—content and relaxed like Yuma had thrown a magic chill switch.

"Okay," Zack answered. He cringed as the First Nations giant towered over him.

"I am sorry, boy, for thinking of killing you. But you frightened me, so."

"Me? Why Yuma? How could I ever scare someone like you?"

Yuma paused before answering.

"Because by your very being..." the giant struggled to find the right words to communicate with the young boy. "I am not sure you will understand any of this yet, but if I am right, the next step in humanity's greatest evolutionary leap forward is standing right before me."

"What? What does that mean?"

"You are a brand-new kind of human being altogether, Zachery Goodnight. With you, the surprising winds of change blow strong, and a new door to the future of humankind flies open on your command."

Yuma allowed his mind to swoon with certainty.

"There will be those left behind in the storms to come,

desperately clinging to the flotsam of the past because of your fresh knowledge, your reality. Those who cannot and will never consent to see your vision of the world as it actually exists will be doomed. The doors to the mind you open will be an open portal between dimensions that can never be closed once all humans cross that new threshold with you." Yuma paused, pondering the sheer weight of his insights

"I have been waiting here for you, and only you, my entire lifetime. Centuries upon centuries. And I never realized that fact until this very moment. Harley has convinced an unsighted fool that a new wonder exists. I ask your forgiveness for being so wrong."

Yuma stepped forward, and Zack startled back before the warrior kneeled before the shaken boy.

Harley stepped up, licking his old friend's hands clean of blood as they watched his newest wounds self-heal as he spoke.

"I always knew, as a Time Warrior and Guardian of the Sacred Forest, that I was born to protect this secret world at all costs. For all of us. From all of us. I stand against greed and hatred and bigotry and hunger and waste. I have always understood that I was born to fight every battle as if it were the last to protect its sanctity. And for as long as it took," Yuma's voice lowered with powerful memories and emotions.

"My duty is to understand everything about what our world presents to us authentically from moment to moment and find the harmony we can achieve to make life better for all. To help guide humankind's wobbly destiny forward on this dying planet, along with the help of my scientific advancements, to propel us into the next cycle of reinvention among the cosmoses. But I never expected to be around long enough to participate in the great cosmic shift myself."

Yuma lowered his head.

"I kneel before no one. I never have. But I bow down to you, young master. I have much to learn from your open eyes. And the rest of the world must follow."

Yuma met Zack's piercing gaze.

"Enlighten me, young one. I am here to serve Mother Earth and you, Zackery Goodnight. I swear to you my undying allegiance. And coming from an Immortal, I hope you understand the gravity of that pledge."

Zack shared his smile.

All fear between them evaporated. It was like watching nightmares dissolve when the first rays of sunlight hit the Dreampool.

But a deadly quandary still lingered for this heroic new trio.

How could a solitary giant, a tiny orphan boy, and one amazing battle hound make a stand against the undeniable forces of Pepper Wixx gathering across the lake?

They were all about to figure it out.

-CHAPTER 31-

Fine Etiquette of the Damned

The first gunshot should have struck Henrietta Hoodwinker right in the middle of her crooked nose if firearms functioned underneath the protective Bubble.

The deadly slug would have punched a nasty hole through to the other side of Henrietta's plumed head at such close range.

But the bullet flattened immediately at the hammer strike, and the hot round tumbled harmlessly to the ground only inches from the .38's smoking barrel.

"They're all monsters!" Tim screamed as he swept the convoy, pointing Petty's revolver at the crowd.

Click. Boom! Thud!
Click. Boom! Thud!
Click. Boom! Thud!
Click. Boom! Thud!

Every round collided with the spellbound atmosphere, causing a series of overlapping ballistic ripples in the air as each deformed slug fell to the ground—now blunted like a handful of copper-tipped mushrooms.

Tim flipped. His fragile mind snapped at the sight of the hideous creatures—most dressed in formal attire and all pointing and laughing at him.

Why are they acting like I'm the crazy one?

A tuxedoed ghoul seized the struggling teen as this frightening new take on reality sent the other kids into a panic. They tore at the invisible strands of Pepper's magical spell and

285

screamed.

"*Help!*"

"*Please!*"

"*No!*"

Pepper grinned like a cobra and seized Tim by the throat with one hand.

"Guess who the star appetizer on the menu will be tonight, pumpkin?"

She conjured a blood-red crystal into her palm, and it sizzled and spat in the air between her fingertips. It had an angry, whirring electricity surrounding it. Tim screamed as the ragged jewel seared holes in his cheeks with its sparks.

"My first tip from a master chef, folks. Remember to prepare Umans properly for consumption. First, you must kill their brains before fileting them," Pepper bore down. "Otherwise, the fear can ruin the taste of the fresh meat. Makes it fishy."

Ah-Ooooga! That hideous car horn blared again, startling Pepper out of her high heels.

"What the...?"

Ah-*Ooooga!* it blatted again, demanding silence.

The mad commotion settled as the visitors and townspeople turned around to respect Henrietta Hoodwinker's wishes.

Ah-Ooooga! the horn insisted once more before Henrietta withdrew her hand from the car window.

Pepper scrambled back onto her heels. "What a foolish horn."

"Composure people," Henrietta commanded, a past QOTD herself and sole heir to the entire Hoodwinker fortune. She suffered no fools.

"Now, I insist you stop this maniacal behavior, Pepper. As Executive Director and President of the Royal Council of Necromancers, I am giving you a direct order to cease whatever nefarious illegalities you are engaged in immediately! We do not kill innocent Uman children like this."

"Oh, really? Since when, sis?" Pepper Wixx wasn't buying the standard PR line.

"Since right this instant! Unhand him now! We cannot afford to have the Upside police search for more of your abducted children. Things must change around here if we are to survive and prosper."

Tim was turning a sickly shade of blue as Pepper deprived his lungs of fresh oxygen.

"Relax, woman. 'Let's eat kids!' Or... 'let's eat, kids!' It's all just a matter of punctuation! Besides, no one's searching for anyone Upside. Their trail has vanished, and I've paved over any traces with a truckload of cash. So don't you worry about it, Henrietta. The authorities aren't looking for them anymore. No matter what you think. I'm just like you and your prestigious family—I am very good at what I do, or I wouldn't have gotten away with it this long, sweetheart."

"Indeed. A commoner to the end."

The kid's hopes sank after hearing her confession.

No one was coming to look for them any longer—not even the FBI.

They were on their own as Pepper Wixx continued to strangle Tim.

"Release that boy now," Henrietta commanded.

"Like this?" Wixx replied and opened her fist, and the boy crumpled to the ground like a rag doll.

"Pity on you, Pepper. See how your constant state of distemper misguides all your other fine accomplishments? It erases them. Now, we have one less pretty, pretty specimen of Uman boy for our big raffle tomorrow night. Pity, pity."

"Nonsense. He'll mend. If not, my vultures will finish him with no lingering evidence to worry about. If given a chance, my boys can clean up any mess in a snap!"

At that point, Pepper sensed she was losing respect among the snobbish crowd of royals clutching at their pearls.

What a bunch of murdering hypocritical fools! She thought.

Pepper switched emotional gears and dialed her Knack down to its most palatable settings. Now, any harsh words would be cloaked within the timbre of her voice and softened for public consumption.

"I am so sorry, Henrietta. Excuse me. You are so right. Forgive me and my tantrum, everyone. I was only trying to protect my prestigious new friends from any harm from this Uman scum. They carry such nasty germs these days, you know. Especially the teens. If we knew you were coming this early, we could have prepared our security and prevented this nastiness."

"Nonsense. A silly pop gun intimidates no one down here, Pepper. You know that. You simply overreacted, as you always do."

"Offended might be a better word to use, mother," Shelby threw out a much-needed lifeline from the crowd's edge.

"Yes. Exactly Shelby. Thank you, dear. I could never let such a blatant lack of proper manners by this offensive toad go unpunished."

"Read me correctly, Pepper. This is now the official proclamation of the Board. We will hear nothing more about the thrashing of Uman children down here. Now don't ruin what could be a significant reign for you, Pepper, dear, by being a simple contrarian."

There were a few titters among the aristocrats.

"Now excuse us, but I must call an emergency meeting of the Executive Council to ratify these additional measures. And then it will be the law, Pepper. You understand that?" she pointed a gloved finger down at the stricken Tim and raised a judgmental eyebrow.

"Wait? Where are you going, Henrietta? No hard feelings, dear. Isn't the Board staying with us again this year? I've held all of your reservations open," Pepper purred. "It's a tradition. And I've prepared everyone's favorites, like last time. I even have that spicy Bald Eagle-Eye stew you loved so much last year, Polonius!"

Henrietta struggled to maintain eye contact as she climbed back into her custom Bentley.

"You can't leave, Henrietta. You know how it works here, darling," Pepper tried to tease her back out. "Once you've checked in at Pepper's, you can never check back out!" she winked and giggled, trying to make a musical joke that didn't land.

"Oh no, I'm sorry, Pepper, darling. Not this year, I'm afraid. Different business commitments have come up within the board's new makeup to prevent it. We are staying at the revamped Regency this year. We hear their traditional British Wiccan tea service is life-changing over there," she praised Pepper's only competition in town.

"I would add this, Pepper. After looking around Dark Hollows, you and your subjects live up to your name here. The place looks dreadful. I expected the decorations would at least brighten up this dreary little town by now. Don't let everyone down, darling. The entire Darkside community will be here by tomorrow evening. We must maintain the proper pomp and circumstance for continuity in all things royal. You understand these age-old protocols and customs?"

"Indubitably."

"Well. Then rise to your best intentions, Wixx. Elevate your sense of class, and your reputation will soar among the underclass and the upper-class alike. You are about to become everyone's Queen of the Damned woman. Imagine? A lowly Taub elected as a Wiccan Queen? Now, who would have ever thought that possible?"

As the twisted limos pulled away, Pepper found herself abandoned in the middle of the street, still dressed to the nines, and surrounded only by locals.

"Well? You all heard the noble lady! Do whatever you have to do to make it happen! Get my hometown sparkling! It's time to celebrate my coronation before somebody tries to snatch it away!"

The crowd cheered as Pepper climbed back into her limo, and everyone scattered to follow her orders.

"What do we do with them, ma?" Berk held up the struggling teens.

Beaumont stopped the Rolls.

Pepper's eyes narrowed as she refocused on the squirming captives. She grimaced, pondering their fates, spinning her crystals.

"Let's light them up all pretty like in our catalog and put them out on full public display in those giant buzzard cages I bought online last year. Put them in their new clothes and hang them from the big tree in the park. Hang them just high enough that the fiends can't get their claws into them. Not yet anyway—not before the big raffle."

Pepper's mood elevated as she imagined the demented celebration in twenty-four hours.

"It's time to get this party started!"

-CHAPTER 32-

Follow Me!

Zip, Zash, and Zee zoomed past Yuma to take the lead down the circular stairway and into the menacing darkness that swallowed their party whole.

Like a trio of shimmering mini jets, all lit up and spoiling for a fight, they corkscrewed down the spiraling black steps, scouting for any signs of trouble lurking in the shadows ahead.

Giant, boy, and beast moved much more cautiously as the crumbling steps listed severely to one side and then to the other, like a stack of drunken pancakes.

Someone ruthless had constructed this spiraling stairwell with no handrails or light sources to make the endless descent into the darkness terrifying. In addition, the circular walls surrounding them were several yards away from the centered stairs to provide any kind of physical or moral support.

Pure crystals didn't exist within the solid stone matrix for Zack to use as a temporary light source, so they only had their wits, balance, and Yuma's medicine bag full of crystals for survival.

He handed the boy a clear crystal to use, and Zack smiled as the chiseled gemstone popped to life in his hand.

Harley cringed, as he couldn't help but remember the last time he witnessed that blinding power unleashed.

Yuma sensed his companion's concern and snatched the pulsing crystal back from the boy before it became explosive.

"Hey!"

"Maybe later, Zack. After practice. We need to keep this mountain on top of us for now," he winked.

Yuma's crystals didn't glow half as brightly as Zack's, but their soft inner light still helped them maintain balance in the pitch blackness—their wits—not so much. It was easy for the mind to lose balance first, with no reference points to guide the body forward. Even Yuma hated this vertigo-inducing part of the spellbinding journey down the stairway of death.

"Ahhhh!"

"Am I falling?"

"Is up, down? And down, up?"

"Am I falling up again?"

At points, Zack had to sit to navigate from one damaged step to the next on his bum to keep from toppling off.

This claustrophobic challenge was even worse for the enormous giant when considering the added dimensions of his height and stone-crushing weight.

They sighed in relief when they finally reached the shaft's bottom over an hour later and stepped off the last dilapidated step.

"We made it!" Zack spurted triumphantly.

"Far from it. Calm yourself. And steel yourself. We have not even begun the first part of our descent, boy," Yuma promised.

"Well, how far do we have to go down?"

"All the way."

Then, Zack noticed the dim light blooming from underneath a massive iron door that spanned the opposing wall.

Yuma reached over and pushed it open, and Zack stepped through and staggered back.

"Whaa?"

Instead of finding some dank cell reserved for the insane—Zack stood inside an underground cavern of staggering size instead.

The granite ceiling arched high above their heads as long shafts of sunlight helped tease out the cavern's epic dimensions for the eye.

"Oh, my!"

Zack stared in awe at the geological wonderland before him.

Birds from around the globe flew through the atmosphere inside Mother Nature's secret second sky.

With Zack's rare visual capabilities, this hidden world held even more secrets. He could see Inklings of every description drifting fluidly throughout the soft rivers of air down here, just as naturally as he could see everything else.

Their whimsical life forms coalesced in the atmosphere before him in dazzling displays of their gossamer-like existence while blessing the giant cathedral's interior with their presence.

Zoids, Red Spinners, Planktoids, Fast Movers, Tic Tacs, and even a few Bobokaffayz swam by.

"I ... I never dreamed a place like this could exist before."

Yuma smiled down at the purity of Zack's emotions.

"What do you call this place?"

"I do not. It calls me," Yuma answered.

Zack cocked his head.

"To name it would be to own it, and no one can ever own this."

The sense of tranquility was so pervasive in this magical space that it soothed the boy's overwrought feelings.

"Close your mouth," the giant chuckled. "Believe me. You have seen nothing yet." He promised. Yuma knew the mind-blowing discoveries still ahead for the boy as he prodded the child and dog along.

"Drink your fill here, Zack. This will be the last chance for pure water for a while," Yuma cautioned.

"A while? Where are we going now, Yuma?"

"Down."

"This is down. Aren't we already down? How far down do we have to go?"

"What you must ultimately witness... is much further on. Down that way."

Yuma pointed to an imposing thirty-foot, hand-forged iron cube that prevented all access to an overgrown mineshaft.

Whether the idea for constructing this colossal cage was to keep something in—or keep something out—wasn't apparent. But whoever created this formidable cage ensured it could do either job for millennia on end.

The formidable structure hunched over the pit's entrance like an iron sentry with its hand-forged bars hidden beneath the disguise of thick ivy walls. Yuma spun a combination of rusty cylinders around that performed a clunky dance between themselves mechanically before unlocking. A small side door popped open on the vine-covered cage.

It was only large enough for the twelve-foot-tall Yuma to kneel and squeeze through with some difficulty, but he could stand to full height once inside.

Zack and Harley walked in upright as Yuma reset the locks behind them, and the metal door creaked toward a close.

"From here on... there is no going back," Yuma said. "If you want to turn around, do so now, boy. Below is what I swore to protect for eternity. And this is what we must protect above all else. At all costs, or everything is lost and can never be achieved again."

Zack stared at Yuma and back at the closing door.

"I don't have a choice now. Do I?"

"Right at this moment, you still do. You know that. That is what I am telling you."

"Do I?"

Yuma knew the gauntlet this remarkable young boy was about to face.

The Wait... The Earn... The See... The Be.

Finally, he answered the child.

"No. You no longer have a choice. Not if you are who I believe you are."

The iron door slammed shut behind them and relocked.

Yuma pulled three oxygen masks out of a chest, with extra oxygen tanks and supplies.

"Put these on," he ordered as he strapped on his custom-made gas mask, the size of a laundry basket along with several extra tanks. The colossal face shield muffled his voice.

"Where we're going—we'll need air."

-CHAPTER 33-

Talking Party Decorations

The oak tree trembled as the ogre named Onyx finished hanging the last vulture's cage up in the middle of the town square—just across the street from Pepper Wixx's Children's Home.

Green ogres were known for being the bulkiest and meanest of their species. Still, they enjoyed following instructions, no matter how foul or hideous the deed was.

That last buzzard cage hung up inside the dead tree was Ozzy's. He was flapping inside like a terrified parrot as the monster climbed coolly around the outside, securing it.

Onyx looked like a nightmarish mishmash between a baboon and a lizard—making for one butt-ugly creature. Its purple tongue flicked in and out incessantly, always searching for juicy bugs or scraps of food.

Kate, Coop, and the others were dressed in their new clothes but still shocked by what they discovered inside their cages.

The oversized vulture cages were splattered with centuries of disgusting human remains. The freshest layer of goo was from a small rock and roll band coming out of Boston on a nationwide tour made up of a bunch of celebrity science fiction writers. They never made it home.

Oz couldn't cope with this horrifying hyper-reality.

"Help me," Ozzy whimpered as a discarded eyeball winked back up from the floor.

Their cages were lit with festival lights, each holding

a single trembling captive inside. Even more decorative lights were added by the fussiest ogres. Then creatures that could only be described as trolls swung up from under the bridges to help illuminate the new Uman raffle prizes the way they should be.

The traumatized children curled up inside their filthy birdcages and fell silent. No one dared make a sound inside this new reality. Even Ozzy was left in shock and speechless.

They watched in astonishment as every conceivable monster that ever stalked a nightmare came out of hiding and into plain view in a sudden gush of civic goodwill.

"Those fancy pants are a full day early!"

"Figures! Get me more lights! Lots more!"

When Kate hit emotional bottom and fell asleep, she was in familiar territory, like floating at the bottom of the Dreampool with her friends. But instead of panicking, she tapped down and shot back to the surface on the strength of her willpower alone.

She remembered her childhood pledge.

Survive! Anything!

She called out to the others.

"Wake up. Don't you guys give up? We're not done fighting back yet."

Kate made eye contact with each one as they lifted their heads. Her confidence encouraged them. They heard that rebellious spirit creep back into her voice again, and they turned to look up at her in awe.

"We will get ourselves out of this ungodly mess. All of us! Somehow. I promise you that!" Angry tears gathered, and Kate set her jaw. "It's time for us to fight back with our rules," Kate stated.

"What's that mean?" Pavarty asked, confused.

"Why, no rules at all, sis!" Kate hissed. "Jungle Rules."

"Shh!" Oz demanded.

"Listen to me. All of you. You too, Oz. I've learned a lot of things in my life, and the one thing I've learned is that everything and everyone are afraid of something else, no matter how badass they seem!"

The kids shared concerned looks.

"So?"

"You're not making any sense, Kate," Pavarty doubled down on her confusion. "Monsters aren't scared of us!"

"I'll repeat it so you can all think about what I'm saying. Let it sink in—everything and everyone that has ever lived—is —or was—afraid of something—even these monsters. I know that for a fact," Kate repeated.

"So?"

"I know what I'm afraid of. All of those crazy effing things!" Pav pointed at the menagerie of beasts roaming below with garlands and more lights.

"Me too," Lennon agreed.

"Code-Red! Code-Red! I'm pegging that needle, girls! I'm going to freak out if this is all real!" Jesse shivered in her cage.

"Listen to me. Every one of those things, little or big, has a weakness too. So now, we must figure out what these things are afraid of. What makes them jump? When do they sleep? For how long? When do they go to the bathroom? Anything. That's how we'll use their own weaknesses and stupidity against them. There's always a chance." Kate bolstered her shaken crew. "We will never give up."

"Or we could just shut the hell up and see what happens next. Shh!" Ozzy whispered. "I was right about not leaving the frigging bus, and I'm sure as hell right about this! I'm a horror film expert! Quiet down!"

Kate nodded but ignored him.

"Coop, Emiliano, and Josh see if you can spot any... behavioral patterns with these freaks. Who are they? What are they? What are their strengths and weaknesses in the numbers? How many kinds of things are there? You should be able to see a lot from way up there. Concentrate on Wixx and her closest goons... any repetitions... whatever. Find something we can use against them as a weakness." Kate took over the command. "We are going to get out of here. Together," she declared.

"That dog don't hunt, Kate! Everybody, please just quiet down," Oz pleaded.

"Want to bet, nerd? I bet you we get out of here!" Emiliano shot back.

"Thousand bucks. You're on, my friend!"

"Ten Thousand!" Emiliano countered, happy for the distraction.

"One million dollars. And I want to lose this bet so frigging bad!" Ozzy replied.

Kate repeated herself with a defiant sparkle in her eyes.

"Make them underestimate us. Act weak and scared when they're around but see everything."

"Oh, sure. That shouldn't be hard."

"Who knows? This could even be fun," Kate promised darkly.

-CHAPTER 34-

Welcome to the Threshold

The three explorers wore pressurized oxygen masks now, even Harley, with the constant threat of firestorms still raging overhead as they continued traveling down into the smoky bowels of the earth.

Camouflaged Creeps hid within the crevices and only peeked out in small packs of twos and threes. Now combat-tested by the mighty Great Dane, they no longer dared flash their gang signs until after Harley passed. They would only drop their camo and whip their cowardly stingers around to impress each other.

Many of the surviving Creeps sported fresh battle wounds inflicted by Harley's fearsome bite at their last encounter—with fang marks ripped across their short-circuited torsos—leaving purple gaps in their animated displays.

Word spread quickly among their kind to scatter and avoid the mighty hound and the strange little boy who could level mountains with his mind.

The Creeps had always been wary of Yuma, and now they learned the same lesson from his fearsome hound.

Yuma led the way into the darkness as Zack and Harley followed him down through endless interconnecting mineshafts, spanning centuries of work from overlapping cultures.

They climbed over the rusty bones of mining equipment the size of extinct dinosaurs and passed into a series of tunnels full of burned and butchered human remains. It horrified Zack when the sweep of Yuma's crystals revealed several small skeletons of children his age lying face down in the ashes.

The blistering heat and toxic smoke intensified the lower they sank. They could feel death threatening their lives around every corner—lying in ambush—ready to spark calamity with just a blink.

They struggled through another series of intestinal tunnels when the claustrophobic airless mineshaft abruptly opened into a mad Escher painting of ups and downs.

"Welcome to the Threshold, Zackery Goodnight," Yuma declared. "A world of choices."

Zack realized they had made it to an abandoned realm of ventilated air and intersecting mine shafts, sideways elevators, and overlapping stairwells that resembled nothing like the crude structures built by humans above. Then he spotted the mysterious lights twinkling even deeper in the open void.

Yuma started down a shifting stairwell, and Zack lifted his mask.

"Hey! Why are we going way down here, Yuma? Nobody can live this deep. Right?"

The giant stopped and turned.

"Are you so sure? Look around you. Nothing is impossible."

Exhausted, Zack pulled his fogged-up air mask down and re-adjusted Harley's ill-fitting one, ensuring it would stay secure.

"You need to see this," Yuma insisted.

He turned and led them down into the bewildering abyss of multiple choices.

"This is the reason you are here, boy. The only reason you've been allowed to travel this far."

They ventured into another artificial cavern. Long pit trenches fed by plumes of natural gas illuminated the sculptured bedrock. Overlapping layers of ancient petroglyphs informed the ceilings and walls like a living compendium of humankind's accomplishments throughout the ages.

Zack noticed a spiderweb of golden rails, more ancient than those they had ridden on. Their gleaming design offered subtle hints of their makers' understanding of the earth.

"Get in," Yuma commanded, pointing to a pair of engraved ore carts.

"Nuh-uh. Not again. No. I sure didn't like that ride the last time I took it. Not at all." Zack backed away from the offer.

"Like has nothing to do with it. Here lies your destiny, son. They are waiting for you. Get in. Anything you see down here, they meant for you to see," Yuma promised.

"Who are they? And what if it's not me you're looking for? What if I'm not who you or they think I am?" Zack pleaded. "I'm not a giant like you."

"Well..." Yuma pondered for a second. "Then this ride will probably kill you." The giant smiled. "Big problem solved, either way,"

Yuma tried to finish straight-faced, but a grin kept escaping. "Climb aboard, young man. There is still a world to travel before you get to where you are going."

"Aren't you coming too?"

"I wouldn't have it any other way."

Zack saw the mischievous twinkle in Yuma's eyes and crawled into the front of the first cart with Harley riding shotgun, and they shared a 'here-we-go-again' look and sighed.

"Does this one at least have brakes that work?" Zack asked, still uneasy, as he lowered his air mask back over his face. "Archie really sucked at stopping last time."

Harley moaned in agreement.

Yuma was impressed with this timid young lad's bravery and boldness as he watched the wounded kid nestle himself down against his canine protector.

"These tracks will deliver us nonstop to our final destination in one piece. But do hold on. Both of you. It is quite the ride."

Yuma stepped into the rear of the ore car with one leg and gave three giant strides with the other before hopping aboard and leaning forward like he was on a toboggan run.

The ornate ore carts rolled slowly downhill at first and then faster and faster, picking up an uncanny amount of speed as they spiraled almost straight down.

"Hold on!"

Gravity alone ruled their lives now—either by slamming them around every turn or pitching them forward to hear their screams at the dips.

Yuma hadn't expected to be hit by his personal visions so early inside this last passage of the Cave of Whispers, where the Blue Lava flowed uphill.

He hoped to witness Zack's initial reactions to his extraordinary visions. But he didn't get the chance when his own hallucinations stampeded into him like a buffalo herd.

Flashes of dead avenging enemies howled straight for the giant from out of the open plains of his subconscious, screaming and shrieking his name.

"Yuma!"

"Yuma must die!"

"Kill the Immortal!"

The fastest of the spirits chased his corkscrewing ore cart down through the spiraling tunnels beside him, ripping away at his flesh with their hunting knives.

"Yuma! You owe me your flesh!"

"You devoured my heart! Return it!"

Zack snapped around in the front at the giant's terrified screams behind him. He could feel the intensity of the warrior's invisible terrors rising out of him in a tsunami of overwhelming pain and death as the golden carts threatened to shudder off the rails with his tortured anguish.

But around the next bend, Zack's bright future discovered him. The blinding new insights rushed out of the darkness in sharply delineated lines of thought embedded with unspoken meanings for this special boy.

He saw past the ancient warrior as if the great giant and his ore cart didn't exist. He saw past himself.

Zack gazed out into a peaceful transcendental state, catching a fleeting glimpse of a place and time that looked like it might conceal paradise.

He heard the peal of a child's laughter that sounded like his own—and then it was gone—faded away—hidden behind the dancing vapors of darkness.

All hope was dashed. Those simple, captivating sounds of lost joy had recaptured his broken heart temporarily. And then, more brief glimpses of a bright paradise reappeared, blooming out of the gloom again, only to disappear once more, leaving the boy crestfallen.

These are the special days I've never lived.

But when his mystical visions reappeared for the third time and then the fourth, the fifth—he realized what he was witnessing.

He watched the elegant transition of time flowing from one day into the next. These beautiful transits of the sun represented the few precious days we are all gifted within a single lifetime to be truly alive and present—if we are lucky enough to recognize it.

It was a rare capability in a child so young to decipher one of life's most challenging but glorious lessons and appreciate it so at such a tender age. But this intelligent, intuitive little boy grasped it all.

Never take a single day for granted ever again.

And life is far too precious a gift to leave the key to your happiness in someone else's pocket.

But any self-illumination this bright came with a tremendous shadow of burden.

And Zack Goodnight recognized that he wasn't prepared to endure the great responsibility that awaited him alone.

-CHAPTER 35-

The Forces of Light and Darkness

Zack remained unconscious inside the hurtling ore cart, lost in a state of transformative bliss. But Yuma was getting his soul ripped apart by an army of invisible marauders in his cart.

His ghostly adversaries swirled and spread their thin gossamer army out in parallel lines in front of the speeding carts. Once assembled along both sides of the track, they formed an endless gauntlet as a blood test of the Time Warrior's courage and commitment.

The ore carts thundered around the next corner, and the undead spirits attacked.

"Murder him!"

"Peel his flesh!

"Inside out!"

A hundred serial killers trumpeted the cries for Yuma's death as they crowded the tracks for any chance at leaving a lasting mark.

But Yuma rushed past the restless spirits at sixty miles an hour, leaving the disappointed spirits nothing to swing at but their horrifying past as he whizzed by, a citizen of the future. They howled in desperation as they were sucked back down into the depths of the hateful vortex they spun out of.

A last volley of arrows pierced Yuma's flesh, but he broke each one off and threw them overboard with disdain. At last, this part of his excruciating nightmare ended as the carts took an unexpected dip and curved around another blind corner. It corkscrewed between several horizontal levels as the

305

sudden blast of hot wind tore at Harley's mask.

The confused canine whined—but not out of fear—he didn't like what he saw when he glanced down at Zack's glazed eyes. The boy was still unconscious as they plummeted deeper underground, with no one in charge of the brakes.

But Zack's happy continence changed as he watched his future unfurl. Bright blasts of color and confusing flashes of kaleidoscopic images flowed over him. Strange music and unfamiliar voices enveloped his soul as if they owned him.

"Where am I?"

"Who are you?"

Every life lesson was stolen from a future he couldn't conceive of yet.

Behind him, the gut-wrenching toll taken on Yuma had only been half paid.

The giant warrior was reduced to a quivering mess as he watched the spirits of his decimated army rise out of Eel Lake. His army of giants was twisted and burned—but whole again. The specters of a hundred dead Time Warriors levitated high above the water's surface before hurling their burned corpses against his ore cart as he sped past.

"You promised to save us!"

"You lied!"

His eternal tormentors laughed as they dragged Blue Feather's lifeless body from under the water and hurled her corpse against his speeding ore cart. She clung to it like a splattered bug, and Yuma's mind crumbled.

"These torments have never gone this far!"

Putrefied flesh now horrified Blue Feather's once sun-kissed complexion, as if someone had reassembled her from digested pieces.

"She is dead! This thing is not my wife!" Yuma howled.

"Oh, noooooo. You are wrong! We kept Blue Feather alive just for Yuuuuuma!" the ghosts taunted. "We know you loved her, sooooooo!"

"Yumaaaaaaaaaaa!" Blue Feather's tormented voice

choked off as leeches crawled from her mouth.

"You deserted meeeee!"

Yuma cowered in fear.

"You deserted all of ussssss!"

The giant fell back against the speeding ore cart, pleading with the clinging ghost of his dead wife for understanding.

"I do not know how I survived! I should have died with you! I should never have turned my back on Wixx!"

Zack snapped out of his rapture at the screams of the old warrior. He spun around and witnessed the man's ancient battle wounds again opening all over his body. The frightened boy grabbed the giant's hand and tried to comfort him with his steady gaze.

"Yuma. Yuma! Come back to me!" the boy called out across the great divide.

Zack witnessed the enormous price the dedicated warrior was willing to endure for his service. He was suffering through every profound loss in his long life to reveal what needed to be seen by the young boy.

Then something even more miraculous happened as bolts of electricity snapped between the carts.

Inside their respective minds, things zinged, and synapses zapped. Yuma and Zack were both shot backward in time together.

They floated high above ancient battlefields filled with raging giants fighting the armies of evil far below.

Boy and Time Warrior observed things from a higher perspective among the clouds as the past began repeating itself in stutters of color and sudden death below. They were now just wispy spectators to what transpired all those years before in violent Dark Hollows.

The Forces of Light fought to defend the Sacred Forest's precious resources throughout all the ages of conquest and invasion.

Both sides of the lake had clashed throughout the

intervening centuries, hidden underneath the Bubble of Mother Nature's protected lands—only to see the Forces of Evil driven back from the pristine shores every time—led by Yuma and his brave legion of defenders.

Together, Zack and Yuma witnessed the Dark Side's last defeat at the hands of Yuma's immortal army—everyone skilled in every deadly form of hand-to-hand combat—from ancient to modern.

Afterward, all creatures, big and small, were treated with dignity in their defeat, hoping to foster a lasting peace between both sides in the Time Warrior's truce.

Zack and Yuma observed the quality of medical care provided to all the wounded creatures below, no matter their creed, color, or station.

Then the vanquished threw an armistice celebration between the combatants in Dark Hollows after that last war ended. Everyone left alive on both sides of the lake attended.

Zack watched as the ultimate betrayal of honor and decency among combatants unfolded before them.

He saw the evening's special-event caterer—the world-famous chef, Pepper Wixx— poison Yuma's food.

Yuma and his army of immortals fell unconscious almost immediately once they tasted her delicious concoctions without a single weapon being unsheathed.

The indoor thunder produced by a hundred leviathans collapsing onto the polished oak floors of the Regency was breathtaking in every sense—like an entire forest fell by an ill wind. And after the dust settled, Pepper Wixx proudly announced she acted independently.

"Honor is for the stupid!" she bragged to the stunned crowd as the giants snored and the evil cheered.

Captivity followed for all the captured giants. Wixx held them underground in specially dug caves and paid the ogres extra to beat them twenty-four hours a day to weaken them when Wixx's potions no longer worked on their ever-adapting metabolisms.

A quick series of mock trials followed, and then the actual torture began—lasting days, months, maybe even years. No one could tell anymore underneath the Bubble. Time flowed in such strange ways down here. This was the place where that antiquated concept was scrambled and followed its own rules.

Wixx found it challenging to torture an immortal giant that could self-heal on command. She wondered how anyone could ever kill one of these immortal beasts when even chopping their heads off didn't always work. So, she studied ancient writings, did her homework, and devised a novel idea for their extinction.

She had the town construct two gigantic catapults to strict specifications.

The old witch was beaming with patriotic pride that distant Fourth of July night as her happy mob surrounded her, chanting her name like a rock star.

"Pepper Wixx! Pepper Wixx! Pepper Wixx!"

Dazzling displays of Wiccan-inspired fireworks lit up the night in celebration.

Floating high above, Zack watched as an unconscious Yuma below—bound and helpless—was winched up by a team of trolls.

They dropped his massive body into the bucket of one of the oversized catapults—already captive inside an enormous straight-jacket.

Wixx nodded, and her sons poured buckets of hot tar over his head from the safety of the great scaffolding above.

"Aghhhhhhh!"

"Wake up, you horrible beast! It's time to fly and die!"

The sedated giant screamed against the searing pain, but Wixx had bound him beyond his strength, and he could only yell so loud—rattling the mountainsides with his agony.

"Yuma! You are the monster that set our precious coal mines on fire! Guilty!"

She gestured for more hot tar.

"Ahhhhhhh!"

"You are guilty of killing my husband and sons and thousands more of our people! Guilty!"

They poured tar into his open mouth.

"Aghhhhhh!"

"And you infested my pretty lake with giant eels to prevent me from ever crossing it! Guilty!"

"Ahhhhhh!"

"You and you alone have kept my people and me from achieving our manifest destiny. You delayed us for all these years, and for what? So, you and your kind get to live over in that paradise while we rot? You primitive, pitiful old rain man. You have no education, possess no true magic, or knowledge of Wiccan spells in your sad medicine kit of head-hunter tricks. You are nothing more than a privileged backward heathen lost in the wrong century! Why do people even respect such a fool when you're just a sad charlatan? Guilty!"

"Guilty!" the rabid crowd of freaks and monsters screamed back.

"Let me ask you all a riddle. How do you kill something that can live forever? Something that can self-heal from every wound and disease from the inside out? Know how?"

"How?" the crowd roared back.

"Easy. Watch and learn!" Wixx nodded, and Berk and Moody dropped torches on the giant, setting his body ablaze.

"Aghhhhhhh!"

"Nothing can grow back together if there aren't enough pieces left! Right? Well, we're about to find out."

"Observe!" Archie's disembodied voice startled them both from overhead.

"Who said that?" Yuma spun.

"Probably, Archie. He does this kind of stuff all the time."

Then they heard Wixx screaming below.

"Go feed your stinking fish!" Wixx yelled as she launched Yuma into that Fourth of July sky, where he became the first screaming fireball.

"I wish, I wish upon a falling star that you... die!" Pepper screamed, and the crowd of monsters cheered at the nasty surprise.

The shrieking comet arced up over the calm surface of Eel Lake, where he would soon plummet back down into the eel-infested waters, thousands of feet away from his initial launch.

"I don't need to watch this." Yuma turned away from listening to his horrible screams—experiencing the agony of his tortured flesh again.

"No. Look!" Archie's disembodied voice commanded. "This is the important part."

Something took shape in the sky as they watched. It wasn't fireworks—it was something else.

Yuma and Zack witnessed small minute particles of light coalescing out of the nothingness and swarming down from every treetop within the Sacred Forest toward the screaming comet.

The pinpoint-sized motes of light bound themselves together into a dancing carpet of energized light beams. That twinkling cloud merged to form and reform as it shot higher. Once they intercepted Yuma's burning body as a unit—they congealed into something more tangible than the air around his burning body.

The lifesaving cloud resembled a pale, electrified halo of ever-expanding soap bubbles. Their soft, lucid formation began quenching the flames while floating Yuma down on an extended trajectory across the lake.

Once over the sacred redwoods, the whimsical lights vanished underneath him as if they had never existed. Yuma fell back to earth, landing with a proper giant's thud, cratering the wet ferns on his fiery impact before passing out.

Zack and Yuma heard the disappointed 'Boos' roll back across the lake from the unhappy town after not seeing a splash.

It took Yuma a moment to ponder.

"This is how my life was spared?"

Today was full of one mind-bending astonishment after another for both the giant and the boy.

"It was the Inklings who saved my life."

"Yes. It was."

With that mutual revelation, they emerged from their time-traveling trance and back into emergency consciousness.

That's when they realized they were still hurtling down the golden tracks to nowhere.

-CHAPTER 36-

The Royal Council

Henrietta Hoodwinker delivered a familiar rant before the Royal Council behind closed doors inside the New Regency's revamped ballroom.

Talented artisans had recently replaced the exquisite parquet floors within the towering dining hall after the extensive destruction caused by a hundred poisoned giants collapsing onto the floor on Armistice Day. Henrietta was still livid about the dishonorable subterfuge involved in their capture and murder—and livid was an actual face color in the hollows, as her vexed complexion took on a ruddy sheen whenever she was distraught.

"Kidnapping Uman children for profit is one thing. It happens. But killing the worthless simply because they're unwanted or misshapen is something else entirely. You all witnessed that witless, classless barbarian's actions. And you want to make that living embarrassment our Queen for the next hundred years? Our new symbolic leader on this side of the Atlantic? What about our ultimate legacy worldwide? To our ancient homelands?" she demanded answers from anyone brave enough to speak up.

Oliver Poole, the shape-shifting soul thief from Dragonia Falls, tried to make a case.

"Be reasonable, Henrietta. As far as the Uman children go? Really? Haven't we all done the same thing ourselves?"

He gestured around the table as hands shot up.

"Guilty."

313

"Guilty."

"I mean, if we're honest about it, darling. I remember a tender stew you whipped up at the last minute on All Souls Day in the Fifties. The doorbell rang. We l heard a chorus of 'Trick or Treats!', and before you knew it, we were all snacking on the most delicious youngling stew that was positively...

"Enough, Olly. That was then. When our palates were much less informed. We have modern tastes and rules now. After all, it is the twenty-first century, not the twentieth, fifteenth, or twelfth, and the Upside's world's law enforcement has grown mighty in its powers of observation. We are far more informed than ever before, and there is no excuse to unleash their fury against us ever again if we're smart. Not if we want to co-exist with the Upside world harmoniously someday."

"Pipe dreams!"

"Speak for yourself."

"I am doing that, young man."

"Let her talk!"

"She has the floor."

"But dear Henrietta, it is Wixx's turn, after all!" Geoffrey the Wizened was the only ghoul brave enough to mansplain in front of haughty Henrietta. Being a self-made warlock of some renown—inherited wealth didn't impress him much. And he wasn't fooled by meaningless family names conjured on the lam centuries ago.

"Why should we worry? It is merely a silly ceremonial post. There can be no true royal bloodlines among the Damned, now can there? We have corrupted our lifeblood since birth. You know that as well as we do. Not even your infamous lineage has remained pure, has it, darling?"

"Oh, dear." Henrietta jolted at the insult. "You all know she will never relinquish her powers when her term ends? Or return the Ring of Bartholomew once she discovers its additional powers? We all know her for what she is!"

Sadie Scrimshaw from Gizzard Flats cleared her throat

and spoke up.

"I agree with them, Henrietta. Pepper has earned that right to be our temporary Queen because of her cunning alone. Never underestimate that powerful witch. She will protect us all in times of danger."

"Hear, hear!" some cheered.

"Remember this," Sadie said, flipping her hankie around for emphasis. "It was Pepper Wixx who won that war against them, giants. Single handily. That fierce witch slaughtered them proper."

"All except one."

"Yeah. That one."

"It's only a century in office, just like your term, darling, and then it's over! Merely a piffle in time for us," Geoffrey offered.

"Bring her in then and let her speak for herself," Sadie suggested as the Board turned in her favor.

"Administer the test now. If Wixx doesn't qualify on at least ten of the List of Thirteen Supremacies, then she doesn't qualify as a Wiccan leader. Simple as that."

Ambassador Polonius snorted his agreement.

That's when Pepper Wixx burst through the ballroom doors, startling the life out of the undead.

"Uh!"

"Oh, dear!"

"Surprised, old friends! I know how that feels!" Wixx waved and noticed the new color of Henrietta's sensitive skin.

"Well, here I am! I believe divining the future is one of those thirteen essential requirements! Prognostication-knowing what's going to happen next!"

Pepper Wixx strolled proudly into the room, wearing a different ensemble to everyone enchanted by her. Shelby stopped in the doorway behind her mother, casting her own bent shadow over the secret preceding's.

"You were about to summon me? And, here I am, ladies and gentlemen, unexpectantly and at your disposal, standing

315

by for more of your asinine tests. Shelby, please read the Wiccan Society's list of Supremacies to be worthy of being a proper witch, so we're all on the same page?"

"Certainly, Mother. Number one- Spellcaster- casting and receiving; Two- Telekinesis- moving objects with the mind; Three- Electro Kinesis- firing energy bolts through crystals or other substances; Four- Beguilement, mind control; five- Shape-Shifting, from human to animal or visa-versa; six- Casting Curses; evil and good; seven- Mastery of Astrology, understanding the stars; eight- Prognostication, divining the future."

"Aha! Check that box off our list, Henrietta. I appear before you unsummoned."

"Nine- Speak in Tongues to demons or dragons; ten- Audible Assault- flooding a mind with voices; eleven- Conjuring- making something from nothing; twelve- Enchantment, bestowing magical powers onto other people or objects, and finally, thirteen- Transvection, free flying."

"Thank you, Shelby. Now, how would you like to proceed with this political charade? Is there a special order to this insulting madness?" Pepper singled out her supporters among the aristocrats and dialed the Knack to full power.

"This isn't just about you, Pepper?" shaken Henrietta backtracked.

"Really? I beg to differ. I would say this is all about me. Very much so. Darling."

"It's about the future of witchcraft itself—our future as a successful society. Moving forward in the right direction and not falling behind again because of our self-deluding deviant behavior!"

"I am showing you all the future right now as we speak. I am that future you keep talking about. As I live and breathe it every day stretched thin between both worlds."

"Come on, Henrietta. Sit. Give her a chance."

"Test away." Pepper raised her arms over her head, with two black crystals spinning in her palms.

A startling thunderclap jolted the room from the rafters, and crimson raindrops fell from a dry ceiling.

"Oops. Sorry friends. That's a premature Eleven, my bad," Pepper apologized, and the indoor rain stopped. "I couldn't hold it in any longer. You know how it is, ladies. Now, what else do you gents need to see so that we can end this chauvinistic nonsense? I need to prepare for tomorrow's events."

The Board murmured amongst themselves.

"Well. I know. How about a number thirteen, Pepper? The highest of the Supremacies. We have never seen you fly?" Henrietta challenged, remembering Wixx's weakest link.

"You want to see me fly, huh?"

"We all do. Have we ever flown, dear? I don't remember a single time."

"In a jetliner, maybe!" someone snarled.

"You don't even own a proper Scorch, do you?" Henrietta pressed.

"Here. Use mine, madame!" The Baron snapped his triple fingers, and his customized Scorch ignited and flew out of the stand. It floated across the ballroom and hovered, waiting for instructions. Its green flames charred the Regency's lacquered floors within seconds, with continuous sparks bouncing off the inlaid surface.

"No one with taste rides these destructive implements indoors anymore, Baron. What are we, farmers? They're named Scorches for a reason, my good man."

Pepper stood her ground as the Scorch danced toward her with another improper gesture from the Baron. Still, Pepper halted its progress halfway across the ballroom with a steely glare and a raised eyebrow.

"Thank you, Baron, for your... overt sense of masculine generosity."

The Baron bowed, Pepper flinched, and a bowl of Muskrat soup jumped up and dumped over The Baron's head, startling him and the entire room.

"But what makes you males believe that a woman needs that vulgar insult of a conveyance to fly?"

Her sudden resentment frightened the leathery aristocrat the most.

"A herd of superstitious, frail, Uman men imposed that wicked lie upon women of a certain age. Then used it to taunt, insult, and make crude jokes about us behind our backs forever. Well, I don't need your silly props to achieve the perfection of full transvection!"

Wixx raised her arms and rose straight into the air on a gust of wind, and the Board gasped as two fainted while she hovered there.

Pepper hummed a familiar tune, kicked off her heels, and danced through the air, clutching her stolen jewels in her fists.

"Women never needed men or brooms to learn how to fly anywhere!" she laughed down at them as she rose higher into the rafters. "We just needed the opportunity to have a chance!"

The Board gasped and applauded as Wixx floated high above them as if she had been winged all her life. No one in memory had ever achieved solo, unaided flight this way, whether witch or warlock.

The stunned Board couldn't believe their eyes as Pepper waltzed around, humming her coronation tune to herself.

That's when Berk and Moody thundered indoors, running down the long hallway, carrying good news and clouds of dust. Shelby heard the familiar hoofbeats and ran out into the hallway to slow the stampede down, and she pointed up and covered her lips with an index finger.

"Shhh!"

Leaning in to watch, the brothers were stunned when they saw their mother soaring around the room like an elegant bat.

"I didn't know she could fly?"

"Way to go, Ma!"

318

As Pepper lowered the levitating crystals to her side, she drifted back down until her toes touched, then slid effortlessly back into her high heels.

"Next?" she asked with a cocky smile.

Everyone sat stunned inside the ballroom. And with nothing left to say, they erupted into a standing ovation—even Henrietta.

As the official historian, Henrietta knew no witch like Pepper Wixx had ever existed before among their kind. There were ancient stories and superstitions, but no one had ever flown without a Scorch.

Shelby's loud throat clear from the hallway, drew the animated crowd's attention as she limped triumphantly back into the ballroom.

"Excuse me, Madame Chairperson, may I have a private word?"

Pepper shot Shelby a surprised look as her stepdaughter limped past her with a big smile and over to Henrietta.

Is this another ambush? Am I being set up by my daughter? Pepper feared.

"What is going on with you two? I must get home and prepare," Pepper insisted as the two women whispered conspiratorially.

This is such nonsense. After flying so majestically in front of these ground squirrels, this should be the end of all tests. Any other spell pales in comparison.

When Henrietta turned back with a crooked smile and Shelby stood back, Pepper expected the worst.

"There is one more unanticipated test. It seems before you start your reign." Henrietta nodded as Berk and Moody thundered in, pushing a heavy metal cart that flapped with a dusty tarp.

"Well, Pepper, if you are only half as powerful as your amazing gifts appear, darling—then perhaps you already sense the importance of this extraordinary surprise your sons have just discovered for this special occasion," Henrietta teased.

319

"Idiot stepsons. And I hate surprises of any kind, especially theirs. No one can read their feeble thoughts."

"Aw, Ma. Yes, you can."

Her boys stopped before her and whipped off the tarp—leaving Pepper speechless.

"Ta-dah!" they chimed in unison.

Before Pepper sat a complete set of jewel-encrusted dragon eggs—each over six feet tall—seven of them making an entire litter.

This discovery was so recent that the eggs were still embedded in a thick matrix of colored crystals. Only the sturdiest gigantic gems served as a proper dragon's nest.

The bejeweled surface of the seven eggs resembled gigantic crystalline geodes turned inside-out, with jewels on the outside. Their unique colorations represented the rainbow's entire spectrum in one nest—red, orange, yellow, green, blue, indigo, and violet.

It was now Pepper's turn to be enchanted.

"Happy Birthday, Ma," Moody cooed.

"It's not her birthday, stupid!" Berk corrected with a quick backhand. "She's going to be a Queen, dumbo! And every Queen should have dragons to command." Berk bowed at the waist, and his miner's helmet clanged off.

"Well, Pepper. Can you conjure a brood of dragon chicks back from the dead?" Henrietta challenged. "You realize the cultural significance? No one in over a hundred years has accomplished it."

It took Pepper a minute to reply as she read the room and listened to her most devious thoughts.

"Sure. I'll take a swing at it, Hoodwinker. But let's keep this all our little secret for now. I don't want to disappoint my fans by not producing results on such short notice. Bad show biz—you understand? But this might just tie in perfectly with my party plans," Pepper responded, seeming more intrigued than ever by this legendary surprise.

The unexpected sparkle in Pepper's eyes made the board

320

members shudder at the chilling thought of Pepper Wixx with a squadron of fire-breathing dragons at her disposal.

What will happen once we surrender the tiller of our fate into Pepper Wixx's hands?

Pepper smelled the wisps of terror spiraling like sour incense inside the ballroom.

Oh, if you horrible snobs only knew what was coming next? She chuckled.

-CHAPTER 37-

Illumination

The tandem ore carts roared out of the gloom of the last tunnel like two Indy cars drafting across an imaginary finish line in search of glory.

Just a few more inches, then... triumph!

Victory!

The end of the gauntlet.

The end of the run.

The finish line!

But no one onboard besides Harley was conscious enough to appreciate that glorious fact.

They were speeding down the last set of rails ever built to reach the bottom of the Big Silence. This was the end of the line.

These impervious tracks and their gravity-defying mules had performed flawlessly for centuries in this subterranean world. The exquisite design and dependable carts allowed them to slow roll to a natural stop, applying no further braking to scrub off the last bit of speed.

Both carts unlatched and stopped independently, using only gravity and exquisite math equations to provide a flawless landing every time.

This built-in ingenuity benefitted everyone onboard because Yuma and Zack remained unconscious after enduring the tremendous G-forces exerted on their bodies and minds. They were both still lost within their distinctive visions, hidden behind fogged-up masks—and unaware of their fate at the end of the line to nowhere.

Harley, always vigilant, along with Zip, Zash, and Zee, only catching up at the end, remained alert and on guard as Yuma and Zack slept at their final destination, which felt like the center of the earth.

Harley sniffed the air and nudged his mask off with his paw. The moisture-laden oxygen was breathable without wearing the ill-fitting contraption, which was fortunate since Harley could not pull it back if he had been wrong. But he wasn't wrong—he followed his trusty instincts like always.

The only illumination in this low-ceilinged cavern was the bioluminescent hummingbirds darting about the place and casting dizzying streaks and shadows everywhere they searched.

The exhausted hound sat dazed and confused at the end of the long, mind-bending road trip and didn't notice the first noises tiptoeing towards them in the dark.

When he did, his ears sprang up to capture and locate the sounds. He cocked his head back and forth like a radar dish, trying to pinpoint the subtle noise's direction and speed.

It was a slow shuffling sound, like something was sneaking in behind the rain curtains, yet still invisible to the naked eye.

Creeps? Harley remembered the Humanspeak for those atrocities and growled.

Grrrrrrrrrrr.

The mighty dog readied for another sneak attack. But his keen nose ordered all defensive instincts to stand down— even before his vision could perceive what was lurking behind the shadows.

But then, tiny shape-shifting life forms began drifting into focus, shuffling towards them through the perpetual underground drizzle.

Glittering human-like silhouettes came shuffling to life out of the darkness as the agitated trio of hummingbirds swirled around in midair to investigate. As they appeared, the birds' bioluminescent streaks illuminated the ghostly apparitions in fast strobes of flyby light.

Behind! Surrounding! Harley knew by training.

But the courageous hound didn't bark at the materializing shapes, even when their torches began popping to life. He had already smelled what he needed to know.

Harley released a slight whimper and bowed his head in reverence as he waited for whatever was about to happen—to happen.

The dreamlike moment started haltingly as several small silhouettes emerged from the darkness in bursts of more bright torchlight. Their golden light burned more brilliantly than any natural flame but without the threat of searing the optic nerve.

Faster and faster, the bizarre, tubby little creatures continued to materialize by the dozens, with each shimmering figure holding a clear crystal torch high above their hooded heads. They whispered and chanted a strange, hypnotic melody in a continuous, harmonious drone of rising and falling notes, transforming its shape and tone with every modulated phrase. And their collective timbre was so harmonically soothing to the ear that it stimulated the mind's inner workings before rewarding it with waves of joy.

Here was the source of the eternal enigma—for these were the voices heard within the Cave of Whispers for all the years. These incredible three-foot-tall creatures reproduced the sounds of the living universe, singing a soothing lullaby back onto itself in a continuous loop of life-affirming celebrations.

Physically, they appeared a spirited cross between a translucent troglodyte and a puffy Water Bear—if those absurd-looking creatures possessed human-like appendages.

There were differences in age, weight, color, and shape, but other than that, they were all bald and resembled each other as if they were from the same oddball litter.

324

These golden creatures featured neither eyes nor ears on their heads—just simple bumps and unformed, colorful hints of either extremity on their translucent heads.

And their mouths were long and tubular, like the rubber snout on a child's water balloon, changing shape with the lilting chirps of every delightful note they produced.

Each possessed seven fingers on their delicate hands as they gestured in time to the music. Their long, ink-stained fingers were the most graceful feature on their stout and dimpled little bodies, and they cloaked themselves in exquisite golden robes with hoods, unblemished by even a hint of soil or moisture.

These were not some subhuman, slimy semi-aquatic creatures living in the perpetual muck and rainfall like the Creeps, but a species of fully evolved holy beings who spontaneously repelled water away from their gold-flecked bodies before any contact could be made. They were each surrounded by a full-length body halo which could only be seen when the waters bounced off, and their gilded robes remained immaculate no matter where they traveled.

As they drew closer to the carts, Harley saw that everything about these exotic, subterranean creatures was golden, which seemed as pure as their intentions.

Their reflective skin glistened with bright flecks of gold—shiny nano-flakes embedded within their flesh as part of their distinct DNA structure. This transcendent flesh held the purest form of natural gold in existence—one hundred percent biological gold.

Harley's eyes danced back and forth like ping-pong balls at a championship match as more and more of the tiny monks materialized before him in groups.

Hundreds chanted and sang as they circled the ore carts. Every sightless creature held up a bright crystal torch that seemed to help them explore their pitch-black environment as the slanted chamber revealed its timeless secrets without a struggle under the sudden exposure of so much light.

Incredible murals spanning hundreds of thousands of unknown epochs of humankind's existence smothered the ceiling and walls. The most profound works were engraved, carved, knitted, or painted with such undeniable artistry that each complicated artwork still held onto its awe and meaning even today.

Every recorded thought throughout the ages was compiled in this spectacular space in some form and protected and exhibited with our forebearers' artistic grace and engineering savvy.

Zack was startled awake when his body started rocking again, and he began screaming.

"Help! She's still coming! I'm falling!"

When his eyes fluttered open behind the mask, Zack discovered himself and an unconscious Yuma were sprawled across a shuffling mass of thousands of those tiny creatures marching in step. They were held only four feet above the ground by hundreds of little hands as the singing monks carried them above their heads like a colony of musical ants raiding a picnic.

Zack feared these unknown critters were kidnapping them for food. But he relaxed when he made eye contact with an unruffled Harley trotting protectively beside him. At that point, Zack surrendered his fate to the winds and allowed himself to enjoy the bizarre ride.

"Look at this, Harley," Zack called out. "You're always out front, showing me the way."

"Yup!" Harley barked back, and Zack smiled because he understood it.

Zip, Zash, and Zee flew escort in front of the undulating procession as if they knew the destination, and Zack discovered that crowd-surfing, while weird, was also extremely fun.

"This is kinda cool!"

They moved underneath single engineered stones larger than most apartment buildings framing their path, forming a winding intestinal tunnel that snaked downward into a crystal maze. The monk's lush harmonics vibrated inside the void with the sounds of universal optimism and balance.

Zack saw a compelling new light source in the distance once they turned into another corridor.

"How does light exist this far down?" Zack wondered.

That uncanny glow promised the existence of another extended cavern just ahead, and Zack prayed it marked the end of this impossible quest.

"Is this it?"

When they rounded the bend, the glare from the brilliant cavern's interior shocked his light-sensitive eyes. But as his vision cleared, he saw the hooded creatures had carried him and the unconscious giant into an underground world that opened before them into an epic panorama. Before him lay the most startling secret kingdom in all earthly existence—the holy realm known as the Inner Jewel.

The curved crystalline rotunda arched over six hundred feet above them at its peak, with every millimeter of surface twinkling back in some form of refracted gem light.

A magnificent waterfall tumbled down through the center skylight, releasing a silvery veil of whitewater unrivaled by any aboveground.

But the surprise of surprises was that after cascading down inside this brilliant crystal chamber, the waterfall crashed over the top of a spectacular crystalline egg the size of a modern skyscraper. This exquisite jewel rose over four hundred feet tall as it floated upright in the cavern's epicenter.

When the tiny creatures lowered them from their shoulders, Zack and Yuma discovered themselves sitting on the top step of the grand crystal staircase that fell away into the uncharted inner world that scurried below.

"Where are we now?"

Zack knew he couldn't trust his eyes any longer, and he kept blinking to see if the channel would change on his overimaginative mind.

"Nothing I see makes sense anymore."

Zack continued rubbing his tired eyes.

"Am I still awake? Or conked out? Have I died?"

That's when the boy felt the giant's huge hand engulf his shoulder, and he looked back to see the legendary Yuma's finest grin.

"Congratulations, son. You have made it to the Brink."

-CHAPTER 38-

There Be Dragons

Jesse sobbed uncontrollably inside her golden cage of horrors when she heard the commotion erupting from behind Pepper's lodge across the street.

She snapped off a few dead tree branches to get a better view, but it was hard to miss anyone the size of Berk and Moody trying to tiptoe with a big metal cart banging around in the middle of the night.

"Pssst! Something's up," Jesse sniffed back tears and called down to Kate, who was just stirring herself. "Look, Kate," she pointed. "Those two idiots are up to something no good."

Kate and the others climbed to their feet but couldn't make out any details.

Tucked away inside her basement, Pepper was strategizing with a handful of her campaign managers about defeating Yuma and yet still entertaining everyone without losing the crowd's enthusiasm—when the back door slammed open behind them. Everyone at the table squealed and dove to the floor, fearing Yuma's inevitable revenge until Pepper spotted her sons walking in.

"You two idiots! I said sneak it in!" Pepper snapped as she dusted herself off.

The brothers uncovered the dragon eggs with a deflated flourish before the surprised co-conspirators, producing a sharp gasp around the war table.

"Tah-dah."

"It is true, Pepper! You weren't exaggerating."

329

"I've never seen a proper dragon's egg before, let alone seven. I thought they were just fables?"

"Of course, it's true, Nathan. I just told you I had dragon eggs not five minutes ago. Aren't you paying attention?" Pepper chastised. "Alright. Are we all clear between us, then? What the proper order of events are tomorrow? One- my coronation parades. Two- my crowning and the important ring transfer, and then three—we light the fuse... and Kaboom."

"Yes, Mum," they bowed.

"And I want you to reconfirm that we have received all my online shipments for the big reveal?"

"Yes, mum. All electronic special effects, video systems, cameras, big screens, etcetera are in perfect operating order and charged up and ready to go on your command?" the computer geek, Percy Bex, answered.

"That's wonderful news, Bex. Alright. Get out of here, losers. I have some major miracles to perform overnight if I'm going to pull off a real showstopper tomorrow night."

Pepper began examining the eggs even before her henchmen exited the underground room.

"What are you going to do with them all, Ma?" Berk wanted to know as he watched her tap the eggs with her knuckles.

"Why, the first thing, my darling, is to reduce that haunted forest across the lake into a pile of ashes. After that heathen watches the rest of his life burn down around him, then I will unleash my new pups on that evil bastard that killed their mother and my proper sons so long ago."

"Who was it killed the last dragon, Ma?"

"Who do you think, idiot?"

"You?"

"No, fool! Yuma! The real demon that lives across the lake!"

"Sorry, Ma. I was just asking."

"I know. I know. We're all so excited we're agitated."

330

Pepper patted his cheek as she calmed herself and reexamined these extraordinary gifts with a magnifying glass. She kept paging through her collection of ancient dragon lore on her phone and looking up popular reincarnation spells for reference.

"First, I'm going to do my homework. And then I'm going to unleash a fistful of dragons and shove them straight up the world's keester!" she howled in delight.

Even the caged kids across the street could hear her triumphant cackle.

But any giddiness was short-lived once Pepper inspected inside the colorful structures. The seven eggs sparkled like living jewels on the outside, but Pepper soon realized they were damaged by smoke and fire. Any hatchlings appeared poached on the inside from contact with the intense underground flames.

"Nothing but parboiled dragon chicks. Useless to me. Just like you two!"

Berk and Moody's mood tanked.

Pepper Wixx hadn't felt a disappointment this sharp for centuries, except for Yuma's recent survival.

"How old do you think they were, Ma?" Berk asked, sniffing back a green tear.

"Do I look like a...?" she killed her angry response.

Pepper felt an actual pang of remorse shooting down an abandoned nerve ending.

She realized the significance of this incredible gift and understood how hard Berk and Moody must have labored to discover these rare gems in time for her coronation.

"I'm sorry, boys," she patted their dour faces and brought up a blood-red crystal from her pouch, and turned to reinspect her precious gifts.

She hoped she might find a spark of biological life to work her dirty deeds with. But one after another, the results were the same. Each damaged egg held only the petrified remains of a dead dragon chick inside.

Until she reached the red one.

When Pepper gazed inside the enormous egg, something blinked back with six yellow eyes. The witch was staring eyeball to eyeball with a living dragon chick so desperate to hatch that it vibrated the egg as it thrashed for its life inside.

Pepper squealed and dropped to her knees as the jagged jewels covering the outside shattered off.

"Oh, my!"

"What, Ma? What?"

Berk couldn't believe anything could frighten his terrifying mother. He snatched the crumbling red egg off the cart and drew back to hurl it away.

"No! You idiot! Drop it. No! No! Forget that too! Scratch everything! Do not drop it, sweetie!"

Pepper chilled her shrill, and Berk froze in place, panting heavily as a very confused Moody danced around in panic.

"What scared you so bad, Ma?" Berk wanted to understand and smash something for her.   "Did it hurt you?"

"Put that egg down gently... my sweet, precious son. You were both right the first time, you wonderful, wonderful boys."

Berk lowered the egg back into the nest, and his mother kissed him on his furry chin and grinned victoriously.

"Thanks to my feeble-minded morons... surprise people! There be dragons in Dark Hollows again!"

-CHAPTER 39-

The Brink

Yuma relaxed when he discovered himself back inside the sanctity of the crystal caverns again.

He plopped his weary body down on the top step of the grand musical staircase, and it blatted out a couple of dissonant chords in response.

Plunk, blannnk!

And when the exhausted giant stretched out, the moody steps answered with two more impertinent notes.

Plunk! Plenkkk!

Yuma ignored the disrespect and released a long exhale—displaying his deep satisfaction after completing another arduous expedition to the center of it all. His recent wounds still wept at the memory.

"The Light in the Dark has arrived safely. That is all that matters now." Yuma felt triumphant in this achievement. "Whoever thought it could be a child?"

Zip, Zash, and Zee zoomed back up the crystal stairway to rejoin their team, and the hummingbirds landed on Yuma's shoulders like tiny, glowing epaulets.

Zack and Harley were still speechless and frozen in place at the top of the Grand Crystal Stairway. Neither had moved a muscle—staggered by what lay before them.

Worlds were spinning within worlds here.

From their vantage point, they had a mind-boggling overview of this entire vaulted underworld. The crystal cathedral soared over their heads in a soaring dreamscape of such immense scale that no human being had even dreamed of it before—not even in the deepest depths of the Dreampool. Not like this. Not as it honestly existed.

The shimmering air inside resonated with the perpetual dream chants of the tiny creatures parading below them as every crystal structure within this looking-glass world vibrated and shimmered in sympathetic harmony with their unbroken incantations.

The arch of the grand stairway provided the only entrance into this spectacular, sparkling underworld, and the wide stairs descended for over a mile before reaching the shores of the molten river that supported the great jewel.

The shimmering, four-hundred-foot colossus was held upright in the center of a ring of concentric circles wrapped around its base like a serpent—as if the symbolic snake was cherishing the last egg on earth—or the first.

Birth. Life. Death. Renewal.

"What in the world... is this place? What is this all about, Yuma? Zack finally asked, still as confused as he'd ever been.

"What in the world... I like your take on that, Zack. You have not lost your good humor yet," Yuma chuckled at the boy's expression. "That is good."

"I don't think I ever owned a sense of humor to lose. But I think I've lost my mind now," Zack answered. "Or you lost it for me somewhere, Yuma."

The warrior chuckled again at the child's natural grit as he watched the intelligent boy fight for his mental equilibrium this far down the rabbit hole.

The giant shot to his feet, beating against his chest, and opened his long arms before him.

"Welcome, my boy... to the wonder of it all! Behold, the only secret more important than yourself, now."

Zack was breathless

"I..." was all he could muster.

"There is not another soul living on this planet who knows this inner world."

"Really?"

"But now... you do."

"Wait... what about them? Who are they? What are they?" Zack asked—still mesmerized as he gestured to the thousands of robed creatures shuffling along like happy penguins far below on the bright crystal boardwalks.

"I still do not speak their language fluidly, but these holy creatures call themselves the Illuminators. As far as I know, they are born sightless and deaf, yet they sing these wonderful tunes and trek wherever they choose by torchlight. They are the keepers and transcribers of the world's collective wisdom and knowledge. And they capture and preserve all planetary knowledge and record it here inside the crystal vaults."

"For who?"

"I believe for you."

Zack's eyes gleamed as they captured everything at once.

"The Illuminators possess the ability to see the past, present, and future. And they share those insights with all species, including humankind, whenever they feel the need to step in."

"How?"

"By releasing the information into the Dreampool, we all share. They are the ones who divined life's daily need for sleep as we developed to help tame our messy destinies. The Illuminators alone maintain the precarious balance between the physical world and the encroachment of the dark."

"How?"

"No... no one understands how they do what they do, except themselves. They do not pass those secrets along. Not even to an Immortal."

"And... that?" Zack pointed up at the colossal egg-shaped jewel itself.

"They romanced that out of the purest crystals ever discovered on the planet, and they discovered that beauty right here underneath the Sacred Forest. They refer to that as their

Eternity Stone. I simply call it what it is... the Big Egg. The end-all and be-all. Which came first?"

He took a moment and allowed the confused boy time to absorb this new mind-numbing information as Zack gazed off in amazement.

There was a long pause before Yuma spoke, pointing out more details.

"That great egg possesses its own inherent powers. The Illuminators inscribe the accumulating history of all life down to the finest detail on the stone's surface in their elegant shorthand. You'll learn that the earth's stability above relies on maintaining this Eternity Stone's balance below. It's like gravity, and life cannot exist without both."

Yuma dropped the weight of the world's problems onto the boy's slight shoulders.

"If the Illuminators are discovered or the Eternity Stone unearthed and compromised..."

"What? What will happen?"

"That will turn it into the Calamity Stone that Wixx predicted it could be. The thing she craves most. And as Time Warriors, we must never let Wixx, or anyone else like her, be the authors of our doom or our future."

Zack couldn't grasp the scale of responsibility that the giant spoke about in this confounding place.

"And who are you, again?" Zack asked. Never feeling he knew or understood the correct answer. "I mean, really? Who are you?"

"I am Tupac Yuma, The Time Warrior. Protector and Guardian of the Brink, Father of the Sacred Forest, Punisher of the Wicked, and Revenger of the Wronged. The One Who Walks Between!" Yuma thumped his chest with each of his sacred obligations.

"I am the firstborn son under a howling moon. My father's tribe was the Tawantinsuyu. Inca. Tupac Yuma was my given name at birth, while those in my past had called me by other names when they believed I was a thunder god—

which I am not—but I prefer Yuma, as I always have."

"Then who am I?" Zack asked. "I'm just a nobody. With no name. No place."

"Nonsense. Why you are Zackery Goodnight of the Four Winds Tribe—born out of love and sacrifice. The solemn Earthshaker who can move mountains with his mind and see across the spectrums at will. The boy who will cross every divide laid down before him. The Light in the Dark. The boy who will change the entire world with only his kind eyes. And the next chosen Time-Warrior of the Crystal Guild."

"No way."

"Make no mistake. The Elders only present this exalted position upon new candidates who hold themselves to the highest levels of courage, integrity, and reverence for life. That is who you are, young man. That is who you are about to become. And that is who this world is about to reckon with."

The more Zack listened, the less he understood.

"There have been few Time Guardians summoned to duty. And at least one guardian must exist to eternally protect Mother Nature and the Illuminators' sanctity by maintaining the proper balance for all."

"And that's me?"

"Once you have sworn your undying allegiance to the Elders, you will assume your duties with the same bravery, dignity, and respect that all Time Warriors have always displayed. And at that moment... you will become immortal."

Yuma let the last depth charge sink in.

"What? Like, the forever and ever kind?"

"Close enough," Yuma promised.

"How old are you again?"

"Older than dirt, but not as old as sand," Yuma grinned.

Young Zack tried comprehending what he felt he already knew in his informed heart.

"But in return, you will lose your simple path forward in your human life," Yuma warned.

"So?"

"And every special connection in your life that might have ever existed in the Upside world. Those opportunities will be lost forever, as well, my boy."

Zack smiled.

"No one will even miss me."

Yuma was passionate as he swept his arms wide open again.

"Nonsense! You are now a true Time Guardian of this world!"

Zack wasn't impressed.

"Sheesh. Give me a break, Yuma. I'm only nine."

"I know, Zack. I know how you feel, boy. Even now, I still have more questions than answers. You being the prime example."

"Why me?"

"Who knows? Because just as I reached my own elevated plateau in my learning and believed that I had achieved most answers to life's imponderable questions, you arrived and showed me I knew nothing all along. You've wiped my expectations clean, Zackery Goodnight."

Yuma's demeanor darkened as he thought of all the world-shattering changes the small boy was bringing with him to both unsuspecting worlds with his knowledge and visions of the future.

"I'm sorry if I messed everything up."

"You rush in like a whirlwind and blow my world apart with a single puff. Looking back, it makes my quest for ultimate knowledge seem frivolous without having your gifts of Truesight."

"That can't be close to true. You've kept both worlds safe forever."

"But never by myself. And now you."

Yuma sat silent momentarily as the seed of that dark realization sank in.

"I have been nothing but an unenlightened fool—even when the truth was right in front of my eyes, I couldn't see it. I have been wrong about everything. I have re-made the same avoidable mistake that all fallible, uninformed humans make. Repeatedly. And yet, I judged everyone else as inferior. Superior and infallible was how I felt I deserved to be treated. I am a legend, after all. But all I feel now is disappointment at myself. My silly pride made me blind and vulnerable. In my mind, I felt I was a much better being than this."

He paused before he spoke, and the giant's eyes brightened as he felt a new vision taking shape in his heart that suggested a new path.

The Wait. The Earn. The See. The Be.

"Together."

"What?"

"Together. Somehow... you, and I, and Harley will discover the answers we seek."

Yuma noticed in the middle of his epiphany that Zack had tuned him out.

"What are they all doing down there?" Zack pointed at the gigantic egg and the tiny Illuminator oarsman surrounding its base, urging the molten gold to flow inside the snake-shaped channels.

Zack felt trapped inside an insane dream that he might never awaken. He'd lost his grip on reality and was mentally free-falling.

Yuma noticed.

"Let me introduce you to the leader of the Guild. Then you might understand what's happening here," the giant suggested. He lifted the little boy and slung him across his back like a quiver of precious arrows.

Harley bounded down the musical stairway just ahead of them—racing Zip, Zash, and Zee to the river glistening below and plonking out his own style of canine road music as he went.

Plunk. Plunk, plunk, Harley riffed a merry tune.

About halfway down, Yuma stopped short provoking another sour note, and he urged Zack to climb off and try the rude musical steps.

The giant hoped to lighten the frightened boy's mood in this beautiful and magical place.

"Is Dr. Briscoe making me see all this?"

"No.

"Am I drugged and strapped down on a table somewhere at the Institute?"

"No.

"Is all this just another mind experiment I won't remember?"

"No. Go. Dance!" Yuma prodded. "Every warrior should dance in celebration of their life every day. It is the way. Go ahead. Dance. Never be embarrassed. Anyway, they do it all the time down here."

As soon as Zack stepped onto the first crystal step, it sang back to him in a lovely, shimmering tone; only this time, the stair lit up on contact.

The little boy giggled with each colorful foot tap and bright step, finding an instant delight in the otherness of this whimsical crystal world.

Rippling rhythms of light bloomed inside the clear quartz stairs wherever he danced upon them.

"Whoa! Those nasty stairs have never done that for me, little big man!" Yuma shouted.

The monk's chanting inside the crystal cathedral halted for the first time in a millennium.

There was an audible gasp from the Illuminators, followed by a profound silence as they listened.

The sightless Illuminators dropped their hoods and turned as one, simultaneously witnessing the same awe-inspiring spectacle. It was almost as if the blind monks could see for the first time in their long uninterrupted lives of eternal night and song.

The shaken flock returned to their regular duties but kept stealing glimpses over their shoulders as Zack continued his long musical descent toward them.

The Illuminators began singing again, refilling the cavern's open spaces with resonance. But now, a new sense of awe and fun was rising inside their heroic music that complimented Zack's intensity. They heralded the boy's spontaneous entrance down the melodic stairs.

This was an unforgettable moment for everyone present.

The Illuminators grew increasingly excited when suddenly individuals broke free from their tasks, a breach unheard of before Zack's appearance, and ran to embrace him.

Zack kept drawing closer and closer—but then grew shy and started dancing back up the stairways, replaying the same refrain in reverse.

But once the boy stepped off at the final landing, every Illuminator rushing in reached out to touch his clothes. And once they connected, they spun on their heels and followed him like instant cult members.

Yuma couldn't believe what he was witnessing. Even a giant didn't stir up this kind of excitement after centuries.

"Curiosity? Or is it sincere reverence?"

Zack couldn't understand what he was experiencing, either.

This place is weird.

Why do I feel at home here?

How?

Yuma led the boy and dog onto the elevated walkways forming concentric channels around the great stone. The air hung thick with a constant mist and steam billowing up from the hissing gold-laden channels below.

Not a single drop of moisture touched any Illuminator's bald head. Even here, the perpetual showers fell straight up and away from them, with the golden-flecked creatures staying immaculate and bone dry as always.

But Yuma, Zack, and Harley were as drenched as if they went snorkeling.

Soaring forty stories above their heads loomed the most magnificent hand-cut jewel ever produced.

"And what... is the point of all... this again? Zack pointed up at the skyscraper of all gems.

He couldn't find the words to describe the scale of what he was looking at any longer.

"That is the Eternity-Stone, Zack. Only the Grand Master can answer your questions about it. If he chooses."

Yuma guided the boy through the billowing mists and over to a solitary monk dressed in dry robes isolated on a remote landing.

Unlike the others, the grandmaster's robes were crimson and gold as he sat cross-legged and alone at the base of the towering rotating stone.

The small holy man turned from his sacred writings on the Eternity Stone at Zack's respectful approach, and the creature's lovely halo twisted with him.

Yuma urged the reluctant boy forward while hanging back on the sidelines with Zack's growing mob of fans. Everyone displayed respect and reverence for the holy creature.

Up close, the tiny golden Grand Master appeared melted down in layers over time, growing softer and wider with constant usage, like a pair of worn-out slippers.

He was older than all others by eons. And his long, golden fingertips were stained to the elbow with the glowing inks from millennia of transcribing the world's greatest joys and sorrows onto the Eternity Stone.

When the Grand Master stood and reached out to take Zack's hand, the rain stopped falling onto the boy's body at once.

And then, with no warning, a precise Lucid Pulse of towering emotions surged between the old master's body and Zack's mind. The ancient Illuminator acted as if electrocuted, and he cartwheeled away before Zack caught him.

When their bodies touched again, a magical bond

formed, and the Grand Master shared his revelations to the entire flock telepathically in a bright flash of empathetic insight.

And in that hysterical moment, the chorus was stunned into complete silence, and the holy chanting inside the Crystal Caverns halted for only the second time in a thousand years.

But after a beat—the Illuminators began singing again with a newfound joy and happiness until they collapsed into fits of wild, unbridled laughter. And their voices sounded like the trilling of a million tinkling silver bells.

-CHAPTER 40-

Essence

The Illuminators held one teaching sacred above all others: their eternal search for purity in all things.

The purity of crystal.

The purity of thought.

The purity of knowledge

The purity of intention.

The purity of execution.

The purity of spirit.

The purity of devotion.

The purity of deed.

The purity of love.

The purity of expression.

The purity of joy.

Whenever these emotional creatures laughed, they launched into their bliss with total abandon. The unexpected, remarkable sound of a single, laughing Illuminator was among the most thrilling experiences anyone could ever experience. And with thousands erupting at once, it was a delight to ear and spirit alike. No living creature captured the joyousness of life so profoundly in a simple, cheerful laugh.

"Therefore, we are!" they trilled to each other in their mysterious language.

Zack was unprepared for the flood of overwhelming positive emotions that swept over him. The awe-inspiring sense of celebration in their heartfelt sentiments gave the boy his first goosebumps.

Even Harley's fur stood on end as the air became electrified with happiness.

And the giddy Illuminators would not, could not, stop laughing. Their Grand Master was the worst of the bunch, as Zack's revelations had reinvigorated his tired soul and thrown his holiness into a state of foot-stomping hysterics. Zack tried to steady him from falling over, but the tiny holy man kept dancing.

The ancient philosopher gazed up in Zack's arms and smiled at the pure-hearted soul, who towered over him like a giant. It was as if the sightless monk could see him as he reached out and stroked Zack's face.

Another Illuminator tried to steady their Grand Master and froze on contact, falling into the same blissful state.

Then a third monk grabbed the second's shoulder, and the domino effect followed. The revelations swept through the crowds of laughing monks as the sights and sounds of the world revealed themselves to them in overlapping waves of excitement.

Yuma felt left out of the big party.

"Why are they all laughing? What is happening?"

Thousands of delirious creatures waddled in from every direction—all sharing in the same wonderment and delight.

"Hey! What about me?" Yuma pleaded.

Harley was howling along with the others as Zip, Zash, and Zee tumbled in gleeful spirals.

That's when the jealous giant reached down and folded Zack's tiny hand into his.

The giant was startled as the rain fell away from his body in a massive halo of reverse raindrops, and he froze when a blinding searchlight snapped on only inches away from his eyes.

"Aghhhhh! I'm blinded!

He squeezed his eyes shut and held onto Zack's tiny hand without crushing it.

And as his vision cleared, Yuma perceived the actual

world, just as Zack Goodnight had lived it every day since his birth. And it was as unnerving and remarkable as the young boy had described it. Clouds of gossamer-thin Inklings shimmered past him like an atmosphere full of ethereal thoughts.

Merely by touching hands, the Grand Master accessed the vast uncharted spectrums of all Zack's visual realities. And the holy man gifted these unexpected delights with his flock.

The third awakening is here! They proclaimed telepathically—announcing a new high holy holiday.

It all seemed impossible, but beyond perceiving every visual frequency, Zack could see spatially and temporally—simultaneously—even in opposing directions.

"I don't know why I'm like this. I was just born this way." Zack answered the unasked whispers flooding through his mind.

The beguiling air dancers came visible in every size and shape as they coalesced in and out of existence before Yuma while filling the crystal cavern's vastness with their everyday lives.

Three dimensions became four. Then five. Six, with other tantalizing clues lingering nearby.

"How many more are there?" Yuma asked as his new vision grew wider and wider.

He realized Inklings didn't physically fly through the atmosphere like a bird, bug, or plane. Nothing that mechanical.

Inklings existed on an entirely different spectrum and frequency of life than all earthbound lifeforms. Here were ancient sky beings that had existed eternally and flourished within the fabric of our atmosphere's electrochemical makeup long before the continents had even cooled.

A high environment, radiation-resistant transitional lifeform nourished by the shifting oceans of pure air and magnetic waves that swirl around our planet like a shield against the deadly solar winds—allowing other organisms to thrive below.

If anyone could physically capture the fourth-dimensional beauty of a single note of music, then seeing an Inkling would be like listening to a symphony with your eyes.

Boy and giant's roles were suddenly reversed, and Yuma's sophisticated brain was reeling in confusion.

"Drive anyone mad. Indeed, boy!" he yelled to Zack, trying to maintain his balance.

As he saw more, his consciousness continued to dilate like the iris of a camera lens.

He realized that every human mind that ever existed was ignorant of this amazing truth at the heart of all our misconceptions about Mother Nature. Balance and harmony were everything at the center of it all.

Misidentified as demons, sprites, angels, foo fighters, flying saucers, Tic Tac UFOs, and UAPs throughout the tumble of all the years by humans, these elegant, mysterious life forms, no matter their exotic nature and shape, were always of this earth.

Not visitors—nor extraterrestrials—but daily co-inhabitants on our tiny blue lifeboat of a planet.

Fish and whales live in the sea.

Humankind and animals live on the land.

Birds and insects fly through the sky.

But only the Inklings exist within the very fabric of the air and heavens above.

Yuma wiped away a tear as the ecstatic monks continued singing and dancing.

When Zack realized what was happening because of him, he chuckled.

"That's funny. Now, everyone understands?"

Zack felt vindicated—the sanest person in the room for once.

"Just like I've always said... everyone else has a problem. Not me. Maybe they won't label me loony tunes anymore!" Zack grinned. "The jokes on you guys!"

The young boy grew eager to present his truth to the

rest of the world.

He was the first human born to behold the center of coexistence and all its meaning.

Zackery Goodnight became The Light in the Darkness before Yuma's eyes, and the staggered Time Warrior summoned enough of a voice to ask questions.

"Do they know we exist? Are they intelligent? Have feelings?" Yuma asked.

"Yes, they do. And families," Archie answered as he appeared out of nowhere.

The sight of the ghostly country boy startled the giant.

"Nice to meet you—face to face again. It's been a long time," Archie said.

The shimmering entity appeared angry, and Yuma didn't understand whose magic this represented.

"Don't you remember me, Yuma?" Archie teased. "You should. Reach back. Reach way back and think."

-CHAPTER 41-

What Now?

It grew late in Dark Hollows. No one was paying attention to the pretty Uman party decorations any longer. Their brass-caged novelty wore off as soon as other prize livestock and demented decorations began pouring in from all over the hollows in tribute to the new Queen of the Damned.

Kate was concentrating on the oversized lock on the cage door. She was trying to determine the size of the key needed to open such an antiquated lock.

"Jesse?" Kate called up to the higher cages.

"What?"

"You still have that cat claw hair clip?"

"Of course... right here. Like always."

Jesse reached back, pulled the black cat metal clip out, and flashed it.

"That is such good news!" Kate chirped. "Emiliano?"

"Yup?" he answered from below.

"These bars are too thick and solid to pry open. Can you use that computerized brain of yours to scan the insides of that keyhole and maybe figure out how we can make some kind of key?"

"I don't know. Sure, I'll try anything if it means getting out of here. What are we going to use?"

Kate scanned her cage of horrors for any artifact or bone large enough to fashion into a key when her eyes fell on her sneakers. "You think a slab of thick rubber might do?"

"Who knows? If it's strong enough. Any bones in

349

here are too brittle. I'll get back to you." Emiliano explored the lock—purpose-driven now; he gained some badly needed momentum.

"Kate, stop it," Pavarty called down from her cage. "Maybe Ozzy has this right! We shouldn't make any more waves. Quiet down."

"We'll be alright, Pav. But we've got to do something to get ourselves out of here."

"How can you know that? Pepper will go, gangster, if we run away! And then, what? Party over—out of time, guaranteed girlfriend!"

"It's okay, Pav. I understand, hon. It changes nothing... but I understand," Kate replied.

"Don't do anything! You'll get us all murdered!" Ozzy whispered. "It's not up to just you anymore, Kate!"

"Oz... we have to save our own lives if no one is coming to help. There's no one else to do it. We're on our own, just like always. That simple."

"I'm not giving up my life over nothing!"

"Up to you two. But I'm getting us out," Kate tried to sound confident, even though terrified.

Ozzy sunk back into the glop of his cage, trembling. "Please don't do this to me."

"Psst! Hey Kate!" Emiliano called back.

"Yeah?" Kate answered.

"I've calculated the rough measurements. Feels like a simple bolt lock design inside. Probably just click open once we get something seated inside it properly and hit the pin. But what do you want me to make it out of?" Emiliano asked. "There aren't any bones in here strong enough to make a key this huge."

"This," Kate tossed down her pink sneaker toward his cage without thinking. She should have warned Emiliano.

Instead, the sneaker sailed past his cage and bounced onto the ground, disappearing behind the reviewing stands being constructed below.

"Oops! Oh, no!"

"Well, I guess I don't need just one shoe."

She pulled off the other sneaker and held it out for Emil to zero in on.

"Let's do this right the first time—unless you want to give up your own."

"Barefoot, down here? No thanks, that's insane." Emil didn't like that choice.

"Thanks for making me feel better about my decisions," Kate replied.

"Toss it, girl."

Kate kissed her last sneaker goodbye.

"I drop on three. One... two... three."

She let go, and the shoe spun slowly through the air, and Emiliano fumbled at it at first. It threatened to tumble out of his cage before he tackled it in the goo.

"Got it! I got it."

Everyone let out a sigh and a small cheer as they watched.

"Jess! Toss down your cat claw," Kate asked.

"Absolutely no way, girl," Jesse shot back.

"What? Why not?"

"I'm not throwing my last line of personal defense to fumble fingers down there. No offense, Emil."

"None taken, Jess."

Emiliano felt the same way about his lack of reflexes. Being a proud, unathletic nerd didn't bother him in the least. He had his intellectual muscles flexed instead.

"Listen? What if I just draw it out on the sole, and you cut it out yourself, Jess?" Emiliano broached a face-saving response.

"Deal, dude!".

"And I'll do all the transfers in between," Kate added.

"Wait? Oh no. That means I still must throw it back up to you, right?" Emiliano began worrying again. Still, he shut down his distracted brain and let his mechanical instincts take over. He went to work, etching the rough shape he envisioned into the sole.

"Coop?" Kate called over to the vulture cage beside her. "See anything?"

"Nope. Nothing. I saw a truck driver leave his engine running when he popped out, but he returned and drove away. Since then, nothing. Just more of those things showing up!"

Coop slumped inside his cage, staring down at the random night stalkers cruising below and pointing up at the pretty Uman cages.

"Looks like we're the freaks down here."

"I already knew that feeling before I got here," Kate replied.

"What's the plan after we get out of these disgusting cages? Ech!" Pavarty asked.

Kate watched as sparks of rebellion re-igniting inside her friend's eyes. "We'll need some big ass wheels to make a clean getaway from these cretins, and you know that, right? Those big suckers are fast!" The sassy Pavarty of old resurfaced.

"But wait. None of us can drive yet."

"I don't know how."

"I might, but not a stick."

"Neither do I."

"I can drive," Coop insisted. "That I can do. As long as the floor mat's not covering the accelerator, I can drive like Steve McQueen!" he bragged.

"I like Vin Diesel?"

"Him too."

"Yeah. Some of us were there that night, hotrod. That wasn't driving, fool! That was crop-dusting," Pavarty smirked. "Maybe we should nickname you Pegasus. You had that pretty pony flying high in the sky that night, boy!" Pavarty relived it in her mind's eye.

"Pssst! Hey, Kate! Finished!" Emiliano called out from his cage below and held the critical design up for inspection.

"Wait. But that's just a big rubber hook. That doesn't

look like a key! It doesn't have teeth?"

"Tim? Does that look like any kind of lock pick that might work?"

Tim opened his swollen eyes and sat up, still suffering from the physical assault.

"Yeah. Maybe, man. It's a big enough pick. Why not? Try it."

Emiliano held the sneaker up with the new design etched into the waffled bottom.

"Time to play catch again?"

"Batter up," Kate said, stretching her arms out as klutzy Emiliano tried the same.

"Alright then, boys and girls. On three. You throw to me on three. One, two, three..."

Kate nodded.

Emiliano flipped the canvas shoe up, heel first, and it tumbled through the air like a sick frisbee. But once Kate snagged it, a small, hopeful cheer erupted from the other cages, except for Ozzy's.

Kate took another deep breath and prepared herself for the crucial toss to Jesse above.

"Ready, Jess? On three. One... two... three!"

Kate flipped her remaining sneaker up to Jess—who snagged it with one hand. She took her cat claw hairpin and shredded away the canvas's outer skin before carving Emiliano's crude design out of the thick rubber sole.

"Hey, Kate," Josh called down. "What can I do?"

"Just keep looking beautiful, Joshy. That's good enough for now."

"That I can do." Vacant Josh slid back down and checked back out.

They were silent for a few minutes as the once sleepy little town teemed with nightlife below.

"Hey, Kate!" Jesse called out. "Check this out!"

She held up the makeshift rubber pick with the sneaker's distinctive sole embedded on the surface.

"It looks like Captain Hook ate a waffle!"

"Beck-beck-bagokkkkk!" Oz imitated a rooster. "Might have more *cluck* with a rubber chicken, people!" Ozzy could never let a chance to burn someone pass.

Jesse released a brief prayer and shoved the oversized pick into the lock. After an awkward jiggle or two, it slid inside as if built to specs.

"Not bad, huh?" Emil boasted, satisfied with his handiwork.

After several rough attempts, the rubber pick kept twisting inside the keyhole.

"Ha!" Ozzy laughed as his nasty prediction came true.

"You want to bet it works, Hollyweird?" Emiliano challenged the TV addict.

"Bet it doesn't, fart-beak!"

"Double everything you've ever owed me or nothing!" He offered a sucker bet that the great Oz couldn't refuse.

"Done, dork!"

They even air-shook on it.

Jess continued applying pressure on the twisting rubber pick—rotating it even more than before as it began twisting and creaking forward until the ancient lock surrendered with a satisfying clunk.

"It's open! I opened it!" Jesse tried to stifle her volume and excitement.

"What?" Ozzy couldn't believe it. "No way!"

"Genius!" Josh yelled.

"Way. What did you expect from a genius? You owe me big time, boy!" Emil grinned.

"What do we do now?" Jesse asked.

"Think!" was the only thing that a surprised Kate had ready to offer.

Now that they could escape from their disgusting cages, they needed to hatch an actual battle plan to get themselves out of town unnoticed and safe. All nine of them —not counting Zack.

"Let's think about this some more before we do anything stupid. Everybody think now. Think outside the box!"

"You mean think outside this stinking cage?"

"Yeah. That's exactly what I mean."

-CHAPTER 42-

The Fires Down Below

Archie shimmered in and out of the essence like an Inkling himself—appearing pliable and able to shift back and forth dimensionally at will.

"I remember you, son," Yuma whispered with a fresh horror shading the timbre of his voice. "I recognized you the minute I saw you."

The sight of this slight boy terrified the warrior as his memories of a century ago came flooding back over him with no warning. "It was you."

Archie flashed his familiar gap-toothed grin. But this time, there was a sinister edge to it as he lowered his brow.

"How do you two know each other?" Zack asked.

"It is a long and terrible story, son."

"You can tell me anything, Yuma."

"Tell him." Archie urged with a new, murderous glint burning behind green eyes.

Yuma paused, unsure how to start.

"Good people have run Wixx and her deviants out of every mud hut, tepee, village, hamlet, and city that they ever lived—no matter the continent, century, or society, in the Upside world. But, once those fugitives assembled down here, they couldn't believe their good fortune."

"Until they met you," Archie interjected, and Yuma's face changed with the telling.

"Not at first. I was drawn away from the Brink on another campaign for the Illuminators for a while. That

356

is when these vermin first invaded the Sacred Forest in the late sixteen-hundreds. They ran and sought any refuge from the relentless bloodhounds hunting them down in the Upside world. That is why they despise the dog now. They have cowered down here like bedbugs ever since. Hidden underneath a cloak of invisibility that Mother Nature has conjured over these lands to protect everything good and innocent below."

"Like the Illuminators?" Zack asked.

Yuma nodded and continued.

"And more. Once entrenched, these predators multiplied uninterrupted. They've been growing here for four hundred years like an unchecked plague."

"And you couldn't stop their evil from spreading?" Zack asked.

"Oh, make no mistake—my army of giants stopped them every time from going any further. And not one polluting monster has ever laid foot on our shores. We slaughtered them by the thousands. If you've ever seen their graveyards, you'd understand the scale of the carnage."

"I have."

"But there are only so many giants left in the world, and the evil dead kept overwhelming us in endless waves—year after year—until the worst of them outsmarted me by using my sense of honor to defeat us."

"And now, only you are left alive out of all of them," Archie added.

"Yes."

These horrid memories always floated just below the surface of his everyday life.

"Wixx and her minions continued mining on their side of the lake. The deeper they excavated in their unyielding greed, the closer they were to discovering the Illuminators' sanctuary."

Yuma paused.

"Can you imagine what would happen to those

defenseless golden creatures and the Eternity Stone if Wixx ever took possession of them?"

"What?" Zack asked.

"Chaos. On a global scale. The earth's balance would wobble and fall—civilizations would crumble. It has all happened before, and if we are not careful, it will happen again."

Yuma seemed to plead his case to a hostile jury of two.

"I had to stop them from ever attaining that holy knowledge, and that is when I decided."

Zack witnessed the events as they transpired now, just as if he were standing next to Yuma back then.

"I trapped you right here when I set the first backfire," Yuma spoke to Archie as he remembered. "There was no way for me to warn any helpless, enslaved people. You were under the strict whip of the Overlords, and I couldn't give away my ultimate plan and risk failure."

His eyes pleaded for understanding from Archie for his desperate wartime actions. With no response, Yuma hung his head in shame.

"That's when I killed you. And all the rest. The good along with the bad."

He raised his head and stared back at Archie.

"That's where I last saw you. Burning alive."

He remembered spotting that panicked cluster of little boys working as slaves alongside other captured creatures when the fires broke out. The enormous flames trapped them on the far side of the Top Shelf Mine as they all tried to scramble to safety up the incline.

Ogres and creeps scrambled over the top of the boys, knocking Archie's lunch pail out of his hand in the mad scramble for safety.

A. McGregor III.

Zack remembered reading that name on the miner's scorched lunch pail at the Top Shelf Mine with Archie just before it exploded.

Archie McGregor?

"That's me, boyo!" Archie winked, answering without Zack saying a word aloud.

Heroic Archie was shoving and pulling the younger ones over the top of a berm—his eyes searched for any avenue of escape.

That's when he spotted the enormous Native American warrior staring at him from across the chasm that divided the center of the mining levels like a chimney.

"Why isn't he running? I remember thinking to myself." Archie said. "Then I realized why."

The giant standing in the shadows held a torch in one hand and a bucket of steaming pine tar in the other.

Their eyes met momentarily before Archie turned back to help his screaming brothers. The panicked ogres continued to knock them aside, and they all tumbled back down the berm when the first massive flashover happened. Roaring flames consumed everyone in less time than it took to remember all their names.

The underground inferno grew fierce once provoked by the tar trails dripped strategically throughout the tunnels by Yuma. There was no fighting back against the intense firestorms once they reached the subterranean gas pockets. Only years of death and destruction followed.

"I remember you, boy. You are the brave one." Yuma said with tears rimming his eyes. "And I am sorry I stole your young breath away so early. I have never sought to kill the innocent, but there is always... collateral damage in war."

Yuma bowed his head.

"Collateral. That's a butt ugly word to say out loud. What does it mean? Things happen? Children die? And what about my little brothers? And my uncles? And my father? Do you remember them too?" Archie asked. "You killed them as well. Like they mattered to nobody. Do you remember their faces? Because I can't anymore."

"Every night since," Yuma answered honestly. "Which

359

Necromancer reanimated you, or are you a wandering soul?" Yuma asked, no longer sure who he was confessing to any longer.

"Couldn't tell ya', bub. All I know is that wherever I go, there I am!" Archie shook his head and grinned, lightening the dark mood.

He bowed at the waist, which made Zack chuckle, softening the strange reunion between murderer and victim.

"That's us!" Zack added, like he was part of the act.

"Why are you here?" Yuma asked.

"I'm not sure anymore. I thought, at first, it might be for revenge."

The boy's eyes narrowed.

"It would be well-deserved but regrettable timing," Yuma answered.

"Then, I thought I might be here just to haunt the living daylights out of you forever!"

"I would not like that either—and you would soon grow bored."

"But I don't feel anger towards you anymore, Yuma. Just pity for all your wasted time," Archie said. "You never discovered the truth."

"But now I have. It's standing beside me."

The spirit of the young country boy realized he no longer held contempt toward his family's killer. Both eternal entities, somehow sensing their unique connections in the here and now, with Zack and Harley as his bridge to the future.

There was still so much to learn about the collision between the natural and the supernatural dimensions to come.

"The truth? I don't understand why I'm here, Yuma. The Inklings invited me but haven't told me why yet," Archie admitted.

"You're both here to help... me," Zack said confidently.

The hidden strength in the young boy's voice surprised Yuma and Archie. The frightened little boy seemed timid no longer. It was like watching a cougar cub discover its claws.

"We will stop them. Together. I know that for a fact now."

"Just how do the four of us accomplish that, son?" Yuma prodded the boy.

"Well, I don't know... how... just yet. I just know we will."

"In the meantime, I will continue with other plans."

Yuma stood and took a knee, still towering over them.

"Quite an odd tribe Mother Nature has thrown together to protect her world, wouldn't you say?" Yuma said with a straight face.

Harley barked, and Yuma understood, bursting out into laughter before translating.

"Harley just joked—No worries. Now we have a proper gathering of giants!"

-CHAPTER 43-

Next stop, the Twilight Zone

Zack, Harley, and Yuma were rocketing back to the surface a hundred times faster than their tortuous descent by foot.

Their swift ride up from the bowels of the earth felt as mind-boggling as every other marvelous discovery made inside the Illuminator's complex underworld of balance and counterbalance.

They stood on top of nothing more substantial than a few petrified planks tied together as Zip, Zash, and Zee spiraled high above them in the vertical shaft.

Somehow, the rushing platform floated even keeled aboard a rising column of whitewater up through the interior of a shiny marble well, thousands of feet deep. And yet, the trip was as smooth and scary as a hi-rise elevator without cables.

The finely polished walls flew past them in a gush of wind as a series of brilliant engineering choices compensated for their shifting body weight.

"Ding! Next floor, the Twilight Zone!" Ozzy would have shouted if he had been aboard.

A bright pinpoint of light high above their heads grew larger, hinting at a star-filled night sky waiting above as they drew closer.

As they shot toward the lip of the stone shaft, their velocity didn't diminish, not even by a fraction, and the hummingbirds flew out first.

"Uh, Yuma? We're not slowing down."

362

"Hang on, Zack. This is where it always gets interesting."

There was a surprising injection of even more whitewater at the last second, providing a final burst of speed before the launch.

"Uh, oh!"

"Have as much faith in the Illuminators as they have in you."

And in those frightening last seconds, the headstrong geyser gentled and drained away into a complicated set of preordained side channels—while maintaining a safe and stable platform ride to the upper rim for the passengers.

The trio stepped off the floating deck and back into the heart of the Sacred Forest with the three Z's already waiting for them.

The colossal geyser spun away in a thrilling display of suction—leaving nothing behind but a glimpse of its diminishing whirlpool swirling hundreds of stories below.

Zack was startled when several surface boulders shuddered beside them like they were alive. And then, as if by magic, they rolled back into place using an ancient hydraulic gearing system triggered by the water's rapid retreat—recovering the secret elevator shaft with a living carpet of nature.

No one would suspect a portal existed underneath fifty tons of moss-covered stone. The stealthy enterprise blended back into the forest floor as if never disturbed.

That's how the Illuminators rolled. They employed simplicity and complex elegance in all their staggering works.

"Geez." was all the staggered Zack could muster as he shook his head.

"I agree—every time. But clear your head. We have much to do before tomorrow night," Yuma ran towards his lodge as an exhausted Zack, and Harley loped after him.

"What happens next?" Zack yelled.

"Everything!" Yuma called back.

"What do you mean?"

"War! If I know Wixx, she will attack me tomorrow night during the eclipse! I have been expecting her!"

"But we've got to sleep first, don't we?"

Twenty minutes later, Zack and Harley snored by the waterfall pool behind Yuma's lodge. The giant was still awake and standing chest-deep in the frigid waters cascading down from the batwing mountain tops. These thundering whitewaters were the source of the purity bathing the Eternity Stone far below.

Yuma was regenerating his damaged flesh by grabbing boulders the size of VWs out of the river and heaving them thirty feet away. One after another, he hoisted and hurled these enormous boulders into a growing mound, as if making practice shots for the next big game.

"Remember, no matter what happens tonight. No matter what you see, nothing will be real unless you believe it down here," Yuma warned, pointing to his heart. "Do you understand?"

Zack stirred.

"What?"

"That is when Wixx will have you where she wants you. Sometimes you cannot believe your eyes, only your heart in these battles. Wixx might have grown all-powerful, as they say, but she can never defeat a pure heart like yours. Never. No matter what silly old-world spells she slings against us."

Yuma poked the sleep-deprived boy with a wet hand.

"Do you understand me, Zack?"

"Then why don't we just attack her first? While they are all still sleeping?"

"Because you're not quite ready yet. But if you listen to me, you will be."

Zack sat up. He saw his position inside the natural world in a new, strategic way. He knew now what was at risk if they failed in their mission and left their fate in the hands of the marauders who planned to attack from across the lake.

This moment of resistance was about so much more than his own story now.

Yuma dropped the problems of the world onto the lad's tiny shoulders. And the terrifying weight of those realities loomed larger than even the boulders perched on Yuma's back.

"Why are we the only ones who can fight back against this evil?" Zack asked, feeling small and outnumbered.

"We are the only giants left, remember?" Yuma answered as he tossed another monolith into the river, and Harley barked in agreement.

"We'll need a miracle, won't we?" Zack said.

"We found it when we found you," Yuma replied, stretching his sore back.

There was a long pause—fueling more worry inside the boy.

"Is it true that Pepper Wixx can raise the dead?" Zack asked, but he already knew the answer since he could now read the giant's mind.

Feeling the brief mental intrusion, Yuma stared at the powerful boy for a second, then tossed another boulder, where it exploded like a deep-water depth charge.

"Wixx is a filthy Necromancer. The bane of all magic. Of all creatures. The scum of the earth. Yes. She can do all that. She can raise the dead. Prolong the suffering for all. That is what she strives for. Nothing less. And she only produces pain because she enjoys it. There is no other reason for the brand of suffering she inflicts except for her sick retaliation against all forms of life. It's simple-minded revenge she seeks because her lives were cut so short, and she thinks she deserves more."

"You mean Pepper Wixx is already dead?"

"Yes, child. Many times, over."

"Who killed her?"

"I did." Yuma smiled with grim satisfaction and threw another boulder. "Every time."

365

-CHAPTER 44-

Darklight

Sunrise officially heralded Queen of the Damned Coronation Day.

But long before daybreak, the improved Pepper Wixx was preening before her full-length mirror. She used the Knack on herself to a pleasing, self-delusional effect as she groomed.

She tried on dozens of gowns for this evening's royal activities, even though she was hours away from attending the official event. Pepper couldn't help but reinvent herself—she was that excited.

"Ladies and gentlemen, I present the new Queen of the Damned!" Pepper curtsied to her glorious reflection. "The one and only Queen!"

She stopped choosing at an exquisite black lace gown with a blood-red fascinator adorned with iridescent peacock feathers. Then she bejeweled herself with skull-shaped pearls, and dazzling crystal spider broaches on a scarlet sash.

Everyone else in Dark Hollows was snoring after a late night of decorating fury. That included the emotionally exhausted children inside their cages.

But Pepper Wixx was wide awake as the sun rose—ready for the dawn of the most thrilling chapter of her long life.

"Why don't they just give me the crown right now and get it over with?" she asked the sun while standing on her balcony and surveying the decorated street.

The denizens of Dark Hollows had done their hero proud overnight. The locals had transformed the place from top to bottom, with bunting and new banners of scarlet and black tangled in decorative party lights twinkling by the thousands all over town, with hundreds of royal flags fluttering everywhere.

Pepper turned at a distracting flash of movement on the far side of the lake.

"What was that?"

She spun her deck telescope around for a better look and saw Yuma scampering to the top of a towering Sequoia that grew down by the shoreline.

"Getting yourself ready for the new day, early riser? This morning won't be as boring as your last! I promise you that," Pepper said, removing a dark crystal from her clutch.

"Let's start my special day off with a real bang," she grinned. "How about a little Darklight to go with your coffee beans, you South American savage!"

As soon as she spoke, the impulsive Darklight hissed in her hand and spat out two sizzling black beams that sliced open the belly of the pretty pink morning like a blade.

The twin rays bit into the giant's shoulder with their fangs bared, and Yuma lost his grip.

"Aghhhhhh!"

He crashed through several stories of bone-crunching branches on his way down—frightening the nesting birds along the way—until he crashed into the ground two hundred feet below.

"Ugghhhh!"

"Bullseye!" Pepper danced a happy jig on her balcony as she watched Yuma crawling away from the shoreline and out of the line of sight of her telescope.

"What's that, Yuma? You want a second helping? Why sure, darling! Anything for you, sweetie! I'm all about serving!" she screamed, firing another blast of malignant Darklight toward the fallen legend.

The sizzling twin beams hit the base of the redwood tree trunk simultaneously, splattering their anti-light against the red bark in spirals of dark energy. But no matter how intensely they hissed and thrashed, they could never penetrate the mighty tree's impervious outer layers.

The Darklight swept the forest, but as physics demanded, their intimidating light beams couldn't bend around corners as they sought to reacquire their target in a perfect line-of-sight shot.

Yuma lay with his back pushed up against the giant tree he had nicknamed Little Sister when he first arrived on these shores, when she was still a young sapling. Her epic size now shielded him, providing dependable cover as he tried to heal from his fresh wounds and broken bones.

He ran the damage checklist.

Broken back and ribs—check! Broken fibula—check! Fingers on both hands—check!

The shattered giant needed a few minutes to plan his next move and recover—but that's when Zack wandered into the laser sights of the Darklight.

The twin beams shot across the forest, seeking Zack like a death ray.

Sssssssssssssssssssss!

The hooded beams flared wide to strike when Yuma dove in front, snatched the boy into his arms, and rolled away. He absorbed another strike, protecting Zack—shielding the boy from harm as they rolled onto their feet.

"Whoa! Hey! I was just looking for you," Zack said, shaken, unaware of the danger.

"Run!"

The Darklight's fangs struck Yuma's shoulders again as the giant and boy ran for safety.

"Agghhhhhhhhh!"

Wixx heard his painful bellows echoing across the lake,

and her dark spirits soared in jubilation as a bleary-eyed Shelby ran into her mother's room.

"What was that? Is that him? Did you get him?"

"Victory tastes marvelous this early in the morning. Doesn't it, dear? Like a cup full of kittens."

She withdrew the twin beams, pocketed Yuma's filched Darklight, and calmed herself as she tried to regain her regal composure before her stepdaughter.

"Let's not spoil any surprises for later tonight, dear... but..." Pepper couldn't help herself and turned and screamed across the lake. "My Half-Time show's going to absolutely kill you, Yuma! I mean, murder you!"

Wixx slowly returned to her morning, and Shelby fell in line as her sleepless handmaiden.

"Today is my day, Shelby, and no one will ruin it for me, including myself."

Yuma limped to the gorge by the waterfall, threw himself into the deepest pool, and floated face-up, letting the pure waters soothe the new wounds ripped across his back.

"I'm sorry, Yuma. I never meant for you to get hurt. Not ever!" Zack's tears clouded his vision.

"Think nothing of it, son," Yuma coughed, wincing. "Comes with the territory."

"Was that Pepper?"

"Wixx. Yes."

Zack plopped down with Harley beside the pool, both feeling guilty about the giant's newest injuries.

"How can we ever fight against something as evil and powerful as that?" Zack asked.

The brutality of the sudden violence frightened him.

The boy thought he understood what had to be done. And he knew why now. But he had no clue how to go about achieving any of it.

"Take heart, young Zack. That was my fault. I let my guard down. That was one of my own crystals that ran

369

home and bit me. It knows better than that. Wixx appears to have stolen my medicine bag when they captured me. She just discovered their purity is far superior to any old-world necromancer's gnarled wand. I am sorry. I did not think about that when I should have. She is commonly preoccupied with baking at this hour, not testing new weapons."

The open wounds along his back and ankle were healing—bones began stitching him back together as Zack watched in amazement.

"I'm so afraid now, Yuma. I don't know what I can even do to help you fight that. How can anyone ever fight back against something wicked like that if she can do this to you?"

Yuma paused from tending to his wounds and turned.

"It only takes character to stand up, son. You face it head-on—using your intellect, wit, willpower, intuition, talents, and perseverance. Those are the strongest forces on this planet besides love to defeat evil. Anyway, it used to work that way before you came along. Try following that inner character and see what happens next."

"What?" Zack felt bewildered.

It was only then Yuma understood the child's confusing paradox.

Here was the little boy who could see everything in the universe yet still couldn't see his place in the transcendent plan as it glowed up ahead because of him.

"Sometimes, the only way to see in the dark is to close your eyes, son, and reach out."

Yuma threw another boulder against the others, testing his revitalized muscles for flexibility and forming a towering testament to his pain and recovery.

He reached into his new medicine gag and retrieved several white crystals. Yuma tossed them into the turbulence rushing past the boulders, one at a time.

"Can you spot these clear stones? Underwater?"

The crystals were invisible to the naked eye.

"No, no way."

"Even with your eyes tuned on high?"

"No. Not yet."

The giant leaned in and whispered in case Wixx was listening.

"Are you ready for your next life lesson, little brother?"

"I guess?"

"Never trust only your eyes. Not even yours. I want you to pinpoint where each of those crystals landed with your mind open and eyes closed. Can you try that?"

"Why?"

"Just try it. Practice, my boy. Clear your head of all else and focus your mind as if our lives depended on it."

"And Harley's too!"

"Especially Harley's."

-CHAPTER 45-

Monster Mash

Coronation morning passed slowly for the kidnapped teens inside their squalid cages. They were still trying to develop any workable escape plan as the overdecorated little town woke up to do Wixx's bidding.

The over-anxious Queen-to-be fussed over every minute detail with her abused staff in tow. Between banquet preparations, dragon-raising, and impending war—her party platter was packed pretty full.

Minutes trickled into hours, but the momentum began building as the day drew closer to noon as more extraordinary creatures began streaming into town.

Tiny Dark Hollows was soon bursting at the seams with all kinds of wandering tourists.

The once deserted streets and zig-zagging alleyways were now lit up for a proper holiday party of the dead.

A grand assortment of beasts, ogres, monsters and mutants, ghouls, geeks, and zombies filled the landscape like a Grimm Brothers nightmare mixed with Mayberry R.F.D. All coexisting peacefully—mostly—while rubbing shoulders like crowds at any county fair.

Name any mythical creature or cryptid in human folklore and those creatures existed in the flesh inside Dark Hollows for this occasion. No matter their legends, these demons, ogres, goblins, trolls, witches, wendigos, and warlocks all showed up for this rare centennial celebration. Along with vampires and werewolves—always undercover, of

372

course.

There was even a pair of reanimated Egyptian mummies that showed up in a tattered Calistoga wagon—holdovers from a Wild West show that wandered down here by mistake over two centuries before—never to be seen again until today.

Witches of every nationality flew in on custom made Scorches with fancy silver stirrups—their brooms spitting out nasty green sparks from their bristles, singeing the necks of any critters walking below.

"Hey!"

"Put a muffler on it, witch!"

Outgoing Queen, Prudence of Moribund Bend, was sitting for the last time on her throne in the middle of the town square.

She gobbled up the praise as well-wishers rushed by, thanking her for her service to the Witchling community.

After a century as their Queen, she carried herself with great nobility. Not bad for a wanton ax murderer and abusive animal torturer from Wisconsin. She was proud of having served her fellow deviants with no relapses.

But no one was feeling the joy inside the revamped New Regency ballroom.

The Royal Board of Governors kept trying to convince an over-caffeinated Pepper Wixx to sit down and listen to their counseling. They needed to explain the intricate ceremonies before the official crowning could occur thereby transfer all additional powers to her. There were meticulous, moment by moment plans to be followed to coincide with the moon's temporary disappearance tonight.

But Pepper Wixx refused to understand why they had to wait for nightfall.

I prefer to attack Yuma during daylight hours, she confided only to herself.

"All this pomp and rubbish is just a lot of fillers and fluff if you ask me for everybody to sell more frog dogs in a bun!"

Pepper said, and she threw down the schedules.

"There is a proper protocol we must follow. Now stop acting like a commoner, Pepper, and start acting like a true Queen and consider your new station in life!" Henrietta snapped.

She must have made her point, because, after an awkward pause, Pepper picked up the scattered papers with a quick flick of a crystal and began thumbing through the contents while levitating.

Henrietta was so relieved that she flushed lavender in the excitement.

"Just think of it this way. The entire day's celebration is being thrown just for you, Queen mum," Henrietta bowed.

"About time," Wixx said, causing everyone to squirm.

Outside in the town square, Kate and the others had unlocked all their cages by tossing the shoe key back and forth. They were surrounded by hundreds of monsters in the middle of the day, and there wasn't much chance they could escape without being seen.

They realized they had to wait until nightfall if their crazy getaway was going to work. There were no other options available.

During the night, Coop had developed a risky and sickening concept of escaping through the surly crowds of freaks and actual geeks, no matter the time of day.

He believed that if he slathered himself in just enough cage gore to vomit, like the walking dead parading below him, he might just be able to climb out and walk around—just another butt ugly creature cruising down the strip.

"I mean, look at them? Which one would even notice?"

"Are you insane?" Kate balked at the whole scheme.

But Coop had the stomach and the guts to test his theory. And the timing couldn't have been better. Lennon had just spotted keys left in a delivery truck's ignition just down the street.

"This might be our only real chance of getting a set of wheels large enough to drive all of us out of town. We have to take the chance now."

"No! Not yet!"

"Listen to me. I will do anything to get us out of here, Kate," Coop promised. "I've got to try it now. It's put up or shut up time."

Coop scooped a big handful of glop off the floor and plopped it onto his head, and the viscous fluids swallowed it whole.

"Oh! Gross!"

"Ooooooh, man!"

"Nasty!"

Coop dug one eye clear and then slathered even more horrible muck all over himself before gathering his courage to give his disguise a live-action road test.

"Wait! Not now," Kate gestured. "Not in the daylight!"

"We have to take the chance. What better time? It's going to work, or it isn't. Let's find out now, not later. Fortune favors the bold."

Coop waited until firecrackers went off nearby, and when the crowd's attention turned, he took his chance and dropped from his cage, whose new brass plaque read: 'Pretty Boy - Strong Back.'

Coop discovered he could shuffle along among the other horrific transients with his head held high. He wasn't even drawing a second whiff.

Should I be offended?

Coop hopped into a red Pepper Wixx bakery delivery truck that Lennon had pointed out from her cage. And just like she promised, the keys were still dangling inside the ignition.

"Score!"

Coop shot a gore-soaked thumbs-up to Kate out the truck's window, almost taking out a passing troll.

"Hey, punk! Watch it!"

Kate waved back, acknowledging his signal, and started

coaxing Oz out of his cage.

Coop's thumbs-up went beyond good news, and everything seemed to go as planned. All they had to do now was smear their bodies in gore just like Coop and make it down to that bakery truck across the park and drive themselves out of town.

That was it—simple as that. Five minutes tops.

Then Kate spotted the game changer striding their way.

Queen-to-be, Pepper Wixx, was crossing the street from the New Regency with her royal entourage in tow. The crowds began following her as she strolled toward the reviewing stands. The same stands that sat just below their dead tree featuring them as the backdrop for the evening's ceremonies.

"Oh, no! Not now!"

Kate and the others watched as any chances of escape dwindled before their eyes.

"I told you!" Oz moaned and slammed his gate closed.

"Get back in, everybody," Kate commanded.

"What?" Jesse was already half-covered in the muck and astonished by the order for
retreat.

"Get back inside your cages! Now!"

"What are you talking about?" Pavarty had just exited hers.

"Now! Everybody! Get back in!" Kate snapped again.

"No way!" Emiliano and Josh disagreed at the same time.

Lennon and Tim swung back into their cages as ordered.

"We've got to make a run for it now, Kate. We're already out!" Jesse climbed around to the backside of the tree to be less noticeable.

"Get back! It's too risky. She's coming this way! We're her special prizes and she'll notice if we're not here! And then everyone will be looking for us! Now get over here and get back into those cages. Just don't lock the doors," Kate commanded. "There will be a better time. I promise when everyone's not staring up this way!"

She waved down at Coop, trying to gain his attention. He didn't realize that Wixx was headed straight for him as he waited below in the idling truck. He was revving the engine when Wixx and her party strolled by her familiar truck with the unfamiliar driver. She gave him a big thumbs-up as she passed by.

"Hey! Take the day off, driver! Haven't you heard? You're working for a Queen now!"

Coop nodded back from the shadows as the witch passed by.

Kate held her breath and the escapees continued climbing back into their cages. She worried that Coop could still be spotted and devoured on sight.

That's when she saw Coop's slimy head reemerge from the driver's side window, smiling straight back at her over his shoulder, and she almost sobbed.

He mouthed something she couldn't quite make out under his disgusting mask and then gave her a quick wave goodbye, threw her a kiss, and drove off down the street.

It was Kate's turn to be floored.

"What? No."

Coop drove cautiously at first through the clogged the streets. So he began honking his horn and gunning the engine as he sped out of town, making his perfect getaway all alone.

Kate couldn't believe it.

Any hope of escape had just driven out of town. She scampered back into her cage, and swung the cage door closed behind her, making sure that it didn't rattle or latch.

And she made it just in time as Wixx and her royal procession crossed the street into the crowded square. The new Queen limped up into the reviewing stands, riding a cushion of applause and cheers as their latest hero and icon.

The frightened teens were now all back inside their

vulture cages—except for one, whose enclosure hung as empty as his promises.

Kate prayed Pepper wouldn't notice his absence as the excitement swelled with the full orchestral fanfares beginning below.

The future queen barely glanced at the special cages as she turned her attention to her subjects and sat down in her box seat, then nodded for the royal procession to begin.

"Let's go!" Pepper ordered. She was already bored with the pomp and circumstance of office. "I'm your Queen of action—not words! Let's get this part over with."

The customized hearses fired up their spit-shined engines and rolled past the reviewing stands one by one. interspersed the small marching bands playing demented little ditties in between the reveals of each vehicle.

The endless procession of hearses was astonishing—showcasing the most exotic cars. Still, Wixx couldn't have been less impressed.

She summoned her son Berk to her side on the podium and whispered.

"Is everything okay at home? Did you mind the new baby and feed and burp him every half hour as I ordered?" she asked.

"Sure did, Ma. But if something's just a day old and can eat seven live rams, four three-hundred-pound sows, and forty-five chickens... is that still a real baby, Ma?"

Pepper noticed that Berk's clothes appeared scorched around the head and shoulders.

She patted his horrible face and then slapped it hard to turn his savage breath away from melting her makeup.

"Reminds me of you when you were just a big, ugly baby. Now get some stronger chains, by tonight. He's a growing boy, and we've still got hours to grow him out. I calculate we'll see another big spurt between now and midnight!" she chuckled.

Berk had never seen his mother looking this lovely or

this happy before in any of her incarnations. This Pepper Wixx seemed intoxicated with joy.

"You're going to be a real, good Queen Ma!" Berk praised.

"I'm going to be the only damn Queen, son," Pepper vowed. "There's never going to be another Queen after me. I guarantee you that."

Berk understood the threat this woman posed to anyone who ever opposed her—including her own demented bloodline.

She ate them for dinner—alive or dead.

He hustled off to make a more extensive set of chains for the surprise guest star of the evening.

Strung up high over Wixx's head, Kate couldn't help but stare over at Coop's empty cage as the molasses-slow procession continued to roll by below with regional cheers or jeers for every vehicle and marching band.

She was crushed. Kate couldn't believe that he would ever desert them like that.

"Is it me?"

Nonsense! Her inner voice replied. *Stop blaming yourself. You are not a victim. Not even to yourself.*

That's when the dead blue hand shot in and grabbed her by the throat.

-CHAPTER 46-

Weapons of Mass Destruction

The heavy timber doors slammed open as Yuma, Zack, and Harley rushed past his underground forges and dashed through several industrial-sized rooms before arriving at a long underground stairway that led downward to a fortified vault made from impeccably crafted titanium.

Yuma winked at Zack and clapped his hands three times in front of the imposing mechanical stronghold, and the oversized door yawned wide like a hungry kitten.

"I'm far too busy to remember passwords anymore," he explained.

Once inside the crypt, Zack discovered himself surrounded by a vast armory filled with an unfathomable collection of weapons. Yuma had stored these dusty armaments underground, in organized rows according to weapon type, ballistic results, and assault functions, for centuries by the looks of the cobwebs.

From the most modern machine guns to outdated Gatling guns and blunderbusses, this fortified armory of mechanized weapons of mass destruction displayed every model of death ever produced for bloody profit.

Swords, pikes, spears, crossbows, bows and arrows, blowguns, hatchets, tomahawks, and knives of every size and description adorned the walls or filled standing racks in complete collections.

"Wow! How cool. Can we use all these in the war?" Zack asked.

"Useless. All of them. Every single one. Unless your only goal is to kill or maim at point-blank range, the firearms will not work. Since that is the reality, I suppose these crude-edged weapons might do a better job. But nothing more and not for long."

"Why not?"

"Modern weapons do not work by Mother Nature's command. Therefore, bullets and gunpowder can no longer kill the undead. Especially underneath her Bubble."

"I wish she could do that for everybody."

"She is trying."

Yuma gestured behind him to another wing.

"But with these beauties, you do not have to destroy reality to harvest your best results."

Zack walked among row after row of tall racks displaying nothing but bright crystals, lighting the chamber with an endless assortment of unique shapes and colors. It was a different level of armory altogether.

"With these telepathic stones—you simply shift the perspective—dramatically."

The lively crystals shimmered even brighter with Zack's presence.

"With the purest of these crystals, you will shape and amplify your intentions into any shape or form of thought you desire."

"How?"

"By centering both your mind and your heart. Linking them. If we are lucky and if we practice, you will master these skills in time."

"Can I pick one up?"

"Yes, yes, of course. These are yours now. Everything down here is yours, Zack," Yuma said. "Regrettably, you will need to know how to use every one of these crystals as time passes. They each have specialized uses. But remember, they hold dangerous wonders within, not to be trifled with."

Zack flickered his fingertips over the tops of several

stones, producing a single harmonic chord between them like the Crystal Stairway.

He picked up an orange-colored crystal with thin black markings twisting around the inside. The moving stripes and swirls were pacing as if trapped and ready to pounce.

"It looks like a tiger," Zack grinned as he held up the fierce light. The gnarly jewel growled back.

"It is whatever you need it to be," Yuma informed, watching his student intently.

The crystal roared again like a big cat, and a perplexed Harley growled back at the aggressive jewel.

"I like this one," Zack smiled up at Yuma.

"You must drill with it conscientiously. Like any weapon, it can still kill you, even when sheathed and unloaded. Practice and familiarity are everything. Understanding when to use each one intuitively is even more important."

Zack held the ragged jewel out and dry-fired like a space blaster.

"Pew! Pew!"

"Make no mistake. I do not want you near the battlefront when it begins tonight."

"Pew! Pew! Why not? Maybe I can help. Pew!"

Yuma leaned down to recapture the boy's wandering attention.

"Do you understand me? This is not your fight, Zack. Not tonight. Not yet. It is all mine. Your only responsibility is to protect the Illuminator's world below at all costs. And you cannot do that in the middle of a battle. Do you understand me, boy? Emotion can play no part in your decision-making processes from now on."

"I understand, Yuma. But what can I do if something happens to you?"

"Your duty, I hope," Yuma declared. "As we have planned."

Zack dropped his head.

"Do not worry, son. My job is not to die to protect our

world... but make sure that Wixx and her type do, instead."

Zack looked back up and sighted along the crystal's length.

"Pew!" he shouted one time too many times.

A bolt of live energy snarled across the room in a flash of orange and black, reducing a rack of heavy weapons to glowing taffy.

The hair-trigger fury startled Zack, and Yuma cocked a wary eyebrow.

"Trust me, boy. Intentions are everything. Keep your mind clear. Control your amplified thoughts. Clear intentions, not emotions, coupled with logical lines of sight, will conquer any spells that hideous creature can conjure. But we must not forget that Wixx has stolen some of my most powerful crystals. Therefore, we proceed with caution face to face. But take heart. None can match the magnitude of the powers you possess."

Zack handled the other colored crystals with unexpected results.

One danced, one spun, one spit sparks and exploded in dazzling bubbles.

"If Wixx ever got her hands on any of these, it would prove disastrous. So, if something happens to me, and they overrun us tonight—in that case—you will need to destroy this entire armory and all the crystals inside. Do you understand?"

Zack nodded his head, but he didn't.

"Like the mine with the Creeps?"

"Exactly. We can never let Wixx possess what I have hidden inside this armory. She could unleash World War Three with just the mechanized arsenal alone," Yuma warned.

"Then why did you bother to collect all that stuff here in the first place?"

Zack waited for an answer that was slow to come as Yuma took his time to respond.

"That's the right question to ask."

Yuma glared at his growing stockpile of death and

destruction before slamming his fist in frustration.

"I was preparing for the wrong future. But you have removed the centuries-old blinders that stopped me from witnessing what was happening before my eyes. And I will thank you every day of life for lifting that curse, Zackery Goodnight, and for this great privilege."

Another unspoken moment passed inside the silent vault, their breathing the only sound. Yuma spoke first.

"Now, while we hold only the purest of intentions—we must prepare for war."

-CHAPTER 47-

Phase One and Done

Kate seized the skeletal arm with both hands and chomped down hard—tearing a massive chunk of blue flesh and veins from the desiccated forearm before spitting out the quivering mass.

She fought for her life like a rabid bobcat and returned for another bloodless mouthful when she heard-

"Kate, Katie! Stop! Shhhh! Shhh!" a familiar voice pleaded. "Calm down, Tempest. It's me."

"What?"

Kate fell back, speechless.

"Coop?"

She had never been this happy to see anyone in her life.

"Sorry about that. I probably could have made a better choice, right?" he apologized as he stashed the zombie's arm.

"You think?" Kate snorted.

"Coop's back!" Oz whispered to everyone.

"No way!"

"Way!"

Only seconds before, Kate thought her life was over, at the bottom of the food chain—now she was trying to stifle her joy.

"Life is so beyond weird."

"I know! Look, I'm sorry it took so long to sneak back. There were a couple of detours, But I stashed the truck outside town in an old auto graveyard and hid the keys under the driver's floor mat in case I don't get back with you guys for some reason."

"Don't even think that!"

"It's cool! I'm here now. Phase one and done. We got getaway wheels and a full gas tank to get out of here!"

He swung down onto a branch beside her cage, and Kate grabbed his hands from inside to stabilize him. But she just wanted to touch him, slimy or not.

"Are you for real?"

"Sure, smells like teen spirit in here."

"That was too close," Kate sighed.

"I know. I'm sorry. Timing is everything, right?"

"Our timing positively sucks."

"Sorry."

"Don't be. It worked out. What do we do next?"

Kate was unsure now that everything had changed.

"Pepper is sitting over there, just below us," she nodded. "Shouldn't we wait?" Kate asked.

They peered around the cage and saw Wixx snoozing below on her new throne as the endless procession continued marching by as her official bodyguards, Moody, and Berk, kept swigging beers in huge steins.

Only the width of the walkway surrounding the tree separated them from contact with the rear of the reviewing stands.

"Yeah. Let's give these fiends more time to celebrate before we ruin their party. They'll redefine getting drunk tonight. I guarantee it. Then, once they're partying like maniacs, which they all are, we'll make our getaway," Coop stated confidently. "You wouldn't believe what I've seen, Kate."

He'd run out of breath yet staring back into Kate's eyes emboldened him. That's when Coop noticed something gawking up at them from behind the reviewing stand.

Whatever the purple creatures with funny noses and swollen tongues were called in these parts, the inquisitive four-legged beast with the swirled nose stared up at the raffle cages and read off the brass plaques in front of each with some difficulty.

"Pretty as a picture," it drooled.

"Suitable for farm or housework!"

"Try One! Get one free! You'll like it!"

Coop swung back into his cage without being noticed, careful not to secure the door as he ducked inside.

The critical purple critter wandered away, unimpressed with the greasy-looking Uman on display as he scratched off each box on his auction bid.

The sweltering afternoon heat dissolved into an unnatural lavender evening, lit by twinkling party lights as the festivities grew. Legions of regional cryptid marching bands descended from every cranny to pay honor to their future queen as they marched by at the speed of clotting blood.

Kate gazed out between the thick cage bars at the full moon as it rose higher in the sky.

The earth's shadow stalked relentlessly across the bright face of Luna like a celestial predator, initiating the start of another Bloody Moon cycle on this repetitive and twisted holiday.

The furthest stars seemed closer here compared to anywhere she had ever known. The Bubble's organic shape focused and magnified everything overhead a thousandfold when seen from underneath its protective lens.

"Do you think we'll ever get out of here alive?" Kate sighed, searching for someone else's self-assurance to lean against for a while.

"There's no other choice," Coop replied and stood up in his cage as the others listened.

"Let me put it to you this way, Kate," Coop whispered, still improving his hideous zombie disguise. "I have slathered vulture poo, cryptid eyeballs, bone marrow, and shredded human ligaments over my entire body—every orifice. I have partied with the local undead and met their mama, and I know what uncooked goat entrails taste like now! At least, I hope that was a goat that those big guys shoved down my throat along with the green frog guts brew. So, the quick answer to your question is... yes! A big resounding, fat yes! We are getting the hell out of here!"

Kate giggled at Coop's maniacal rant as his whisper vanished and his volume raised.

"Shhh."

"Because I... *we*... will do anything... absolutely anything... to get ourselves out of this... ridiculous nightmare! If I need to tear them apart with my bare claws and eat these things, I will!"

"Shhhh!"

"Keep it down, madman!"

Coop appeared as demented as the murderers lurking below, yet the others knew he'd risked his very future by leaping back into the fires of this blazing madness a second time just to save their lives. And that went far beyond courageous. That was self-sacrifice.

Kate adored the crazy new glint in Coop's squinty eyes.

"Let's do this," she agreed, and Kate's spirit soared back into warrior mode along with his.

"Slow your roll. We've got the wheels stashed now. Now we have to figure out the right getaway to get us *all* out of here in one piece. Together. Let's bide our time like my grandmother used to say. There's no reason to rush our next chess move against these clowns. We've already learned that lesson. When it's completely dark, and we're ready to exploit a distraction, we'll strike out of here together like a bunch of drunken zombies!"

Coop's aggressive tone bothered Oz.

"You mean to set out, don't you, Coop? Like in run away? To freedom? Not like strikeout with our fists, but like run away, run away? Right, Coop?"

Ozzy feared Cool Hand Coop could ruin everything if he were left in charge. But Oz wasn't about to be left behind, either.

"Remember," Kate cautioned the others as they settled

back down to find a way out. "The best gift any enemy can give you is for them to underestimate you," Kate stated boldly.

"And who in their worm-addled brains *wouldn't* underestimate this goofy bunch?" Coop laughed. "Just look at us!"

Everyone was in on the same cosmic joke, as even Pavarty, Emil, and Jesse choked back a chuckle at the gruesome sight of this posse. Their new clothes were smeared and filthy from the disgusting cages, with thick ooey-gooey gore patches in everyone's hair.

"Hold tight, killer clowns. We'll split this bizarro world just as soon as these goons aren't paying attention to us with those goofy eyeballs."

-CHAPTER 48-

Queen of the Damned

"Under the dark of a dying moon, dripping blood from its beating heart, let this sacred ceremony begin and give your new reign of terror a befitting start!"

Pepper Wixx fidgeted on the cushions of her new throne, waiting to be crowned. But outgoing Queen Prudence seemed frozen after uttering that last incantation. She held the black coronet suspended high above Wixx's coiffed head without moving a muscle.

"Pssst!" As the spellbound audience watched, Wixx tried to get Prudence's attention without moving her lips.

But Prudence was biding her time—waiting for the total eclipse to complete its slow caress of the moon before placing the ebony crown down upon her successor's head.

"Just drop it, sis," Wixx growled.

"Shush, Pepper! It's a timing thing. You, ignorant serfs, couldn't possibly understand the delicate intricacies interwoven into the deep tapestry of Wiccan royalty. The exact conjunction makes it binding," the veteran scolded the crass upstart. "Unimpeachable."

Once the earth's shadow covered the lunar surface, the satellite blushed a deep red in embarrassment, and the crowds "Oohed" and "Awed!" as the new Blood Moon dominated the night sky.

Prudence wrapped up the ceremony by removing the ornate Bartholomew ring from her gloved hand and slid it onto Pepper's extended finger.

A surge of new energy shot into Wixx's body, electrifying her while leaving Prudence weakened at its loss. Though staggered, she continued the ceremony.

"Ripped from the finger of a dying saint and sustained below throughout the years, I grant you the Bartholomew ring to protect us and bind us and keep safe our deepest fears!" she proclaimed.

Everyone squirmed as transferring powers diminished Prudence physically, but she continued to execute the last of her official duties with a panache.

"From this day forward, and a hundred laps more around that hideous sun... I anoint you Pepper Wixx, the Queen of the Damned. Now let us celebrate your new reign and have us some wicked fun!"

Hats filled the air, and whistles and cheers went up from every corner of the packed town. Ex-Queen Prudence continued speaking. But no one was listening any longer as she fled the stage, and Henrietta Hoodwinker stepped in and filled the void. She led the rowdy crowds in another round of cheers for their new Queen.

"Huzzah!"

"Hooray!"

Pepper finally knew what it felt like to be gob-smacked for the first time in her many lifetimes sitting on her new throne. This was one of the most satisfying feelings she had ever experienced.

"Wixx! Wixx! Wixx!" the crowds chanted.

"I like the sound of that!" Pepper squealed, and they roared back their approval when she hugged their flag.

Wixx had never dared dream that a day like this would ever come—a day when she would be exalted into High Witchling royalty without having to steal it first.

And yet, here she was—the new Queen of the Damned.

She stared at the radiant Bartholomew ring as if it belonged on her finger. A sadistic Roman warlock had ripped it off the finger of a tortured saint two thousand years before, and its powers over life and death were now Wixx's to use at her discretion.

"I never thought that consuming the living could be so rewarding?" She murmured to herself as she felt the new layers of protection shielding and reinforcing her body.

"I am never taking this ring off again."

Queen Pepper Wixx stood before her new subjects with both arms raised high above her head, milking the chanting reactions until she snapped her head awkwardly, as if possessed by serpents.

"By the blood on the moon and the pain in the stars, I accept your pledge of allegiance and promise to leave behind scars!"

Most in the crowd howled and cheered, but a few creatures groaned and mocked Wixx.

Troublemakers. Peaceniks.

She smiled as she cataloged their faces to add to her growing enemies list. Her goons would soon hunt them down to eradicate any pockets of resistance.

"To my old fans and my new subjects alike, thank you, one and all. Thank you to the Royal Executive Board for allowing a silly commoner to ascend to this lofty and prestigious post. Although to be truthful, it should have happened a long time ago."

The crowd roared at the uptight board's reactions.

"I mean, face it. Upside, I'm already a superstar!"

The throngs howled and started rapping her familiar TV jingles.

"I promise I won't wear out my welcome, ladies and gentlemen. But I have some fabulous new ideas that I want to share with you all tonight." She turned the Knack on full force.

"Go ahead, Pepper! Anything you want! You're our hero!"

"Well, thank you, Glippy. That brings me to my point. We never finished what we started after winning the last war, right?"

"You won that one, Pepper! You alone! Not them!"

The audience jeered at the cowardly board members.

"Well, thank you, yes, I know that, but we left one giant thing undone in our rush to success," she yelled.

"What's that?" they screamed back.

"Why, the final sacking of the Sacred Forest and the grand opening of my new resort called Wixxland!" she exclaimed, and they roared back their approval. "And... the final annihilation of Yuma!"

The mention of the legendary monster that still existed across the lake dimmed their enthusiasm.

Wixx grew upset with the crowd's timid reactions, and she began taunting her audience.

"Do you idiots want to continue living in this filth and squalor? When the only thing preventing us from that glorious new Paradise is a single ugly giant! The only immortal giant left alive, mind you, because I alone killed the rest! For you! And tonight, I will reclaim that long-overdue privilege and destroy Yuma—for you—for me—and for good!"

An uninspired cheer went up from her cabinet.

"But it's Yuma you're talking about, Pepper!" the cryptid with missing limbs called out.

"So what? Once that gigantic rat's gone, those untapped lands are ours forever and ever. Then we can jumpstart our conquest of the Upside world again! Including the discovery of the Calamity Stone! I can smell it over there."

"How'd that work out the last time, Pepper? War!!" someone called out.

"Well, there'll be zero giants left to worry about after tonight! Not even one! That I guarantee you!"

Her squad of goons began intimidating the crowd, and the captive audience responded to her speech under duress.

"Listen to me, all of you. I can still remember just like it was yesterday when our kind couldn't show our faces in public anywhere in the world. No matter what continent we lived on. No Uman ever wanted to listen to anything we had to say. They denied us the basic right to walk among them in freedom in their precious Upside world without being judged and attacked. Thousands of us were crushed and drowned under stones or set aflame and hanged across every continent because some superstitious idiot's crops failed that year in England, or their mules grew colicky in Massachusetts! Utter nonsense! We're the ones who've been abused throughout time! Not them!"

The crowd turned surly and spun back into her arms again.

"Sixteen-ninety-two! Salem Village! Ring a bell, folks? That is our eternal rallying cry for our war against the filthy Umans!"

"Sixteen-ninety-two!" Someone started the chant, and a ripple went through the crowds as they swelled toward the stage to pay tribute to their evil past.

Henrietta and the executives exchanged uneasy glances at this mood shift into unscripted territory with the dangerous return of this vengeful subject.

"Our kind died by the millions across the centuries on nothing more substantial than the hysterical whims of superstitious and pious holy men. And for no other reason than that. Some of our finest witches and magicians would still be alive today to help guide us if it wasn't for these pious Umans hoarding everything!"

The crowd was hers again.

"But then we got luckier than those that never fled Europe. Here in our colonies, they turned on their innocents while we smart ones fled and found the perfect shelter down here, thanks to Henrietta's dear father."

Henrietta blanched at the reference.

"Umansssss," Wixx hissed, drawing the word out, making it sound evil and nasty. "Why, I've got house slippers older than the longest-living Umans!" she wisecracked, and her audience roared.

Some timid council members left the stage as the agitated crowds drank in the hate speech and surged forward.

"Umansssssssssss!" she hissed again. "A tiny, insignificant blip of a species that won't be missed when history is re-written by us—the last true survivors of the world!"

The re-engaged mob cheered again.

"Some of our feckless leaders on this stage allowed this unnecessary Purge to happen against us for centuries! But those long days of suffering and ineffectual leadership are over, my children! Look around you! Umans are now the same scum they said we were, if not worse than they ever imagined us all to be! Watch their nightly news! They are the monsters destroying their stupid lives—preying like packs of cannibals on each other, mowing each other down in huge numbers because they're misunderstood or upset. Boo-Hoo! Umansssss and their spoiled children are the only authentic monsters left to fear. Not us! They are the true scourge of the universe! Just look at them!"

Wixx gestured dramatically up to the vulture cages behind her as an example of the Uman threat.

But instead of some frightening examples of rampant Umankind—the audience saw only nine shivering children, and the crowd's angry mood deflated like a leaky party balloon.

Nothing could be less menacing than the sight of this pathetic, shivering bunch of Uman pups.

Each orphan was smeared in vulture poo and bloody guts, appearing as fragile as any defeated creature could. Nothing was even appetizing about them at this point. They couldn't frighten a caterpillar.

It jolted Pepper out of her rage when she saw them peering back from their cages with helpless, puppy-dog eyes.

"What were you thinking? That's not good optics, you idiots." She blamed Shelby and her sons.

Wixx could feel the many eyes of the board on her, and she dropped her head in embarrassment.

"Oh, dear. This will not do at all. This is not how I envisioned my party."

Wixx could read Henrietta's sarcastic expression from across the stage.

No more speechifying to these fools. It's showtime, woman.

Wixx turned to her musical director.

"Maestro Hermann! If you'd be so gracious and accompany me with a little night music, I'll wrap this all up, my friends!"

The crowds hushed as the classical music swelled from the orchestra, reinvigorating the night with its turbulent beauty.

Pepper Wixx raised her arms above her head and vaulted majestically into the air in time with the music, and every creature present gasped at the legend-making sight.

"What?"

"She can fly unaided?"

"Hooray!"

Wixx swirled with the building fanfare.

"Our future is boundless together. I promise you that!"

She dove close to their heads, and three creatures fainted.

"Everybody up! Get up and dance this night away! Dance to meeeeeeeeeeee!" Pepper swirled up into the sky.

The dazzled crowds had never seen a witch flying unaided without a traditional Scorch. They all understood that Pepper was a powerful woman. Still, no one suspected she was harboring these secret superpowers.

"No, Scorch?"

"That's impossible?"

"Nope! That's the future, right there!"

Wixx circled each cage.

"Take heart, children. Your suffering is almost over. Somewhere in this crowd are your future parents! Lucky you!"

She waved her crystals around each child, drowning them in blasts of fresh suds.

"We can't have a proper raffle looking like this!" she proclaimed midair. "I have a reputation to uphold!"

By the time Wixx was through redressing them—pausing only to add a few specific accessories here and there—she had transformed each teenager into their own best Prom versions of themselves.

She draped Kate in a refined version of the prettiest gown of her dreams.

This is perfect. How can she know my favorite color?

Wixx aimed her stolen crystals—levitating the startled teens out of their cages and down onto the stage below.

The crowds ate up the showmanship.

"Look! Flying Umans too!"

The kids panicked midair on their second visit with uncontrolled weightlessness, causing awkward spins and collisions. Still, being a natural dancer, Lennon took this rare opportunity to pirouette into the sky like a fairy, captivating the surly crowds below.

"I want to win that pretty one!" a ghoul screamed and threw more crystals onto the stage to a very busy Shelby, who was hawking more raffle tickets than ever to build up the growing stockpile of precious jewels.

"Now dance, my pretty little Umans! Dance so that all my subjects can see and bid on you, just like the privileged get to do!" Pepper commanded.

She twirled around them as each child landed on the stage, paired with the nearest unchosen dance partner, and sent to perform like marionettes attached to Pepper's strings.

Wixx slammed Kate and Tim together with just a slight nod. Josh and Coop swirled away as a duo, with Oz and Jesse paired, leaving Pavarty dancing with Emiliano.

They left Lennon spinning like an angel in the sky, high above the stage.

Conductor Hermann's dark waltz added another layer of sophistication and grandeur to the down-home country festival, elevating the moonlit night with his dark necromantic fanfares.

Pepper Wixx was overcome with emotions she thought

were long dead within herself.

This must be what love feels like.

She swooned and soared as no witch had flown before. It was a terrifying yet magical moment where the melancholy melody encompassed them all.

Forced to waltz together like puppets, Coop resisted whatever dance button Wixx had pushed. As he did, he found he could peel himself away from his partner, Josh, as everyone else continued to swirl madly around them in broad sweeping circles.

Coop straightened his tie, and when Kate and Tim twirled by, he tapped Tim on the shoulder, and the couple spun to a stuttering stop, temporarily ejected from the wispy spell as well.

Lost within the center of her bliss, Wixx's spell dampened as her emotions spun away on the waltz's romantic drive.

"May I have this last dance?" Coop bowed, and Tim relented as any gentleman would.

Coop stepped back into the intricate swirls of the dancing spell. As he and Kate clasped hands together, they began waltzing and twirling as if they'd been dancing together their entire lives.

Tim didn't want to miss this magical moment of freedom. So, he extended his hand out to Josh, who stood nearby.

"Why not?" Josh smiled and accepted.

Tim had found his new dance partner.

As Pepper Wixx danced through the air, she held the audience captive within the moment.

"Listen, I'm sorry for even risking this," Coop said, "But I'd never forgive myself if I didn't at least take the chance to be with you at least once more before we died," Coop apologized.

"So, I guess I just found out what you believe in?" she smiled.

"Uh, yeah. Guess so."

"And I would never forgive myself if I didn't do this." Kate leaned in and kissed him.

They lingered nose to nose as they whirled around the stage floor before levitating back up into the air, and the majestic night music built towards a powerful crescendo.

That's when Pepper Wixx opened her eyes and remembered just how much she hated the concept of the Uman's sense of romantic love and their precious need for bogus happy endings—along with everything else, the stinking vermin believed in, like cherishing babies and little puppies. She grimaced, watching their wholesomeness appeal even to her unworthy hordes.

This is my party. Not theirs. I am the star. Not them.

"Stop!" she frightened the orchestra into a few tuba squawks

"Enough!"

Wixx spiraled down over Kate and Coop, who landed on the stage again, once startled back into their horrible reality.

"Welcome to Dark Hollows, lovebirds. Where every fairy princess becomes a wicked witch, and every heroic prince becomes a cowardly lion," she purred. "And just remember this, my pretties, from here on out... silence is golden! Or I'll tie all your tongues down to your chins and let you drown in your own spit. Now kneel in front of me, Umans! Kneel and pray that I don't kill you both right now."

Wixx used the power of her stolen black crystal and shoved them down to the stage in coils of barbed sparks.

The crowds' spirits fell, most disappointed at this sad and violent ending to the whimsical moment.

"Ah, man, it was just getting good."

Wixx hurled the children back into their vulture cages with a wrist flick and locked the cages again.

They were reduced to fancy-dressed raffle prizes again.

"This is our time! You've had yours!" Wixx spat at the frightened teens.

The hometown celebrity began working to reestablish

her connection to the hometown crowds again.

"Now, folks, for your viewing pleasure, I have that unfinished business to attend to. So, sit back, relax, and prepare to get thrilled right down to the dead marrow in your bones as we watch Yuma die."

Henrietta scuttled over from her chair to Pepper. The board members were growing concerned.

"Pepper, darling. Muddy waters are best cleared by leaving them alone," Henrietta cooed as if trying to quell a gathering storm.

"What does that even mean?" Wixx asked.

"Maybe we should just leave well enough alone across the lake for now. You've already won that war for us. Why start another so soon during your virgin reign? It's not considered good form, darling. He has no standing army to fight back. You have made us safe by exiling him. Whether you planned that, it has worked out well for the rest of us," Henrietta pleaded. "He will die over there in shame and banishment. What else do you want?"

"I want it all, Henrietta. I want him to die a painful death and stay dead. But only after I tear him into a million pieces. Then I want his thick skull skewered onto the tallest redwood for my ravens to pick clean and use his skull as proof that giants don't exist anymore."

"My dear. Really. What a crude way..."

Wixx leaned in and hissed before Henrietta could finish.

"Do you really want to understand? For one to be defined, the other must perish! Do you really want to climb onboard this train to hell with me, sis?"

Henrietta recoiled as Wixx's eyes rolled back, and she floated.

"Get out of my sight."

Henrietta slunk back to her chair to bear silent witness to whatever calamity was about to transpire.

The new Queen nodded offstage to Moody, and he

lowered two large projection screens from underneath the branches.

"Welcome to Pepper-Vision, folks!" Her amplified voice filled the town square.

"My dear subjects, the living future surrounds us daily, roaring past on their freeway above. A Uman future that we are no longer allowed to participate in!" Wixx started reciting her prepared speech. "Well, my friends, that old-fashioned rubbish stops today! We must seize life by the throat to reclaim our future!"

Wixx reached down and squeezed a remote hidden inside her sleeve, and five hundred drones suddenly lit up the sky.

The impressive new armada was hovering just offshore, startling the screaming crowds. The audience went insane as the humming hi-tech invaders turned visible, with brilliant LED sequencings lighting up the shoreline.

"Oh!"

Everyone gasped as the brilliant display of quadra-copter illumination mimicked astrological shapes in the sky in 3D.

Wixx squeezed another button.

The automated dragonflies raked the crowds with their rhythmic, pulsating lighting magic—illuminating everyone below like celebrities in an 80s disco, and the cheering mob bounced in time to the sugar-coated music.

Wixx frowned at the childlike delight still alive in so many hideous monsters before soaring up among her fleet of synchronized drones to catch sight of the giant's startled reaction.

"Buckle up, boys and girls, and get ready for the Half-Time Show!" Pepper sang as she waved to all her fans below.

"Behold, the prophecies of our future come roaring back to life in all its multifaceted glory!"

She punched another button, and giant letters formed across the airborne billboard of drones. Its hi-tech message

towered a hundred feet high above the lake.
"TIMES UP, BIG BOY!"

-CHAPTER 49-

Duel of the Titans

The last giant on earth stood on the banks of Eel Lake alone, dressed for battle.

A million spiders had manufactured his simple battle tunic overnight, and the remarkable gift shielded the mighty Time Warrior in several defensive layers of gossamer-thin fabric. Yet neither bullet, arrow, blade, lance, or flame could penetrate its finely spun armored weavings.

Yuma applied his war paint in symbolic colors, representing humankind in bright slashes of red, yellow, black, white, and brown. Then, he prepared his weapons to make his stand on the untouched shores of the Sacred Forest—maybe for the last time—as a solitary fighting force of one.

That's how it appeared to Queen Wixx on her side of the teeming lake, with the crowds urging her fleet on. Everyone celebrated while watching the zoomed-in close-up of the giant projected on the new Pepper-Vision screens and broadcasting Live from the advancing drones.

Even Yuma couldn't ignore the latest attempt to bait him when the message towered a hundred feet tall.

'TIMES UP BIG BOY!' - 'TIME TO DIE!'

"Get my message, heathen?" Wixx's amplified voice screeched across the lake, "You're going down, Mister Boogeyman!"

Pepper Wixx had been planning this revenge-fueled extravaganza for quite a while.

"Look! Look at that old squaw man! What's he wearing now?" someone in the crowd shouted.

"I think he's camouflaged like a tree!"

The audience howled at the sight of the ancient warrior's battle attire.

Yuma stood on the shoreline, wearing redwood shin guards and forearm protectors while carrying a tall wooden shield in front of him, all carved from the invincible Sequoia bark.

He gripped a lance the size of a sapling in his other fist. After years of underground growth, the spear featured a multifaceted quartz blade that grew naturally at its tip. Twelve Time Crystals of varying shapes and sizes grew inside the straight shaft while multicolored feathers adorned its length.

Yuma named the trusty weapon Thunapa—Thunder in English—and they had cultivated it underground for generations before the Illuminators presented it to him in his youth.

"Maybe he's going to make-believe he's a dogwood tree and bark!" the blue tailor from Badazz Junction laughed at the sight. The crowds barked and began yipping and howling at the moon like a pack of cartoon hounds.

But not everyone in Dark Hollows was so arrogant.

Those who had fought against Yuma knew better than to mock this elite warrior and holy man—or underestimate any of his incredible powers. Provoking him seemed a foolhardy move to the brightest—yet to everyone else, it was just another wonderful surprise gift from their malicious new Queen.

One way or the other, a legend was falling tonight—because if Pepper Wixx wanted to poke this sleeping bear as part of her grand celebrations—then everyone standing on her side of the lake had better-

"Duck!" Wixx shrieked as debris collided with her midair.

A tornado of destruction swept in—amputated rotor blades flew past, sent spinning like humming buzz saws. Someone had destroyed Pepper's expensive fleet of drones and hurled their shattered carcasses back across the lake as trash.

"Yuma!" Pepper screamed.

The shrapnel rained down on the surprised crowds below, followed by explosions and life-threatening wounds, but the demented partygoers thought it fit Wixx's black humor, and most demanded more mayhem.

The Pepper-Vision screens buzzed with the first images of the fleets' destruction—televised several seconds after unfolding events.

A shell-shocked Wixx noted the severe time lag in the feed.

"Never trust those online reviews!" she hissed to the crowds and flew higher for a better battlefield view.

Yuma laughed as he cleared the air of any remaining pests with a simple point and flick of Thunapa. The giant had destroyed most of the pesky drones several seconds before they broadcast their dying transmissions to the large Pepper-Vision screens.

"Your move!" Yuma bellowed from his pristine beach.

Wixx spun a ragged crystal, and the deadly cloud of debris streaking by her instantaneously transformed into a flurry of harmless snowflakes.

"Ooh! Yay!" the crowds cheered, sticking out their tongues to capture a taste of the magic.

But Pepper Wixx was enraged, embarrassed, and no longer in a celebratory mood.

"You will never insult me again with your feeble folk

powers in front of my kind, you cur!"

Wixx zapped her hatred for Yuma into every drifting snowflake, infecting each with her malice before they could hit the ground. The abused water crystals exploded into snowdrifts of fat, wiggling maggots. The moist piles of white larvae swelled and then double-popped into full-grown adult locusts.

"Ooh! Someone's spoiling for a fight, folks! What do you think? Want to enjoy shoving back for a change?" She called down to the merry crowds below.

"Yeah!" they roared as she spied Yuma striding boldly along the beach.

She snapped her fingers, and the monstrous cloud of locusts vibrated their crispy wings and lifted off in a unified swarm that enveloped the sky.

"Time for a midnight snack, everybody!" she called out, and the crowds cheered as the pestilence rose around them.

"Quick, take a picture, take a picture!" an ogre yelled as dozens of locusts flew out of his snow-filled mouth.

Wixx's cursed plague rose to meet their maker, where they engulfed her in hatred before swarming away toward the lush green shores across the lake.

Wixx spied Yuma standing out on the shoreline, and she spun the Darklight Crystal up into her palm and fired—its twin-headed blast shot down from the sky.

Yuma ducked at the first flash of the anti-light, sending rocks and debris flying away from his feet as the giant leaped out of harm's way.

The twin laser bolts hissed as they sizzled across the forest floor, searching for him in vain, as Yuma dove and rolled behind the protective bark of Little Sister again.

Yuma staggered at what he saw coming next.

The massive swarm of insects rose up across the lake and flew directly toward him with their hungry intentions given wing.

When Yuma absently drifted within sight of the

Darklight, it struck out hard, slamming his shield with the sudden force of a double-barreled lightning blast.

Its violent contact slid the giant backward, digging his feet deeper into the soil as the relentless beams thrashed against his shield. But Yuma leaned back against the willpower of his stolen crystals with unwavering force. Now it was his turn for decisive action.

Yuma stared skyward—undistracted by the deadly beam's unceasing attack—holding his lance overhead, and he began chanting—summoning any powers from the electrical fields of the natural world to come forth.

Thunapa's length rippled with light and began to rumble when, without warning, Zip, Zash, and Zee whizzed past overhead, head flying in battle formation.

The staunchest defenders of the Sacred Forest were there to protect their giant and homeland at the first signs of trouble.

The fearless trio penetrated the hungry clouds and devoured as many oversized pests as possible, intercepting them like miniature antiballistic missiles in midair. These tough magical critters rarely slept, and their specialty was eating bugs at speed, no matter the size or time of day.

What the supersonic hummingbirds couldn't consume or impale, they sliced in half, streaking by with their razor-sharp beaks held wide open, dispatching several giant insects at a time as their dead husks littered the lake below.

The songbird community living within the Sacred Forest witnessed the courage displayed by the tiny trio of heroes, inspiring them to act. They voted with their hearts as they dove from the treetops to join in defending their secret world.

Wixx hovered above her raucous hometown crowds, growing more confused by the second as she witnessed her assault cloud diminishing in density and becoming thin and grey. It was like someone was swirling an eraser over a dirty chalkboard in the sky.

"What kind of reductive nonsense-magic is this? No one can fight back against a plague of locusts! No one in history!" Wixx screamed.

Only a few mangled stragglers were dangling in the air–hovering on broken wingtips–as the hungry eels surfaced and dined.

The angry crowd of monsters and doomsayers 'Booed!' at the apparent defeat of their shadowy swarm as it dissolved back into nothingness.

"No way!"

"Lame!"

They expected so much more from their new Queen of the Damned and their home team.

Everyone began comparing scorecards. Rounds one and two had gone to Yuma, and Pepper's blood boiled.

He had humiliated her for the last time in front of her hometown crowd and the Board.

"Well. It looks like our imposter has bitten off a lot more than she can chew," Henrietta whispered to the rest of the shaken board below on the stage—but Pepper heard her.

"We'll just see about that, sis!" Wixx promised.

-CHAPTER 50-

The Reckoning

"The nerve of that amateur butcher! He's ruining my party!" Wixx exploded after being shown up by Yuma on her most memorable night.

She had no way of knowing that the giant warrior had nothing to do with that last decisive victory. He had cast no magic spells except for washing the sky clean of those rude drones.

Any credit for her defeat went only to Zip, Zash, and Zee and their brave community of hummingbirds, along with all the other songbirds of the Sacred Forest.

No magic was involved to covet, except for the sacrificial love displayed by all. The tiny birds defended their nests with guts, smarts, and determination, which is its own kind of magic.

"I won't allow this backward pagan to spoil my reign," Wixx seethed. "Never! I have trained for this fight all of my lives!"

The spectators watched in amazement as Wixx summoned forth the second great plague from the earth as she began chanting in the forgotten language of Taub, and her babble of tongues multiplied the size and ferocity of the new curse to biblical proportions.

Hordes of locust, bark-beetle, and murder hornets rose from the polluted soil in numbers a thousand times greater than the previous swarm.

The audience grew hysterical at the sight of the

levitating spectacle. Then, on her command, the growing cloud of death and destruction rose to fill the sky with pestilence again as far as the evil eye could see.

Yuma staggered back at the apocalyptic sight billowing up from across the lake. This second wave appeared large enough to swallow the entire forest as it unfurled before him like a bad dream.

The giant raised his lance to the sky in tribute—ramming it three times onto the earth.

Boom! Boom! Boom!

The crystals embedded along the shaft of Thunapa glowed hot, then faded in intensity as a cooling breeze rose off the lake.

It wasn't Yuma's magic causing the stiff wind to blow. It was the sheer biomass of a million wings beating toward him. This new menacing swarm was so dense that its size alone forced the rapid displacement of air away like a hurricane.

Yuma stood alone in the howling winds, waiting for any sign of Thunapa's powers to rejuvenate. Yet, nothing seemed to happen as the Time Crystals embedded in its shank failed to ignite.

The swarms swept toward him—unchallenged and gaining speed.

It confused the giant as he slammed his lance harder into the soil, demanding a reply.

Boom! Boom! Boom!

The crystals glowed, then dimmed once more.

"Nothing? Am I too late?"

Zack stayed hidden underground inside a stone bunker with Harley, where Yuma had stashed them for safety, far away from the battlefront of the shoreline.

"Remember, you stay down here until I summon you," Yuma had commanded.

"What if I can't hear you down here?"

"You will hear me. I can guarantee that."

The giant brushed the hair off the little boy's sweaty forehead. They'd only just met; still, Yuma felt an honest kinship with the brave homeless wanderer.

"You stay here and do not act until you hear that command. Not a moment before! Understand me? Timing is everything now. Do nothing but practice until then. Learn to use those special crystals as if our lives depended on them, son, because they do. So, think, and remain focused. Everything depends on you now. I will call you when it is time to act."

The giant slid the heavy lid closed, flashing one last smile before sealing them underground in the fortified crypt.

"Hey? How can I open this thing up when I need to?"

"You figure that out as well!" came the distant reply.

"Oh, great. Something else to learn."

Across the lake in their fancy cages, the teens were still dressed formally, although far less elegant than before. They stood slack-jawed as the sky above them grew darker, and the clouds of rising insects engulfed them inside their open cages.

"Eek! Help!"

"Noooooo!"

"Stay off of me!"

Kate knew this was the moment of distraction they had been waiting for.

"We go now! No B.S.! Now or never!" Kate yelled to everyone as they passed the sneaker key from cage to cage again.

The showdown mesmerized the crowd, and no one was paying attention as Kate swung open her door, and the others held their breaths, unlocking theirs.

"Wait! Kate!"

"What?"

"Sorry, but you can't leave here looking that good?" Coop said.

"No time for a compliment, Bub?"

"Just look at your pretty selves," he gestured to their

new clothes. "You won't make it out of this park," he promised as their only veteran of escape.

"Oh, no," Kate said.

"Oh, yes."

"Oh, no!"

"Oh, yes," Coop promised, grinning like a madman. He plopped a handful of entrails onto his head again—transforming himself into a horrifying new monster with cool-whipped hair.

He forced the thick gunk from his eyes and gagged.

"Twwwwwwh! Try not to swallow... twwwh!... too much of this green bile stuff," Coop mumbled as he slathered on more gore and stuck random gull bones and undigestible bat wings into his hair—scavenging for anything he could find to cover up the sight and smell of his Uman flesh living underneath the revolting disguise.

Pavarty stared at her lovely, one-of-a-kind gown with resignation.

"This is just so typical of my life. If I live another million years, I swear, I will never-ever look this perfect again," she sighed.

"I think you look pretty perfect all the time," Josh replied from his open door.

"What?" Pavarty asked, astonished. "Me? Was that you, Josh?"

"Yes. You, Pavarty."

"Nonsense. I'm just a... weird collection of ovals."

Josh smiled beneath the beginnings of his horrible disguise.

"Ovals are the perfect shape. Orbits are ovals. Eggs are ovals. Everything perfect is an oval. And all orbits are symmetrical things of exquisite beauty," the handsome teen promised.

"What?"

The hideous glop swallowing her head was the only thing that could extinguish Pavarty's smile.

"Why, thank you, Josh... (glub)."

She never got to acknowledge the rest of his compliment as she gagged.

Josh read that as a negative reaction. The pretty boy had never made anyone puke before.

"Woop-ehhh!" Pavarty retched again and couldn't bring herself to slather any more goo onto her face—so Jesse obliged and hurled some neighborly glop her way.

"Here! Free makeup!" Jess grinned.

"Ooh! Gross, sister!" Pavarty squawked.

"The word gross can't possibly ever define this..." Emiliano replied, covered in phosphorescent entrails. "Any of it!"

Yuma stood before the advancing plague, unsure of his ability to summon his magical powers for the first time.

Is it because my army is dead?

Was the magic inside them all along and not me?

He squinted at the Crown of Swords wavering high overhead. They twinkled in the blowing treetops—every weapon clashing and clanging together as if in dress rehearsal.

The wind off the lake intensified as the plague roiled closer

Yuma thrust the blunt end of Thunapa down into the earth, demanding to be heard

again.

Boom! Boom! Boom!

The chaos caused by his impacts thundered the mountaintops as the Time-Crystals exploded and glowed white-hot, burning with a fierce authority at last.

"Took your sweet time, Thunapa!" Yuma admonished the ethereal weapon. "Growing as weary of war as I?"

A fresh wind blew in from behind him—as well as the one from offshore. He felt squeezed between the colliding vortexes.

Is this the trap?

Yuma turned in surprise to face a tornado of leaves swirling behind him—and that's when the bats exploded out of the forest, followed by thousands of seagulls—each species squawking orders as the acrobatic gulls and bats joined in the deadly fight against the winged intruders.

"Scabs and boils with this nonsense!"

Wixx wasn't taking any more chances, with her numbers visibly dwindling again. She needed reinforcements.

Still hovering like the angel of death above her mobs, the witch split the night sky open with her crimson crystal and began chanting an old Druid curse. That's when she spotted the rare Tiger Crystal she sought on the stage. Wixx dove straight down out of the sky to retrieve it—eliciting another big- "Oooooh!" from the captivated crowd.

"Watch out! Make a hole for the Queen!"

She skimmed only inches above the reviewing stands, plucking up handfuls of random crystals from the growing pile in front of her throne before soaring back into the sky, seeking new inspiration, before spotting all the birds roosting below.

"Call to duty, boys! You're all drafted!"

Wixx blasted double-barreled beams of multicolored light into the flocks—unsure of the outcome.

The ravens and vultures squawked and shrieked as her erratic beams bit into their bodies—launching every scavenger into a panicked flight high above Dark Hollows.

The ravens transformed as they flew through her convoluted web of intersecting X-rays. They expanded midair, plumping into muscular, armored versions of themselves. But now, these demonized ravens displayed fangs on either side of their reinforced metal beaks and extra talons.

"Now that's a proper murder of Crows!" Wixx bragged to her appreciative audience below.

Any vultures hit by the beams doubled in size as

well. Only now, these deadly versions came armed with talons as long as steak knives protruded from their wingtips and advanced cartilage spikes crowning the tops of their ulcerated heads—everything fashioned for impalement and disembowelment.

"Don't come back unless you're carrying that big, ugly giant's head in your claws!" she ordered the mutants and turned back to the crowd. "Cravens and punctures! I adore adding new creatures to my menu! I'm just like Mother Nature! Only more powerful! I can do in seconds what takes her millions of years!"

Kate dropped to the ground, barefoot. She was the first down and smeared in goo and slime—no longer dressed like anyone's version of a fairy-tale princess. She shredded her designer gown to free her legs in this last dash for freedom.

The reviewing stands had emptied as everyone rushed to the shoreline to watch the new battle lines form

Tim jumped next, still in pain, but he was the tallest, and he helped the shorter kids along with Coop and Ozzy.

Pavarty found time to rethink their self-made disguises as they waited for the rest to assemble. She readjusted or added gross details to everyone's homemade Walking Dead costume as they dropped. Tim resisted any improvements.

"Trust me, Skater boy. Look at them. All those butt ugly things have a certain flair, just like you and I!" she said, pointing various chic creatures out. With a go-ahead nod, Pav continued to add whatever details she could find—discarded hats, gloves, and any extra bones and eyeballs they had lying around in the stands. She contributed so many layers of detail that even Ozzy chuckled at his motley crew of rejects.

With only cage remnants, feathers, eyeballs, viscous fluids, and a few regurgitated fashion accessories to work with —this was the inspired work of a budding design genius.

"My best work yet!" Pav bragged, now surrounded by the monsters of her making. There was a distinctive elegance about them all now.

This group would dominate any Cosplay convention, but inside this living nightmare, funny didn't exist.

"Alright, that's it! I'm done!" Pavarty tried to clean her hands.

"If we're caught now, we're deader than we already look," Emil said.

"What monster couldn't resist us? We're wearing all their favorite flavors, aren't we?" Ozzy trembled.

"Nope! That's why they left this waste behind."

"Remember. From here on out, if anything comes up to you and talks, you just roll with it," Kate ordered. "But don't talk back. You got that, Lennon?"

"Okay."

Coop agreed.

"If we get split up for any reason, I stashed Pepper's red delivery truck at the car graveyard on the outskirts of town that way, and I hid the keys under the driver's side floor mat."

"But I don't know how to drive! What if nobody makes it out alive but me?" Ozzy moaned.

"Neither do I," Josh and Pavarty admitted.

"I do. And so do Coop and Tim," Kate tried to encourage them. "And I will see all of you in that truck, okay? I promise. But right now, let's stay tight like we're all just a happy pack of zombies out celebrating a good time and watching the end of time together. Okay?"

They all nodded.

"Bring it in!" Kate gestured.

Everyone fist-bumped. Kate, Coop, Pavarty, Jesse, Lennon, Tim, Emiliano, Josh, and Ozzy followed up with a big group hug—maybe for the last time.

The slimy squishing sound produced when squeezed together was disgusting.

"Eck!"

"Ooooooooooh!"

"Gross!"

"I told you! Gross is not a strong enough word anymore.

Not down here! Not by a long shot!" Emiliano gagged.

"We stay together. Alright?" Kate demanded, and the pack of fake undead headed out together into the heart of Dark Hollows.

"Remember what Coop said—fortune favors the bold. Let's go."

Yuma waited on the other side of the lake, studying the newest wave of horrors flying into battle. He paused before unleashing the power of Thunapa again.

Whip-smart ravens are born to fight dirty, and their advanced survival instincts allow them to read their enemies' vulnerabilities and adjust their attack on the fly. But these new mutated cravens were even larger and more determined than their counterparts.

They aimed for the gulls' vulnerable eyes and the bats' fleshy ears and wings—tearing hundreds of them apart as they slashed by flying at speed.

Even the maneuverable hummingbirds had difficulty diving out of the way of the robust new species of attack birds.

The combined flocks of the Sacred Forest took heavy casualties as these armored freaks slayed the brave defenders with abandon and filled the already dark skies with death.

Their superior numbers allowed easy penetration of the bird's defenses as the first locust touched down on the green shoreline.

"Never!" Yuma bellowed and raced forward, twirling his battle lance over his head. He washed the beach clean of the first locust clouds with a sweep of his lance. Then he spun back around and sliced and diced through the advancing waves of winged freaks that attacked. He destroyed the cravens and punctures midair as if he'd been practicing for this unending onslaught his entire life.

After each impalement, he would sling the carcasses off his lance to feed the eels.

Yuma rammed the mighty Thunapa into the ground once more.

Boom!

Lightning flashed, and thunder split open a clear night sky as something dark and wonderful began spiraling down from the heavens to help.

Thousands of eagles, condors, hawks, falcons, owls, harriers, and osprey materialized overhead, establishing an impenetrable formation of birds of prey.

They tucked their wings and dove into combat, using their superior flying abilities and deadly talons against the vicious monsters swarming below and attacking the smaller creatures.

The avenging eagles and hawks defended the other birds as fiercely as any sibling protecting his family from bullies—and the sky rained enough black feathers that night to stuff a thousand pillowcases.

The somber crowds lining the shoreline of Dark Hollows groaned as their horrid marauders appeared to be thwarted in every attempt at conquest.

"Hey! What gives?"

"We haven't even taken a bite out of their shoreline yet! Have we?"

The crowds grew angry at such an embarrassing display by their decimated demon flocks.

No matter the insane distractions happening above their heads—Kate kept her eyes locked on the path of escape. She steered everyone in the same general direction they'd come two days before as they bullied and charmed their way through a maze of inebriated monstrosities.

Every thing in town stood frozen in place, transfixed by the legendary aerial battle just offshore.

A family of goblins shoved their way past the disguised teens, trying to get a better view, and ended up separating the orphans in their wake.

"Nope," Kate whispered and swung the entire group

around, still arm in arm. They made a full three-hundred-and-sixty-degree sweep, recollecting the lost members of their tribe in one uninterrupted move, never missing a beat, like a zombie marching band.

Hovering alone in the sky, Wixx grew impatient with the nasty turn of events. She descended next to her throne, where everyone tried to console her.

"Enough!" her over-amplified voice boomed across the lake, and the crowd quieted on her command.

"That was just a tiny appetizer to whet our appetites before we tackle the main course of revenge to be served up hot tonight. How do you like your giants cooked, my subjects? They can be pretty gamey!"

"Bloody!" the crowd roared as they ping-ponged emotionally back into her corner again.

"Then look up into the night sky like you owned it again, folks! Because we do!" she commanded. "That's my moon, now!"

Wixx nodded at her sons and the workforce on the street. Each monster held the end of a network of long, thick chains that stretched across the road and disappeared underneath her lodge.

Something powerful thrashed indoors against the other end of the snapping chains, and Berk missed his mother's first cue.

Wixx cleared her throat, agitated at his ineptitude, and nodded again with more emphasis.

"Now, stupid!" she finally shouted.

"Oh no! Sorry, Ma! Heave-ho boys!" Berk and Moody grunted, and all seven ogres gave the chains a monstrous heave.

Wixx grinned in premature victory as the ground began trembling beneath their feet, and that tremor grew into a furious rumble, quaking the entire town.

"Ohhhhhhh!" the crowds reacted.

"I return to you... your past and your future!" she

proclaimed, and everyone cheered. "My vision of that new tomorrow conjured tonight just for you! My poor, long-forgotten people!"

Pepper's basement exploded, sending a blast of bricks skyward, leaving a jagged hole behind.

"Witness my children! For I am the only reason to look up into the sky again! My bloody sky!"

A plume of green flames blasted out of the hole, and the ogres dropped the glowing chains and bolted down the street as the last living dragon climbed out of the basement, roaring like a nitro-fueled superstar.

Rrrrrrrrrrrgggggggggghhhhh!

The red dragon unfurled its four scalloped wings and flapped them overhead while spewing a stream of unstable gas flames, setting several fast-food stands on fire. For only the second time in his force-fed life, this young dragon belched internal fire from within.

After a series of powerful beats to synchronize his new wings, the newborn chick the size of a school bus took off, silhouetted against the oversized moon in search of his mother, as the stunned crowds gasped in amazement and admiration.

"Meet my newest boy!" Wixx screamed as she flew up face to face. With its six disturbing yellow eyes, the simmering youngling hovered next to his adopted mother. They bonded high above the heads of the masses, with the young dragon's chains still dangling from his neck like a severed umbilical cord.

This outrageous dragon pup had been force-hatched into existence through willpower and a bevy of Taub bewitching spells within only hours of first discovery. Wixx's toxic replacement for mothers' milk was to force-feed the chick livestock to achieve full size within twenty-four hours. The very existence of a dragon this size was a miracle, and he was a sight to see.

"And he's all mine!"

Not as imposing as some legends, this newly hatched creature still towered over anything more significant than an elephant, and his upswept wingtips added more height.

Wixx stared into its six complex eyes and saw they shared her favorite color—spoiled lemons.

"My darling boy, just look at you. Born belligerent. What a mess. Who could ever love such a horrible face except your new mother?"

The young dragon answered by spraying an arc of fire across the sky, and the crowds roared back their appreciation before ducking as the sticky flames splattered below, obliterating several more concession booths.

"Whoa!"

"Look out!"

"What are you going to call him, Pepper?"

"Bob!" someone shouted out.

"Methuselah!"

"Beelzebub!"

The thought hadn't crossed her mind.

"Yes. I will name him... Caesar! King of the World!" Wixx anointed her newest child.

"Yeah!" the crowds screamed, cheering at his very existence.

"Caesar! Caesar! Caesar!" everyone took up the chant.

"That's not all, folks! This show has just started! Watch this!"

Wixx pushed another button hidden on her sleeve, and thousands of spitfire drones shot out of the new smoking hole one at a time. They flew into a pre-programmed attack formation in the sky as thick as any conjured plague.

"Online delivers anywhere! Anytime these days! And their drivers taste just as fine as you'd expect for home delivery!" she laughed.

Pepper Wixx's updated spitfires carried lights and infrared cameras aboard like the others, but these burly upgraded versions also packed heat.

421

"Somebody said they liked their giants bloody, but not me. I prefer mine well-done! Observe!" Wixx yelled, and thirty-foot tusks of flames shot out of every drone.

Each militarized model carried two mini flamethrowers aboard, and four rotating quad-blades made their flight patterns pinpoint accurate, allowing the vectored rotors to transform into chainsaws on request.

"Dragons and drones! Here is the future I promised you! Our future combined with our past!" Pepper screamed, and the astonished crowds roared in approval as legends soared high above Dark Hollows again.

"Dragons and drones!" the public started chanting. "Caesar! Wixx! Caesar! Wixx!"

The dragon hovered next to Pepper, and she whispered into its twitching ear and pointed across the lake.

"Destroy the filthy Uman living over there that killed your mother. Avenge her and avenge me and mine. Fly, sweet Caesar, fly! Wreak havoc, as only you were born to do!"

The perceptive young dragon spun in the sky as if it understood and flew off to catch up to his pre-programmed step-brothers—both seeking fire-breathing revenge against the legendary target.

"Buckle up, folks! It's going to be a hot time in the old forest tonight!" Wixx sang, and the crowds went wild and joined in the song.

Yuma didn't understand the shape of what he saw rising behind the wave of scavengers and drones in the over-crowded sky.

"Only one creature looks like that... is this even possible?"

Yuma had killed the last dragon himself. And yet here rose another more than a hundred years later.

"Draygore, must have been the mother?" Yuma never realized the gender of one of his fiercest foes. "How many dragons does Wixx possess? Some dragons laid dozens of eggs." He worried aloud.

The untrampled forest vibrated with the thundering power of negative energy flying its way, and the once-protected animals of the Sacred Forest trembled in fear.

Yuma intentionally held back the most ferocious grizzly bears, cougars, wolves, coyotes, foxes, stags, and elk populations in reserve—ready to sacrifice them only as a last resort. But the sight of a living dragon terrified even the fiercest of these apex predators, throwing their survival into doubt.

Except for a few ancient tortoises, no living animal had ever witnessed a fire-breathing dragon before.

The physical reality of seeing such a powerful beast flying overhead made even the bravest of these fearless brutes cringe when confronted by the unbelievable scale of the brutal monster for the first time.

Caesar circled above Yuma with only a few short wing-strokes, and the warrior dropped to his knees, taking cover beneath his oversized shield.

The beast turned and flew past at supersonic speeds, raining fire down in a continuous shower of flames while spewing its hatred across the entire beachfront, incinerating every innocent sapling growing there.

The extreme heat blast boiled the living sap out of Yuma's protective shield. Still, the thick, heat-resistant redwood held firm against the blistering assault.

Caesar soared past Yuma and swung around in the crowded sky to make another strafing run on the giant. Yuma's lonely battle allowed the hi-tech spitfires to land for the first time.

The crowds in Dark Hollows cheered at the shocking dragon spectacular overhead as the conflict raged far out across the bay. The murderous assault was being broadcast via PEPPER-VISION again as the Invasion Channel flashed fancy graphics, and the Jabberwocky Twins sputtered gibberish, trying to keep up with the ever-changing odds.

The grizzlies and eagles tried valiantly to combine their inherent strengths and get their anger airborne—planning a surprise attack together. But several giant eagles and condors attempting to lift a six-hundred-pound grizzly into the air failed with miserable howls of pain with every try.

Their only plan was for the massive eagles to drop the giant grizzlies onto the dragon's back while still in mid-flight—like suicidal time bombs bearing fangs and claws. They hoped one or two of their most ferocious bears might physically tear the dragon apart in midair. But they couldn't achieve proper aerodynamic lift-off.

The condors and eagles hoisted a few brave dire wolves airborne, but not in enough numbers to justify their howling self-sacrifice against this ferocious killing machine.

The animals of the Sacred Forest watched helplessly as the dragon continued his fiery assault on Yuma. There was nothing left for them to do to halt this rampaging nightmare.

"Stand down!" Yuma commanded as he saw the bravest bucks take a step forward. They felt weak and hopeless and cringed back into the tree line as the red dragon whooshed by for another attack.

Still hunkered underground, Zack continued practicing live firing his crystals, with Harley cowering at the unexpected results. He absently sizzled his finger when he heard Yuma's voice bellowing up on the surface.

"What did he say? Was this the last signal, boy? He never said what the words would be, did he, Harley?"

You will know when you hear it! His mind reassured him in the timbre of Yuma's words.

"Wait?"

A neglected thought shattered Zack's concentration.

"What about my friends? What's going to happen to

Kate? Coop? The rest?"

The boy's mind flooded with the images of drowning babies from his dreams, and his friends' faces were floating among them.

-CHAPTER 51-

Rise

Yuma sprinted across the beachhead, with his curved shield covering his head and back like a fireproof tortoise shell as the dragons rained fire down from above. He dashed behind the protection of Little Sister's girth and dove into his closest elevator, discarding his smoking shield to lighten the load.

Nothing but his incineration or a miracle would quench the dragon pup's fury now.

The giant slashed the counterbalanced ropes, sending him soaring to the tips of the redwoods in seconds while the confused dragon continued searching for him below.

Jumping out at the top, Yuma thrust Thunapa overhead, and lightning shattered the sky as the thunder roared its approval.

The Time Warrior sang an ancient chant. The Song of the Center had gained new meaning as he combined its insights with other tribes' wisdom over the centuries, but its open invitation remained true.

"Show me the magic!" Yuma demanded from the sky, and his command became thunder. "Show me the magic!" His voice boomed, summoning the ultimate powers of Mother Earth and the Great Creator.

A sudden crack overhead parted the clouds, revealing an unidentifiable speck circling high in the heavens. That sinister dark form took shape as it spiraled down from the stratosphere and pierced the upper membranes of the Bubble.

"What is that?" someone screamed in Dark Hollows.

426

"Is this part of the show?"

That's when the Thunderbird swooped out of the electrified sky—demonstrating its legendary size and scale by carrying a Killer Whale in her talons like she had caught a trout.

Why would you interrupt my hunt? Her piercing side-eye chastised Yuma as the deadly myth whizzed past.

Lightning flashed, and thunder crashed along the leading edges of her painted wings as the glorious Thunderbird caught sight of the crimson dragon circling below.

Inside the fortified chamber, Zack discovered new light skills. Each crystal glowed inside his fists, scattering a shimmering rainbow of light inside their underground bunker as the sounds of war raged above, and Harley ducked.

"I sure hope Kate and the others are okay?" Zack could only think of his friend's well-being now. "But how could they be alright if it's all-out war? They'll be killed, right?"

Harley whimpered back, not capable of explaining how bad things had become.

Another bone-jarring thud exploded overhead as trees toppled aboveground. The dense stone crypt muted the violence, but the earth still shuddered with destruction.

"How am I supposed to concentrate when I can't think of anything but them?"

Try. Yuma's calming voice resonated in his mind.

He took a deep breath and refocused on aiming crystals with his eyes closed while firing at moving targets like a firing range. After another volley of precision firepower, Harley groaned and pawed at a bumpy stone protruding from the opposite wall.

Zack understood, reached out, and pushed as the stone popped open, revealing a rusty wheel hidden behind it. He spun it a few times, and the immense lid hoisted over their heads like a moon-roof and opened with a grinding shudder.

But instead of catching a breath of fresh air—they were met with a face full of hellfire.

Red flames lit up the interior of the bunker as firestorms raged.

Zack caught only glimpses of the deadly action from his ground-level vantage point, and he found himself driven to see more outside—disregarding any sense of danger or larger responsibilities.

It horrified him as he watched a squadron of drones torching the once untouchable beachhead. Then, without warning, a column of fire exploded out of the sky, driving the boy and dog back underground into the safety of the vault. That's when Zack spotted the screeching red monster for the first time as the mythical beast flew overhead.

"Holy moly."

Zack knew Harley was as shaken by this nasty turn as he was. Everything in their battle plans had to change with the threat of this formidable new weapon.

The frightened boy spun the wheel back with both hands, and the rolling lid ground shut, but not before Harley leaped out, leaving Zack alone inside.

Thud!

"Harley! Harley!" Zack called out, but he knew it was useless.

He'll be back. His soul comforted him. *You know him.*

The boy closed his eyes and whispered his new mantra.

"Whatever will be, will be. Don't believe what you see but believe what can be. Believe in Yuma as much as he believes in me. The hardest part is still to come," Zack whispered the simple refrain, steeling his courage.

The Briscoe zombies were only three blocks away from the edge of the town and executing their escape plan to perfection when they spotted the Thunderbird circling in the sky and staggered at the sight, they stopped short, just as a bunch of drunken ogres strutted by. These hulks were led by Onyx, one of the green-striped ogres that had caged them.

"Uh, oh. Look who's coming?" Coop nudged Kate, recognizing the ugly creature by his spiky top knot.

"Oh, no. Not that one with the drool!"

"That ogre has sniffed every one of us!"

"He licked me! He already knows what I taste like!" Ozzy moaned.

"Everybody, look down and get moving. Eyeballs to the ground. Make yourself as revolting as possible," Kate ordered.

The disguised teens drooled and vomited, acting like a pack of drunken zombies as Kate dragged her leg behind her.

Onyx strode by and snatched the barefoot Kate off the street, throwing her onto his back like a party favor.

"Ooop!" Kate startled.

"Sit back and enjoy the ride, gimpy. We know where the best parties are! Don't we, boys?" Onyx bragged as they headed in the opposite direction. "Will you look at the size of that thing coming down?"

"Hey! Whoa, stinky!" Kate growled and pounded his ridgeback as he held her on with one hand. "Eech! Let me down now, creep!" She tried to disguise her voice.

"How do you always get the pretty ones, Onyx?" his buddies quizzed, sizing up his next martyr with her slimy complexion.

"Simple! I don't ask!" he bragged. "They can't say no that way! What are they going to do? Sue me?" Onyx laughed.

"Put you in jail?"

His posse roared in agreement.

"Let me down!" Kate improved her growls.

"Hold on. You got to see this first, sweetie! You ain't going to believe it. Wait? Don't I know you?" Onyx took a big sniff over his shoulder of her bare foot. "Hey! Where do I know you from?"

Coop and the others had spun back around to help like before. But Kate motioned for them to continue moving forward as the drunks carried her away into the packed crowds—knocking any smaller goons and children out of their way.

Kate couldn't risk using her human voice to protest anymore, so she signed to the other kids—*I'll deal with this! I'll meet you there! Go!*

Coop didn't understand ASL and wasn't about to lose her again. He ran after the retreating ogres, blowing his zombie cover with undisguised speed. But once Kate spotted him, she became furious—more at him than even her sexist monster kidnappers.

"Get back!" Kate roared and snapped her fingers, insisting he save the others.

"Get back. That's the party spirit, little lady," Onyx replied.

Coop watched as the merry pranksters carried her deeper into the crowds, like they'd found their long-lost sorority sister.

"Oh, no. No-no, no-no, no-no." Ozzy sputtered, trying to stop himself from overreacting. But then, as a surprise to even himself, he bolted after Kate.

"Ozzy!" Emiliano yelled.

Oz dashed past the retreating Coop without stopping to ask permission.

"Fortune favors the bold!" Oz kept repeating to himself as he ran towards danger and not away from it. "Fortune favors the bold!"

"Oz! No! Don't, man, don't!" Coop growled.

It was too late. Ozzy was all-in like the horrid gambler he was, and he chased after Kate as Coop gathered his frightened herd into an alley.

"Listen to me, slimes. We stay together! No one else runs away! Now let's go," Coop regrouped the team, and they resumed their bad acting as they limped out of town without three of their own.

The blood-red dragon continued to blowtorch the shoreline as Yuma stalked and shadowed his way to the top of another Sequoia, unseen by the flying nightmare. The ancient medicine man lashed himself to the branches to witness the impending duel between the Titans.

Wixx dove to the safety of her throne when she saw the legendary shape circling above her and ready for attack.

"Is that a thunderbird?"

The sudden appearance of the mythological beast froze Wixx into inaction and disbelief.

"Who could conjure such a thing?"

The hungry super bird released her meal reluctantly before nosediving toward the troublesome dragon flying below, and the terrified orca screamed all the way down as it plunged into the lake right in front of the behemoth's snout.

The sight of the plummeting whale distracted the startled dragon before noticing the immense shadow engulfing him from above. That's when Caesar flipped onto his back midair and realized the Thunderbird was diving at him in full attack mode, with talons the size of bulldozers outstretched, and its eyes fired lightning bolts with every blink.

The ambushed dragon's only choice was to roll away in the air and dive for the ground to gain more speed and find cover.

Yuma vaulted to another treetop and thrust Thunapa into the sky, commanding the weather to rise stronger to support the great battle.

"Show me the magic!" he bellowed, and his voice reverberated across the hollows as the converging storm fronts and storm clouds gathered along the mountaintops upon his authority.

Wixx watched with alarming concern as her smaller dragon seemed to be on the losing side in this mythological heavyweight dogfight.

"This isn't how it's supposed to go! This isn't what I planned!"

Wixx wasn't taking any more chances, with her fragile vision of the future crumbling before her eyes.

As chaos reigned supreme—crowds cheering—dragon and thunderbird dueling in the skies overhead, and the once impregnable Scared Forest burning—Pepper Wixx was ready to launch her Doomsday scenario against the solitary giant.

"Face to face!" she demanded as she shoved Shelby aside and stepped onto the pile of raffle crystals. The scattered jewels on the stage flared up, glowing all around her by the thousands as she absorbed their amplifying powers into her veins.

Coop risked a panicked look over his shoulder. Even lost inside this rattling nightmare, he still couldn't believe what was happening in the skies behind them. The escapees all ran through the dead forest searching for the stashed delivery truck, and they kept tripping over their feet while freaking out about the fierce aerial battle behind them.

"Is that really a dragon?" Pav shrieked. "A freaking dragon?"

"It's not a Shetland pony!" Jesse cracked.

"Don't look back! Never look back!" Coop ordered, just as he face-planted.

Yuma summoned the whirlwinds to howl stronger, twirling Thunapa above his head and conducting the storms like a maestro, throwing the fire-breathing drones into a demolition derby of whirring self-destruction. The fierce weather continued to rain an avalanche of dead branches on top of the explosive drones—guaranteeing their extinction with a few clean puffs of air from Mother Nature.

The Thunderbird snagged Caesar's long neck chain as she jetted past and stopped in midair—spinning the dragon around in a wide circle.

Dizzy Caesar vomited flames, creating a ring of fire in the sky as the more experienced Thunderbird dodged and returned fire with blasts of sizzling electrical bolts.

The savvy Thunderbird released the spinning chains and flung the smaller dragon far up ahead, and fired again.

Wixx's eyes rolled white, and she trembled, standing within the power grid of the scattered crystals. The planks to the stage vibrated underfoot, losing nails. Then the ground rumbled as the blood-thirsty crowds cheered and screamed for more destruction and pain, as if riding a diabolic new amusement park ride.

Drawing on the additional powers of the Bartholomew Ring, Wixx closed her eyes and summoned the world of the dead as she'd never been able to before—challenging the universe's natural balance with her simmering jealousy and fury.

"Rise up before me, my children of the damned! Rise up with your anger and your hate! Assemble before me, to walk among us again, and hand deliver an overgrown goon—his most hideous fate!"

The ground splintered and yawned open across town in response.

Even Wixx's voice had changed now. The Bartholomew Ring's abuse caused her vocal cords to sear, and her eyes and skin festered, both glowing snail grey.

She flung her arms wide, and the dying oaks lining the lake exploded out of the ground and flew into the surf, one after another in a dutiful row.

Mangled bodies of every kind of creature reanimated under Wixx's growing powers. They squirmed and vomited out of their graves, interrupting the feasting maggots and leeches as they scampered back to resurrected life on her royal command by the power of her ring.

Most skeletons struggled to free themselves from centuries of ensnarling tree root—or had to break off bones to answer her call—but they rose from the ground by the thousands under Queen Wixx's command.

The crowds screamed in delight as the dead relatives buried beneath the town's streets rose from their graves into the middle of a party.

"No way! Joe, is that you?"

"Whoa! Nana?"

"This is excellent!"

The cemeteries surrounding Dark Hollows emptied—even the mine shafts gave up their dead. Thousands of broken bodies scurried to the surface like cockroaches seeking a crumb.   Queen Pepper Wixx now held sway over the living and the dead as she soared into the sky.

"Look, Yuma! I've raised a limitless army of pawns! Where's your army? Oh. That's right. I checkmated them!"

Coop and the six others had made it outside town limits, minus Kate and Ozzy. They ducked as the Thunderbird screeched by in the background, and the dragon howled in pain over the center of the lake, exchanging fire for electricity.

"Whoa! Are you kidding me?" Josh spoke up.

"Forget about that! Our ride home is right over here!" Coop yelled when he rediscovered the auto graveyard. He began searching the maze in the dark for the red delivery truck he had stashed nearby hours before.

Wixx took charge of her growing army of the undead from the air and pointed to the opposite shores.

"Make it all mine!" she commanded. "And bring me his head!"

Her legions scavenged for weapons before scurrying aboard the uprooted oaks, ready for the ultimate invasion against the Sacred Forest to begin.

The vengeful sorceress floated godlike above her troops, silhouetted against the shimmer of her unleashed powers. She gestured with an index finger, sending the entire fleet sailing north across the lake to invade and destroy those untouched lands.

Yuma was up in the swaying treetops, dancing among the lightning bolts, when he witnessed the depth of the old necromancer's powers assembling her forces across the lake.

"Wixx has been studying."

He watched more twisted oaks explode from the ground into the surf line. And the undead continued to scramble out of their graves before scuttling aboard the next wave of invaders destined for his shores.

Wixx had conjured an entire wartime flotilla out of nothing—one large enough to crush any army—and her reserves of the undead seemed limitless.

The sideways rains and swirling winds decimated any remaining attack drones within the Sacred Forest. But the aerial battle between the dragon and Thunderbird raged overhead, causing widespread destruction across acres of pristine forest as the two warring behemoths tumbled through the treetops.

Back on the crowded streets of Dark Hollows, Onyx, and his partying posse still held Kate captive. They stopped along with the rest of the spellbound audience as the two legendary creatures retook to the air.

And that's when Kate saved her life and jumped off the ogre's back, sprinting away barefoot.

Ozzy searched everywhere for Kate, shoving his way through the monstrous crowds like a zombified gorilla. But he cringed as a massive troll strolled past him, gnawing on a human leg as you'd snack on a turkey drumstick at the State Fair. The same creature was wearing part of Officer Petty's old grey uniform. Oz was sure it was Petty's because the surly guard's name was embroidered on it, and the old school Briscoe reformatory badge still dangled from the torn pocket.

He could only hold his breath as the long-haired troll strolled by with his snack, dragging a long, protesting chain behind him.

"That could be me next?"

Oz felt terrified and melancholy at the same time.

"Bye, Officer Petty," Oz whispered. "Can't say I'm going to miss you, dude, but you sure didn't deserve this."

"Where am I going again?" a hollow voice rang out from behind.

When Ozzy turned, he was staring face-to-face with Petty. The now-deceased corrections officer was at the other end of the troll's chain, with the links twisted around his neck like a leash.

"Wha?" Ozzy froze.

"My shoes, ma! I still got to get my proper dress shoes!" he shrieked into the boy's face. "Hey, I know you!" he growled and seized Oz by the throat. "Help, Master!" Petty screamed.

The old guard had died two days before, on that first terrible night, only to be resurrected by zombification the very next day by Wixx and her inner circle. Petty was now a full-time bondservant of Dark Hollows until he paid his final dues.

"Help! Look! Look who I caught, master?" Petty croaked.

Ozzy cringed as the old guard cried out again, leaving the nonviolent teenager with no other choice.

Oz hauled off and punched Petty square on the jaw, just like in the movies, and the undead creature staggered back from the heavy blow and dropped like a bag of hammers.

"Hm! Guess that does work sometimes!"

Only then did Oz realize Petty was lying in the street naked. He was being paraded around like a pet Uman by that ugly troll ahead. The same troll was turning around to check

436

on the sudden deadweight on the chain.

"Too much information! Too much information!" Ozzy couldn't handle what he saw anymore and bolted away from them both. He barreled over monsters of every description, knocking them out of his way like bowling pins on Halloween Night, when a sleek zombie intercepted his path and tackled him to the ground by the knees.

When Oz rolled to his feet, ready to fight back for the second time tonight, he realized his slimy opponent was Kate.

"What? How could you...?"

"Good to see you too, buddy! Now run!" she commanded. "I've got ogres after me!"

"Mine's a troll, I think! But I could be wrong. Run!"

At that point, Oz did what Oz did best and split. He sprinted past Kate so fast that time travel existed as she struggled to catch up.

Yuma beckoned the north winds to howl across the lake, blowing the headstrong armada of death back onto the same polluted shores they had launched. And the winds summoned the tides.

But Wixx countered the move, and her unending fleet of the undead surged ahead against the weather—the entire fleet energized by her singular power.

The zombie armada lurched forward across the lake, making steady progress against the strength of Yuma's natural resistance.

A glowing Wixx smiled.

"You cannot change the inevitable!" she screamed, feeling her powers intensify as she leaned against Yuma's.

"Outmatched and outwitted again!" she hissed. "Ain't life a bitch... and then you die!"

Three of the tallest Sequoias crashed into the lake on the northern shores, startling everyone with their delayed concussions.

Boom! Boom! Boom!

The fallen victims included Yuma's beloved Little Sister, and their impact sent a series of waves rushing back across the lake to meet the fleet.

Wixx watched as the shadow of the giant emerged from behind the towering curtains of spray on the screens below.

The remaining spitfire drones showed Yuma's crystal lance still glowed white-hot after felling all three redwoods with a single swipe of his weapon.

"Uh oh," the celebratory crowds reacted in genuine fear for the first time.

Then Harley stepped out behind Yuma dressed in full battle armor, including a metal helmet spiked with antlers and battering horns, sharpened for impalement.

The greatest of all battle dogs snarled as the enemy of the undead continued their slow advancement across the storm-tossed lake.

'Over *your* dead body.' had real meaning to these loyal warriors. For these two lifelong, back-to-back friends, it was the only way they knew how to live—or die.

Yuma grinned at his fearless comrade. "Here we go again."

And Harley released a startling howl into the wilds as thousands of homeless dogs stepped out of the forest together.

An army of grizzly bears, wolves, foxes, cougars, and even a few extinct dire wolves backed them up—and they all roared as a unified pack.

Yuma jumped onto the deck of their lead destroyer, Little Sister, as Harley ordered every underdog to follow. Once aboard, he assigned duty stations along the branches according to size and specialties.

Little dogs, the real ankle biters, stayed low in the limbs, with the larger canines remaining high along the length of the trunks. Big cats could prowl wherever they wanted to go, like always. Within minutes, the Apex predators defined their offensive and defensive positions along the massive branches of the sacrificial redwoods.

Yuma raised Thunapa to the sky and summoned the weather to propel all three redwoods forward. Then, with more effort from favorable winds, Yuma had these monumental trees surging ahead to ramming speed like a trio of dreadnoughts racing to destroy the invading flotilla.

Wixx gave the signal, and the town's giant catapults fired a barrage of fireballs into the advancing fleet while also destroying her formations.

"Wait, my Queen! We are hitting our army too!" Shelby cried.

"So what? Fodder! I will destroy the entire world, even if that means all of you, too!" she smiled.

Yuma gave another spin of his lance, and the north winds reversed for a fraction of a second—but that was more than enough to snap the tallest treetops in the Crown of Swords like a beach towel, launching every weapon skyward towards the invaders.

A hundred giant warriors' blades flew across the lake as one. The winds of war propelled them back into battle one last time to help fight the good fight.

In that glorious moment of reborn purpose, the magical weapons rained down on the invading army below—each reborn weapon defeating the brittle enemy with every slice, chop, and impalement.

Coop was losing his mind inside the delivery truck, looking for the keys.

"Where are they? I know I put them right here! Why can't I find them anywhere?"

He kept searching as the others ran in behind.

"You haven't found them yet? Are you kidding me? That freaking dragon's angry, man!"

"No! I'm not kidding! I know I put them right under the floor mat!"

Coop kept searching.

"Uh oh," Josh pointed outside.

In the light of the fireballs, they could just make out that dozens of other delivery trucks sat abandoned here that looked like the familiar trademark.

"You're in the wrong truck, man!" Emiliano yelled.

"Keys! Search! Now!" Coop snapped.

The kids scattered like the Happy Trails Racing League and began hunting for the lost keys in every other red truck—when a piercing whistle froze them mid-stride.

"Oh, no!"

"We're dead!"

"Run?"

A creepy fist held up the missing truck keys and jingled them.

"Look familiar?" a winded Kate asked, and everyone squealed.

"Kate!"

Their reunion was short and sweet. They welcomed her and Oz back into the fold, and Coop held onto her longer than the others as he buried his slimy head in the crook of her neck.

"Thank you for coming back."

"I know. See how good that feels?" she smiled.

There was a moment of reconnection and joy, and then reality slammed them back to their senses.

"Alright! Get in, get in! We gotta go, go, go!" Coop ordered, as he wiped a tear and hopped into the driver's seat. It was then he realized he didn't have the keys.

Kate held them up as everyone climbed aboard.

"Sorry. Do you want to drive? Ladies first," Coop offered.

"No. You drive Wyatt Cooper. I love second chances." Kate winked and pointed uphill.

"Floor it!"

Coop fired up the old delivery truck, found first gear, and peeled away from the car graveyard in a cloud of dust.

Yuma's redwood destroyers slammed head-first into Wixx's fleet, pulverizing them on contact with their mammoth scale as the three sequoias shattered the brittle oaks mid-lake. Dogs, grizzlies, wolves, and cougars launched their massive counterattack as the undead tried to scamper aboard the unsinkable redwoods.

Yuma fought back, wielding both Thunapa and sword alike, as he dispatched the living dead back into nothingness—three or four bodies at a time. There would be no rejuvenation of these hijacked souls once he pulverized them and the eels made bones into fertilizer.

The battle-weary dragon and the Thunderbird still clashed high above the audience's heads. Both legendary creatures now displayed significant battle wounds as they flew past each other. What once seemed an unequal battle had proven much more unwieldy than that.

Zack remained alone inside his secret bunker, testing his nerve and resolve. He wore a crisscross bandoleer he had fashioned for carrying the different crystals he pre-selected as his best first responders.

The concussive sounds of war kept hammering the ground above as the fireballs hit all along the shore.

And then Archie sat down inside the hole next to him, smiling with his familiar gap-toothed grin.

"Uh! Where have you been?" Zack seemed angry, yet unsurprised.

"Sometimes it matters more where I'm not," Archie teased, content to exist on the other side of life.

"I'm just worried about all my friends across the lake. They're in great danger now, aren't they? What can I do for

441

them?"

"Nothing if you're here."

"Can you find them?"

"I suppose? I would just have to try."

"And how would we do that?"

"Well, wherever we are, there we are, right?"

"Yeah. That's how it's worked so far."

"I just close my eyes, and there I am."

"Show me!" Zack commanded and grabbed Archie's forearm.

There were several soft snaps and sizzles of synapses merging. Then, a final crystal popped, and Zack observed two distinct realities before his eyes. First, he saw his present existence, still trapped inside the bunker. And yet, Zack also perceived the outer edges of another physicality inside his head. He was also flying just outside a speeding delivery truck on the other side of the lake.

Both confusing worlds overpowered his already overburdened senses, and he experienced vertigo with the competing sensibilities colliding in his brain. His inner ear no longer knew which reality to reestablish balance, making him seasick.

"What am I seeing now? Am I here, or am I there?"

"Close one eye," Archie suggested, and when Zack did that, it was as if he was floating outside the truck somehow, staring back at Kate through the windshield. Or at least his mind's eye was.

"Zack!" Kate screamed in shock and delight as Coop jumped on the brakes and they skidded to a stop on the deserted road.

Zack's hazy image floated just outside the vehicle, with one of his eyes closed in a perpetual wink.

"What the wha...?" Oz couldn't find the words to finish as he leaned forward to stare at the familiar ghost.

"Are you alright, Zack? Where are you? We can come to get you! We have a truck!"

"No! I'm safe. But you're not."

"No kidding, amigo," Emil said.

"You must rescue yourselves and the babies right away! Yuma is going to destroy Dark Hollows tonight. Soon."

"Yuma? Whose Yuma? What babies?"

Pavarty tapped Kate's shoulders and pointed to the dozen empty child car seats lining both sides.

The spooky crimson delivery truck was a customized, soundproofed kidnapmobile—designed from the ground up for child abduction by Pepper Wixx herself.

"Has anybody spotted those other orphans we found locked upstairs behind the purple door in cages like us?" Jess asked.

"No."

"Not a one."

"They weren't even in the catalog."

"I didn't see them. I don't think so. Just us."

"That means they're all still locked up back there. That must be who Zack is talking about."

"If they're even still alive?"

"Zack, there must be something we can help you with right now?" Kate pleaded, concerned for the little boy.

"No, Kate. Thank you. But doing as I ask means a lot. Save the innocents. It's what we were born to do. I know that now. Don't worry about me anymore. I've found my forever home. I hope you do, too—all of you. Be happy and safe," he wished everyone as he disappeared.

"Zack's dead!" Lennon started crying.

"No, no, I don't think he is, sweetheart," Kate soothed the girl, still shaking at the mind-shattering truth she'd just witnessed.

"Be brave, Zack." Kate threw the last kiss.

She wiped away tears and stared at Coop.

"What was that? A curse? A trick? A ghost?" Coop asked.

"I don't think so. Something more wonderful than that. I think we have to turn around, Coop."

"What?"

"We can't go back there now. Those monsters will kill us! We're almost out of here?"

"We have to," Kate insisted. "You heard Zack."

"What?"

"No."

"Listen to me. We are the only hope those poor stolen babies have left. If anybody understands what being abandoned is all about, it sure better be us."

"But Kate..."

"It's why we were here with Zack. I'm as sure of that now as I've ever been sure of anything in my life. We're the only backup he could ever count on. Now turn around, Coop. We've got to go back to Dark Hollows."

-CHAPTER 52-

The End of the Beginning

Hunkered down inside his bunker, Zack opened both eyes as he released Archie's arm.

"See? Wasn't that fun? Zipping back and forth?"

"Not really. My stomach doesn't feel good. What do I do now?"

"Don't you think you should peek outside before doing anything else?"

"No, Arch. Yuma ordered me to stay down here. Hidden. Not to believe whatever I saw—including you! To protect... you know?" Zack nodded toward the ground, not daring to say the Crystal Kingdom or the Illuminators' name aloud.

"But how long can you pretend to protect something without knowledge first? You can't learn anything unless you lift your noggin up and inspect what's going on around you for yourself. Without having to be told about it by somebody else?" Archie said. "I hear nobody's eyes work better than yours! I expect your brain's pretty keen, too. Keep using them."

Zack felt torn. Yuma made his orders crystal-clear about when and why he should evacuate the bunker. But Archie always found an excellent reason to peek around every corner when it counted.

The boy spun the stone wheel, and as it lifted off the slab a few inches, Zack heard the screams coming from the center of the lake. Massive fireballs rained down along the once pristine shoreline, and the night sky filled with cravens fighting eagles and hummingbirds fighting punctures, while

445

high above them all, the dragon and Thunderbird still battled to the death.

Using oversized binoculars, Zack spotted Yuma, with Harley fighting beside him, on the back of Little Sister.

Air, land, and sea were engulfed in all-out warfare underneath the protective world of the Bubble.

Wixx's unholy invaders gained the upper hand against Yuma and his menagerie of predators as they boarded the redwoods in the middle of the lake by the hundreds, while back onshore, their undead comrades continued to scuttle out of the cemeteries like cockroaches in search of crumbs and the army of Creeps followed.

The getaway truck pulled a U-turn and skidded to a stop in the shadows just outside the town, where the spellbound crowds still clogged the streets, watching the war overhead.

Coop studied the crowded landscape, plotting their only course of action as he revved the engine.

"Hang on tight, folks, we're going off-road!" he yelled.

The inexperienced driver floored it, and the delivery truck bounced through the twisted backyards and alleys that paralleled the streets as his rattled passengers got knocked around.

Coop cut the wheel hard when he spotted another crowd forming, flew past the haunted well, circled behind the orphanage, and zoomed past the swing sets, still swaying with the spirit children onboard.

"Look at that!" Kate pointed.

"What? You're still surprised by this place?" Coop asked. 'Hold on!"

He sped between the properties, crashed through the hedges, and landed on the circular driveway of the children's home. Once he skidded to a stop, everyone jumped and ran up to the front porch.

Coop remained behind at the wheel of the getaway truck—revving the engine and on the lookout for any trouble as more fiends filled the streets.

Kate discovered the front door was locked. But Oz wasn't dealing with negative barriers in his life any longer. He hit it running at full speed, and the door exploded at the insistence of a new superhero on the block.

"Quick! Upstairs! Third floor!" Jesse shouted, leading the way, with Pavarty and the others searching downstairs.

"Look!" Josh pointed to the messy office. "Gather all the computers and files! We'll nail these suckers!"

"Brilliant!!" Emiliano beamed.

Jesse searched the vacant, haunted second floor with the handprints on the bay window before sprinting upstairs to the purple doors on the third landing.

The sounds of vengeance raged outside and thumped the walls in the claustrophobic stairwell, rattling the picture gallery. And just as Jess reached out to open the purple door, Kate caught up and grabbed her arm.

"Are you sure about this?" she whispered. "Anything could be waiting inside there now."

Jesse considered, nodded, removed the cat's claw hairpin, and slipped it over her knuckles.

"On three."

When she slammed the door open, it hit the wall with a bang, startling everyone—including the handful of broken toddlers cowering inside.

Half a dozen uncared-for children shivered and cried as the dragon screamed past the broken windows.

None of these neglected cryptid children was older than four, and the youngest was still in diapers.

"Come here, honey," Kate cooed as she snatched up a bent little girl with dark hair and furry ears.

Every surprised rescuer scooped up at least one child, and that's when the little blue girl standing next to Kate tugged her skirt and signed in ASL.

"We need our babies."

"What babies?" Kate signed back, proud that this

valuable skill set had come in handy again.

"Come on, girl, we got to go, go, go, Kate," Pavarty urged.

"Wait!" the blue girl signed.

"We'll get you another doll, sweetie. I promise!" Kate responded, trying to hustle her out.

"No! Shelby locked our babies in the dollhouse," the little girl replied with dancing fingers and pointed.

Kate glanced to the end of the long room and saw an oversized dollhouse built there.

Abused dolls of every shape and color filled the plastic windows and adorned the fun house's fake flower boxes.

"Alright, but we have to be fast if you want your baby doll."

Kate dashed to the other side of the room and found the playhouse stuffed with generations of abused toys.

"Quick, find your doll," Kate encouraged, holding the little girl in her arms.

"Here he is," the youngster signed and bent over a crib.

That's when Kate heard the mewling. It was the sound she had heard before downstairs.

She glanced around and saw cribs and bassinets scattered among the piles of naked Barbies. But inside every toy crib squirmed a living, breathing cryptid—infants of different forms and functions, and every child had their mouths taped shut.

These were Wixx's unwanted leftovers. The castoffs. The 'permanent uglies,' as Pepper called them, to their faces before disposing of them like rubbish.

Many of the kidnapped creatures had health problems or deformities, be they Uman, wendigo, ogre, troll, or witchling. They could never be adopted for profit. Instead, Wixx would recycle them for spare parts—each unwanted infant predestined for the murderous underground root cellar.

Silence is golden, after all, and when they pulled the tape off their mouths, they found out how noisy these yowling little creatures could be.

When Tim ducked inside the dollhouse and spotted the squirmy little beings howling inside—he recoiled as if snake bit.

"Geez! What? We just risked our lives for these things! No way! I'm gone! Who's coming?"

"Get a grip!" Kate barked as she scooped up a blue-striped infant. "Nobody is born a monster. Nobody. Now pick up a baby, and let's get out of here and go home!"

"Home? Really?"

"Let's get out of here!"

Across the lake inside his bunker, Zack watched the battlefront creep closer when a terrifying screech came from overhead. The intensity of the primal scream startled everyone as they all saw the thunderbird crash and cartwheel down the beach—its left-wing sizzling and fractured.

Caesar hovered high above the larger but helpless predator, content to barbeque the legendary bird from a distance and dodge her lightning bolt eyes.

"Noooooo!" Zack screamed as he rolled out of hiding, focusing his powerful Lucid Pulse through his tiger crystal in a bolt of amplified energy.

The lightning bolt beam lashed out with a fierce roar and knocked the hovering dragon backward across the sky, startling Yuma and Harley in battle and shattering the nearest undead in front of them like peanut brittle.

When the Lucid Pulse hit the unsuspecting Wixx on the other side of the lake, it knocked her off her feet as the town screamed at the sonic icepick driven into their eardrums.

"Ahhhh!" they all wailed in a fresh chorus of pain.

"You will never stop me, Yuma?" Pepper screamed as she scooped up a handful of new crystals and flew back into the sky as if she owned it.

"I'm going to kill you tonight all by myself! Face to face, you butcher!"

No one ever expected to see old Pepper Wixx flying out over the lake to battle in hand-to-hand combat against the last giant on earth tonight, but this was an entirely different Pepper Wixx than had ever existed before, and her enslaved army of mindless fiends heeded her rallying call without question.

"Murder!"

Lost in the swing of another furious sword slash, Yuma spotted Zack running down to the beachhead alongside the thundering herds of bear, elk, and stag reinforcements. They all rushed to defend the downed Thunderbird, no matter the outcome.

"No, boy! Not yet! I need my hands on her first! Not yet!" Yuma bellowed, and the mountains trembled as Zack looked back briefly but kept running.

The giant pointed, and Harley understood without words. Yuma helped the battlehound shed his armor as they both sprinted back. The more armor that flew off, the faster Harley could fly until he was in a desperate sprint to save young Zack's life. His canine army of underdogs filled their ranks behind him and continued their brutal fight against the undead, crushing the animated skeletons with bone-chomping glee.

The yellow-eyed dragon sprayed another blast of flames at the wounded Thunderbird, and the Thunderbird used her undamaged wing as a fireproof shield against Caesar's impressive power.

Zack sprinted onto the decimated beach, but the elk and bear calvary got to the sand first to defend the downed legend. They encircled her with their enraged protection as the surprised dragon paused its attack, shaken at the sheer number of creatures gathering against its extinct form of tyranny.

The elk and moose lowered their massive racks and

interlocked them, forming a single defensive shield around her. And the grizzlies bared their fangs in an outer ring of support. Every apex predator was ready to die defending their lands.

"I said no!" Zack screamed, and another Lucid Pulse shot out of his mind and into his crystal, knocking the red dragon out of the sky. It splashed a hundred yards offshore in a blast of water and steam. When a dazed Caesar resurfaced, the drowning animal was squealing for its life—now covered in eels hanging off its body like giant leeches.

The eels loved the flavor of raw dragon flesh and pulled the struggling monster underwater.

When Zack reached the wounded Thunderbird, the bear and elk opened their perimeter to allow him entry—and that's when Harley sprinted in and intercepted his path.

The gigantic hound snatched Zack up by the scruff of his shirt like he was a pup and kept running.

"Hey! Put me down, Harley! Hey!"

The noble dog wasn't listening to anything now but his instincts as he bolted up the scorched beach with the protesting little boy—headed for deep stone cover as fireballs from the catapults continued to rain down around them.

That's when Yuma looked back and spotted Wixx flying out over the lake as he slowed his dash back to the boy.

"There can be no other way. This must be it."

The Time Warrior couldn't waste this rare opportunity for the final faceoff they knew was long overdue.

Yuma watched Harley bolting away with Zack up the beachhead while the dragon drowned in the lake. His predator army continued to fight back gallantly, holding the line against the onslaught of bones and decayed flesh, fighting to climb onboard Little Sister.

Yuma felt confident for the first time at their chances and turned back to confront his old nemesis head-on for the last time.

Caesar struggled to catch a breath underwater against the ravenous eels and rose out of the lake on the sheer strength of his four wings alone.

The dragon whipped clumps of eels off his body with every wing flap as he broke the surface—with the heavy metal necklace continuing to dangle like anchor chains off his neck.

At that moment, the dragon spotted Harley sprinting away with that vicious little boy in his jaws, and Caesar craved immediate revenge against that pain-inflicting cub.

Flying solitary over the lake of calamity for the first time was the most liberating feeling of freedom Pepper Wixx had ever known. While she craved the smell of fresh air, the smell of burning timber brought even more joy to her twisted senses.

"There he is. Look at him, still fighting at his age. What a fool."

Wixx saw Yuma slashing toward her below, and she fired down, striking his recovered shield. The explosive collision staggered the giant backward along the tree trunk, but even her reinforced beam couldn't penetrate his shield's natural defenses.

The vindictive dragon swooped down in pursuit of the galloping dog—so close that Harley could feel the heat of its breath on his back paws, and that's when the great hound zigged when he should have zagged.

Yuma grinned with fierce determination and released a lightning bolt from Thunapa. But Wixx's invisible defensive shield protected her and deflected the deadly blast away. She returned fire from the air when an unsummoned waterspout swirled up out of the lake between them.

"What nonsense is this?"

Blue Feather's untethered spirit soared out of the dark waters that cleaved between worlds, wearing the same matching war paint as her husband's.

"Blue Feather!" Yuma yelled in joy.

Her untarnished soul reclaimed her customized sword from the winds, and before the scarlet witch could react, Blue Feather thrust her custom meteor blade deep into Wixx's chest with a fierce battle cry, avenging her death in person.

"As a wise Immortal once promised me," she winked at Yuma, "There is never a good time to die," Blue Feather said. "Only the right reasons."

Blue Feather's last cut severed the Bartholomew ring from her finger and sent the immobilized witch spiraling out of control, crashing onto the redwood trunk of Little Sister, impaling her body on the spiky branches.

"Ahhh! It burns!"

Yuma only had seconds to savor the cherished reunion with his beloved's essence before Blue Feather disappeared back into the mysterious folds of the universe.

"You are never alone, my love. Ever."

A mangled Wixx struggled onto her feet as the Time Warrior ran in to finish the job. Blue Feather's spirit had sapped her additional powers and stopped the witch's deadly rampage precisely where Yuma needed her to be at this point—right in front of him—as it was written.

Separated by only a hundred yards of burning redwood branches, Yuma and a revitalized Wixx began slashing a path toward one another—each Immortal eager to bring the gift of permanent death to the other.

"It all ends tonight!"

"So, it is written!"

Harley spun around with Zack when he realized he'd taken the wrong turn by the mossy boulders. There was no choice but to reverse course or get trapped inside the narrow box canyon. Then Caesar caught up, leaving them nowhere to run.

The Great Dane dropped Zack from his jaws as the exhausted six-eyed dragon landed, reared up before them to its full height, and roared.

Harley bristled at the thought of anything harming Zack and charged at the mythical beast, making sure his last stand was his choice.

"No, Harley!" And Zack's mind released an unfocused Lucid Pulse at the dragon. But it wasn't powerful enough. Or perhaps the new-age dragon had adapted to mental combat, as it recovered from the massive psychic blast almost instantly.

The wounded Caesar took in a long, ragged breath—savoring the moment and inhaling enough oxygen to reduce his victims to embers when Harley charged to attack the dragon's exposed throat.

But a tremendous flash everywhere at once froze everything in place. The eclipsed night sky underneath the Bubble exploded in a brilliant amber light.

Everyone on both sides of the lake froze, blinded into believing the other side must have detonated some new superweapon against them.

But as everyone's vision cleared, they watched in awe and amazement as a shimmering leviathan of immense proportions coalesced calmly overhead—in stark contrast to the raging storms still boiling inside the Bubble. The energized mist seemed to form between the tenuous fabric buffering our dimensions—revealing its hidden existence in another startling flash and exposing itself as an Inkling of stunning proportions and complexities.

This happy, living cloud was the same fog bank that intentionally hijacked their runaway bus before saving their lives and suspending them midair and weightless instead of crashing.

That unbelievable Zero-G experience had never been Zack using his new powers.

Zack never lied.

It was this intelligent, glittering creature of the sky who deliberately coaxed Zack and his newfound friends onto this very wrong path——at just the right time in his life—to follow his destiny to change the world with his overwhelming gifts.

The sparkling cloud searched along the sand with the muzzle of what looked like a soft, tornado-like snout as everyone stood immobilized in the blinding wonderment of it all.

The Inkling spun as Caesar attacked—sucked hard and inhaled the pesky dragon with a healthy snort.

Finding himself airborne, Harley tumbled onto the beach instead of into the belly of the dragon, as expected.

The surprised dog spit out sand as an astonished Zack watched in amazement while the young dragon's fires flared briefly inside the glowing gullet of the shape-shifting mist— then winked out permanently after a series of pale pink puffs.

The last fire-breathing dragon on earth disappeared inside the transparent belly of this enormous, defensive Inkling.

Caesar was gone with the wind.

"That's a Great Garth, boy!" Zack bragged to Harley as he realized he had nicknamed these rare species, too. "You don't see those around much! I think because they draw too much attention."

The effervescent Garth floated over to the exceptional boy and nuzzled Zack's cheek with a soft, familiar nudge. The fluttering, affectionate contact felt like the dewy cloud was giving away free butterfly kisses.

Unknown to humankind, this gentle life form had always existed within the fabric of the firmaments. And this individual Inkling had been designated to personally watch over Zack since birth as one of his many protective guardian angels.

The blinding atmosphere inside the living Bubble graciously shifted into a brilliant Inkling blue as these invisible sentient beings unveiled themselves as an entire species.

Most of their miraculous appearances only happened in Zack's times of greatest peril.

There was that dark time a few years before when Zack desperately needed rescue from his abusers. It was back when his latest set of frustrated foster parents left bruises on his backside so severe that he couldn't sit down for days. The authorities never found a trace of those missing sadistic cow farmers from Kansas City.

"Nastiness be gone." He remembered thinking—and they disappeared into the same distinct pink puffs he remembered so well.

"Thank you!" Zack waved to his guardian angel.

These wondrous beings had always protected Zack once they discovered the infant was the first human wonderment born with the gift of Truesight in over a thousand years.

The Inklings had known about Zack Goodnight's unique visual gifts from almost the first moments of his tragic birth. They had followed his existence ever since, hovering protectively over him throughout his uprooted life.

They realized that here was the Light in the Darkness of prophecy.

The See.

The boy who could move mountains with his mind.

A simple child of peace who would bring contrasting worlds together with his life-affirming illuminations and gentle observations about the vast dualities of our existence.

The Inkling's secret plan was to coax Archie's effervescent spirit from the netherworld as a fitting ambassador to help steer the rudderless young Zack along the deadly gauntlet to his ultimate destiny as the defender of the Sacred Forest while sharing their regal existence with the entire world.

Still airborne, Pepper Wixx blinked as millions of innocent Inklings stared into her shrieking soul and read her like a Stephen King horror novel.

456

Yuma noticed the distracted sorceress drifting in the air, and he sprinted down Little Sister's length and vaulted into the sky as only giants could leap.

He grabbed Wixx by the ankle and slammed her down onto the barbed spine of the redwood, impaling her body again like an ugly voodoo doll.

Wixx wiggled and spurted black ooze, cackling with unbridled joy as she struggled to rise. Yuma seized her by the throat with his massive hands and shoved her back down as she summoned her darkest powers to resist his size advantage.

"Now, Zack!" Yuma bellowed under attack, and the hollows trembled with his voice. "Now, boy! Show me the magic! Bend the light!"

Zack didn't hesitate. He spun around, facing the great waterfall behind Yuma's cabin, nodded, and each crystal flared in his hand. They ignited in a colorful array of particle beams. But as Zack concentrated, each vertical shaft bent to his will, forming a perfect concentric rainbow arc as their light turned earthward.

Not only had Zack learned to bend light with his mind wide open and his eyes shut tight—but his curved light beams could strike around corners as they hit every explosive target at the base of the boulder dam simultaneously.

Kaboom! Kaboom! Kaboom! Kaboom! Kaboom!

The boulder dam collapsed, freeing the towering wall of whitewater trapped behind it. The purifying floodwaters had been assembling, waiting patiently for their revenge since dawn.

"Thatta' boy!" Yuma bellowed as he heard the distinctive crystal explosions.

Wixx took that second of distraction, launched her Knack on full force, and transformed into a slithering demon, fighting for her existence, snarling, and shredding Yuma's arms and face with a terrifying set of new fangs and claws.

457

No one realized the scale of the onrushing disaster headed their way but Yuma. His tidal wave descended from the higher elevations, picking up more water and speed as it tore down the river valleys feeding Eel Lake.

Inside the getaway truck, the sudden brilliance of the night sky frightened an already petrified bunch of heroes.

"Slow down, man! Look out! I can't see! Can you?"

"No way! I am not slowing down for anything!" Coop said.

"What's that?"

"How should I know?"

"And those? What's that floating by? And that?" they screamed, pointing out the window as if someone had trapped them inside an alien zoo—both thrilling and chilling at the same time.

"What time of day is it now? Wasn't it just night?"

"I don't know, man! Don't distract me! We're getting out of here!" Coop yelled. His rising panic controlled him, and the noisy babies in the back wouldn't stop howling.

"Whatever they are, we're getting away from all of them right now!" Kate tried to calm everyone to no effect.

She believed she understood what she was witnessing now. Those beautiful visions dancing by the windshield made her confident that Zack had something to do with this rush of fresh magic toppling the old.

This is that extraordinary world Zack described to me! Look! I think I just saw a real bobokaffayz go zipping by! She mused. *And look... that's a tic-tac and a fast walker, I bet!*

Kate brushed away a flurry of tiny, bright gnats that danced around her face, understanding Zack's curse now as never before.

She prayed that all this meant that Zack had found his destiny in this magically disturbing world.

Maybe he's not lost anymore. Maybe he's exactly where he needs to be. Where we all need him to be.

Coop gunned it until their getaway wheels brought them back to the swollen stream they had crossed before. Their Briscoe Institute bus, still squatted in the middle of the rising floodwaters—now a rusting monument to a different time only hours ago.

"Wait? How long have we been gone?"

Coop could taste the copper tang of fear inside his mouth as he slowed and eased the truck gently into the rushing stream.

"Please don't stall! Please don't stall!" he implored.

The fast-rushing waters kept rising inside the low-slung vehicle, flooding the interior floorboards almost immediately. That's when the hijacked truck bucked and died before its time, like everything else trying to escape Dark Hollows.

Yuma pinned Wixx against the redwood as she thrashed like a rabid banshee five times her size. He could have ripped her in half with his bare hands, but he knew that would never be enough. Not even being devoured by the eels could diminish her recuperative powers now.

Wixx knew it, too.

He would have to hold on to her forever.

She loved tearing him apart mouthful by mouthful, relishing the delicious flavor of his immortal blood when Yuma heard a different thunder roaring through the canyons.

Then Wixx noticed.

"What puny magic tricks do you have left in that bag of tricks, fool?"

Yuma grinned in triumph. His simple plan had worked.

"Please—don't hold your breath!"

Wixx finally saw the tidal wave roaring their way.

"No! That's not fair!"

Yuma closed his eyes as the titanic mountain of water struck them head-on, and they tumbled beneath the churning waters.

The artificial wave spit out the three redwood dreadnaughts in the center of the lake like used toothpicks. Luckily, the big cats and canines had evacuated on Yuma's command to Zack long before the roaring leviathan hit the flimsy fleet.

Coop kept tapping the accelerator, trying to restart the stalled truck until he noticed the empty gas gauge.

"Impossible! Oh, man! We're out of gas! We need to find another way up this road fast," he screamed. "Now! Get out!"

"How can we be out of gas? What kind of crappy car thief are you, Coop?" Pavarty screeched.

"It had gas! I added more. We must have blown the fuel line!"

"We?"

Everyone turned at the sudden reverberations rattling the truck from outside. The rhythmic, low-end rumble differed from all the other baffling sounds filling the air—something was thundering closer.

That's when four enormous draught horses charged past them, dragging the remains of the shattered Calistoga wagon and a few mummy wrappings behind—followed by herds of cow, goat, and sheep, as every farm animal escaped Dark Hollows and stampeded uphill.

And the reason for the animals' panic rose up behind them like Godzilla coming ashore. The teens saw the swollen tidal wave pushing the entire lake in front of it, forming a massive wall of whitewater as it roared across the lake on a mission to destroy anything in its path.

"Oh, no. Oh, no. Must go faster! Now!" Oz screamed.

"Go, go, go, go, go, go, go, go!" Kate screamed.

There wasn't time to find another vehicle—they had run out of seconds.

Coop took a deep breath and slammed the accelerator down on a fuel-less engine.

"Now!" Coop raged, demanding it all. "Show me the

Magic!" he echoed the calls of Yuma. He had felt those same majestic words thundering on the winds all night, and that holy incantation reverberated within his soul.

The swamped truck shuddered and bobbled forward.

"What the...?"

"Here we go!"

The delivery truck miraculously picked up speed, moving uphill just as the apocalyptic floodwaters crashed against the outer banks first in its quest to consume everything whole in the southern bay.

"Punch it!" Kate yelled.

Coop floored it just as the mammoth wave broke over the crest of the road behind them. The sounds of the end of the world chased them uphill.

That's when Kate saw a shimmering image of Zack twinkle in her mind-eye again. Distinct. Present. One lovely eye was clamped shut again in a perpetual wink, only this time, he was grinning and giving her a big thumbs up.

Zack watched their getaway from his enhanced viewpoint onshore as he forced the gasless truck up the road using only the raw horsepower of his mind.

His curving light beams fired with pinpoint accuracy from far across the lake—propelling the gasless vehicle uphill and away from the rampaging floodwaters still rampaging below.

"Goodbye, sweet Zack," Kate whispered as she looked back across the turbulent lake and blew him a kiss.

She still cuddled the striped blue baby with wide, golden eyes. Once they realized they were sure they were out of harm's way, Kate shared victorious fist-bumps with her team. Everyone cooed and cared for their newly rescued orphans, including Tim and Oz.

The Briscoe 9 shared looks of shell-shocked disbelief between them.

"Who's ever going to believe this?" Tim said.

"Nobody."

"They're going to have to." Jesse smiled and nodded down at the newborns.

Kate saw Josh curl Pavarty's hand up into his, and she dropped her head down onto his slimy shoulder with a sigh.

Coop couldn't understand what was propelling this truck uphill any longer.

"What's making this thing go?"

"Guts! Get it?" Oz beamed.

"Don't ask. Just keep doing what you're doing!" Kate smiled.

"Go, go, go, go, go, go, go, go!" everyone chanted.

"I'm never letting up again!" Coop yelled back, laughing like a madman.

Kate couldn't help but feel proud of the dependable young man with a deep, abiding affection for his maniacal potential.

"I don't think you should either, hotshot. Now show us what you got, Lightning McQueen! Get us home!" Kate challenged.

"On it!" Coop laughed.

In the future, whenever these special Umans and cryptids looked back on their incredible lives—they all remembered the same fantastic story.

Once upon a time, an army of brave giants appeared out of nowhere to rescue helpless orphans from the real-life monsters—back when dragons and witches still threatened the skies over the Americas.

The last glimpse Zack and Harley caught of Yuma that night was watching the colossal Time Warrior tucked neatly into the curl of the fast-moving tidal wave and riding it like a maniac bodysurfer of old. Enough eels were clinging to the great giant to drown him, but Yuma still gripped Wixx by the throat and wouldn't release the snarling beast she'd become—

even in the face of his own death—and he was smiling.

Out of nowhere, the hijacked Orca suddenly resurfaced in the churning chaos and ripped the screaming witch out of Yuma's hands—swallowing her whole—and Pepper Wixx disappeared beneath the wave as someone else's dinner for a change.

The main body of the rogue wave rose up and blotted out half the sky as it peaked above the shores of Dark Hollows. The sight of the towering doomsday wave sent the already panicked creatures clawing over the top of family and friends as they all tried to escape its wrath as the enormous wave crested, then collapsed on top of the tiny town in one cataclysmic mountain of whitewater. The final wave wiped Dark Hollows off the map as if it never existed with its final devastating blow.

Everything vanished beneath the purifying waters, except for bits and pieces of rubble floating downstream. The cleansing waters churned and eddied for days throughout the embattled lower valley until every trace of their evil existence was purged clean of her shores underneath the Bubble, and the pristine lake waters of the Sacred Forest calmed and settled as they replenished themselves.

Over a short time, life inside the boundaries of the Sacred Forest grew green again as the perpetual firestorms raging below were quenched for a while by the massive inundation, and everything prospered and flourished on both sides of the great lake—having gained a second chance.

Mother Nature always self-corrects—no matter the cost.

The inhabitants living underneath her enchanted Bubble existed now as she designed it—with everything back in balance—both above and below, the ebb and the flow.

The Time Warrior, known as Yuma, although washed away with the rest of the swirling calamity, had performed his duties flawlessly in his last battle.

The living legend had sacrificed his immortal life in the service of Mother Nature, as he had sworn to do.

There could be no better ending for this brave warrior and one of the most remarkable human spirits to have ever lived.

It was a fine death.

Now it was young Zack Goodnight's turn to learn what his remarkable life was about—from the ground up. And with the education he was about to receive from the Inklings and the Illuminators—he was going to enlighten the entire world—one person at a time, the way Mother Nature always meant it to be.

And he wasn't alone any longer. Harley stayed by Zack's side—that was always part of Yuma's plan, along with Zip, Zash, and Zee taking point.

With Archie and the Inklings to support him with their sass and wit, his forever friends stood by to help him sort out the rest of the unknown rules of the universe, one day at a time, just like everyone else.

It was a most glorious destiny that Zackery Goodnight had seen projected for all of humanity inside the Cave of Whispers. Humankind's bright future hovered just over the horizon like a perfect jewel, waiting for discovery once everyone experienced Truesight together through Zack's eyes. And the best was yet to come.

The Wait.
The Earn.
The See.
The Be.

-The End-

-EPILOGUE-

New River Times Latest dispatch for the Spooky Holidays ahead! October 31

It's that crazy time of year again, loyal readers, and it seems that the weird stories keep flooding in. There have been numerous reports about mangled bones, strange decaying carcasses discovered all along the riverbanks, and building materials and rotting timbers.

This unsightly mess seems to be debris swept downstream by recent flooding from somewhere north of town. However, that is impossible since nothing exists above us in this state but pristine open wilderness. The disturbing remains are reported in vast numbers, and the county health examiner has ordered that everyone avoid contact at all costs because of possible health concerns.

Folks, keep in mind that there have also been numerous recent sightings of a cackling killer whale soaring through the air, all up and down our river basin, so it looks like anything goes this holiday. Also, a fresh set of giant human footprints have recently been discovered leading out of the water in Muskrat Bay. The tracks seem to be heading straight back into the wildest of the wilds.

So, dear readers—Bigfoot? UAP reports? Strange lights? Flying whales? Monsters of every description? Just remember what time of year it is, and please take these disturbing rumors swirling about with a dose of good humor.

We all need to howl at the moon sometimes.

-EPILOGUE 2-

The guards standing watch at the Briscoe Institute were stunned when Kate, Coop, and the rest of the missing children rolled up to their gates that stormy night in the same gasless delivery truck they made their escape in.

But who could blame the silent staff with their mouth's hanging open?

These notorious orphans had vanished off the face of the earth over six months ago.

And what kind of tiny monsters held them hostage, making those impossible otherworldly howls?

ABOUT THE AUTHOR

Jack Kincade

After discovering in High School that the world's brightest minds still couldn't explain gravity in our modern world, he took offense and joined the Marine Corps. After four years of that high adventure, he dashed west with his future wife to attend the UCLA Film School and then on to a career in writing and directing in Hollywood where he was lucky enough to be nominated for an Emmy and several other awards while  working as the Supervising Sound Editor on 'Orange is the New Black'; 'Weeds'; 'Glow'; 'New Girl'; 'Hell on Wheels'; 'Chance'; 'United States of Tara'; 'The Dead Zone', 'The Guardian'; 'Judging Amy'; 'V.I.P.'; 'Full House' as well as many, many other legendary shows before retiring in 2018 to write full time on this lifelong project he began working on in 1983.

FROM THE AUTHOR-
I hope you enjoy this extremely tall tale about the brave giants that live inside us all and relish the discovery of these bright new worlds swirling within.

It would mean the world to me if you could leave your honest review on Amazon or Goodreads.
The only way our books stay afloat in the electronic ocean these days. Your reviews.

And you can follow me on agatheringofgiants.com and my Facebook page- https://www.facebook.com/roaminggiants for all updates and exciting new developments as this epic journey continues.

WOULD YOU LIKE TO KNOW WHAT HAPPENS NEXT? PLEASE WRITE TO ME AND LET ME KNOW AT jackkincade@gmail.com.

Thanks for sharing the magic time.
See you all in the Dreampool.
Jack Kincade